Broken Hearts and Mended Love

Carmen S. Bauer

Copyright © 2017 Carmen S. Bauer

All rights reserved.

ISBN-13: 978-1543145496
ISBN-10: 1543145493

The right of Carmen S. Bauer to be identified as the author of this work has been asserted by her in accordance with the Copyright, Design and Patents Act 1988.

All rights reserved. No part of this publication may be reproduced, stored or introduced into retrieval system or transmitted in any form, or by any means (electronic, mechanical, photocopying, recording, or otherwise) without the prior permission of the author. Any person who does any unauthorised act in relation to this publication may be liable to criminal prosecution and civil claims for damages.

This is a work of fiction. Especially all characters, names and actions in this publication are fictitious and any resemblance to real people, alive or dead, is purely coincidental.

To Samuel

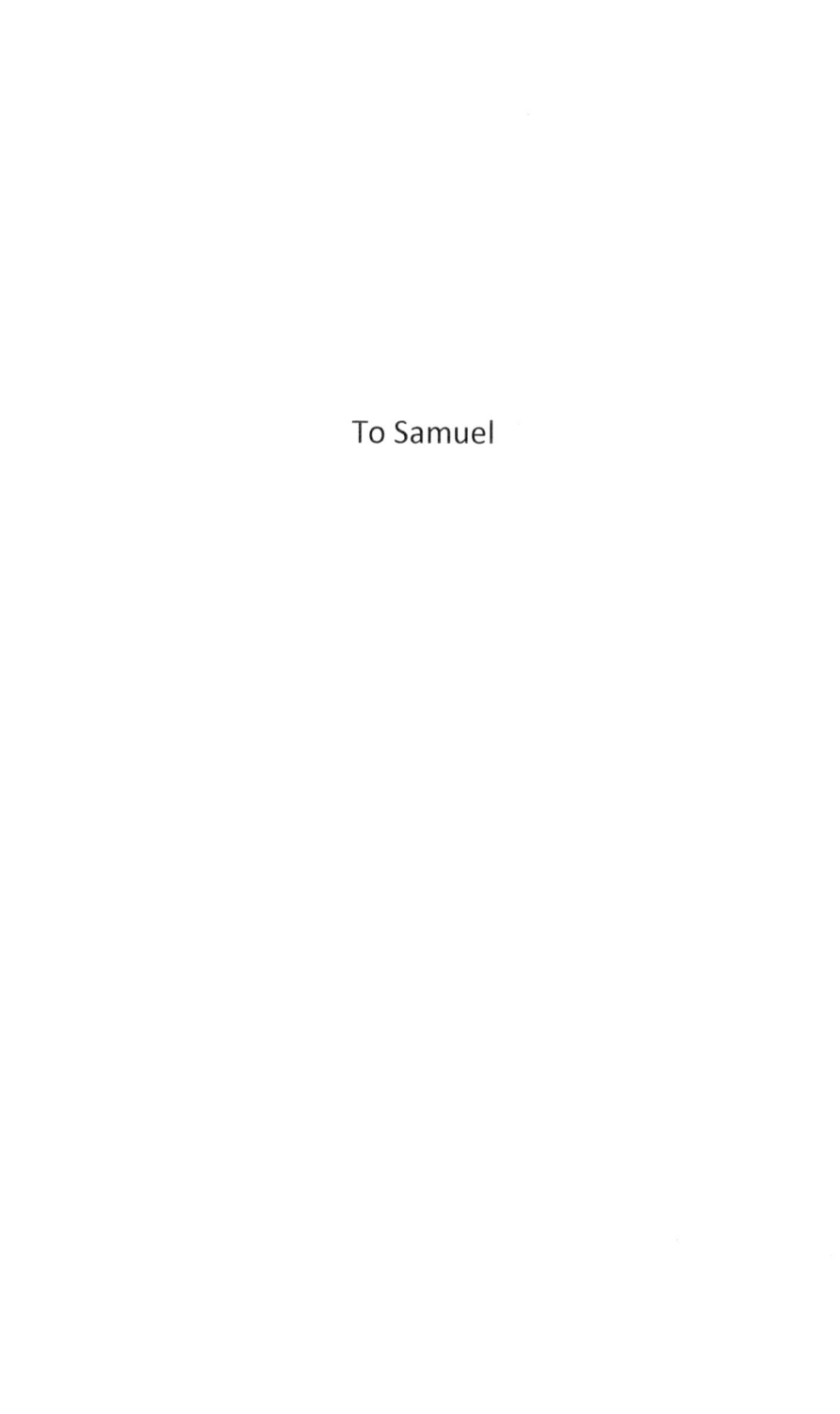

Chapter One

Ashly was tossing and turning in her bed. The thundery weather and the storm making it impossible for her to get the sleep she so desperately needed. Haunted by a nightmare, she flailed until she woke up completely, trying to catch fragments of her dream. All she remembered was that she had been looking down over the lights of a busy city. Darkness was clouding the view, as she stood on top of a skyscraper. It was very blustery and she was filled with the tension of balancing and not being blown over. ...

Before she was able to sort out the bits and pieces of the dream, her unborn baby made itself felt – after almost nine months it wanted to leave the warmth of its mother's womb. Minutes later a clap of thunder made her jump, and at almost the same moment she felt an unfamiliar pain, causing her to wonder if her baby was on its way. When she turned on the bedside lamp, she saw it was shortly after midnight. Following a desire for Rick, her partner of several years, she reached out tentatively for his hand. But what she touched was a cold hand, clenched into a fist. Knowing how angry he could become at times, when things didn't go his way, she was careful not to wake him up and slipped out of her warm bed.

Her initial disappointment of no longer getting any affection from the man she had once so madly loved, quickly changed into joy when she became aware of her baby moving. Looking forward to soon being a mum, she grabbed her dressing gown and slowly walked off to the bathroom.
"Stay where you are," she said, gently rubbing her tummy. "You're not due yet," she continued, speaking softly to the unborn life in her womb and blissfully reflecting on the past few months when she had been excitedly preparing for the arrival of her baby. Her happiness was somewhat spoiled when she saw her troubled face in the mirror. It reminded her of the complicated yet turbulent relationship with Rick. Basically he would have been quite a nice guy if he hadn't succumbed to his excessive drinking which turned him gradually into some sort of a monster. Having been so convinced that he loved her, she had ignored all the warning

signs of his addiction. For a moment, she speculated how their relationship would be like, had he not become a heavy drinker, making her feel so angry and alone, because she couldn't rely on him for any sort of comfort or support.

There was a time she fondly remembered before his alcohol consumption had taken over. Like their first Valentine's Day together – Rick had treated her to a romantic evening out. But those happy days had long gone and made way for times when she felt she was near to having a nervous breakdown, because he was so short-tempered and couldn't control his anger.

His extreme mood swings – one minute he was happy, the next he threw a tantrum – were not only very unpredictable, but had made Ashly believe she was somehow responsible for his compulsive drinking. Of course "Mr. Big Boss" was always in denial about his illness and never wanted to face the truth that he had issues with alcohol. Whenever she had pleaded with him to seek professional help, he had refused and simply blamed her for being the cause of his drinking.

"You drive me mad with your fabrications and accusations. I've got to go and get myself a drink!"

"Rick, come on – it's not my fault that you're

addicted to alcohol," she had argued her case until one day she had realised it was all part of the game that he was never at fault.

Over time, she had become fed up with trying to hold him back from running to the pub. He was unstoppable once he had his mind set on rushing for a drink, coming home late, his breath stinking of gin when he wanted to make love with her.

"Ashly baby, I love you. I need you. I'll kill myself if I ever find you seeing someone else," he had slurred his speech, drawing near Ashly to hug and kiss her. She had flinched, appalled as she couldn't stand his foul breath of alcohol and the smell of his cheap aftershave. Fortunately he had abstained from molesting her on that occasion, but it was then that she found out he was obsessively jealous.

"I'll kill him! Admit it, you're having an affair with that bloody art student of yours..." he had gone on and on...

His lousy character traits, such as jealousy and anger, drove her mad. This was just another one of his techniques – he did something to upset her and then used her distress as justification for getting drunk.

"Don't lie to me. I know you were out, dating that little smart ass," he had given Ashly a volley of aggressive verbal abuse. And as if that wasn't enough, he boastfully added, "I checked the mileage on the car!"

"Bollocks! You know quite well this isn't true. Don't waste my time with your jealousy!" she had answered. Having had a tough day at work she hadn't been prepared for such stupid arguments with him. But Rick never gave in easily. Relentlessly accusing her of betraying him, he had also made it clear that he didn't like children – not even his own.

"You sanctimonious bitch!" he had shouted at her, when she had cheerfully told him the good news that she was pregnant with his child, "It's not my child. Who knows who you've been in bed with!" His whole demeanour had been as cold as ice, and the anger in his voice had made her shiver, leaving her totally lost for words. She knew immediately one thing for sure – she had screwed up. Having stubbornly ignored his freak-outs, for fear of him causing another scene, turned out to be a big mistake! By doing so, she had let him get on top of her. And then, the news of her pregnancy had changed everything at a stroke.

Ashly sighed deeply when it became clear to her that she and Rick really had nothing in common apart from their child, which wasn't even born yet.

The thought that it might grow up without a father – just like herself – had been preying on her mind during the whole pregnancy. Under no circumstances had she wanted this to happen. A child needs a father, she always believed. But at what price? She had dithered for months over what to do. Yes, in hindsight, she should have left Rick, but instead she had clung to the illusion that, once the baby was born, he would change. 'Then again,' she now asked herself, 'was that likely?'

Another clap of thunder broke through the turbulent night and interrupted Ashly in her thoughts. Her pain intensified. Feeling her baby moving and turning, brought her back to reality. She instinctively knew that it was making its way into the world, leaving her with no other option but to ask Rick for help.

"Rick," she shouted, "Rick you've got to get up! The baby is coming. We must get to the hospital."

But Rick, having been on a pub crawl, was so soundly asleep that even the loud thunder didn't affect him. As usual, it wasn't easy for Ashly to wake him. She became more and more anxious that he would let her down, as he had done so many times. Fortunately this time her worries were unfounded. Rick mumbled something while getting out of bed and, springing into action unusually fast, he hurriedly dressed, and raced Ashly to the nearby hospital without further vicious comments.

A few hours later Ashly gave birth and the very moment she heard her baby crying she sank relieved back on to her pillow, knowing everything was fine with it.

"It's a boy," the nurse smilingly said and placed the little bundle softly on Ashly's tummy. It was the most wonderful moment in her life, one she would savour for ever.

"Jake, my little Jake," she said, overcome with emotion while gently stroking her new baby. Totally absorbed in her happiness, she couldn't take her eyes off him. After all, she thought the little sweetheart was a reward for all the misery and hardship she had been through with Rick.

"Now we go through life together," she whispered caressing the baby – her little son!

◆◆◆

It wasn't long after she returned home from the hospital that Rick raised hell again for no apparent reason. Although they weren't married, he wanted her to be the ideal wife, putting Ashly under pressure to pander to his whims.

"Everything is always about you! Don't you know how deeply you hurt me with your chauvinistic behaviour?" she wanted to know.

Apparently he didn't! He was as selfish as ever, seemingly pleased playing "Mr. Big Boss", and making Ashly feel inferior. The whole world had to revolve around him and he made damn sure everybody knew he came first. When he had an important get-together, he demanded that Ashly ironed his white shirt immediately. But when she, tired from nursing the baby, asked him for some help in the house, he usually cleared off to the pub, calling over his shoulder,

"The hoover is too heavy for me – do it yourself if you want the house clean."

"Try not to fall over on your way to bed later," she shouted after him.

It was hard for her to come to terms with Rick being so unsupportive. However, she suppressed her fury and decided to refrain from further utterances.

'Let him play his silly little games with his mates, but not with me,' she thought.

At times Ashly vacillated between hope and despair. It was impossible to guess what Rick would come up with next, as, when he wasn't drunk, he was the most loving and amazing man Ashly could ask for.

"You know baby, sometimes you've got to lie to keep things nice and neat to protect your feelings," he apologised sweetly for any wrong-doing, gently brushing a strand of her dark hair off her forehead.

Ashly looked at him, puzzled. 'What is he up to now?' she asked. "If you really love me, you wouldn't lie to me," she told him.

In a clumsy attempt he continued to explain that he was cross with himself and admitted drinking too much.

"I'm so sorry. I'm so sorry," he repeatedly said.

"You keep saying "sorry" – I simply wish you would stop drinking."

"I will! I'm going to do something about my alcohol addiction. I'll give it up."

'Aha,' she thought. She had recently intimated that she was fed up with his ill-mannered behaviour and threatened to leave him. Maybe her announcement had born fruits? She was prepared to believe him.

"I understand that drinking changes me into someone intolerable even if I'm a nice drunk," he tried to be funny. He must have sensed that Ashly was still attracted to him and knew exactly which buttons to push to keep her sweet. Seeing the perplexed expression on her face, he hastened to reassure her, "Honestly. I swear – I won't drink any more."

Was he telling the truth or was this just another of his lies? She vacillated – did she perhaps do him an injustice?

"I don't want to be this way. I know, I need help," he pleaded and looked at her with such an appealing expression that she succumbed to the temptation and surrendered to his promises.

For a few months he did indeed manage to stay sober and even occasionally took a fatherly interest in his son. But, as one would expect, the peace didn't last, because he started to drink again and fell back into his old habits: frequently stomping off to the pub and coming home late totally drunk. The slightest whimper from Jake or tentative question from Ashly could set off his tirades of name-calling and capacity to argue over the smallest of matters. Clearly Ashly was angry with him and herself for having trusted him. She resented that he had broken his promise, but despite all her misgivings she hung on to him and resorted to excuses for his bad behaviour.

It wasn't always easy for her to recognise the warning signs before his behaviour escalated. Rick was a master of disguise and an inveterate liar, and it was sometimes difficult to distinguish the truth from his lies. One minute he would say he loved Ashly and show affection to her and his little son, Jake. But the harmony never lasted long. The next minute he would punish her by withdrawing his love and giving her the silent treatment. By the time she had fully comprehended the degree of his alcohol abuse it was already too late – Rick had developed an incredible tolerance of the amount of beer and gin he was able to drink, and sooner or later he vented a stream of insults towards Ashly.

"You smart little bitch, you! Who'd give you a second look?!" he blustered in drunkenness, aiming to make her feel she wasn't good enough. "Nobody takes a second-hand bitch with a bastard!"

Despite his stinging words Ashly ignored the ridiculous spectacle he made of himself. What was that phrase she had recently heard on TV? *When he goes low, you go high*... With this in mind, she would have loved to tell him what an idiot he was, but then decided it wasn't worth responding to that drunken retard.

'He doesn't do it wilfully. It's the alcohol which changes his whole personality,' she kidded herself, still hoping that the man, she had once fallen for, would – as promised – get his drinking under control. But the contrary was the case. His alcohol consumption increased over the following months and so did his verbal attacks. Whenever he had a bad day, he mindlessly took out his anger on her, and her strength to withstand him was starting to wane fast.

"You're nagging me with the crap you talk," he snarled at her, barely disguising how drunk he was. "I'm working hard at building sites and you? You're nothing! All you do is sit on your ass and chat all day long with your smart students. And that makes you think you're something special, eh?"

She stared at him in disbelief.

"I think it's the drink which makes you talk like this. Before long you will have to seek professional help!" she warned him.

"Oh really – if you say so," he said, tottering as he stood in front of her, posturing with his hands on his hips to keep his balance. "Of course, you know better being an academic. Then tell me why you have difficulties getting on with other people?"

That just did it!

She choked back a flash of anger and decided to ignore his attack.

Yes, it was true – she hardly went out with friends, because she felt unable to confide in them the reality of what was happening in her life. How could she explain to anybody that she, a well-respected art historian, lived with an alcoholic and that she, despite all odds, stayed on in this failing relationship? So she played along, telling everybody how busy she was with her work and how demanding her baby Jake was.

◆◆◆

What bugged Ashly more than anything else was the fact that Rick constantly tried to drive a wedge between her and her mother, Iris. And he almost succeeded in the two women becoming estranged from each other, had Ashly not foiled his persistent attempts.

"Your mother causes trouble. I don't want to see her any more!" he threw at her more than once.

"I'm sorry that you feel that way," she replied with overblown sincerity. Did he seriously imagine she would cut off all contact with her mother?

"Yeah, tell your mother, the old busy-body, to piss off!"

Ashly should have known that Rick had a real knack of upsetting her. If she responded now to his abusiveness, it would merely fuel his bad temper. No matter how hurt she was, she didn't want that bastard to see her tears!

Fortunately Iris was well aware of what was going on between her daughter and that scumbag Rick. All too often he had offended her and she simply couldn't bear the thought of her daughter suffering at the hands of that alcoholic or even getting drawn in his addiction. Despairing at his distressing boldness and the drivel he was spouting, she had reluctantly stopped setting foot in Rick's house. The only time she saw her grandson was when Ashly came to unburden her heart to her.

"Rick gets so furious when I see friends and spend time with them," Ashly shared with her mother, "I wish he were dead."

"Don't be silly! Wishing him dead is no solution. Why do you stay with him? He is such a nasty piece of work and you should take a stand before his drinking gets totally out of hand and he becomes even more abusive," Iris expressed her displeasure. She was convinced her daughter needed to be rescued from the clutches of this fiend. In her opinion, Rick was rotten to the core, not even caring for his own son, but living on Ashly's gentle disposition and bonhomie, draining her emotionally. "He will destroy you!" she warned her.

"Yes, but what do you suggest I do?" Ashly didn't really expect her mother to answer. She hesitated – should she confide in her that she was still magnetized by Rick and how easily she believed him when he promised to change his attitude and showed more affection towards her.

As if Iris had read her daughter's mind, she said, "Wake up, darling. You're conducting an imaginary relationship – one that's nice in theory, but doesn't work in practice."

"He isn't always nasty. Sometimes he is quite nice, taking me out for a meal or on a holiday," Ashly made excuses, instantaneously feeling a flash of guilt coming on in allowing him to get away so cheaply for his behaviour.

"Do you not think you're merely being deluded by such gestures after he has thrown a tantrum?" Iris put her finger right into the wound. With a stern look at Ashly, she went on, "You let him bamboozle you with all his false promises. Can't you see it yourself?"

Following her mother's emphatic appeal, Ashly was contemplating over her relationship with Rick. A sudden nostalgia for the times she had spent with him flooded over her. He had pushed her – a bit too quickly for her liking – into a relationship, passionately remonstrating that he would kill himself if she ever left him. Like so many other women before her, she had fallen for his charming smile until she had recognised there was nothing more beyond it. Rick was extremely good looking, but inside shallow and conceited, hitting the bottle and obsessed with jealousy. And as he always portrayed himself as good and women as crazy, it wasn't easy to see behind his façade.

She took a deep breath. For a moment she visualised how Rick, when he was in a good mood, played with little Jake and talked to him in his soft voice. Why can't he always be like that? Why can't he make more effort to get his heavy drinking under control and become a loving partner and father? She found herself still harbouring the ludicrous thought that her tricky relationship could be mended and her little family would be safe and happy. Could she not see that Rick had thwarted her optimism many times and sent her spirits into tailspin? His drinking was taking their relationship into a descent on a downward spiral!

"Just because he can't control his alcohol consumption doesn't make him a bad person," Ashly defiantly replied. She tried not to think about the fact that she still hadn't made up her mind whether or not to leave Rick.

"Honey, this isn't the man you'll get the 'Happy-ever-after' life with! Don't you think you have covered long enough for him? This man doesn't deserve to occupy your mind or life any longer," Iris stopped, but not for long before she continued, "Don't look so worried. I'm only trying to help. I'm very concerned about you, and as you know there's always a home for you here."

"Mum, you don't need to worry about me. I'm fine," Ashly said with a forced smile.

"Darling, it's useless to feign happiness. I can tell that you're not happy!" Iris said, because her daughter's gloomy look had raised her concerns. "You either take measures to improve your life with Rick — which by the way I think isn't possible — or you leave him."

Ashly sighed. It was hard for her to realise that the years with Rick had been wasted. Then again, she could count the times she was really happy with him on one hand.

"What choice do I have?" she asked, discouraged by the fact that her mother was probably right — a happy life with Rick seemed totally out of reach.

"Leave him! His alcohol abuse isn't just a flash in the pan!" Iris admonished her.

"Leave him — as if that would be so easy."

"Yes. Leave him!" Iris stuck to her guns. "I can't understand why you don't stand up to this man, who is so relentless and ruthless, and simply leave this relationship behind."

Why didn't she leave? She knew herself that the chances of Rick changing into a loving partner and father were almost zero. Still, Jake, he needs a father came to her mind... She felt somehow queasy. The thought about the actions to come perturbed her. How catastrophic would it be if she left Rick? Her life – wouldn't it be plunged into chaos? She would have to reshape her and Jake's world.

While she was still worrying, what impact her decision would have, Iris spoke on,

"Come on darling, lighten up. That low-life has nothing in common with you. You're an intelligent woman with a degree in arts, who speaks several languages fluently. You, with your gentle nature, and he with his bravado – he's the exact opposite of you!"

"Yes, I know. It took me some time to figure out that opposites attract but not necessarily for ever," Ashly agreed with a wan smile.

"I'm sure there is someone out there who suits you better!" Iris tried to encourage her daughter and quipped, "Look on the bright side – the prospect of sleeping in your own bed, without having to put up at night with this abusive drunkard, inhaling his stale breath..."

Ashly nodded slowly. Her mother's well-intentioned words didn't really convince her.

"What about Jake? I don't want him to grow up without a father... Jake needs a father..." Ashly said haltingly. Having missed out on a father herself, she knew what it was like to grow up without one. She had always felt rejected and the sense of anxiety and insecurity stayed with her all her life. It still hurt when she remembered how her schoolmates ran into the arms of their fathers and were lifted with hugs and kisses. She had longed for a complete family and would have loved a father, but later accepted how her life played out. As for Jake, she cherished the hope that Rick would become reasonable – at least for the sake of their son.

Ashly looked at her mother – would she believe how concerned she was about Jake or would she uncover her self-delusion?

"Don't make excuses to stay!" Iris replied promptly. "Do you really want to go on living a lie, covering up for that drunkard? You will sooner or later have to resign yourself to the fact that this odious man will never change and Jake *has* to grow up without a father!"

Slightly confounded by her mother's words, Ashly considered how to reply. She remembered how nervous she had been about making mistakes raising Jake more or less on her own, because Rick – apart from when he was in a good mood – never shared any of the responsibility of parenthood. So far, all her anxiety was groundless, since her little boy was – just like her – good-natured and no bother.

"*Min älskling,*" she said in Swedish soothingly, with a look at her little son sleeping peacefully on the sofa beside her. She had always avoided speaking to him in a baby-like manner. Instead she talked to him in one of the foreign languages she fluently spoke, calling him *mein Liebling* or *mon chéri* or *min älskling* – all meaning my darling. She was sure that his development would benefit from teaching him different languages, every day a little bit more, by showing and explaining to him in one of the foreign languages everything that came into her mind while she carried him around in her arms.

"Gib' die Hoffnung niemals auf," she whispered softly in German. "Never give up hope," she explained to her mother.

Iris, normally worried about Ashly overdoing things, treasured the moment, her daughter fondling the toddler, and was cautious not to spoil it.

"I have great respect for your attitude, but I don't agree that Jake needs a father," she said, trying to encourage Ashly. "I brought you up on my own and it didn't do you any harm."

"Yes," Ashly replied, "but it wasn't always easy for me."

"Darling, it won't be easy for Jake either, but it

won't be impossible. Don't worry, we will manage," Iris tried to reassure her daughter.

Ashly glanced at her watch. She wanted to be home before Rick.

"I've got to rush, mum," she said, while hurriedly lifting Jake and saying goodbye to her mother.

"Take care darling – and remember: The time for avoiding the truth has passed...." Iris called after her.

◆◆◆

Her mother's persistent criticism gradually sank home. Considering her situation dispassionately, Ashly realised she ought to split up with Rick. But she wanted a neat and tidy end of the relationship and was waiting for a suitable opportunity.

Weeks turned into months and Rick didn't change. On the contrary: by becoming more and more furious, he repeatedly caused Ashly to cry in despair. One day, in a last-ditch attempt to save the rotten relationship, she had prepared his favourite dish: steak, baked beans and chips. Hoping that a civil conversation with him at the dinner table was possible, she cautiously broached the matter which had been occupying her mind.

"I'm beginning to ask myself whether our

relationship has a future. You don't seem to have any regard for my needs or feelings," she paused and tried to catch his eyes. Rick stared brazenly at her and after a long minute of silence, she continued, "You don't seem to notice I'm unhappy."

"I don't know what you're talking about." His tone was dismissive.

"I go to work, make dinner every night as well as doing all the shopping and cleaning, never mind looking after our son. And what do I get from you? Not even a hug or a bunch of flowers or at least a thank you," Ashly tried to explain.

Rick looked as if he couldn't care less what Ashly had just said. With his face darkening and tension sharpening his voice, he huffed,

"So what?! You won't catch me wearing a pinny or waving a feather duster!"

"This isn't fair on me and I don't think it would hurt you to help with the shopping or washing up once in a while," Ashly went on, trying to stay calm.

"I don't care! Why do you always bother me with your girly stuff?!" he uncompromisingly blustered. And then his temper flared and before Ashly had a chance to say any more, he was on his feet.

"Come on – get real!" he shouted, and continued to insult her further by adding, "And by the way – your dinner tastes like shit! You can't cook. You should go

on a cookery course instead of hanging out with that smart little student of yours!"
Then, in a final display of his despicable temper he threw his plate at her, missing her head only by inches, before he slammed the door and ran out to the pub.

Ashly was once more left speechless. What further proof did she need? Shaking after the violent freak-out she had just witnessed, she realised that this wasn't the affectionate home she wanted. Rick's never-ending squabbles and lies were simply too much! She had no strength left to cope with the constant clashes any more. Her nerves were frazzled and she started crying. All through the night she racked her brain how to make him stop his drinking and get their relationship back on track. In the end she realised there was only one way to stop her suffering: leave this toxic relationship as quickly as possible.

Then came the moment she snapped: Not a single day longer did she want to waste with that man. Rick, having turned so nasty, didn't deserve another chance. Jake was three years old when she explained to him,
"Enough is enough – we are going! I have tried my

best, but this relationship isn't working! I don't want to be exposed to this man's recurring and offending humiliations any longer."

She was extremely relieved at having actually made the decision to leave and wasn't expecting Rick to suddenly show up, creating a scene on the day she was moving out. But he stood at the door, attempting to hold her back when Ashly told him that the relationship was finished.

"Piss off!" he said brazenly, hardly able to hold his balance because he was so drunk. "I don't give a shit what you do."

The beer must have stoked his anger, as he went on bellowing,

"If you leave me now, you'll regret it bitterly."

His brown eyes glittering dangerously, he grabbed her by the arm. "You walk out now – you're not coming back!"

The situation was simmering and about to boil over. Ashly however remained level-headed.

"I won't want to come back. We are done! Get out of my way. Immediately," she shouted back, forcing her way past him with Jake in her arms.

"You'll never survive without me. This isn't over!" he threatened her with a smug grin. And then, he contemptuously added, "Don't come running back!"

Hastily opening the door, she yelled,

"Don't worry. I won't! I hope our paths never cross again!"

Having beforehand arranged to stay at her mum's house, she just wanted to get out and get away from Rick as fast as she could. It was a breezy day in autumn when she and Jake left, never ever to see Rick again.

Chapter Two

Iris had always lived on the other side of town in a tranquil environment. She owned a small house that, at one time, had been painted yellow with brown window frames, which had faded over the past years and was now in desperate need of repainting. But, as she was living on a small widow's pension, decorating the house was not one of her priorities. However, the faded colours of the little bungalow perfectly reflected the autumnal colours of the scattered leaves being swirled around the street by the wind at the very moment when Ashly and Jake arrived at the house with their few belongings.

The outside of Iris's home was enclosed by a highly colourful garden, echoing the owner's passion for gardening. There seemed to be no order in what was growing – the variety of flowers was simply stunning and it was reminiscent of a jungle. People walking by were fascinated by the wilderness and blaze of colour and often stopped to admire. As it turned out, Jake, who was always keen to explore the world around him, loved to be with his grandmother in this heaven on earth. He was especially enamoured of the word "deadheading", not knowing what it actually meant. Dressed up like a pirate he sometimes dashed through the garden, shouting "Yeah deadheading – I'm coming!" whilst waving his little plastic sword over the plants. Iris was often worried about her plants being mangled but usually couldn't resist laughing at her grandson's performance and explained to him that "deadheading" was the gardening term for removing faded flowers from plants.

The inside of the house was cosy and comfortable – not very tidy, nevertheless it was a place where one felt "as snug as a bug in a rug". And at Christmas particularly the house looked like something out of a fairy tale – warm, nicely decorated, and smelling of cinnamon, almonds and cakes. It was built in the early 1920s and still had the original kitchen, except for the wood stove which had been replaced. Very little had been done to the inside, apart from some wiring and plumbing when Ashly's father had been alive. There were some tales of ghosts in the house – children from the neighbourhood often talked about the spooky presence of a little girl and her mother. Iris didn't pay too much attention to what she called "kids' talk", but sometimes she felt a cool breeze on her back when she was in the kitchen. One day in particular she thought something was watching her and had a funny feeling that someone was behind her. Yet, when she turned around she didn't see anything unusual, and she thought it wasn't an evil presence, because whatever it was, it wasn't intrusive. Even though Iris had never encountered anything scary she felt relieved when her daughter and grandson came to live with her.

◆◆◆

Apparently, Iris's old house was an idyllic place for Ashly and her son to live and to finally forget about all the unhappiness with Rick during the past years.

'This is so much better. No more arguing, no more fighting,' Ashly thought, looking forward to find the rest and peace of mind she so urgently needed.

For Jake, lively and curious as he was, the new home was a paradise: His grandmother had collected a lot of stuff in her lifetime – soft toys, dolls, figurines, but above all, countless books. And she was also a great storyteller. Especially on cold or rainy days, Jake and his grandma snuggled up on the settee, where Iris made up stories or read to him from her collection of fairy tales. Either way, they always started with "once upon a time" and ended with "and they lived happily ever after".

When, years later, Jake discovered that his granny's stories were just made up, always starting and ending with these lines, he was pretty disappointed. But at the time he couldn't get enough of her fantastic tales, all relating to strange creatures, such as giants hopping around the world in seven days or building massive bridges across the water to meet their sweethearts, or fire-spitting dragons living in countries far, far away. As a little boy, he was entranced and never tired of listening to his granny's voice, telling him stories of ghosts haunting old castles, or of creatures coming at night and eating all the plants in the garden.

"SNAP," Iris snapped her finger, "and all the plants are gone."

Many nights he sneaked into his grandmother's big bed under the window so that he was able to look out and see the sky at night. The room was always filled with a heavy, lingering scent which tickled his fancy and prompted him to drift away into a world of dreams and fantasy. He was fascinated how some stars glistened like diamonds on a blue velvet cloth.

And they seemed so close – he just needed to reach out and take one down. Often he fantasised about living somewhere else in the depths of the universe. Was there life anywhere out there? He assumed it was quite possible as there were so many stars – why should the Earth be the only planet with life? What would that life be like out there?

"Granny, do you believe in little green men?" Jake once asked Iris, lying beside her on her big bed under the window.

"I believe in you, little man. But as far as I can see you're not green, or are you?" she replied with a smile.

"But granny! If I stop breathing I will turn green," Jake insisted.

"No, you'll turn blue and then you might die," Iris responded.

"But I don't want to die. I want to be like these green men."

"Why is that?"

"Because they can do things which nobody else can do," Jake whispered and nestled up to her.

"Like what?" Iris asked. But her grandson didn't respond. He was absorbed in thought.

"Do you know that everybody has a guardian angel who is watching over you?" she started a new thread. Gently stroking her grandson, she explained,

"You have to give him a name and call him whenever you need him."

Jake turned around. "You mean those figures which appear on tombstones?"

"Well," Iris replied, "that's the impression we humans have of angels."

Her little grandson was hesitant. He tried to picture an angel.

"Do they live out there in the universe, on one of the bright stars?" he wanted to know.

Iris was slightly nonplussed. Yes – where do angels live? As she had no answer to her grandson's question, she tried to avoid responding directly. Instead, she said,

"Angels used to be part of people's everyday lives and children grew up with angels as their invisible companions."

'Invisible companions?!' it flashed through Jake. "I want one. Wilfred. I will call him Wilfred," he whispered and, no longer listening to his grandmother, he fell asleep.

◆◆◆

Sometime later, when Jake had started school, he came home one day and talked enthusiastically about his new friend Wilfred. Ashly and Iris speculated who this friend was, who so suddenly popped up.

"Who is Wilfred?" they asked as Jake had never mentioned him before.

"He is my friend at school," Jake explained with a secret smile and the seriousness made everybody believe him.

"Where does Wilfred live?"

Without hesitation, the boy answered, "Not far from here."

The two women looked at each other frowning – they had no idea what to make of Jake's story. And he felt amused to see their baffled faces. However, sooner or later they became suspicious, because Jake never invited his friend back to the house for a sleepover and always conjured up excuses as to why he didn't bring his friend home. Being so imaginative, he related his adventures with his friend so convincingly that there was no doubt that Wilfred was real. Later in life he would laugh when he remembered this episode of his childhood. Wilfred had been his imaginary friend and he had almost persuaded his mother and grandmother that he existed.

◆◆◆

Jake, always eager to do things in his own way, made a real effort to learn to read by finding out what all those funny characters meant, before he even went to school. Many times he sat next to his granny at the kitchen table, a big white sheet of paper in front of him and a red pencil in his little hand. Eagerly he sketched the pencil over the paper, trying to copy the letters from an old birthday card. Iris was always there to help, either holding his hand to draw the letters, or explaining to him how to pronounce them. It didn't take long until he was able to read and write.

"That's a cinch!" he smiled after having finished reading his first whole children's book.

It was very obvious that he thoroughly enjoyed the company of his grandmother. Unfortunately – in his opinion – he couldn't spend too much time with her, because he had to go to school one day.

"Why do I have to go to school, granny?" he innocently asked Iris.

"Because you will learn things there which neither your mum nor I can teach you," she explained with a resolute look.

One could see in the boy's face how much he doubted what his granny had just said.

"But I have learned so much from you and mummy. I do not need to go to school," he remarked smartly, and, typical for children of his age, he enunciated each word distinctly. He was convinced that nobody could teach him better than his granny and mum. Besides, had his granny not always told him, if he believed in something and strove for it with all his heart, then dreams would come true? With a heroic pose he often stood in front of the mirror, making faces and desperately wishing that he could stay at home. Yet, it was all in vain – he had to go to school! Not that he disliked the school, but he thought it was a waste of time because there was nothing which really interested him – nothing, apart from a girl who caught his attention one day.

Chapter Three

Jake was six years old when he spotted her in the school playground. She looked different, because of her long red plaits, and the freckles on her face made her look cheeky.

"I am Claire," she said, flashing him a smile.

His brown eyes curiously roamed over her.

"Hi, I am Jake," he replied slightly timid. "I have not seen you here before. You must be new to the school."

"Yes, I just moved here with my dad, in the old house at the end of the street," she explained.

He blinked his eyes when asking her, "Where is your mum?"

"She died some years ago. I live with my daddy," she answered, quickly adding, "See you later in class." And then she hurried into the school building, leaving Jake in suspense, wondering how things would go for him.

Shortly after, the two found a place to sit together in the classroom, right under the teachers' nose where they visibly showed their lack of interest during lessons, because they figured out tasks long before anybody else. Jake was over the moon when he realised he had found his match in Claire – she too was very talented and extremely sensitive. So far it hadn't been easy for either of them to find other kids, who shared the same enthusiasm and dynamic interests, and consequently it had been quite difficult to establish long lasting friendships. For the want of a friend Jake had already invented an imaginary friend. Wilfred, as he had named him, was gradually fading away, since Claire had become his true friend. Nevertheless, in the beginning he told her about his adventures with Wilfred. But being so sensitive and smart Claire very quickly sussed out her new friend.

"You are such a tease," she said with a big smile on her face, whenever Jake told her another of his stories about Wilfred.

As it turned out, the two six-year-olds got on very well together, and they became even closer friends by their shared experience of being shunned or bullied by other children, because they were perceived as "strange" being so outstandingly bright. While the other kids often tried to entangle them in a brawl by pushing and elbowing them, Jake and Claire always stayed amazingly chilled despite all the provocations.

Nonetheless, Jake, not really nettled by violence and childish behaviour, persistently went on quizzing his mates with what they regarded as stupid questions, like:

"How far is it from the earth to the moon and back?" (And Jake wasn't satisfied to only ask how far it was to the moon. No, that would have been too easy! He wanted to know the return mileage as well.)

But his well-meant tricky question-and-answer games during break-time didn't win him any points and he was often frustrated, because he was accused of being nothing but a patronising little squirt. Yet, Jake couldn't understand – he never thought of himself being lofty or pushing to the front, nor did he intend to boast about his achievements. On the contrary he just thought it was funny to know a lot and couldn't understand why some of his classmates turned against him, blatantly laughing and yelling at him,

"Watch out, here comes the smart-ass Jake!"

"It's not fair! I am not a smart-ass. I do not always

know all the answers," Jake grumbled when kids had poked fun at him and made him feel ridiculous. Claire tried to console him and curb his frustration.

"Don't pay any attention to them," she said with an angry flush over her face. Pulling him aside she whispered, "You know, my daddy always tells me: no one can make you feel inferior without your consent."

"But why am I accused of being a windbag and an attention seeker? I am not like others in the class, stubbornly arguing that black is white," he went on complaining.

"Well, you know, some people just like to belittle other people because they are envious," Claire explained.

Jake, being quite a busy little mind, wasn't convinced. "If I can be nice and wise, why cannot others be too," he argued.

"Some people simply cannot stand the thought that someone is cleverer than them," she replied.

"I suppose this is true," Jake agreed. "But only because I am thoughtful does not mean I am *dazzling with intelligence*." He embarrassingly giggled about his own, made-up words.

Claire didn't respond immediately.

"Don't take things too personal. You cannot force people to like you," she spouted, adding with a warm smile, "I like you. Isn't this enough?"

"I like you too," Jake responded.

After a reflective silence he was back to his usual self, coming up with another piece of his knowledge.

"Did you know that gunpowder is made of animal poop?" he asked her with a knowing grin.

"No", she answered perplexedly.

"Gunpowder was invented in China and is made of sodium nitrate which is basically animal poop," he explained eagerly. "No animal poop – no war!"

"How come you know all this?!" Claire asked him with an astonished look.

"My mum and my granny tell me all these things," he replied proudly and continued with enthusiasm, "If my granny does not know the answer, she looks it up in one of her big books."

Indeed, Jake was so astute that he always found something to ask his mum or granny. Iris was more than once taken aback and sometimes even worried, because, with his immeasurable thirst for knowledge, Jake acted more like an adult than a young child. Even so, his constant questions kept her old mind busy and she always tried to answer her grandson's questions to the best of her knowledge. But many times she simply didn't know the answers.

"Wait," she would then say, lowering her glasses and taking an interest, "I will look it up in one of my big books." She would then disappear to search her many bookshelves for the appropriate book, reading her findings out to the boy.

❖❖❖

As if it were fate, Jake and Claire had met at school and it was no surprise that the situation at school would shape their friendship forever. Claire, just like Jake, was extremely clever and she felt the same way as him – school wasn't really challenging. As quick learners, she too was always several steps ahead of others and easily got bored. Then, instead of following the class, the minds of the two little Einsteins were often inclined to wander. For their teachers it was rather a nightmare having to put up with such seriously clever children, because they simply didn't fit into the mould of their expectations. Seeing their faraway look, the teachers knew that the two geniuses needed to be occupied with more advanced work while at the same time they had to teach the other children. Subsequently this proved almost impossible and would put an even greater strain on the teachers.

Jake, being genuinely modest, realised very quickly that it wasn't easy for his teachers to keep him busy. He himself didn't like always being the first in class. As he didn't want to show off, and, in an attempt to make life easier for his teacher, he took his granny's advice on board and toned things down. He did this by deliberately giving wrong answers which, unfortunately for him, created even more problems. Despite all his attempts, some kids still thought he had a cocky attitude and accused him of being stuck-up, refusing to work with him. And yet others saw Jake as a stimulus, immediately identified with him, and endeavoured to become as bright as him. His teachers, however, feared that the whole class might polarize into pro and anti-Jake.

◆◆◆

In the course of the time especially Jake's precocious behaviour became so apparent that the teachers couldn't bear it any longer, but expressed their concerns to the headmaster. Then came the day when Ashly was called to a meeting in school. The morning the letter arrived in her house, she was very nervous.

"I wonder what this is about," she said to her mother. "I hope Jake hasn't got into trouble and that he didn't get up to any nonsense!" She was concerned, because she knew that not all Jake's classmates appreciated his performance.

Iris tried to calm her daughter down,

"I wouldn't worry too much. What does it say in the letter?"

"That's it! It doesn't say anything except that the headmaster wants to talk to me about Jack's behaviour," Ashly explained.

Iris tried again to allay Ashly's worries and said,

"Jake is like a cat, you don't need to worry about him. He'll always fall on his feet, come what may." After a short pause she added, "Anyway, I believe that Jake is being looked after by a guardian angel."

"Well, I wouldn't be so sure about that," Ashly replied. Being more level-headed, she didn't share her mother's beliefs in supernatural powers or miracles. Especially after her relationship with Rick had fallen apart, she realised that miracles don't just happen.

"Don't you remember the case with the football a little while ago?" Iris asked.

A vision of the incident, Jake almost being killed, flashed into her mind. The boy had been playing with his football and, while running after the ball onto the street, he had nearly been knocked down by a car which seconds later raced past. Iris had been at the front gate when she saw the speeding car coming. She would never forget how she froze because of fear for her grandson. And then the miracle happened – Jake jumped back and was saved. "That was his guardian angel!" she had sighed.

"You're probably right, mum," Ashly answered, turning her attention to the letter. "Still, I hope that Jake didn't get into a fight."

"But why would he?" Iris asked, looking at her daughter in astonishment.

"Well, you know – that day he came home from school crying so badly, because some kids had teased him. You comforted him and told him to always refrain from violence but instead stand above things and see them from a different perspective."

"Yes that's right. If you look at a situation from above it becomes very small. One shouldn't get involved in violence. This is never an acceptable solution."

"Even so, sometimes one is given no option and, in order to defend yourself, you have to know how to use your fists," Ashly argued.

"No, I don't agree. The best way is to learn how to negotiate and to run. You shouldn't get roped in to fights. What if you injure somebody? And what if

43

that results in death?" Iris responded, glancing sceptically at her daughter.

But Ashly was no longer listening. She was too concerned about why Jake's headmaster wanted to see her.

"Stop worrying, Ashly darling, that's only misleading your imagination!" Iris said.

"Yes, you may be right," Ashly agreed. For a moment she stood quietly in front of the window, watching the heavy rain. Then, turning towards her mother, she added, "My mind is already astray, leading my attention to faulty assumptions."

A quick look at her watch, reminded her that she was late for work.

"I've got to go to work," she hastily grabbed her bag for university, and hurrying to the door, she shouted to her mother, "Don't let Jake know about the letter, mum."

Chapter Four

The few days between receiving the letter from the school and the appointment taking place felt like an eternity for Ashly. In the past weeks she had encountered some trouble at her workplace and additionally had been accused by a client to have brokered a fake painting from Paul Horton for him.

Ashly liked the artist because of his distinctive naïve style and its pastel, strong colours, leading one into a world of myth and magic. Many years ago she had met him in person at an art exhibition and would never have thought that he could paint such wonderful work. The vivid colours of his paintings were even better in reality and later she had decided to buy one of his pictures for her mother's 60th birthday.

Fortunately, the dispute with that client was settled when his accusation was proven wrong. Nevertheless, the whole incident had caused Ashly sleepless nights and the stress and worries of the last weeks showed on her face. She was very nervous when she arrived at the school and entered the principal's room. The atmosphere was very friendly, and, when she sat down at the round meeting table, she became aware of a man whom she had never seen before.

"May I introduce you – this is Mrs. Mc Kenneth and this is Mr. Lund. And my name is Robert Wilson", the headmaster said, glancing at the two adults with a wan smile. After a short introduction he continued,

"Both your children, Jake and Claire, are extremely intelligent and I would like to discuss with you what we can do in order to best enhance their performances without adversely affecting the other pupils in class."

'Ah, it's only that!' Ashly thought and was of course very pleased to hear that Jake's teacher seemed to appreciate her son's intelligence. She looked expectantly at Mr. Lund, a rather small man with dark brown, slightly wavy hair. What was he going to say?

"Yes I know, my daughter Claire is a naturally gifted child despite me not being able to look after her all the time." His voice was very pleasant, deep and hoarse. He spoke slowly, and Ashly thought she could hear a Scandinavian accent. Swedish was her first impulse. Then again, his full dark hair made him appear more Slavic than Swedish or northern European. She also noticed a sparkle in his eyes. She knew that radiance. She had seen it many times in people born under the star sign Gemini. For a moment she forgot why she was in the headmaster's office, lost in her thoughts about this man and, secretly captivated by his voice, she got the impression that he was quite a pleasant fellow.

'He looks nice! I hope he isn't Gemini. They are supposed to be thinkers, very inquisitive but not hot passionate lovers.' All these thoughts flashed through her mind, while she fixated her gaze on the man sitting opposite her.

"It would be a shame not to acknowledge that Claire and Jake are very bright and way ahead of the other pupils. Sometimes this can be very disruptive to the class," the hard voice of the headmaster called Ashly back to reality.

Ashly knew about the talent of her son and hoped that Jake's classmates and teachers would show understanding.

"I am aware that being too clever can sometimes lead to difficulties at school and I appreciate your efforts," she said slowly, with an indifferent expression.

"Well," Mr. Wilson began to speak, "in Jake's case it is a bit complicated". He paused as if to look for words. "His teachers have the impression that he sometimes deliberately makes errors which makes teaching very difficult, and, if not having his own way, he can at times get quite heated."

Now Ashly felt unpleasant. She didn't like the implication of Mr. Wilson's pronouncement. As she hadn't discerned anything like that about her son, she didn't quite know what to say. Was the headmaster suggesting Jake was a difficult child?

As if Mr. Wilson had read her mind, he went on to explain,

"Don't get me wrong. It is our duty to look after all pupils – not just the bright ones. Jake may be a little bit out of place. It is at times difficult for the teachers to judge what he really knows and where he purposely makes mistakes."

"I'm sure it is," Ashly asserted in a wryly way. "So how can you facilitate his educational needs?"

She looked at Mr. Lund, seeking help. But Ulrik – as Ashly would later learn his first name was – sat on his chair, stony-faced and rather detached looking.

'Typical,' she thought disdainfully, 'he looks as if he has nothing to do with it all. It's not his child so he isn't bothered.'

"You should know that we really do our best!" the headmaster emphasized. "Jake's class teacher is already managing a balancing act. She is very eager to give the eight-year old the impression he is not different and yet to challenge him by giving him special tasks in class. In addition, Jake has another highly talented classmate, namely Claire, which makes it a little bit easier to hold usual classes."

"What do you mean?" Mr. Lund questioned, lifting his head.

"Well, not being challenged can prove extremely boring for gifted children. Perhaps another form of education would suit your children better," Mr. Wilson clarified and explained after a pause, "As Jake and Claire are both extremely clever, we try to include them in the teaching, for example letting them help other pupils who do not comprehend the learning material as quickly as your children do."

He looked meaningful at Ashly and Ulrik, and then continued, "We should avoid continuously giving the pair special treatment. That's why I invited you here today to talk to you both about your children's talents and perhaps find a solution to the problem "

"Like what?" Ashly and Mr. Lund asked in unison.

"They could for example go to a special school with other gifted children. There is one not too far from here, at the edge of town," the headmaster explained calmly.

Ashly looked again quizzically at Ulrik and she thought she could see some movement in his face. Indeed, he wasn't happy at all about the headmaster's proposal. Another school would cause inconvenience and involve more hassle for him, being a single parent. He had chosen this particular school for no other reason than it was close to home and he wouldn't need to arrange for Claire to be picked up. So far he had been able to combine his lecturing work at university with his daughter's school requirements. But what if that was going to change – what then? Heavy objection started to rouse in him. He cleared his throat and began to speak,

"To be honest – I don't like that idea. As far as I know my daughter likes it the way it is. So why change it?"

All eyes were directed towards Ulrik. Then Ashly, nodding her approval, spoke on,

"I know from Jake that he likes to help the other kids in school who are not as gifted as he. As long as he isn't showing off with his intellectual abilities, it seems to me all right where he is now."

"Well, it was your son who has already run into trouble being so clever. That's not the first time Jake got into fights and lies about it," the headmaster countered, glaring at Ashly with hard eyes.

'Hang on', Ashly thought, feeling very uncomfortable again, 'what's going on here?'

"And not only that," Mr. Wilson went on, turning towards Ashly with all his weight and leaning forward, "Jake shows little interest with routine and repetitive tasks", and then, turning towards Mr. Lund, he resumed harshly, "your daughter as well, Mr. Lund! Both children show demonstrative boredom which makes teaching in general sometimes very difficult."

The situation started to become somehow tense. Ashly had taught her son from when he was a toddler, now the headmaster implied that it was all wrong. She felt as if she was being bullied and struggled to find the right words.

"What are you doing as a school to help my child get along with his classmates?" she insisted on knowing with a straight look at the headmaster.

"Well, as I already explained – we do our best," Mr. Wilson said with a smug smile on his face, "Even so, we cannot just keep your children entertained by always providing more challenging tasks to them than the rest of the class."

"Your school is certainly not a platform where children are being *entertained*," Ashly objected indignantly. It seemed that Mr. Lund had left the conversation to her, as he kept quiet and it was for her to continue, "I don't expect you to fulfil impossible tasks. And I don't want my son to attend a different school. Surely there must be other options."

This time it was Ulrik who nodded approval.

Mr. Wilson looked at his watch. This meeting took much longer than anticipated and he wanted to finish it as soon as possible.

"There are several alternatives. Such as skipping classes, alternatively being excused from regular class on certain days, or attending school on certain subjects in higher classes, or taking part in special classes for gifted children in the afternoons in a special school," he outlined his proposals, emphasizing that all were tentative suggestions.

'I wonder why he didn't tell us sooner,' Ashly thought. She was a bit fretful and said aloud,

"Yes, where there is a will, there is a way. I don't mind if Jake is excused from regular class from time to time. I can teach him at home."

Mr. Lund was more reluctant.

"I will have difficulties if Claire is attending another school or skips classes. I'm a single parent and I'll be unable to align this with my work schedule," he objected heavily.

The headmaster tapped with his fingers on the

table, becoming more and more irritated at this lengthy discussion. It was almost lunchtime and he wanted to end this meeting.

"I am sure there will be a solution to your problem Mr. Lund. Maybe Mrs. Mc Kenneth can help and look after your daughter as well?" he glanced expectantly at Ashly.

Ulrik also looked at Ashly, waiting for her to answer.

"Why not?" she replied. Smiling approval, she continued, "Jake and Claire seem to get on well with each other, so why should they not skip classes? I suppose I can manage looking after another child for a few hours per week."

Mr. Wilson was very relieved – at last a possible solution!

"Well," he said with an appreciative expression on his face, "I will consult with the teachers and inform you about the outcome. You will hear from me soon." He stood up from his chair, wished the parents well, and left in a hurry.

◆◆◆

Both parents left the building rather silently. On their way to the car park Ashly wanted to know from Ulrik what he thought of the headmaster. When he looked at her she noticed again the sparkle in his eyes.

"I'm not too sure what to think," he said slowly. "Mr. Wilson made some good proposals and we have to see how they will work out." For him the problem – if it had been one – was solved satisfactory.

Ashly, however, tried to make her point,

"Our children are already special. They shouldn't be made more special." Looking askance at Mr. Lund, she went on, "They should really be mixing with other children, who may not be such quick learners, and learn to respect and interact with children from different backgrounds."

Standing in front of the Swedish man, she was waiting for a reaction. But he seemed to be far away with his thoughts.

"Sorry, what did you say?" he politely asked seconds later, with his look now targeting Ashly.

"Well, what would Jake and Claire gain with a special treatment for gifted children?" she raised her concerns. "Become even more gifted? What good would that do later in their life?"

"I don't know," Ulrik replied calmly. "I haven't had a chance to think about it."

"Our two kids are already experiencing difficulties as minors because they are so clever – how will that be when they are adults?"

Ashly had a lot of questions yet Ulrik was seemingly not in the mood to answer them. He was more interested in Ashly, her appearance, and the way she handled things. She was dressed in an effortlessly chic style with a touch of sex-appeal. Under her elegant black jacket she wore a low-cut white top. Her black hair was drawn back in a ponytail which, together with her red lipstick, underlined her feminine appearance. She looked amazing and that made her even more appealing to Ulrik despite the fact he hardly knew her. He was curious what she was doing for a living, since she seemed to have time to look after her son.

'She's probably married to a rich husband,' he suspected. And then his curiosity got the better of him and he asked straightforwardly where Ashly was working. What a surprise when he heard that she was a single parent too and she worked as an art historian at the university.

"I wonder why we never met," Ulrik said, and, noticing Ashly's look of astonishment, he explained, "I work at the university as well. I lecture archaeology."

"Archaeology," Ashly exclaimed cheerfully, "I once wanted to study that. But then I saw a picture of a rather imperial looking archaeologist, standing very relaxed over a find with his black shiny boots on, while all the natives were doing the hard work barefooted. That had put me off and instead I studied arts and became an art historian." She paused and then added with a winning smile, "After all, I think I'm not so much into digging but more into studying the artefacts that people have already found."

"Ah, so you like more the ancient things above ground, whereas I am more interested in what is below the ground," Ulrik remarked with a very distinguished Swedish accent in his voice.

"You are from Sweden!" Ashly was happy that she finally figured out his accent. "How come that you are over here?"

"My late wife was from here. We met on a holiday in Egypt. Well, I was working there and she was on a holiday," he clarified with a touch of melancholy.

"Your late wife? What happened?" Ashly asked considerately.

"She was killed by a gunshot while on a holiday in the Middle East two years ago," he explained quietly.

"Oh my god – I'm so sorry. That must have been terrible for you!" Ashly was visibly distressed.

"Never mind, life goes on," Ulrik tried to smile and added abruptly, "I would very much appreciate it if you could look after my daughter from time to time."

"Yes of course! No problem." Ashly was pleased that she could help that poor Swedish widower and his daughter.

"We can make all the arrangements when we get the final decision," the two adults agreed, and, after bidding goodbye to each other, they took off in opposite directions.

Chapter Five

As soon as Ashly came home, Iris was of course curious to find out how the meeting in school had gone on. When Ashly told her mother about a nice Swedish man named Ulrik, who had been at the same meeting, Iris became even nosier and was dying to know more about this man.

"Is he single? And where is he working?" Iris was very concerned about her daughter still not having found the right man to share her life with and feared for her daughter's future.

"Yes, he is single and he is an archaeologist lecturing at the university," Ashly told her mother.

Iris wasn't too pleased. She was somehow worried. The countless freak-outs of Rick were still present in her memory and she didn't want her daughter to be hurt again. Knowing nothing about Ulrik she simply assumed if a man, being the same age as her daughter, was still single, there must be something wrong with the fellow.

"What's wrong, mum?" Ashly noticed doubts on her mother's face.

"Well, I'm only afraid you may have become attracted to the wrong person again, darling" Iris expressed her worries. "It's not so long ago that you had come out of a relationship with an alcoholic." She paused, and glimpsing at her daughter she went on, "I would be very pleased if you would meet a man with whom you could be happy with."

Ashly rolled her eyes. This was so typical of her mother. She badly wanted a man on her daughter's side, a son-in-law. Whereas Ashly was sure that her mother wanted more a *son* than an *in-law*.

Indeed, Iris always wanted to have another child, a son. Unfortunately it hadn't been granted her. Ashly's father died on one of the many battlefields, never came home, but was buried somewhere unknown.

"I hope this, what was his name – Ulrik? – doesn't let you down," Iris said and had difficulties pronouncing the Swedish name.

"Mum! So far he has only asked if I can look after his daughter Claire from time to time, as he is a widower – nothing more!" Ashly said firmly.

When she heard the word "widower" Iris became all of a sudden very attentive.

"A widower – why is that?"

"His wife got killed when she was on a holiday," Ashly said without intention to tell her mother more about Ulrik. But when she saw her mother's questioning look, she quickly added, "She was shot in a holiday complex."

"How awful," Iris shook her head and commented resentfully, "the world is not a safe haven any more."

As she herself was a war widow for so many years, she totally condemned warfare. Being very agitated, she went on to voice her opinion,

"Now you can't even go on a holiday without having to fear for your life. I'll never understand why people are prepared to kill and to be killed and even seem to have pleasure shooting each other dead."

"There is a lot in this world you just can't change," Ashly stated.

She knew it would be a never ending story talking with her mother about guns and war. Whereas Iris never stopped to get to the bottom of injustices and wrong doings, Ashly wasn't so much bothered to alter the world. She, like some of the neighbours, regarded her mother unfairly as somehow stubborn and difficult to argue with. No wonder that there was plenty of gossip about Iris. A lot of it had to do with the fact that she didn't care what other people said. Iris had her own mind, and, following her own heart, she simply did what she wanted.

◆◆◆

A few days later Ashly picked up her son from school when she caught sight of Claire for the first time.

"Who is that girl over there with the red plaits?" she asked Jake who jumped in the car.

"That's my friend Claire," the boy answered. His little face beamed with pride. He was so delighted to have found a friend with whom he had so much in common and, like with no one else, he could share his interests.

Ashly thought it might be a good opportunity to tell Jake about the meeting at school.

"You know, I had recently a talk with Mr. Wilson, your head teacher. And since you are so bright we considered that you might skip some classes. You would stay at home and your teachers will give you extra work, more challenging and problem-solving stuff to be done at home, and I can supervise you."

Jake looked a bit baffled. He didn't like this idea, because he thought he then wouldn't be able to see Claire. Ashly noticed a big question mark in her son's face.

"What do you think?"

"What about Claire?" He glanced suspiciously at his mother.

"What about her?" Ashly put the safety belt on and started the car.

"I don't want to be without her," Jake hesitantly remarked.

"Well, I have agreed that Claire can stay with us on those particular days," Ashly said while steering the car through the narrow streets towards home.

"Cool!" Jake was very excited. "When is she coming?"

"It's not decided yet on which day – maybe on Wednesday afternoons," Ashly replied.

"It doesn't matter which day, as long as we can spend the time together," Jake spouted. He was thrilled by the thought that he would eventually be excused from classes, where he felt bored anyway, and his mum or granny would teach him. But not only that – Claire would stay with him and they could spend a lot of time together.

"Granny was right," he suddenly said, smiling secretly, "If you strive for something with all your heart it will come true." And after a little pause he added, "sooner or later."

◆◆◆

And so it happened that not long after the meeting at the headmaster's, Claire spent the future Wednesday afternoons with Jake. The first thing he did, when she arrived, was to introduce her to Iris.

"This is my granny – you know – the one with the big book."

"Hello Mrs. McKenneth," Claire said very politely. Iris realised the girl's handshake was rather soft and she didn't like it. 'Oh well that will have to change,' she thought and said aloud, "Welcome to our house Claire."

There wasn't much time for a talk, because Jake took over and dragged Claire away to show her his room filled with books and toys.

"Wow," pointing at the big wooden chest standing at the window, she exclaimed, "That's a treasure chest!"

"No," Jake objected, "that old thing is full with junk. Look here..." He opened the chest which was filled with all sorts of things, like Gameboy, soft toys, stones, chess, card games, and much more.

"You have an amazing collection of little treasures," Claire said, admiring the contents. "I wish I had such a trunk at home."

Jake, looking slightly confused, waited for an explanation.

"Our house is full with old stuff from all over the

world," she told him. "My dad says the figurines, tables, and knick-knacks are valuable antiques and I'm not allowed to touch any of the pieces."

"My granny has a lot of old stuff in her house as well, but I can touch anything I like," the boy said confidently.

He loved his granny's house with its nooks and crannies and its spider webs hanging from the ceiling in the hallway. The fact that it was old gave the house a very distinctive smell which was hard to describe, because it was mixed with the scent of the masses of flowers from the garden. No wonder that Iris's old home provided the perfect playground for the two kids. After Jake had proudly shown Claire his room upstairs, with the treasure chest being emptied and every item thoroughly inspected, they ran through the house where they spent quite some time playing hide and seek until Iris called them for a late lunch.

"Well, well," she said, trying to look serious, "you are supposed to have classes and not run through the house."

"Yeah," Jake exclaimed, "granny can you please tell us one of your stories. You know the story about the ghost in the house."

"A ghost in the house?" Claire asked in astonishment, her green eyes wide open.

"Yes," Jake emphasized, while he sat down on the table. "Did you not hear the noises when we were playing hide and seek?"

"No," Claire shook her head. Doubtfully looking at Jake and his grandmother, she said, "You are kidding me."

"No, no. Wait till you hear this." And then Jake started to tell a fantastic story, "One night I woke up because I heard some strange noises. They sounded like footsteps and I followed them down to the kitchen. There was also a strange breeze, but no window or door was opened. I heard a woman and a little girl talking and laughing…." – He started to giggle and at this stage his grandmother interrupted him.

"Enough!" she declared. "There are no ghosts in this house. You will scare the life out of your friend. And by the way – if there were any ghosts you definitely shooed them away with all the noises you've made."

Claire sat at the table, peering at Jake and his grandmother, and she didn't know what to make out of it all. Was there a real ghost in the house? She thought if so it was totally exciting.

"Yes! We could play ghost hunting," she proposed, being enthralled by the notion of catching a ghost. But Jake had a different idea.

"Oh granny, please, tell us the story about the little boy. You know the one who used to live next door – he came by and told you about the ghosts. Please," he beseeched his grandmother.

Iris hesitated. She didn't want to get the kids excited and was therefore not very keen on telling a ghost story. She wasn't too sure about the whole ghost stuff anyway. There had been some really strange things going on in her house. Then again, she found it surprising that neither Ashly nor Jake seemed to have been bothered by the noises at night. Maybe it was just a mere figment of her overly active imagination?

"Just as well that your mother couldn't arrange to have time off today and it's up to me how we spend the day," she tried to avoid the subject. "Once you have done your extra homework from school, I'll read you a story as a reward – a fairy tale, not a ghost story."

"Yeah," Jake exclaimed, and, turning towards Claire, he added with a serious ring in his tone, "You wait and see – all my granny's stories end with 'and they lived happily ever after'."

Unexpectedly Iris had been left alone with the two kids and she hadn't been able to prepare for such energetic children. Nevertheless, they had a good time together. She remembered a quote which she had recently read in a magazine: 'A creative adult is a child who survived.' And that was how she felt with the two very lively children in her house – she was young again and she enjoyed it.

While the youngsters huddled up to her on the settee, she told them the most wondrous adventure about a fairy in a land far away and the two kids listened attentively, eagerly following every word she said.

"And they lived happily ever after," Iris finished the story with a smile, leaving the comfortable couch to walk to the kitchen.

"See, I told you – my granny's stories always end up with everybody living happily ever after," Jake said aglow with joy and nudged his friend chuckling.

As it was a nice sunny day, it was really a shame to spend the rest of the afternoon inside the house.

"Come on, let's go in the garden," Iris said, with an inviting gesture opening the back door.

Jake and Claire were reluctant to follow. But since they weren't sure what else to do, they stepped behind her into the backyard. It didn't take long before both the children became absorbed with the colourful plants and the garden's wildlife. Iris smiled when she watched her grandson explaining to his friend about deadheading and creatures munching plants.

"My grandmother has some really poisonous plants in her garden," Jake spoke glowingly about his granny's nature resort, as he called the garden. His excitement of discovery was undeniable while he pulled Claire along.

"Here for example, this Foxglove, or see here that blue one – Aconitum is its name. That's an extremely toxic plant, also called Monkshood because of its flowers being shaped like a hood." He visibly enjoyed giving Claire a little lecture on his grandmother's plants. And Iris felt great, as her grandson seemed to share her passion for nature.

◆◆◆

It was late afternoon by the time Ashly arrived home. She was greeted by her son, jumping into her arms the very moment she came through the door, and telling her excitedly what a great time he and his friend had enjoyed with granny.

"Yes," Claire, standing a bit timid in the background, confirmed, eagerly nodding, "Since my mum died I haven't had as much fun as today."

The girl's words warmed both Ashly's and Iris' hearts, causing a feeling of sadness and compassion.

"Well, you know, you are always welcome at our house," Iris said, gently putting her arms around Claire.

Before Ashly, who was filled with melancholy at the thought how dreadful it had been losing her own father when she was only a young child, could say anything, the doorbell rang. It was Ulrik, picking up his daughter. Just as well. Both women were glad of the distraction which occurred so fortunately at the right moment.

"Don't let the man stand outside the door," Iris instructed her daughter. "Come on in, Rick" she said to Ulrik who was used to people shortening his name and didn't mind Iris doing it as well.

"It's Ulrik," Ashly reminded her mother, "His name is ULRIK, not Rick."

"Never mind," Iris responded and gestured for the man to come into the living room, while she sized him up. Her first impression was that he was quite attractive, though she wasn't able to say what exactly it was that made him likeable. He looked fresh-faced and appeared calm and friendly, as he walked into the house. His full dark brown hair matched his brown eyes. Iris instantly noticed the sparkle in his eyes and was curious to know more about him. Since Ulrik had just finished a hard day at work, he only wanted to pick up his daughter and go home. Therefore he very politely refused the offer of a cup of tea. Iris fell immediately for his husky voice and it was meant honestly when she said to him "see you again" while walking him and Claire to the door.

◆◆◆

"What a nice man," Iris was all enthused about Ulrik. Ashly wasn't answering and hence Iris spoke on, "Isn't he?"
"Well yes, not too bad," Ashly mumbled. For a moment her mind was occupied, thinking back of Rick. So many times he had insulted her and tried to make her feel inferior. Her life with him had been an emotional roller coaster and she didn't want it to happen ever again. In hindsight she concluded that he had simply been a man with an unstable nature, fraught with all sorts of problems which he had tried to solve by compulsively drinking. And Ulrik – was he different? She wondered what he was like. He didn't appear as a pushy overachiever, but seemed to be very laid back.
Her mother interrupted her.
"Did you see the sparkle in his eyes?" Iris tried again to get her daughter's attention. "Is he Gemini? People with the star sign Gemini are said to have the gift of the gab. Whereas this Ulrik is rather

quiet, isn't he."

"If you want to know when his birthday is – I haven't found out," Ashly replied. She knew her mother would like to know Ulrik's star sign to check whether he would be compatible with Ashly.

"I don't want to judge him, but doesn't he look more like he's from Eastern Europe than from the Northern part?"

"Yes, mum!" Ashly really didn't want to talk about this man.

"I like Ulrik," Jake interrupted all of a sudden with a big smile on his little face. "He tells such cute stories about the ancient world."

"How do you know that? You never met him before, or?" Iris and Ashly were both surprised.

"Claire keeps telling the whole class what she learns from her daddy. Did you know that in early times there had been many gods?" he asked the two baffled women. "Apparently, the ancient people had different gods for a variety of occasions and they worshipped all these different deities. This is called 'Multi-Theism'. And then, some decades later, the ancient gods were all abolished gradually, and one god was installed. This is why we speak of 'Mono-Theism', because there is only one god in each of the big religions". Jake chirped along, looking at the women with a big smile on his face.

"Wow," Ashly remarked, "Claire taught you that?"

"Yes," Jake answered, fervently nodding. He seemed to get much fun out of presenting his knowledge to his nearest and dearest, because he continued,

"Did you know that the Romans used to burn the dead at the stakes? Unlike Christians and Moslems, they didn't believe that a dead body had to be in one piece in order to ascend into heaven."

"No," Ashly admitted and was amazed by her son's knowledge. 'No wonder his teachers say Jake is difficult – he really knows a lot,' Ashly ruminated, still keeping the conversation with Mr. Wilson in mind.

"Well, well, little man. Is there anything else you like about that Rick – alias Ulrik?" Iris enquired, waiting eagerly to get to know more about the Swedish man who had appeared so very polite and well mannered.

"No, not really, I just like him the way he is," Jake answered hesitantly and after a moment of silence he left the room to play upstairs.

Iris gave up. She realised that neither her daughter nor her grandson fancied talking about Ulrik.

'If I was younger I could become infatuated with that friendly man,' she thought and went to read her newspaper.

◆◆◆

The next time when Ulrik picked up his daughter, Iris didn't let him get away so easily. She drilled him with questions.

"Ah," Ulrik said with a smile, "the *Irish questionnaire*." As he understood that Iris was genuinely interested in him, he took the questioning from her in good humour and answered whatever it was, she wanted to know, with a wink.

Of course, the first thing Iris quizzed him for was his birthday.

"My birthday – you don't really want to know when my birthday is," he warded Iris off, laughing. "I'm older than you think."

Yet, Iris wasn't easily deterred. She could be quite persistent at times.

"No, no, I don't want to know how old you are but on which day you were born."

"I was born on the 14th of June," he disclosed.

"So you are Gemini – I knew it!" Iris exclaimed, darting a knowing look at her daughter.

"Yes," Ulrik confirmed. He couldn't understand why the elderly lady was so cheerful.

Iris went on wisecracking. "The 14th is the same day as my birthday," she explained.

"Oh, is it?"

"Yes, but my birthday is a few months later," she

said with a little smile.

He laughed, "And now you want me to ask you how old you are?"

"No, no, I suppose you are bright enough to imagine that I'm of an age where I have a bus-pass," she replied amused, after a small pause resuming, "So now I've found out your birthday – tell me more about yourself, what about you birthplace?"

"I was born in Malmö," Ulrik answered, "It's the third largest city in Sweden and the sixth largest in the Nordic countries."

"Malmö?" Iris could hardly pronounce the name of the Swedish city.

"Yes, my family still lives there."

During the further conversation Iris bombarded Ulrik with her questions, trying to find out more about him.

"No it wasn't because of lust and passion or for personal fame and glory. Since I was always interested in history I studied archaeology," he answered Iris question as to why he was so interested in ancient remains and their stories. "Digging and discovery of ancient civilisation is a very fascinating part of my job."

"Is this where you met your late wife – at university?" Iris nosily inquired.

"No, I met her in Egypt where I had taken part in

some excavations," Ulrik seemed hesitant to continue. For a little moment he dipped into the past, remembering Kate as she walked by the excavation site and being very interested in ancient Egyptian history. Later they met again at the swimming pool of the nearby hotel. She was climbing out of the pool when he caught sight of her. Her beautiful body was hardly covered with the wet bikini and with her drenched long red hair she looked ever so sexy. A beautiful woman and he had instantly fallen in love with her. Somehow Ashly reminded him of Kate, although on the outside they had nothing in common.

Iris was patiently waiting for him to continue.

"Ja," he said in Swedish, but then continued to explain in English, "we got married and then we tried very hard to have a child…," he suddenly faltered, remembering the day when he received the phone call that his beloved wife had been shot dead. Taking a deep breath, he spoke on, "Claire was five years old when her mother died."

"I'm so sorry for your loss," Iris said kindly "It must have been terrible for you, especially when your daughter was so young and you had to raise her on your own."

With a weary look at Iris, Ulrik asserted,

"I did what most people do in such a tragic situation

— I stuck my head into work. I gave up the digging and discovering and became a lecturer. Fortunately there was a vacancy and ever since then I'm up to my neck in work."

"This explains why you couldn't go back to Sweden," Iris assumed. "What about your family there?"

"My parents are both pensioners. And as you probably know yourself — pensioners never have enough time. Apart from that, they are relatively old and I didn't want to leave Claire with them."

Claire nodded assiduously.

"Sure, I preferred to stay with my dad," she declared, holding on to her father.

"After all, that may have been a wise decision of my daughter, because otherwise we would never have met," Ulrik said, warmly looking at his daughter.

"Yes, and I wouldn't have met Jake," the girl confirmed with a big smile flickering across her face.

"That's right." Putting his empty tea cup on the table, Ulrik asked politely,

"Any more questions, Ma'am, or am I allowed saying good-bye now?"

"Of course, I forgot that you may have had a long and hard day," Iris acknowledged, tickled pink by the Swede's wits. "It was great talking to you. But I have one more question — what about the family of your late wife?" She deliberately prolonged the conversation because she liked his voice so much.

Ashly was somewhat ashamed by the persistence of her mother. Did she not notice that Ulrik looked tired and wanted to leave? He was however a nice person and respectfully responded to Iris request.

"Very briefly, because I really want to go home. Both my in-laws died many years ago. One sister-in-law still lives over here and both my brothers-in-law live abroad." He guessed that Iris was dying to hear where the two brothers-in-law lived, so he continued, "one lives in Japan and the other in the Caribbean."

"Oh dear," Iris summed it all up, "That's quite an interesting family."

"Absolutely," he confirmed, "they're spread all over the world. Listen, now I really must go." And looking at his daughter, he asked her, "Ready to go?"

Claire nodded.

"Yes unfortunately. I liked it very much here," she said regretfully. Unlike her father she was reluctant to leave.

"Don't worry. You'll be back next week," Iris said warm-heartedly and tenderly hugged the girl. Then she turned towards the Swedish widower to bid him good bye.

"Well Ulrik, it was really a pleasure talking to you. Have a nice evening."

"You too," he replied, having arrived at the front door. "And thanks a lot for looking after my daughter."

Chapter Six

"I do like that Swedish fellow. He is so unassuming and really easy to get on with." Iris started the conversation with her daughter after Ulrik had left. She was beguiled by his charm and acumen.

"What was his name? Rick?"

"No, ULRIK," Ashly enlightened her mother again.

"Oh well, Ulrik. What a coincidence – the similarities of the names," Iris pointed out. Noticing her daughter's frown, she hastily continued, "Well, we shouldn't get the names mixed up. I think that charming man Ulrik is a much better match for you than Rick ever was!"

For a moment Ashly was confused. Her mother's observation on the men's names hadn't occurred to her yet. Yes indeed – Ulrik with his sparkling eyes was a nice guy and not to be confused with that bully Rick.

"Why do you not see him more often," Iris

interrupted her daughter's thoughts. "He is Gemini – a good match for you," she went on. Firmly believing her daughter and this polite Swedish man would make a good pair, she would have liked them to be together.

Ashly raised her eyebrows. She hated it when her mother tried to talk her into doing something. Obviously she had her own views on how and with whom to spend her time.

"Live to your own expectations and don't care what other people say," she quoted her mother, "You always told me to live my own life."

"Yes sure, honey. But like all mothers, I only want what is best for you. That's a mother's role in life," Iris objected, flinging a meaningful look at her daughter.

"Mum, you only want me to marry a safe and, what I think, a boring man!"

Ashly was annoyed. Having been single for some time now, she did of course not want to stay that way. Unlike her mother, who wished for a man committing to a serious relationship with her daughter, Ashly didn't want to rush into things. Since she had broken up with Rick, she had been going out a lot. Almost every time she ended up getting to know very interesting people, yet "Mr. Right" wasn't amongst them. She wasn't completely happy with her life at present. Everything went smoothly – a little bit too smoothly, according to Ashly's taste. Something to spice up her life was missing. A love affair perhaps? Nothing really serious – just a man to have some fun and excitement with. Yes, a little adventure to give a bit of zing to her life would be fine, but that was difficult to explain to her mother.

"A safe man needn't be boring," Iris didn't give in.

"I see! So why did you never get married again?" Ashly challenged her mother with a fierce glow in her eyes. She knew quite well that Iris had never really followed rules for her gender: Marrying again had definitely not been an option for her. Ever since Ashly's father had died, Iris kept her life to herself. She didn't want people to stick their noses in her private affairs. Ashly was the long-awaited and only child. Her mother naturally indulged her and even more so when she was brought up without a father.

Iris was in her mid-30s when she had given birth to the baby girl and Ashly was almost the same age as Claire when her father had died. Being a single parent at that time was definitely not easy. People sometimes came up with either really weird advice on how to handle a toddler, or were speculating why the little girl had no father. Fortunately Ashly developed rapidly and grew into a confident young woman. Since she was very talented, she received a grant, enabling her to go to university and starting her own life.

In all these years Iris never let her love life show to Ashly. Of course she had the occasional little affair. There had been men trying to comfort her, though she never allowed that and always stayed independent. Above all, there was only one man, she had genuinely loved, and that was Ashly's father, she so dearly missed. There had been times when she thought she could just snap her fingers and her beloved husband would be back with her. But sadly, through his death she had learned in a very brutal way that she could never get the affectionate moments with him back. Consequently she had spent as much time as possible with the daughter she limitlessly loved.

Ashly knew it wasn't fair on her mother to speak in such a harsh manner. She understood quite well the hardship of her mother's life; that she was reluctant to get vulnerable and therefore lived a very quiet life. Still, somehow Ashly wished her mother would stop treating her like a child.

Seconds later she said,

"Mum, I know you only mean well for me. But you don't win any points if you always tell me what to do." Ashly went over and embraced her mother tenderly. "Don't look at me like that. I want you to think of me as an adult. I'm not a little girl. Yes, Ulrik is a nice guy. There is nothing wrong with him, but there is something about him, and I can't explain to you why I'm not drawn to him wholeheartedly."

Iris nodded and meeting her daughter's eyes she replied,

"Honey, you will always be my girl – little or grown up. We don't have to talk about anything. Not if you don't want to. Never mind, I only believe that you shouldn't be so hard on that charming Swedish widower."

◆◆◆

A couple of weeks later Ashly found a note in her pigeon hole at her workplace. It was from Ulrik asking her out for a date, 'Can I treat you to dinner on Friday next week?' the note said.

It had taken Ulrik some time until he had the courage to ask Ashly out. And although he would have loved to date her, he never dared to ask her directly. The invitation via a little written message was easier for him than facing Ashly in person, as he feared she might decline his request. Now the ball was in her court, and all he had to do was to wait and see, hoping of course that she would accept.

From the very first time when he had met her at the headmaster's office, he was attracted to her, seduced by her feminine charm. He thought himself lucky that Ashly had agreed to look after Claire on their home schooling days, and he always enjoyed being close to her during the short time at her house when he picked up his daughter. Unfortunately Iris was always there and she seemed to dominate the conversation, besides he was much too well behaved to simply ignore the peppy lady and her boundless questions.

Ulrik was no adventurer when it came to emotions. The next time when he picked up his daughter at the Mc Kenneth house he was a bit apprehensive, because so far Ashly hadn't responded to his dinner proposal. When he knocked at the door he thought everybody would hear his rapidly beating heart. He almost froze, and then fortunately Jake opened the door and called Ulrik in. As if Ashly had sensed his internal turmoil, she said right away with a smile on her face in almost perfect Swedish that she was pleased to accept his invitation for Friday evening. She really took Ulrik by surprise!

◆◆◆

The time until Friday seemed to pass rather quickly. Ulrik plunged into his work, only to leave earlier on Friday to get ready for his date. In the early evening he drove his vintage white Volvo to pick up Ashly.

"*Hej Ulrik,*" Ashly welcomed him in Swedish. "Let's go." And on the way to the car she asked, "Where are you taking me?"

"That's for me to know and for you to wonder," Ulrik replied with a wink as he opened the car door for Ashly. He was looking forward to his rendezvous with this charming woman, hoping that the recently opened pub-restaurant, situated in the old part of town down by the harbour, would turn out to be the right place to have a quiet intimate dinner.

It was a short, enjoyable drive. As it was early summer the air was quite warm, trees and bushes alongside the road showed their full colour potential, the skyline of the city sparkled in the sun, and there was that distinctive smell of the salty sea when they approached the road leading to the harbour.

Ulrik was a little bit anxious and had butterflies in his tummy – this attractive woman, sitting beside him, he inhaled her perfume. In former times he would have talked too much and too quickly when he was nervous. Luckily that had settled over time.

As he was driving very smoothly, Ashly took much

pleasure in the ride in the old Volvo with the man who smiled at her so winsomely. While she was very relaxed, Ulrik was frantically searching for a topic of conversation. All sorts of thoughts raced through his mind, at the same time having to concentrate on the traffic. He was all churned up inside – like coffee grounds which had to settle. Then he forced himself to calm down.

"How are you getting on with your work?" he finally managed to start a conversation.

"Well nothing special at the moment," Ashly replied rather reluctantly, as she was so much enjoying the view of the landscape in the beautiful summer evening. "At the moment I'm working on an interdisciplinary project. We are looking at hidden messages, such as postures and body parts in paintings and sculptures." She stopped – would he understand what she was talking about? "You know, in the fifteenth and sixteenth century a man's leg painted over a woman's thigh was for example a clear symbol of sex," she explained.

This was definitely not one of his favourite subjects. Nevertheless he said politely, "Aha, sounds interesting".

"Yes. If you ever come across of Michelangelo's works, you may be able to see it yourself. Apart from this, it's a job paying for my expenses," she replied aloud while silently observing, 'he has such nice hands.'

Ulrik's hands were not very muscular, rather soft and small with round, well-proportioned fingers. The skin appeared smooth, warm and gentle.

'A thin wrist indicates mental sensitivity,' she remembered one of her students had told her recently, when they were talking about how difficult it was to sketch hands.

There was no time left for a further conversation, because the eating place was within sight and Ulrik slowed down the car. After having parked the Volvo at the waterfront, he said,

"I hope you like the restaurant. The menu has a great variety of choices."

"That sounds good to me. I love good food and I'm not too difficult to please." Ashly smiled and was curious how the evening with Ulrik would unfold.

◆◆◆

The Alehouse, as the pub was called, was an insiders' tip. It was a little family operated place with an ambience that exuded romance and, despite being somehow hidden, it was very busy. Ulrik had chosen it because it was allegedly a seductive spot at which couples could create connections whilst dining superbly. Tables were hard to get. Nonetheless, Ulrik had been fortunate – he had reserved a table for two for eight o'clock. The furnishing was plain and simple, whereas the tables were laid out beautifully with candles, white dinner plates, elegant cutlery, and exquisite glasses. The mood lighting was dimmed, but enough to see clearly what was on the plate. In spite of its plain interior the service was excellent and the food was indeed scrumptious: aged steaks, fresh seafood and other delicious dainty entrées as well as desserts.

Ashly had ordered fish and it tasted so fresh as if it had just been caught in the sea outside the restaurant.
"I like fish," she said in Swedish, trying to practise the language, "especially when it tastes as delicious as this one."
"We have a lot of fish in Sweden as well."
"Sure you have – there's plenty of water," Ashly laughed.
"No, I mean we eat a lot of fish. Apart from that, Swedes are very inventive when it comes to Fish," he made a pause and then added, "and vodka."
Ulrik noticed Ashly's questioning look.
"Yes, we have soft Swedish candies called 'Swedish Fish' and some people soak gummy bears in vodka," he explained.

"Ugh, yuck! That sounds horrible," Ashly grimaced.

"It doesn't only sound horrible, but it tastes disgusting," Ulrik agreed. "It's not for me – I like a good meal better as well as a good wine."

"Me too," Ashly approved whilst holding her glass of excellent white wine up. A little while later she said, "You have some nice landscapes in Sweden."

Instead of answering, Ulrik caught her eye and asked,

"Have you ever been to Sweden?"

"Yes, a long time ago. When I was a student I travelled through Europe. I was in Malmö as well."

"Oh, have you been to the festival in August? It starts off with a crayfish party. People go really crazy. They wear colourful hats and eat tons of crayfish. We could have met there and then," he said jestingly.

"No, unfortunately not. When I was in Malmö there was no festival and no bridge over the Sound."

"*Ja, ja* the *Sundet* as we call the straight between Copenhagen and Malmö. That was opened in July 2000. You must have been to my country before that date."

"I can't remember when exactly it was. All I remember is that the people were very friendly and the landscape was stunning."

"Just like the people here," Ulrik commented, "and

your country. This little place has so much to offer," pointing to the window, he continued, "Have a look outside – is this scenery not beautiful?"

Indeed. From the restaurant one had a breathtaking view over the water. A couple of big ships, far outside on the tranquil sea, were on their way to the harbour. The spectrum of colours was dazzling. The blue sky was in stark contrast to the lush green of the rolling hills surrounding the white seashores. In the far background a few clouds were hanging over the dramatic sea cliffs. And the sun, breaking through the clouds, reflected the mountains on the water.

"I can only agree with that," Ashly said while her gaze rested on the view outside. "One forgets so easily how wonderful this little jewel is when one lives here."

"You don't need to go on holiday – you have everything to relax right outside your doorstep, so to speak," Ulrik observed.

Ashly took a deep breath. 'Maybe he is right,' she thought. Nevertheless, she was yearning for a holiday, adventure and excitement.

"How strange that I've never heard about the Alehouse before. It's such a lovely place to eat," she remarked after they had finished their meal.

"A friend of mine recommended it to me. And I'm

pleased that you like it," he replied. On balance, it seemed that he had chosen the right place and he was relieved that so far the evening had turned out delightful. As Ashly was somehow easy-going, he felt totally relaxed in her presence. In the course of their tête-à-tête he had discovered that they had quite a lot in common – their sense of humour, their love for food and wine, and life in general. For all that, he had got the impression that the attractive woman was not averse to flirting. When they left the cosy place they were both in high spirits and smiled.

◆◆◆

The restaurant was only footsteps away from the old lighthouse which was surrounded by parkland from where one had a magnificent view of the Lough. Ulrik didn't want the evening to end here but sought to continue enjoying Ashly's company. A soft evening breeze wafted over the sea. The scent of summer was in the air and it made him feel elated.
"A little exercise will help us to work off our dinner. What do you think of a walk?" he suggested. And with an inviting gesture he put his arm on Ashly's shoulders.
"Yes, why not." Ashly liked walking and she immediately agreed to a little stroll alongside the

waterfront towards the lighthouse. The beautiful scenery caught her imagination.

"You know," she said, trying to put her thoughts into words, "people often say, when seeing such spectacular scenery like this sunset, it looks like a painting. But nobody can paint as good as nature itself."

"Yes you are right. I never thought about it, to be honest," Ulrik agreed. He tried to draw near Ashly. Her perfume drove him mad. Every time she turned her back on him he could smell it.

"This is so beautiful," Ashly murmured, as if she was talking to herself. Being an art expert, she remembered an awful acrylic painting from a Canadian artist which she had recently seen.

"No," she shook her head, "no artist can paint as good as Mother Nature." She didn't really expect Ulrik to answer and, feeling a little bit constrained, she wasn't sure what else to talk about. Even more so, when she suddenly sensed that Ulrik wanted more of her, but she didn't really want to end up in his bed – at least not just yet.

They silently walked side by side to the little park. The view from there was simply stunning: A fantastic interaction of smells and colours and of cloud formations, as they are not seen every day. There was the brawl of the sea and its characteristic smell of salt and decay, of fish, and seaweed. Not to mention the gorse with its yellow flowers and its very distinctive scent of coconut and vanilla which Ashly had already noticed on the way to the restaurant.

'When gorse is out of bloom, kissing is out of season,' she remembered an old saying and was surprised that the bushes were still blooming in June. The bright golden flowers lifted her spirit. Suddenly she was overcome by romantic feelings.

"This feels like a holiday," she resumed the conversation with Ulrik who stood quietly beside her. She kept it to herself that she would have loved nothing more but a little break from the routine of her every day schedule. The lights of ships glittering in the distance did their bit to unleash Ashly's travel lust. Looking straight ahead, her thoughts began to wander. 'Either a holiday or an adventure with an exciting man… or both?' she ruminated and looked at Ulrik. But was he the right man? Or would he not rather turn out like Rick? 'Ul-Rick' an inner voice alarmed her and made her almost freeze instantly.

◆◆◆

Would the evening have unfolded differently if Ulrik could have read Ashly's mind at that very moment? It was that crucial second where he was close enough to touch her. Turning towards her, he was absolutely intrigued by her. There was an aura around Ashly that made her irresistible. She was the kind of person he really liked, striking him as a warm-hearted intelligent woman. His heart started racing with excitement, as he was going to ask her if she knew about Midsummer Night – the most typically Swedish tradition of all, when the sun never sets and Swedes dance around a pole.

"The night before Midsummer's Day is supposed to be a magical time for love," he uttered. For a moment he was swept back to the celebrations in his home country, to the magically glowing landscapes where he saw himself dancing with Ashly under the maypole and later strolling arm in arm to the nearby bonfire. He looked at her, being totally drawn to her, he wanted to hold her in his arms. Yet, Ashly seemed somehow far away, absent from reality and he didn't want to interrupt her. After a while of silence he suggested,

"Let's go back." It was a smart move. Curbing his desire for her, he finally realised it might be better to give her more time and space.

"Yes, it's getting a bit chilly out here now that the sun is setting," Ashly happily accepted his suggestion.

She noticed that she felt somehow comfortable

with him. He had a lot going for him: charisma, pleasant to talk to, and not bad looking. He was an engaging character and she didn't want to hurt his feelings, nor did she want to spoil the fun. She was tempted to turn towards him and hug him but hesitated. Was there more to him than just a pretty face? A sudden reminder of her failed relationship with Rick made her feel uneasy. She tried to put the past away and concentrate on Ulrik. For a moment their eyes met, but she broke off. No, she wasn't ready yet for another man to seriously share her life with. And if any, she was seeking for an open relationship without any demands. Ulrik seemed a bit clingy to her, not exactly what Ashly wanted at the moment.

The situation was a bit reserved when they walked back through the park to the car. Acting on impulse, she said,

"Thank you for the pleasant evening. I had a really good time."

She looked at Ulrik who was a bit perplexed, not intending to let the evening fade away like that. Ashly's sensual elegance had totally captured him. She wasn't at all like any woman he had met since his wife died. At this moment she meant everything to him. Arriving at the car, he leaned against the Volvo, glancing avidly at Ashly. She looked stunning!

His gaze followed her body downwards, her face and neck, her breast and hips, and lastly her legs. He was again very much drawn to pull her over and kiss her. She was so beautiful. Being unavoidably attracted to her, he wanted to reach out for her when suddenly something in her posture said DO NOT TOUCH ME! He instinctively bounced back as if he had been bitten by a snake. A little bit confused he opened the car door for Ashly. And when in the car he tried to strike up a conversation, but the drive remained an awkward silence until they reached Ashly's home. By now it was dark and the light in Iris' living room signalled that she was still awake.

"Well, thanks again for the wonderful evening. See you next Wednesday," Ashly said brusquely, quickly climbing out of the car.

"Yes thank you for your company," Ulrik replied drily, adding in Swedish: "*godnatt*."

And without looking back he drove off.

Of course, he hadn't expected his night out with Ashly would end so abruptly at her doorstep. Surely, he was disappointed. Which man wouldn't be? He had received the impression that she would lean more towards him. Obviously he was all wrong. He was inwardly steaming. Driving home through the night he mulled over what kind of person Ashly was. Good looking and intelligent —she was definitely his choice of a woman. Would he be able to win her over?

"I have to give her more time," he told himself, realising that he had to curb his desire for that woman who reminded him so strongly of his late wife Kate.

When he passed by the illuminated hotels at the waterfront he felt somehow lousy at the thought of his clandestine fling with a married woman. They met frequently to spend a few hours in bed together. Nobody knew about her – not even his daughter Claire. But Ashly was something else and she started to shape things in his mind.

◆◆◆

Iris must have heard the car coming, because she opened the door as soon as Ashly arrived at the house, bursting with curiosity to learn how her daughter's date with that affable Swedish man had gone.

"Mum, you are still up. How did you know I was coming home?"

"I didn't. But I took what you told me about your feelings for Ulrik seriously and didn't expect you spending the night with him. How was your evening, darling?" Iris asked, nosily looking at her daughter.

"The restaurant, the food, everything was marvellous," Ashly enthused. "And I think Ulrik is very fond of me... But..." – there was some hesitation in her voice.

"But – what?"

"I felt very comfortable with him – but I'm not enamoured by him," Ashly went on about her date, sounding tired.

"Why not – He's a nice guy."

"I don't know. I really don't know. Yes, he's definitely pleasant, with his winsome smile and charming looks, but...," Ashly tried to find words to explain it to her astounded mother.

"But – what?" Iris inquired again, eager to know what her daughter tried to tell her.

"I don't know. There's something holding me back from opening up to him. I can't explain it. He seems to be a bit clingy," Ashly looked sincerely at her mother.

"Clingy?" Iris asked with a disbelieving look. "The man didn't appear at all clingy," she mumbled. After a little while she resumed, "Well, then leave it for the time being. I think after all you went through with your last relationship you're looking for emotional support, not just a one-night-stand or sex."

There was nothing Iris wouldn't do to keep her daughter happy. Yet, little did she know that Ashly was by contrast looking for an adventure to add some spice to her mundane life.

◆◆◆

Ever since the night out with Ashly, which had in the end turned out so frustrating for Ulrik, because her reaction had suggested that she wasn't interested in any serious relationship with him, he rather reluctantly accepted that the two just stayed good friends. Accordingly, they went out for a meal from time to time, but it was never as romantic as their first date.

Although Ulrik sometimes felt that Ashly was playing with his heart, he was very cautious not to impose on her, but to make allowances for her feelings. As far as he understood, she must have had a rough time with her previous partner – a bloke called Rick as he had learned in the meantime. Thinking about her past complicated relationship, he was musing whether she may subconsciously mistrust him for the remarkable similarity of the two names – 'Ulrik' and 'Rick'. That would perhaps explain as to why Ashly wasn't opening up to him.

All things considered, he optimistically thought,

'Hey, I'll take you on. See what the future has in store.'

Ashly appreciated Ulrik's patience and was more than happy to have found such a dependable and reliable friend. She just loved spending time with this unassuming man, not being aware that she might be leading him on.

Chapter Seven

With the summer holidays coming up, close cooperation between the adults was required. Arrangements had to be made for the two youngsters who were by now energetic ten years old. At school the children were excited, naturally looking forward to lazy mornings and days. Most of them would spend their holidays as they did every year, including Claire and Jake. She would go to Sweden to see her family there, and he would spend the time with his beloved granny and mum.

Thinking of the forthcoming break, Jake felt a little bit blue this time. The older he grew the more he missed his soulmate Claire when she was away on holiday. Never mind what the other kids did in their holidays – Jake was just happy to be with his friend and to spend as much time as possible together, either gaming or sticking their heads in books, reading. Preferably they hung out in the treehouse which Claire's father had once built in one of the old oak trees in the back of the garden. It was like a secret den with a little porch, only visible when the leaves had fallen in winter, stuffed with pillows and all sorts of publications. Amongst all the books there was one which they especially favoured – *The Little Prince*, by French author *Antoine de Saint-Exupéry* – Basically a story about a little boy from another planet, travelling different planets and meeting different characters, and each chapter containing thought-provoking allegories of the human condition.

Sitting at the edge of the little porch, high above the ground, with his legs hanging down, Jake said,

"This book is full with wisdom. Our parents should read it too!"

"Yes," Claire immediately agreed, "it would make our life easier, wouldn't it?"

The leaves of the old oak tree, covering the treehouse, rustled in the wind as Jake spoke on,

"I guess, I'll never understand adults," and looking at Claire, he asked, "What does the Little Prince say?"

As if by command, the two friends simultaneously quoted from the book: "Grown-ups never understand anything for themselves, and it is tiresome for children to always and forever explain things to them."

Enjoying the warm summer weather, the kids talked a lot about their parents – how stubborn both were. Could they not see that they were a perfect match?

"Why do our parents not get on with each other?" Jake asked out of the blue.

"Well, grown-ups, you know, they can be quite difficult at times," Claire replied.

"Still, why can they not get along?" Jake responded, and looking at the girl, he continued, "We are doing well together, aren't we?" After a moment he added in a low voice, "All the other children in school have a dad – I would like to have one too."

"Yes," Claire agreed gingerly, "we are getting on very well together." She tried to be helpful but didn't know what else to say to Jake. For a moment she was busy thinking about her dad until the loss of her mum came to mind. She could hardly remember her, but she would never forget the good times they had together. ... Claire looked out in the sky – everything looked so beautiful, the white clouds, the birds. ... She herself quite liked the idea of being one family and, feeling a warm glow in her heart, she turned towards Jake and said with a smile, "It would be wonderful if we all could become a family."

Jake couldn't agree more!

As the days passed, it turned out that Jake and Claire had a lot in common which bound them together even more. Neither of them liked swanky, flashy things, swaggering or boasting, and thought that make-up and designer clothes were overrated. Just like Jake, Claire too preferred to stay in the background rather than being in the spotlight. Contrary to Jake, she was more balanced. Her red braids had been cut off some time ago, but her freckles were still there and so was her perspicacity. As young as she was, she had already realised that there were people who, by talking too much, created problems where there were none only to have something they could lament and talk about.

"Language is the source of all misunderstanding," she often pondered lately, referring to one of her favourite books in which she had read a similar line.

Apart from that, both juniors were naturally very helpful and always seeking the truth. Their motto was to be invariably honest, because this was the clearest path through life. A liar would need a very good memory and it was in their opinion much too demanding to always remember *everything*.

"You know, once you start lying you have to invent

more lies," Claire explained to Jake.

"Yes," Jake agreed, "And by doing so you get more into trouble. In the end one is caught in a web of lies from where there is no escape."

"Sooner or later the truth will be revealed anyway," the girl confirmed earnestly. Not in a million years could she foresee how right she would be one day.

◆◆◆

And then came the day when school finished for the long summer break. Claire and her father were in a hurry to get things done. They left soon after, as they wanted to be home in Sweden for Midsummer Eve at the end of June. This time Jake got a first taste of what it was like to be left alone. Fortunately his soulmate was back before his life turned into what he regarded "*misery*".

In the meantime his mother had promised him a good time together, taking him to the newly opened adventure park with many different thrilling fun rides, such as roller coasters, big wheels, and water slides that were turning and twisting Jake around at breath taking speed.

He thoroughly enjoyed the rides until he was attracted to a fun ride called the 'Flying Carpet'. Apart from the flashing different colour lights there was a striking figure with a big moustache and a very colourful turban in the background. The seats were fitted on a giant piece of steel and the whole thing was mounted to a metal device which made the steel-carpet swing backwards and forwards. Just as the ride was going high above the ground, Jake heard a noise which sounded like a metal screw gliding over the steel floor. The noise was very persistent. With each move the so called carpet made, the sound of a screw, gliding over the floor, became more incessant. Jake looked warily around to see if he could find the cause of that noise. For a moment he thought that all screws, which held the construction together, would break loose and that this 'Flying Carpet' would really start to fly through the air. He didn't like that idea at all and was very happy when, after what seemed an eternity to him, he touched the ground again.

"That was exciting," he said rather drily to his mother who had been waiting at the entrance. However, Jake would from now on be very wary of amusement rides.

◆◆◆

Iris felt too old for joining in at the fun park and had instead suggested taking Jake to the old botanic garden near the university. She assured her grandson that he would discover plants from all over the world and enticed him by offering to buy him an ice cream. After his experience at the fair ground he was looking forward to spending a quiet day with his grandmother anyway and happily accepted her invitation.

When they arrived at the botanic garden they were welcomed by majestic scenery – ablaze with colour throughout the park. The wide range of plants, tropical and native, weird and wonderful, and a variety of impressive exotic species of trees, as well as various kinds of birds was truly stunning. It felt like being in paradise.

They took a stroll to the fishpond which was covered with water lilies. Together with the scent of roses and lavender it embellished the air with tranquillity. While they sat down on a bench, Jake said to his grandmother,

"Can I ask you something?"

"Yes, of course you can."

"I don't understand the whole thing..." he paused as if he thought about how to continue.

Iris looked at her grandson and waited patiently for what he had to say. Then after a while she asked him gently,

"What's the matter?"

"My mum – She needs more in her life than just me," he said with his face seemingly troubled.

"Sweetheart, it's not your job to worry about your mum," Iris said. Creasing her face she was astonished where her grandson's thought was coming from.

"But why is my mum not dating Ulrik – does she not like him? I like him," the young boy inquired straightforwardly with a serious look at his grandmother. "If she would like him too, I could have a father and be with Claire all the time. We could all be a family."

Iris smiled – as if things would be so easy.

"Honey, there's nothing you can do if your mum doesn't feel the same way for Ulrik as he does for her. She definitely has her reasons, and apart from that, feelings can't be forced," Iris tried to clothe her thoughts in words. And then, tenderly embracing her grandson, she continued, "You have to respect your mother's choices."

She could see in the boy's face that he wasn't at all satisfied with her explanations. So she went on,

"You'll encounter a lot of obstacles in your life and you have to learn how to deal with them."

Some minutes passed and then the young boy asked,

"What is love?"

Now Iris stalled. She never expected such a question from her young grandson. Yet, she was surprised how deep his thoughts were. She was sure that he wouldn't content himself with a simple answer. How does one explain a difficult matter in plain words to a minor? Iris was searching for words.

"Well," she began to speak, paused a moment and then continued with a smile, "I don't have one single answer to your question and I don't have my big book with me. Love is a paradox; it's not just a feeling and it's a little bit complicated to explain."

"But is it not easy: if I like to be with someone and if I feel happy with that person – is this not love?" Jake wanted to know.

Iris was very astounded about her grandson's logic.

"Well, it's often said you're not complete unless you found the other half…" she trailed off, at a loss for words. "Look little man," she then said, "There are many ways to describe what love is. I love you. And your mum loves you. But the love between your mother and a man is totally different. It always depends on the relationship we have with each other."

Jake took a deep breath. He was baffled and stared at his granny because he wasn't sure what she was trying to tell him.

"Do you mean two adults seeing each other aren't

the same as two children playing with each other?" the boy asked his grandmother with his little brown eyes wide open.

Iris laughed. She was thinking that adults can also play with each other but on a totally different level. 'Attention,' she thought amused, 'my little grandson is on his way to become a teenager.'

"Yes. What you feel for your friend Claire, or for me, or for your mum isn't the same as what two adults feel for each other", she explained, carefully balancing each of her words. "When you're a bit older you'll understand that love can happen quite naturally and at the same time it can be very irrational. It's the source of our deepest pleasures and our deepest agonies."

Dark clouds were gathering on the horizon.

"It looks as if it's going to rain," Iris said whilst getting up from the bench. "We'd better get a move on."

She caught her grandson's eye and flicked her head, indicating to him to follow her. Yet Jake wasn't so easily knocked off the subject.

He insisted, "Did my mother love my father?"

Iris expected everything but not that question. OK, she was aware that sooner or later the boy would want to know about his father who nobody had ever seen or heard from again. For now, she was so taken aback that she sat down on the bench again, only able to think 'oh my god – how do I explain to him?'

"I'm convinced she did. At least in the beginning when she met him," Iris said after a good deal of thought. "The question is however: Did your father love your mother?"

Her grandson stood in front of her, looking a little bit puzzled. Iris felt obliged to clarify and spoke very slowly to Jake,

"Normally we love what we know and what we are aware of. But there are also parts which are hidden when we meet a person for the first time and fall in love. It's not clear what makes adults attracted to each other. Is it the looks, the voice, the warm hands, the clothing?"

"These are all things on the outside," Jake acknowledged. "What about the inside – one's feelings?"

"Oh, feelings can be very deceptive," Iris asserted. "What we perceive as love may in fact be something different. This false love can easily change into hate."

"Did my mother hate my father?"

"Well, I don't think it was hate. Even so, it was very obvious – at least for me – that your father Rick didn't love your mother or even you. Your mother had a very hard time with him especially after you were born." Iris took a deep breath – why not tell the boy the truth about his father? She knew the truth was hard on Jake when she spoke on,

"Your father was unpredictable if not dangerous, throwing a tantrum when he was drunk. He had a mean temper and was definitely not committed to your mother...," she stopped and seconds later continued, "And he was certainly not a loving man. He upset your mummy, until in the end she decided to leave him, as this was the best for you as well."

"So my mum got hurt?"

"Yes very much so," she said acrimoniously, "That man insulted her mentally and was little short of abusing her physically."

"Perhaps this is the reason why she is so restrained with Ulrik?"

"Well, that could be a reason," Iris confirmed in a pensive mood.

All of a sudden the young boy realised the parallels in the names Ulrik and Rick.

"Could the similarity in the names of the two men be the reason why my mother subconsciously rejects Ulrik?" Jake asked, his look resting on his grandmother's face.

"Hm," Iris pondered over her grandson's assumption. Returning his gaze, she said, "It could well be that your mother's subconscious is playing tricks on her, and she dislikes Ulrik all for the wrong reasons."

◆◆◆

When Claire was back from Sweden Jake was of course over the moon to be reunited with her. And for the parents it meant that arrangements had to be made as to who was going to look after the two kids for the rest of the summer holidays. Ulrik had kindly offered to take the youngsters fishing to his favourite fishing lake. Ashly instantly agreed to his plan, as she thought being on the water provided an excellent opportunity to teach the kids about their environment.

As fishing wasn't good in the area where Ulrik lived, he usually went out to a reservoir surrounded by the forest near the McKenneth's home. From there the small angling party could have easily walked to the lake in about twenty minutes by cutting through the forest. Because of the bulky fishing gear and the two kids, Ulrik had decided to drive the car, taking the risk that it was sometimes hard to get a parking spot close to the water. They were however lucky The weather was exceptional and, despite being a calm day, it hadn't attracted many other anglers and Ulrik easily found a convenient parking place too. He was cautious not to take the two ten-year-olds to the deep end of the water. Therefore they hiked to a little bay, surrounded by blocks of stone all covered with white and yellow spots which were small clumps of lichen. From here they walked out to a point on the rocks for deeper fishing.

The gentle lapping of the water and the tranquillity was usually enough for him to unplug from daily life and to recharge his batteries. And normally a tug on his fishing line would push away any stress far from his mind. But, since this was the first time he went fishing with two kids, he had to fully devote his attention to them, making sure that the youngsters were doing fine and that they would enjoy themselves. Sitting on one of the massive rocks, they were listening eagerly when Ulrik gave details on the basic rules of fishing: how to put a rod, reel and line together and attach a fly.
"The rod tip has to be kept as close to the water as possible," Ulrik swung his line in the water.
"Why?" Jake wanted to know.
"This is in order to avoid any slack line," Ulrik was for a moment busy with his reel. "One has to be in direct touch with that fly at all times," he went on explaining, while letting the fly drift naturally on the water.

"Don't be disappointed if you don't catch anything," he continued to point out to the kids.

"Why?" they asked.

"Because the fish usually figure out that what they are given to eat is false and spit the bait out," Ulrik explained calmly. "Keep your feet well away from the line. Don't stand on it", he persisted, while retrieving the fly to keep it in the feeding zone. And pointing to the rest of the slack line on the rocks, he added, "Otherwise the line cannot get back out again in case a fish bites."

Watching how Jake swung his rod in a whipping motion out to the water, Ulrik showed the boy how to coil the line.

"Keep your rod high and steady," he advised him gingerly.

Then he was finally able to sit back, trying to unwind. The latter was easier said than done, as he had to keep a wary eye on the kids who were handling the fishing alone. When after all a fish took the bait and tugged on the line, he quickly got up from his comfortable position, helping Jake who was struggling with his catch.

At the same time Claire shouted words of encouragement. Bitten with enthusiasm she clapped her hands and cheered her friend on,

"Go on Jake. Yeah you'll get the fish!"

Then came the crucial moment of getting the catch out of the water and into the net.

"Look at that!" Jake and Claire were exceedingly delighted when they finally saw the fish in the net. For a moment Ulrik was overwhelmed by his childhood memories when he had caught his first fish. He had been so proud and yet so anxious to get his slippery catch out of the net. Now, he fully shared the kid's joy, especially when Jake caught another fish. Watching Claire and Jake holding a fish was certainly more rewarding for him than catching his own.

As Ulrik had promised Ashly to be back for lunch, the little party had to leave the lake for the day. Of course, Ulrik's announcement to head home didn't go down too well with Jake and Claire. They would have loved to stay longer and catch more fish. Yet, what else could they do but to follow him grumbling with long faces until Ulrik reassured them they would return to the lake soon.

While they walked back through the water to the shore, carefully watching not to slip and laden with all the fishing gear and the fish, Claire joyously said to Jake,

"When I'm grown up I want to marry you." She believed Jake was a hero catching fish and so she added with a giggle, "You caught all that fish – I'm sure that you can feed me."

"Yeah and we will have many children," Jake replied, being in high spirits. He couldn't wait to get home to tell his mum and his granny what a great time they had at the lake catching fish.

◆◆◆

Throughout the rest of the summer break the adults tried to keep the kids busy. Ulrik, Ashly and Iris took it in turns to undertake all sorts of indoor and outdoor activities with them. Basically they all had a wonderful time together and sometimes, when Claire stayed overnight, the two kids hung around so long that Ashly had to admonish them,

"Kids you have to go to sleep or your brains will not function in the morning!"

Prompting Jake to response,

"Don't you worry about our brains." And with a meaningful wink at his friend, he whispered, "Don't listen to my mum."

Everything was going smoothly, especially with Claire and Jake having been so excited by the idea their parents could get together. Fate, however, would take a different turn a few months after the new school year had started.

Chapter Eight

It was near Christmas when Ashly was invited by her friend Claudia to a vernissage in her art gallery which had recently been opened. She had been hesitating to ask Ulrik along. But then she had decided to go on her own. She still wasn't able to say what it was that prevented her from falling in love with Ulrik. Yes, her mother was right – Ulrik was a nice guy, fair and square, a very sociable fellow. She enjoyed his company as much as he enjoyed being with her. Still, there was something that she couldn't explain which stopped her from opening up her heart to him. Maybe her son's assumption was true and her subconscious was playing tricks by confusing her with the names Rick and Ulrik? The thought was heavily lingering in her mind when she arrived at her friend's gallery.

The atmosphere at the exhibition hall was relaxed. It was pleasant, not too crowded with people who bragged about their reputed knowledge of art. At the centre of the presentation were thirty pieces by Russian architect Victor Hartmann who died in 1874, aged only thirty-nine. Appropriate for the exhibits the piano cycle of Mussorgsky's music *Pictures at an Exhibition* played discreetly in the background.

While Ashly walked along the paintings and drawings, a tall, very good looking man approached her from behind and said with an Australian accent, "Art is in the eye of the beholder."

She turned around and looked into a pair of intense blue eyes. For a moment Ashly thought: 'That's it. That's him!' She had always assumed it would be impossible to find a great guy, and then like a miracle, out of the blue, this incredibly handsome man stood in front of her.

"Gordon. Gordon Thompson," the attractive stranger introduced himself, taking Ashly's hand to kiss it. Ashly was completely taken aback and while she lingered in total surprise, the stranger winked at her and flashed a friendly smile. Alas, it was a cool calculated move on his part. He had observed Ashly already at the entrance and learned that she spoke several languages fluently, including Russian.

It took a moment for Ashly to reply,

"I'm Ashly, Ashly McKenneth. Nice to meet you,

Mister Thompson." She was absolutely chuffed. Only recently she had craved for some excitement in her life and suddenly there it was – embodied by this most stunning man standing in front of her. While she was dallying with temptation to draw near him, she heard him say,
"I prefer you call me Gordon."

With a glance of appraisal Ashly noticed that he was someone who put a lot of emphasis on his outward appearance: Perfect white teeth, the skin slightly suntanned; his blond hair was cut short and showed a hint of grey at the temples; his muscular body looked well-toned with broad shoulders which virtually invited to lean on. It was difficult to tell his age, nevertheless this man simply looked gorgeous. Just like the sort of man Ashly had always dreamt of meeting but until now had only seen on TV.

"Can I get you a drink?" the man asked bringing Ashly back to reality.
Her first impulse was to say 'no thank you'. She wanted to freeze the moment and take it all in by just looking at this stunning stranger. But then she thought better of it. This extraordinarily alluring man was so charming she could simply not resist learning more about him.

Without waiting for Ashly to answer, this man Gordon grabbed her by the arm and ushered her to the table with the drinks.

"Let's have some champagne", he said while he lifted two glasses, handing one to Ashly.

"I can hear an Australian accent. What brings you here to this exhibition?" she asked, finally regaining her composure.

"I like art, especially Russian art." And then he asked her with a seductive look, "What is your connection to Victor Hartmann?"

"Oh none – I know Claudia, the gallery owner. She is an old friend from university."

"I see. Well, Hartmann was an architect. He had some good ideas on building and I'm interested in his works."

"Are you an architect?" she wanted to know while sipping her champagne.

"No, I'm not," Gordon answered deliberately with a suggestive wink. "I am an estate agent."

Ashly was disappointed. 'An estate agent – he's just another looser' it crossed her mind for a moment. Then again, he didn't strike her as a man who was on the losing end of life. He was much too well dressed and seemed very distinguished. Trying to figure out if he was married, she searched his hands for a wedding ring. But she couldn't even find a tan line. 'He's not married,' she observed, and at the same moment her heart started racing with excitement.

Gordon was much too conceited to realise that Ashly was deep in thoughts. He had finished his champagne and, without asking her, he took her glass, ordering more champagne.

"This champagne isn't too bad," he remarked while handing her the filled glass. "Normally I drink Laurent-Perrier. It's not so dry like most of the champagnes but has a touch of sweetness."

Ashly would have wanted to tell him that she wasn't bothered about champagne. She liked a glass of wine in a friendly ambience more than standing around talking with a stranger about the different notes of champagne. Yet, this charming, outgoing man drew her into a seductive conversation from which there was no escape for her.

"Have you ever been to France? – Paris the city of lovers, the epicentre of romance," he eloquently enquired with a come-hither look at Ashly.

"Yes," Ashly replied, feeling light-hearted, "a long time ago. I liked it very much."

Wallowing in memories for a moment, she remembered her very first trip to France. She and her friend Claudia had arrived very late, being totally exhausted after having tried for endless hours to get a room. Finally, they had succeeded outside Paris where they took a room in a pension. It was a sleazy joint as they found out later. The owner of the establishment had hastily emptied one room with clothes scattered all over the floor and an awful smell lingering in the air. When, after a week in Paris, Ashly returned home, her mother had exclaimed horrified, "Oh my god – you have bug bites all over your body!"

Placing her champagne glass on the counter, Ashly decided it wouldn't be appropriate to tell that stunning stranger about her encounter with bedbugs in Paris.
"I hope you went with your lover. Pondering on the love-locking bridges, dining at charming little secret places around the *Rue du Faubourg Saint-Antoine*, or going for a romantic evening stroll along the river Seine," Gordon provoked her with a gentle smile playing around the corners of his mouth. Their eyes met for a moment, but Ashly broke off.
"No, I was on my own when I went there," she paused, thinking of her second visit to Paris, and continued after seconds, "to the famous cemetery *Père Lachaise*." When she saw Gordon's disturbed look, she hastened to explain, "I studied art and we

had to do sketches of the different tombs. They look like beautiful little fairy houses."

"One wouldn't think that a cemetery is a romantic place," Gordon considered with a tantalising smile.

"Well, not unless you stroll along hand in hand with the love of your life, looking for a place to be buried together one day," Ashly gave a charming smile back to Gordon. "But seriously – the place has some really nice structural conditions. The narrow winding pathways have their own street signs and names. And a lot of famous people are buried there, like Maria Callas or Marcel Proust and not to forget Edith Piaf. Her nickname *La Môme Piaf* (The Little Sparrow) stayed with her for the rest of her life," she gave an account of her experience in Paris. Then looking at the man beside her, she asked him with a sweet smile,

"And you – have you been to France?"

"Many times," Gordon answered firmly. Avoiding to look at Ashly, he disclosed, "I like to travel and to set up small companies."

Ashly became curious when she heard the word travel – she liked to travel as well. But setting up small companies – how did this work for an estate agent? She didn't want to appear nosy and abstained from asking him further questions.

"Have you ever been to Russia?" this gorgeous

looking man wanted to know.

"Yes, I've been there too, as well as to many other places which I visited in Europe," Ashly responded truthfully. And then the conversation went on about places they had been to in Russia, like the Red Square in Moscow with its legendary onion domes of St. Basil's Cathedral; the world famous Bolshoi Theatre; the Moscow Metro which opened in 1935, an ambitious architectural project with 197 stations; and the Winter Palace in St. Petersburg. They chatted about how extraordinary this vast country is, how remarkably tasty the food is, and how friendly and interesting Russian people are.

Since Ashly was driving home in her car, she declined the offer of another drink. It had been undoubtedly an amusing evening with this stranger from Australia and Ashly was somehow reluctant to leave. But being tired and having not intended to spend so much time at the exhibition, she was searching for an exit option. Hence she dashed to the lady's room and, after returning, she bid goodbye to Gordon who had so enjoyably entertained her all evening long.

"Is there a chance we can meet again?" he asked with his blue eyes looking deep into hers.

In this very instant it was all up to Ashly. Not being

averse to an adventure and agog with enthusiasm, she replied,
"Yes, why not? I would be delighted!"

◆◆◆

Waking up the next morning, Ashly remembered, like wisps of fog, a dream from last night.
'Strange,' she thought because she hadn't been able for some time to recall any dream, since the terrible nightmares, in which she stands on the roof of a skyscraper, had stopped. With her eyes closed she vaguely recollected that there was a tall man with dark hair who shepherded her into an old mansion. Inside everything was covered in dust, making it impossible for her to see what the place contained. While she stood there being lost, her friend Claudia appeared all of a sudden. Glaring at Ashly with hard eyes, she flicked her head emotionlessly, indicating her to look out of one of the big windows. With misgivings Ashly followed her friend's request and saw clearly that the house was surrounded by lush green grass with bushes and trees at the end. And in the middle of the manicured lawns she saw a horse looking at her. ...
Horse being a potent symbol of sexuality – was this a premonition? Ashly was wondering, while minutes

later jumping out of bed. There wasn't much time for her to think about the meaning of the dream. She had to get Jake ready for school. Although it was Friday, which meant that she didn't have to go to work, she didn't mind getting up as usual to take her son to school. She had often thought about moving out of her mother's old house, where she had grown up and which was packed with objects Iris loved so dearly. While getting ready in the bathroom her thoughts carried her to her childhood – just like Jake she had liked to play hide-and-seek with friends in the old house and listening to her mother's tales and made up stories. But, in contrast to her son, she had never been keen on gardening and was always interested in books, preferably mysteries. Moving into a nice, new, open-space house was out of the question. She had become so acquainted with this unusual family set-up and that cosy timeworn place that she simply didn't want to leave it. With hindsight she was glad to live with her mother. Iris was more than just a baby-sitter. Not only did she take the work out of Ashly's hands with Jake but, like a good friend, she also shared joy and sorrow with her daughter at all times.

❖❖❖

When she was back from taking Jake to school, Ashly finally had a chance to look at Gordon's business card, and reeling in thoughts she was totally carried away. Considering her life matter-of-factly, she had a good job, a lovely mother and son, and a comfortable life which lacked adventure, at least a little bit of spice. Her face brightened by the thought of Gordon – what a wonderful evening that had been, spent with such a charming man. When he had kissed her goodbye on her cheeks she noticed his after shave. It was a subtle, pleasurable scent. Not too overpowering but just right for Ashly to like the fragrance and the man who was wearing it.

She started daydreaming – it had been a long time since she had travelled. She would like to do it again – go to all the places where she had gone with her friend Claudia when they were young, enjoying themselves. All of a sudden she became itchy feet, remembering all the wonderful moments she had experienced. Her sudden wanderlust was however no option at the moment, as she couldn't afford it. Instead she wallowed in memories, recollecting as if it was yesterday, how she had met Rick in a holiday resort in Tunisia: It was summer and sunny, the beaches were magnificent, and everybody was in a playful mood. She saw him standing at the beach bar, a handsome tall man with short, raven black hair, shining blue in the sunlight, and brown eyes which made him likeable straight away. Ashly had been totally entranced when he offered her a drink which she of course hadn't refused. If she had only known what a barefaced liar he was, hiding behind a façade of fallacious illusions, and plunging her life into chaos. But she had been oblivious to his alcohol problem and so it happened that they went out together and had continued doing so back home. A couple of times they went back to the holiday resort which was by all means not really a holiday for Ashly. It had taken her some time to figure out that the real reason behind Rick's generous offer was his way of redeeming himself. Every time, when he had come home totally drunk after a pub crawl and created an ugly scene afterwards, he had invited her on what he called 'a special holiday'. But what was so special about always visiting the same place? Ashly had soon realised that there was nothing special, and, after having left Rick, she had decided never ever to go back to such crowded places for her holiday – she wanted something more challenging, and to wake up to the sound of birdsong rather than the shrieking voices of people fighting over the best places at the pool.

Iris interrupted her in her thoughts.

"Sorry darling, I didn't wait up for you last night," she started the talk. "I was too tired. How was your evening, Ashly dear?"

"Mum, you won't believe it – I met a really nice guy, a good-looker."

"Oh did you. Tell me more," Iris went to get herself a cup of tea, while Ashly told her mother about the previous night.

"He is so handsome, so distinguished, and he seems to have quite a lot of money," Ashly gushed about Gordon.

"What does he do for a living?"

"I'm not sure – he said he's an estate agent," Ashly answered truthfully.

"Since when do estate agents have a lot of money – unless they got it at the expense of people's misfortune," Iris remarked with a touch of sarcasm.

"Well, he's from Australia and he said he likes to travel and to set up small companies," Ashly disclosed, aglow with enthusiasm. "He's very good looking and seems to be very generous."

For some strange reason Iris didn't like the implication of her daughter's enchantment, getting the feeling that this stranger may be playing games with her. It simply sounded too good to be true. Her gut told her that she wasn't off beam in assuming there was something wrong. But for now she didn't want to spoil her daughter's happiness. With a dash of concernment in her voice, she advised Ashly,

"Just be careful. I don't want you to be unhappy or to get hurt again like with Rick. You have to protect yourself!"

"Yes, mum. I know," Ashly said, and with an engaging smile she went over to tenderly embrace her mother, "You should see him. You would be delighted."

"I'm concerned as to what he is doing for a living!" Iris pointed out worriedly. "You don't need his money. You have enough yourself. And once I'm gone, you and Jake will not have any reason to worry about money." Iris had never told Ashly that she had taken out a life policy some years ago with her daughter being the beneficiary.

"Oh mum, please don't talk that way. I don't like to think that you may not be with us one day," Ashly said with a sad tone in her voice. She felt suddenly very uneasy.

Before Iris could reply, a knock on the door interrupted their conversation. It was nothing special, only somebody from a charity asking for a donation.

◆◆◆

The following days went quietly until Ashly received a phone call from Gordon. He invited her out on Friday night to a party of some friends who lived close to the seaside in one of those impressive mansions. Needless to say Ashly was very delighted and without hesitation she accepted his invitation.

Iris, although she normally didn't care for the opinion of her neighbours, was totally flabbergasted when a showy Bentley *Mulsanne* parked outside her front garden. It was Gordon, picking up Ashly.
Could he not hold his fire, or why did he come so early? Iris harboured suspicion straightaway, not knowing that Gordon had planned it all. He was determined to say "hello" to Ashly's mother with his ulterior motive being to impress her. Ashly was a little bit ashamed to show such a wealthy man into her modest home. Gordon, however, simply made his way inside, and, when seeing Iris, he took her hand in a very gentlemanly manner, saying with a deeply affected voice in a feigned French accent, "*Enchanté Madame.*" After this theatrical performance, he immediately tried to impress her with his lavishness by presenting her with a richly decorated gift-wrapped box, containing two bottles of his exclusive champagne, and, while standing in the door, he waited eagerly for Iris to appreciate his

generosity.

But the first thing Iris did – and she always did it, when meeting someone for the first time – was look down at the shoes. In a split second she realised that Gordon's shoes were pointed! She never liked pointed shoes, and it didn't matter if it was fashion or not. Pointed shoes always reminded her somehow of the legendary Leprechauns – the swift little creatures with magical powers which were so impossible to catch.

Looking up at Mr. Thompson, Iris admitted that at first glance the attraction was undeniable – that man was good looking. Nonetheless, she saw immediately through his façade. If he had thought to impress her with this exaggerated gesture of extravagance, he was totally wrong. This affected behaviour only stirred her suspicion. 'What is he after?' she asked herself and eyed the Australian doubtfully, rather reluctantly acknowledging his salutation. 'Stick your champagne up your bum!' she thought. And clearly showing her disdain for his apparently generous present, she couldn't stop herself from saying drily,

"Thank you for the nice box. But that wasn't necessary,"

Ashly was appalled at her mother's unfriendly performance. How could she do that! That woman was going to ruin her date with this heart-throb. 'Oh no mother – don't you do this to me!' she thought determinedly and threw an appealing look at Iris.

Meanwhile Jake was watching in the background and only came forward when asked by his mother to welcome Mr. Thompson. 'Hopefully my son doesn't let me down,' Ashly thought, still feeling awkward by her mother's behaviour.
Yet, Jake also played hard-to-get and wasn't very comfortable when shaking hands with Gordon.
"So you must be Jake – the young genius," Gordon addressed the boy while stroking his head. Jake never liked to be touched, especially not by strangers, and so he flinched. In his own eyes Mr. Thompson wasn't genuine, but a phoney who was after his mother.
For a moment Ashly was speechless. She had expected more good-will from her family towards this stunning looking, eloquent Australian.
"Listen," Ashly said, slightly irritable, grabbing Gordon's arm and dragging him to the door, "these two must have had a bad day today. Let's go and enjoy the party."

◆◆◆

Iris and Jake gave a sigh of relief when Ashly and Gordon had gone, leaving a strong smell of his aftershave behind. What a show!

"What do you make of him?" the boy was dying to know from his grandmother.

"What can one say? He's indeed very good looking. Undeniably attractive. I can well understand your mother being spellbound by this man. Blue eyes, stylish haircut, well dressed," Iris resumed. She wasn't sure what else to say in the presence of her grandson, because she didn't want to belittle the Australian stranger prematurely. Still, in her eyes this man was a rather slippery character. What made him show off his extravagance to such an extent? It all seemed very dubious to her.

'It wouldn't surprise me if he turns out to be a bold and sophisticated liar,' she thought and was determined to sooner or later pierce a hole in his façade.

"He is old enough to be my grandfather!" Jake blew off his steam. The prospect that such a man could indeed be his grandfather or – even worse – his father, didn't put him in a happy mood.

"Well, maybe not quite so. He appeared quite fresh-faced," Iris replied, whilst she went to turn the TV on. "But I tell you what – this man is a wolf in sheep's clothing!"

"He is definitely not genuine! Not like Ulrik," Jake had to say what he thought. "That honeyed voice when he kissed your hand. No, no," he added, shuddering with disgust.

"Yes my dear Jake, you can't trust a person who speaks like him," Iris nodded. Turning the sound of the TV down, she bitterly complained, "And then that box with the champagne! He seems to be a self-indulgent man. Did you notice how he was standing over there, waiting for me to fall round his neck and be grateful for the champagne? Well, he didn't impress me!"

"You're not kidding. He seemed so slimy. The whole situation was somehow false," Jake, sharing the same qualms as his grandmother, considered aloud, "I don't think he is genuine. But then again, what are his true intentions? I hope my mum doesn't get into trouble."

◆◆◆

"You look lovely," Gordon said, guiding Ashly to his car and chivalrously opening the door for her, "Sexy, smart, interesting – a very unusual woman."

"Thank you for the compliment," Ashly replied charmed.

It had taken her some time to find something suitable to wear, until in the end she had decided on her little black dress with matching silver jewellery. She was slightly nervous about being appropriately dressed for the party. Though, her fears were laid to rest when they arrived at the venue and she saw the casual outfits of these allegedly rich people. Gordon introduced her to some of the people, but then left her to talk business. After a couple of drinks Ashly felt confident enough to talk to random people – people she had never met before.

The host provided an abundance of food and drink: Lots of caviar, fresh sea food, delicious niblets, and other culinary delights, as well as obscene amounts of champagne, vodka, and whiskey. With a glass of champagne in her hand Ashly mingled with some of the influential people from the art world, most of them Russians, and sustained light conversation, sharing views and common experiences on a variety of art related themes. Whereas her image had been that the people would be glamorous and full of themselves, she detected that a lot of them didn't really show off with their wealth. On the contrary – the majority of these flamboyant people, enjoying the party, just had quirks and habits which Ashly knew already from other people from the art world, rendering them overall quite pleasant. And although everybody she met could tell that she was

"Gordon's girl", no one gave her a hard time.

◆◆◆

There was crispness in the air when Ashly and Gordon left the event late at night. She leaned on to his chest, inhaling the scent of his after-shave with her eyes closed and suddenly experienced that irresistible feeling of sheer lust. Gordon, feeling her warm, aroused body, pressed her tight to his body, and then he couldn't resist any longer but took her face in his hands and kissed her, obsessed with desire. And Ashly passionately returned his kisses and fondling.

She paid no attention to how they got to his place. She was all consumed by wonderful thrilling feelings, looking forward to spend the night with this fascinating man. It turned out that he lived in a penthouse suite from where one had a fantastic view over the town and further beyond to the sea. The apartment, its furnishing, and especially the bed exceeded Ashly's expectations. She thought it was the most extravagant furniture money could buy.

"Would you like a drink?" he asked when they arrived, not wanting to appear too obvious in his longing for her.

"Only if it is non-alcoholic," Ashly, feeling slightly

tipsy, didn't want any more hard drinks. "A glass of water would be fine with me."

While Gordon went to fetch the requested water, Ashly pondered if she should play hard-to-get. She wanted to give Gordon the feeling of conquering something desirable. But it didn't take long for an experienced lover like Gordon to make Ashly change her mind the very moment he kissed her and immediately teased her ear with his tongue. She savoured that instant sensation of pleasurable shivers zinging down her spine, making her crave for more. Minutes later he unzipped her dress and dropped it to the ground. The atmosphere was charged with sensual heat. While Ashly helped him to open her bra, he tore off her red mesh and lace panties, and then carried her naked to his bed which was covered in white satin. It was a dream, soft and comfortable, but felt at first cold on her bare skin.

She looked at him in anticipation as he took off his clothes. An insatiable feeling of pleasure awoke in her like never before. His pristine body was strong, muscular, and hairless. His tanned skin felt like velvet, not quite masculine yet very pleasant. She became aware of how much she desired him – this slim, well-toned body. This lady slayer had everything a woman needed to be satisfied and Ashly could no longer resist giving herself over to him. The love-making clearly measured up to more than she had expected. And the evening with this Australian stranger was turning into a night full of lust and sex, she wouldn't so easily forget.

◆◆◆

When Ashly woke up the next day, the place beside her was cold. Was it all a dream? Then she remembered that she had been a bit tipsy last night and that Gordon had been an excellent lover. Suddenly she caught sight of him, as he sat dressed in a white bathrobe in front of the bed by the window and, whilst drinking champagne, he was watching her.

"Good morning Ashly. Did you sleep well?" He left his seat and went over to the bed, reaching a glass filled with champagne to her.

"Here, have a drink. Champagne stimulates your blood circulation. Why don't you stay the weekend? We could have the entire time to ourselves," he whispered, bending over Ashly, gently kissing her on the neck.

While she was sipping the champagne, she looked out of the big window in front of the bed. Heavy snowfall, unusually early and not expected at this time of the year, made her want to stay in that cosy warm bed. It was nice lying there and watching the snowflakes dancing along the window. Gordon's offer was very tempting, not least of all because he was such a good lover. Ashly didn't need to think twice but phoned home to let Iris know she would stay with Gordon and be back Sunday evening.

Entwined around Gordon she was mesmerized by him. He had given her so much pleasure last night. Now, she enjoyed lying in his arms, feeling his warm, soft body, and watching the snow flurry outside the window. Then she felt her lust returning. Gliding her hand over his pristine body, she was prepared for Gordon to take her again. His skin smelled tangy and spicy – a peculiar smell which didn't bother her at all. On the contrary, she wanted him more than any other man before. Gordon flicking his tongue in her ear increased her feeling of pleasure. Slowly his mouth grazed over the skin of her neck. She felt his breath, his wet tongue. A voluptuous tingling spread through her body and totally captured her senses when Gordon showered her with kisses, while his hands were sliding deftly over her white, slinky body. Then he leaned over and slid into her. Ashly screamed with delight, reaching her climax. They remained entwined, quietly, until his body slowly began to break away from hers.

After a decadent start to the day, Gordon turned

out to be a man who could make extensively love. The kisses on her body, the typical odour of sexual activity, the beating of her heart – it was a bewitching attraction that Gordon had on her, and Ashly knew she had fallen under his spell and was henceforth at his mercy.

Chapter Nine

Jake was furious when he heard that his mother would stay away the whole weekend. Never before had she left him for such a long time for another man. He had always hoped that she would reciprocate Ulrik's feelings and that they would one day get together. If it would have been with Ulrik, the young boy would have happily appreciated his mother staying away as long as she wanted to. But ever since this Australian poser had turned up in their lives everything had changed. It simply didn't feel right and Jake became quite frustrated.

Iris wasn't very comfortable either with her daughter's plan to spend the weekend with a man she hardly knew. Then again, it wasn't up to her to dictate to Ashly the do's and don'ts of her life.
"Jake darling, what do you think if I take you and Claire to the cinema tomorrow?" Iris thought she

could appease the young boy with her suggestion. She herself had not been downtown for a long time, as she tried to avoid the hectic life of the city. Usually she did her shopping nearby, and once a week she went to the local club to play bridge with a group of friends.

To her surprise Jake immediately consented to her plan.

"Yeah, that's a cool idea, granny," the boy said with a big smile all over his face. "I'll phone Claire. She'll be over the moon." And he immediately ran off to make arrangements with Claire.

As Ulrik had a lot of work to do until Christmas, he was more than pleased when he was told about the visit to the cinema and that Iris would look after the two children the whole day. Not having to care for Claire on Sunday, might even give him an opportunity to enjoy his secret romance for a couple of hours. Looking forward to a date, he agreed happily to bring his daughter over to the McKenneth's home in the morning and pick her up later in the day, knowing that Claire would be overjoyed spending the whole day with her friend.

In the blink of an eye Sunday arrived and along came Claire much to Jake's joy. It was bitterly cold outside and the snow had in some places turned into slushy ice. Mercifully Iris spared Ulrik her questions when he delivered Claire to the house.

"The weather has turned really cold since yesterday," Ulrik exchanged a few words with Iris on the harsh winter weather. Despite being so calm on the outside he was dying to know why Ashly wasn't present. Iris must have sensed Ulrik's curiosity.

"If you're waiting for Ashly, you're wasting your time. She isn't in," she said and left it at that. It wasn't her business to break possible bad news to the nice Swedish man. Ulrik, curbing his curiosness, swiftly replied,

"Ah, OK. I have no time anyway. There's a lot of work at home waiting for me." And then he left in a hurry, dashing off to his secret mistress who had so willingly agreed to meet him.

◆◆◆

It was very cosy as always in Iris' old house, and the two kids didn't really want to leave the comfy place. Not even to play outside in the left over patches of snow. After lunch Iris made the trip by bus to the cinema in town tempting for them. She had decided to get the children into a festive mood and had chosen a fantasy film *The Nightmare before Christmas*.

While the little party went along to the bus stop, Jake and Claire were giggling and passing time until the bus arrived by talking in a made up, secret language which didn't make any sense, not even to themselves. To increase their fun, they breathed out into the cold air, guessing what the shapes produced by their breath were meant to depict. Iris, wondering what the words *"pipi-pipi-kaka-doodah"* were supposed to mean, looked quizzical at the two minors, prompting them to burst into peals of laughter. They expected Iris to believe it was Swedish, but she didn't fall for the kid's joke. Luckily they didn't have to wait too long, because the double-decker bus arrived on time; and, while the bus was carefully driving through the wintery weather on some very narrow roads, the trio were looking forward to their day out in the city.

◆◆◆

There was a festive air all over downtown which totally amazed them as the bus approached the city centre. Christmas lights were shining all around the streets and a big richly adorned Christmas tree stood in front of the town hall, spreading a wonderful atmosphere. Iris was totally enthralled by the wondrous sights.

Jake, his face pressed against the bus window, remarked admiringly,

"Wow, the most dazzling and festive light display I have ever seen."

Then the bus took a turn and when stopping at the crossroads, Claire shouted out,

"Look – there is your mother, Jake!" She knocked on the window, pointing towards Ashly who stood there in front of a taxi, passionately kissing Gordon.

Before Jake or Iris could have a closer look the bus moved on. Never mind what Claire thought at this very moment – Jake only caught a glimpse, though the whole scene stung him tremendously and he was totally flabbergasted until they arrived at the cinema.

Fortunately Iris, who normally didn't like animated movies, had chosen the right film. The amazing mix of fright and fun was just right to get her grandson back into a better mood. The light entertainment was filled with animations on a big screen and the two kids were quickly carried away into a different world. And when they left the cinema they had red cheeks from all the excitement in the movie, with its songs and laughter and the little romance.

Jake gently nudged Claire, "See, there is always a happy ending, just like in my Granny's stories!"

And then he ran boisterously ahead, chasing the street pigeons. Iris tried to call him back but Jake wasn't listening. He hardly stopped at the red traffic light and only slowed down because he tried to sneak through the crowd of people onto the street. Iris, immediately sensing danger, hurried after, stretched through the crowd, got hold of Jake's hood and pulled him back. Just in time to avoid the oncoming cab! Her heart dived. If Jake had taken one more step forward, the cab would definitely have knocked him down.

◆◆◆

After that horrifying incident Iris was in no doubt that Jake's guardian angel had again kept an eye on the boy. 'That was his guardian angel,' she thought thankfully. Nevertheless, it was too much excitement for her and on the spot she told Jake off,
"Remember what I have told you! We are instantly going home!"
Grumbling and pouting the children followed Iris to the bus station. It was dark and cold and it had started to snow. While Iris was walking up and down in order to avoid cold feet, she bumped into Claudia, her daughter's friend from university, who was laden down with bags of Christmas shopping.

"What a surprise – Mrs. Mc Kenneth. What are you doing downtown?" Claudia asked, struggling to put all her bags in one hand so that she could shake hands with Iris.

"I went to the movies with my grandson and his friend Claire."

"Where is Ashly? I haven't spoken to her for a while. Is she all right?"

"Yes, she is splendid. Imagine, after so many years she is finally seeing someone."

"Who is that? Do I know him?"

"Ashly met him at the exhibition in your gallery recently."

"Oops, you don't mean Gordon – that wealthy businessman?" Claudia was genuinely surprised and raised her eyebrow.

Iris nodded somehow downcast, "Yes, it's Gordon."

Claudia noticed that Iris wasn't very enthusiastic, "You don't like him?"

"Well, he's a bit of a bragger," Iris didn't hide the fact what she thought of Gordon.

"Oh yes. And if I were you I wouldn't trust him either," Claudia agreed. And when she saw Iris' astonished look, she quickly added, "If you think he isn't the guy he appears to be, then you have to find out as much as you can about him. Listen, my bus is coming and I have to rush. Come and see me in my

gallery and we can talk – but not before the New Year." And with these words Claudia hurried to catch the bus.
Soon after, Iris' bus arrived at the terminal. She and the two children were glad to get on to the warmth of the double-decker which would bring them home. While the kids seemed to enjoy the ride, sitting upstairs in the front of the bus, Iris was very pensive all the way home.

To her surprise Ashly was already in the house but wasn't very talkative. In fact nobody spoke much that Sunday evening. Iris was too tired after that eventful day to have a serious conversation with her daughter. A short exchange of words – "How was your weekend?" – "Thank you, fine" – was all that the two women had to say. Ashly was far too much occupied with her new love and didn't pay much attention to Ulrik who was in a rush anyway when he picked up his daughter.
It was Jake who broke the silence after Ulrik and Claire had left. Being honest by nature he spoke out what everybody, apart from his mother, thought about that Australian stranger,
"I don't trust him at all!"

◆◆◆

After her exciting weekend with Gordon, Ashly was in ebullient spirits. On Monday morning, when she was on the way to her office, of all things she had to run into Ulrik. Claire had of course told her father that she had seen Ashly with another man who was, as far as she knew from Jake, very rich but not trustworthy. It was the last week before the Christmas break and everybody was very busy at the university, getting the work finished before the holiday. Ulrik had intended to see Ashly and invite her out for a drink before he left for Sweden. Now, that he knew from his daughter about Ashly and another man, he was alarmed that the fate of his friendship might be at stake.

"Can you spare me a couple of minutes?" he politely asked.

Ashly, sensing that something prickly was coming her way, wasn't very comfortable with the situation and answered brusquely,

"Yes, but I have to hurry to work."

She didn't make it easy for Ulrik to raise his question,

"I wonder if we could go out together for a drink before Christmas." Standing close by her side in the busy exit corridor of the arts faculty, he would have loved to invite her to come with him to Sweden. On second thoughts she would probably decline once again his invitation. So he immediately dropped it from his mind with great regret.

"I don't think so. Sorry. I have a lot of commitments and work to do," she tried very obviously to put him off. When realising that she shouldn't be so hard on him, she quickly suggested, "Why don't we meet early next year when you're back from Sweden?"

Ashly hadn't finished her sentence when in virtually the same moment Ulrik realised that she seemed to just use him and didn't care one little bit how he was doing.

It was hard to tell whether he felt so frustrated because of the conversation he just had with Ashly, or because he knew that she was seeing somebody else and would have a good time while he was on holiday. Ulrik, like so many men, had difficulties expressing his own feelings and emotions. For all that, he suddenly became aware that a totally new situation had occurred – a condition he never wanted and requiring him to think better of his friendship with Ashly. Up to now, he had maintained a friendly relationship with her, hoping that one day it would develop into more. Instead, the circumstances had unexpectedly changed, and the thought, that she rejected him in favour of a supposedly rich man, who was probably good in bed too, crept deeper and deeper into his mind. This

was getting ridiculous. He wasn't going to make a fool out of himself any longer. No doubt about it – Ulrik was very miserable and with a toneless voice he said to Ashly,
"OK, see you next year."

Heading towards his office, Ulrik was fuming. Damn it! Why had he never insisted on taking Ashly to Sweden for a holiday?! Or taken her out to posh places? Or chauffeured her in a big new car? He tried to convince himself that in the coming year he would make it good. He was a very patient man. Then again, he realised that Ashly had given him the brush-off in favour of an allegedly successful, rich businessman and Ulrik didn't really want to compete with a man he didn't even know.

'It doesn't matter – money isn't everything,' he thought bitterly, 'who cares – if Ashly doesn't like me the way I am, then there's no point chasing after her.' Even as he told himself not to have any bad feelings, he got carried away with his emotions. Barely able to control the rage he felt, he secretly wished Gordon from the bottom of his heart, 'Rot in hell!'

◆◆◆

Ashly had to rush to her office on the third floor because she had to prepare for a lecture on contemporary art. When she entered the room, she found a bouquet of long-stemmed Baccara roses with a letter saying:

'Thank you for the most wonderful weekend. Would you be able to meet again on Thursday? I have an urgent request: Could you translate the enclosed little text for me into Russian? I cannot wait to see you again. Yours love, Gordon.'

And the text to be translated read: *'This is to certify that the painting is a genuine art work by artist ----'*

Spontaneously she lifted the phone to let Gordon know how pleased she was to be seeing him again. Her excitement was however curbed when he didn't answer his mobile phone. After several attempts to contact him, she started to become slightly worried if something might have happened to him. And when she couldn't get through to him by the afternoon, she eventually left a message. Her worries were however in vain. Gordon phoned her at home later that evening and apologised sweetly for any inconvenience he may have caused.

"I would so much like to see you again, kiss your body softly, make you wet between your legs", he started to whisper through the phone in a very erotic style. Ashly had to stop him from going on before he totally turned her on.

"I'm not alone in the house. Spare your fantasies for Thursday", she purred. "I'll see you in your penthouse after work."

Gordon had rendered her all excited. Putting the phone down, it crossed her mind that her mother was normally going to her bridge club on Thursday nights. Who would look after Jake if she was seeing Gordon?!

"Who was that on the phone?" Iris asked when Ashly entered the living room.

"It was Gordon. He has some work for me to do," Ashly exaggerated and seconds later she regretted it when faced with her mother's reaction.

"What sort of work?" Iris sounded very stern. She saw her daughter ending up as a prostitute being with Gordon.

"Relax mum. He wants me to translate some art related texts into Russian," Ashly took a deep breath, "and for this reason he wants to meet me on Thursday."

"So what?" Iris asked.

"Well," Ashly paused. It was visibly awkward for her asking her mother for help. "Could you look after Jake on Thursday?"

"Ashly! That's my last evening with my bridge friends this year."

"I know mum. Please." Ashly looked pleadingly at her mother, and then embracing her, she continued, "please mum. It's important to me."

"Being with my friends once a week is important to me too. At my age I may not have many chances to meet up with them," Iris made it quite clear what she thought.

Ashly felt guilty all of a sudden. She didn't want her mother to cancel her bridge evening in favour of her pleasure with Gordon. But she had an indescribable desire for him. She pined for him, and Iris could see that her daughter was in two minds what to do.

"Well, we'll see what I can do," Iris said, leaving the room to go to bed. She had never been able to deny a request from her daughter. And if it was only for a translating-job – she didn't want to stand in her daughter's way. 'Tomorrow I'll talk to Dorothy and cancel my evening out,' she thought.

So far Iris had left Ashly in the dark that she was willing to look after Jake on Thursday night. It was crazy, as she rarely missed out on meeting her friends regularly once a week. Then again, she had spoiled her daughter all her life and this was no exception. Yet, if Iris had known what Gordon's true intentions were, she would definitely have decided differently.

◆◆◆

It was a rather busy day at her office. Unfortunately Ashly was lacking sleep and because of that she laboured through the pile of work on her desk. She had been torn between her own desire for Gordon and asking her mother to call off her bridge party. No wonder that the last night had been pretty rough for her. All sorts of thoughts had haunted her and forced her to stay awake half of the night. She felt and looked awful today. Her face was pale with dark rings under her eyes.

Iris was immediately full of pity when she saw her daughter coming home from work in the afternoon.
"Oh dear, how was your day, honey? I hope you didn't have too much hassle," Iris was genuinely anxious.
"My day was all-right. The drive back home from Jake's school was a nightmare. Some people simply don't know how to drive in bad weather," Ashly replied wearily.
She was glad to be home and to relax. The fire was burning in the living room, giving off a cosy heat. The Christmas-tree in the corner of the room, which

had been lovingly decorated by Iris and Jake, glittered and its fairy lights twinkled, and there was a soft aroma of pine in the air together with the smell of homemade cookies.

"What would you think if I called off my bridge evening?" Iris asked, handing a cup of tea and some of her freshly baked biscuits to Ashly. And because Ashly didn't answer straight away, she continued, "Does Gordon make you happy?"

"Yes, he makes me very happy."

"Don't you think he is a little too old for you?"

"No, I do not think so!"

Iris realised that her daughter didn't want to talk about Gordon and changed the subject.

"Are you meeting Ulrik before Christmas?"

"No!" Ashly answered decidedly.

"Well, I'm only asking because of the Christmas presents," Iris excused herself, sitting down on the couch next to her daughter. "Then it will probably be the same as every year – we exchange presents late as usually, after Christmas when Ulrik and Claire are back from Sweden."

"Yes mum."

For a moment the living room was filled with an awkward silence. Iris, busy with her tea cup in her hands, said,

"I've cancelled my bridge party on Thursday evening

so I can look after Jake for you."

Looking up she expected Ashly to be delighted.

Of course she was! Overwhelmed with joy and with a gesture of relief she replied,

"Thank you mum – you are wonderful! And I love you!" Turning raptly towards her mother and giving her a bear hug, she continued, "I really appreciate how you are supporting me. What would I do without you?"

"It's ok, Ashly darling," Iris said while putting her hand on Ashly's. Then she went over to her recliner and grabbed her newspaper which she regularly read in order to vent on the injustices in the world, and the topic 'men' wasn't mentioned any more.

◆◆◆

Ashly could hardly wait until Thursday to see Gordon. She had translated the little text for him without questioning what it was for. It had been a dull day, and when she arrived at his suite, Gordon awaited her with a chilled bottle of champagne and two crystal glasses.

"I have fresh oysters," he said while helping Ashly out of her coat, and then went on to explain with a flippant smile, "Oysters are good for your health. They contain zinc and protein which strengthens your immune system. And they are also an excellent aphrodisiac."

"You mean they make me horny?" Ashly remarked.

Gordon bent over her, kissing her along the neck.

"Do you need such a stimulus?" he asked while slowly sliding his right hand straight down between her legs.

Ashly couldn't resist, she gave in to his fondling and enjoyed his foreplay all the way to his bed. She had hardly been able to take her tight dress off before they both sunk into the soft cushions. She felt wonderful – even more so when he positioned himself on top of her and then took her.

"This is awesome," Ashly screamed in ecstasy. "I want more!"

And more she got.

When they finished Gordon rolled over, leaving the bed and swaggering over to the bar in his big living room to get some drinks.

'What a beautiful body!' Ashly thought, while watching Gordon with amorous rapture.

There was no doubt about it – Gordon was an excellent lover and Ashly was asking herself how many women he may have satisfied before her.

"Have a glass of champagne, Ashly," Gordon said while offering her the glass. He left the room only to come back minutes later with a white mink coat.

"Have you ever made love on a mink?" he asked Ashly who was very astonished to say the least. If there was one thing, she was one hundred percent convinced of, it was no cruelty to animals! And she would never ever even go near a fur coat or anything made of fur.

"You are not serious!" she said with a perplexed expression, her voice shook with anger.

"Come on Ashly – it's great to make love on a mink. It gives you additional sensation". Gordon didn't get it and Ashly became even more disgusted. "It's such a beautiful product," he continued while stroking Ashly's naked skin with the fur. "And it's my Christmas present for you."

"No!" she said with a totally nauseated expression. "That's beyond the point. Don't you know how much these cute little animals suffer?" She furiously jumped out of the bed.

The mink sickened her, "Never ever would I wear fur!" A wave of revulsion gripped her. Gordon thought she looked even more desirable as she was standing there naked and so angry. Ashly, on the other hand, had never found her lover as revolting as now. Although she was totally attracted to him, she thought that this cringe-making situation was becoming more than a bad joke. She was totally shattered.

"Take your mink present away immediately," she ordered him.

"But Ashly, what's wrong with you. Don't get so excited about something that feels so luxuriously soft and plush." He tried to calm her down and of course only achieved the contrary.

"You don't get it. You really don't get it!" she yelled at him. "You make me sick with your mink!"

Gordon realised his mistake and gave in because he needed Ashly for further services. He didn't want to chase her away. Not yet.

"All right, all right," he capitulated, throwing the coat carelessly in the corner. "Then let's have some fun without the mink," he tried to pull Ashly back into his bed. But the evening was spoiled. And as Ashly had promised her mother she would not stay out too long, she left Gordon's penthouse shortly before midnight.

◆◆◆

Ashly had decided not to tell her mother about the mink. Iris would have been totally enraged, and, since she didn't like the Australian anyway, Ashly preferred to keep her latest encounter with Gordon to herself.

There were only a few more days until Christmas – the most wonderful day of the year. As every year, the Christmas cards had arrived from friends from all over the world. Iris had carefully hung them all up on a little rope over the living room door together with the little string of Christmas lights. Mistletoe was hanging in the doorway, although no one special was expected to come around to be kissed under it. The front door was decorated with a wreath, which Iris had made herself, and lots of festive figurines had been placed around the fireplace and on the bookshelves.

Ashly wanted to use the Christmas break to get a few things done from her to-do list and of course she was keen on seeing Gordon. She wondered what he would do over Christmas, as they hadn't spoken about it, and hoped he wasn't sulking, having so strongly refused his Christmas present. It was only later that she would find out that Gordon was the sort of man – just like Rick – who would always manage to make her feel guilty, thinking she had done something wrong. For now she was sweet on Gordon, even though he sometimes tended to camp it up. In the meantime she had tried to telephone him a few times and sent him several texts, but Gordon had failed to return her messages. Being slightly concerned about his whereabouts, she considered driving to his penthouse suite, then dropped the idea, as she didn't want to appear to be running after him.

It was one day before Christmas Eve when the postman brought another pile of Christmas cards with a single envelope standing out. Ashly, not recognising the handwriting – it reminded her of an old-fashioned scrawl – was eager to open it. The card was from Gordon saying that he is very sorry but he had to go home to Australia for Christmas, because his old mother wasn't well. He wished her a wonderful Christmas and he would contact her in the New Year when he was back in town.

Holding his card in her hands, Ashly was thunderstruck. She had been looking forward to seeing Gordon over the holidays, and with one stroke he had totally dashed her hopes. This wasn't how she regarded a relationship with Gordon – if it was a relationship in the first place. Why hadn't he told her about his mother? Surely he must have known for some time that his mother wasn't well and that he was going home to Australia. She tried to find excuses for his weird conduct. Perhaps he didn't want to burden her with his private affairs? By all means, Ashly was determined not to let things take their course in future so easily but to talk seriously with Gordon about his strange behaviour. However, as it turned out later – talking to Gordon was like talking to a brick wall and he certainly always knew how to talk his way out of a corner.

Of course the whole incident, which couldn't be hidden from Iris, only cemented her doubts about this Australian lady slayer who was in her eyes a consummate hypocrite. Accordingly, when she saw the card, she only remarked curtly,
"What a flimsy excuse! This man hasn't a spark of decency."
And young Jake agreed,
"Wait and see – he is a con man," he insinuated assiduously nodding.

◆◆◆

Christmas arrived and it was as every year at the McKenneth's home – devoting time with the nearest and dearest in Iris' cosy house. Everybody had looked forward to spending the time lazing about, playing games, cooking together, watching movies, and drinking hot chocolate.

When it was getting dark and the burning candles gave a warm glow to the living room, Iris told her grandson the familiar stories about Santa and how he comes every year to her house to visit them.

"You know, you have to leave cookies and a glass of milk for Santa on Christmas Eve," she told Jake who was by now approaching his teenage years and gradually turning into a sensible boy. Although he didn't believe his grandmother's Christmas tales any longer, he nevertheless loved to listen to them. In the past Iris had always eaten the cookies, when her grandson was asleep, then left some crumbs to indicate that Santa had been there. Once Jake, when he was younger, had suggested leaving carrots outdoors for Santa's reindeer as well. Iris was each time amused and kept up the pretence by going outside, when Jake was in bed, to nibble on the carrots and to leave some gnawed pieces behind as evidence. She didn't need a Christmas present, the joy of her grandson that Santa had been visiting them, was more rewarding than anything money could buy.

On Christmas morning the three family members gathered around the Christmas tree, which had been decorated so beautifully with ornaments, and exchanged their presents. After a long discussion on the pros and cons of modern gadgets, Iris, who had been very critical about children having such things, had agreed to buy Jake a smartphone. It had taken

Ashly her best powers of persuasion to convince her mother how important these devices are, and since Jake wanted such a thing – especially because his friend Claire had already one – the two women had finally decided to surprise him. When Jake unwrapped his long wished-for present on Christmas morning, he was delirious with joy. Holding a smartphone in his hands was really a thrill!

"Cool, now I can stay in touch with Claire all the time," he said, and grinning from ear to ear his face let up with happiness.

After that joyous handing out of presents, they all lazed on the couch in front of the warm log fire. And, whilst nibbling little homemade cookies from the beautiful handcrafted wooden plate, which Iris' husband had once brought back from abroad, they watched *Gone with the Wind*. It was almost like a ritual to watch this heart gripping tale of a love story at Christmas – as it was Iris' favourite movie, she never liked to miss it.

"I love to watch this epic film every year," she explained to everybody who was wondering about her strange custom and, as if she was excusing herself as to why she liked such a tearjerker, she added earnestly, "Christmas wouldn't be Christmas without it. There's nothing quite like snuggling up on the settee, drinking cups of hot chocolate on a cold winter's day, and watching this movie."

◆◆◆

Christmas was as always, yet it wasn't the same. Though the atmosphere was tranquil, it was only because Ashly and her mother had agreed that the topic of Gordon wouldn't come up. Nevertheless, the disappointment with him rested heavily on Ashly and made her feel low. How would Christmas have been with him? Then again, she had her beloved family and somehow Gordon didn't rightly fit into the picture of a sound family with all that happily-ever-after stuff. Could she truly see him as a father for Jake? She wasn't sure for a moment, catching herself thinking that he wasn't a true boyfriend anyway. The more Ashly ruminated, the more questions turned up. Was there more than just the sex which connected her with Gordon?

"Darling, why do you make your life so difficult?" her mother had recently asked and Ashly was wondering if she was right. Could her life be any easier?

"Scratch a lover and find a foe," Iris had recently quoted Dorothy Parker in lieu of better attributes to describe Gordon. Was her mother right? Was Gordon a blessing or a curse? At the moment he appeared rather to be a curse, not being dependable. Then again, Ashly hardly knew the handsome stranger and who knew what he held in store?

◆◆◆

As well as Ashly, Jake too felt a little bit sad this Christmas, despite his new toy – the smartphone which kept him busy for a while. He missed his soulmate Claire more than ever and excitedly agreed to the distraction his mother offered him. She promised him they would build a snowman together, providing there was enough snow, and also to go skating. On the whole, Ashly felt that she had somehow neglected her son recently and wanted to atone for the lost time of the past weeks.

Luckily it was still snowing on Boxing Day. Wrapped up warmly in their winter coats, mother and son took the opportunity to make some snowballs and roll them into larger ones and before long they had the most wonderful snowman in the whole street in Iris' front garden.

Ashly kept her promise. After lunch they took the sledge to the big hill in the nearby park. On their way she showed some sporty talent, towing Jake on the sledge through the light sprinkling of snow that had begun to fall again.

"Just like Rudolph the red nose reindeer," he cheered while visibly enjoying his mum dragging him through the wintery landscape.

When shortly after they arrived at the park it turned out that they weren't the only people, who had been attracted by the cold weather and enjoying the snow. Jake met some of his school mates and they all had a fantastic time together, sliding down the white slope or having a snowball fight.

"Mum, that was a really, really nice day," Jake said on their way home, pulling the sledge through the dark street. He couldn't have been happier.

"Yes," Ashly agreed, thinking to herself that life could be so easy.

Chapter Ten

Gordon called Ashly from Australia on New Year's Day as a sign that he was thinking of her from far away.

"Cheers to the New Year," he said and sounded a bit low. "I hope this will be another chance for us to get it right."

Rushing to answer the call, Ashly hadn't been able to identify the caller because the number was withheld. She listened quietly, wondering who it was and was flabbergasted when she realised it was Gordon. Hearing his voice was like the happiest moment of her life, and she instantly abandoned all her resolution for the coming year with regards to him.

"Happy New Year," she wished him too in a sweet voice. "I saw it on the News – you are the first ones to celebrate the New Year. The fireworks were impressive."

"Yes, that's true. We in the land Down-Under are ahead of everybody else. Did you have a nice evening?"

"It wasn't too bad – as every year Mum and I went to the local pub. We couldn't stay too long because the babysitter wanted to get home to her family."

"Understandable," Gordon said, speaking very quickly all of a sudden, "Listen, somebody is at the door. I've got to go now. Good to hear your voice – I'll call you again shortly." He paused and then added as if he had just remembered, "Tell your mum I asked about her – and a happy New Year to all of you."

"Thanks, to your family as well," Ashly swiftly replied, not being sure if Gordon had heard her last words as the line went dead so suddenly.

"Gordon sends his regards," she told her mother soon after, not expecting her to burst into cries of joy.

"This man Gordon," Iris said tersely, adding with a tinge of mockery, "Always expect the unexpected of him."

"Mum!" Ashly exclaimed, throwing a disapproving look at her mother.

"Well, his whole false air of a gentleman," Iris promptly reacted. She couldn't help but speak out what she made of her daughter's acquaintance. "His ambivalent character – It goes against my very nature how he is treating you."

Ashly didn't answer. She knew her mother – she would voice her concerns for a while and at last concede. Then again, would she ever really accept him?

◆◆◆

Gordon did indeed phone her again one day in her office. It was a nice sunny day in January.

"Guess what," he said and Ashly recognised him by his voice and his Australian accent, "I'm in Switzerland and I'll be back in town in three hours. Can you come and pick me up from the airport?"

Ashly was thunderstruck. She hadn't expected him back so suddenly.

"No, I can't," she replied with a dash of regret, feeling really sorry that she couldn't meet him at the airport. "I have an important meeting with the dean of the faculty this afternoon."

"Never mind, then come and see me afterwards in my penthouse," Gordon suggested, feigning sympathy and instantly making Ashly very happy, only to change his mind seconds later. "No maybe not today. Let me think – what about tomorrow?" His voice sounded noncommittal, leaving Ashly, who was now confused and disappointed, no choice but to agree half-heartedly,

"OK, see you tomorrow after work. Where?"

"Where? In my suite of course," Gordon said sharply and hung up the phone.

After that disappointing conversation Ashly had again a funny feeling that something wasn't right. Doubts started to gnaw on her, not being sure what to make of him – he seemed to fancy himself as a womaniser, giving the impression of an affluent businessman, apparently appealing to a lot of women. Who knew who he was seeing when he wasn't with Ashly? He had prided himself that he knew women and that he was familiar with how they feel and what they want. Did he really deem himself to be a smooth operator with the ladies, including Ashly?

◆◆◆

Although Ashly was full of excitement and could hardly wait to see Gordon, she prepared herself to have a serious talk with him about the future of their relationship. Gordon, on the other hand, had no desire to commit himself and seemed to believe that Ashly was gagging for having sex with him. When she arrived in the late afternoon at his suite, he stood in front of her, looking very pleased with himself.

"Hello Ashly," he welcomed her, lustfully going for her. And when she raised no objection, he manoeuvred her with burning desire to his bed, feeling assured in his role of being a brilliant lover.

"It's good that you're back. I missed you so much," Ashly whispered in his ear, inhaling his beguiling aftershave.

"I'm really pleased you missed me," Gordon showered her with kisses all over her body. "I'll try my best to make up for it." He spread her legs and Ashly was instantly lost in him. The kisses she craved were lavished on her, sweeping her away in her desire for him.

"Oh yes please," she moaned with pleasure when she devoted herself to him. She had indeed missed him deeply all the time he had allegedly been in Australia. Having yearned for sex with him, she could hardly wait for him to go down on her the second time.

"You are so good, so good!" she screamed at the height of pleasure.

Besotted from the love play, she forgot about her resolutions. Gordon was back, the sex with him was simply fantastic, and her great appetite for spicy pleasure was finally quenched.

Resting totally satisfied in Gordon's comfortable bed, she watched how the day was dwindling outside. It was already dark and one could see the lights all over town. Suddenly she caught herself pondering what did she really like about Gordon? He fascinated her with his lust for sex and money, and his generosity. Was there anything more? She only knew one thing for sure – this man had absolutely nothing in common with Rick or Ulrik. And she thankfully believed she had found the man to have fun with – an enticing lover who would add spice to her life. Then again, Ashly was instantly way out of her comfort zone, thinking that she had a right to know why he had let her down over Christmas. What was that thing with his mother?

"But Ashly, dear," Gordon never said darling to her, nor did he use any other term of endearment, "I didn't want to spoil your Christmas with my problems," he said. Glancing mischievously at Ashly, he tried to resolve her doubts.
"Don't you trust me?" she asked him.
Gordon replied skilfully sidestepping instead,
"Yes of course, very much so. You are a very good art historian with an excellent reputation," he flattered while fondling her, and then continued sweetly, "and a very sexy woman."

Ashly didn't know how to react, even more so as she became distracted by his smooching. She didn't want to succumb to his temptation and tried to fend him off. Doubtfully scanning him up and down, she took a deep breath and was somehow appeased when he offered to take her out and show her parts of the town she hadn't as yet seen.

"I'll take you to charming intimate venues where we can drink and dance all night long," he promised Ashly while his eyes rested on her. Oh, how much she loved these intensive blue eyes!

"And by the way, I have a surprise for you," he was waving two flight tickets which he had pulled out from under the pillows, "I'll take you to New York next month to redeem myself for having messed up your Christmas."

Ashly winced for seconds at the sound of the word "redeem" – too many times Rick had used this term, trying to compensate for his rude behaviour towards Ashly when he was drunk.

At the moment she was overwhelmed by Gordon's generosity, and he was delighted how easy he had won Ashly over without fuss or quibble.

◆◆◆

A few days later Gordon picked her up as promised to show her the town's nightlife. Ashly knew some of the places by daylight and never expected that these rather quiet places would become so lively, loud, and a little bit naughty by night. Her hot lover took her to the opening night of a new and very exclusive night club. When they arrived there, the place was already packed with people who seemed to have no qualms about showing off how rich they were. Their lack of taste was reflected in their flamboyant outfits, with ices hanging round their necks on multiple gold chains and big fat rings on their fingers. Ashly was amazed about the gaudiness. She had been so afraid of what to wear when going out with Gordon to such luxurious places. And then, when she saw how careless some people were dressed, she thought it was ridiculous how little sense of style particularly the younger women seemed to have.

Soon she became aware that there were a lot of people from the arts world present, many of them Russians whom she had already met at last year's party. Everybody seemed to know everybody. And a lot of people apparently knew Gordon.

Gordon, who was wearing an attractive dark blue Hugo Boss suit, obviously enjoyed being everybody's darling. He could truly work a room like nobody Ashly had seen before. He was 'Mister Big Deal' and took especially women's imagination by storm. They were magnetised by his glamorous lifestyle and impeccable manners, and adored his presence. His charm worked well with women, who were taken by his charisma, as well as men, because of his chinwags on racing cars and horses. And he could financially afford to impress the crowd by being a star with a know-it-all air and showing all his glory, while Ashly didn't want to draw attention. Indulging his vanity he splashed out on champagne for everybody sitting at the bar, and he must have spent a fortune in that one night. At one stage he went over to an intimate seating area with dark red plush sofas where Ashly saw him talking in a lowered voice to several people. For a moment she thought that she had seen them before at the party last year. That raised her suspicion. Who were these people and why did Gordon not introduce her to them? At first she was reluctant to ask him when he returned to the bar. Maybe she had already figured out that he would lie to her anyway? Or maybe she thought it was best not to know too much of his wheelings and dealings.

She gave it a try, "Who are these people you were talking to?"

"Just business partners," Gordon replied cagey, having no intention of talking about his business matters with Ashly.

"Come on, let's dance," he then said, dragging Ashly from the stool onto the dance floor.

◆◆◆

Ashly thoroughly enjoyed the night out with Gordon, but she had a bad headache the next morning waking up next to him. When she told him that she didn't feel well, he smiled wickedly at her and said,

"I have a good cure for it," and while rolling over her, he added, "sex." And then he began immediately kissing her breasts. Ashly instantly launched into action, positioning her legs expectantly around his waist, while Gordon thrusted himself inside her until she groaned with pleasure.

His lovemaking was as always fascinating, even in the early morning, and Ashly felt indeed better after he finished satisfying her.

"Gordon," she started to talk, turning around and gently tickling Gordon's hairless chest, "I have a son to look after. I can't leave everything to my mother, while I'm enjoying myself with you."

"Yes, I know. Why don't we take him out together?" he suggested. "We could have lunch together and then take him window shopping."

'Oh no!' Ashly thought, 'anything but window shopping.' Aloud she said, "He is eleven years old. I don't think he is interested in shopping, let alone window shopping."

"Good boy," Gordon replied grinning, "I'm not interested either but I thought you, being a woman, would like it."

"No not really. Sometimes, yes," Ashly admitted, not being very attentive as she was thinking what else to do instead. "We could go ice skating," she proposed with a smile.

Gordon wasn't too keen on active sports. He played tennis from time to time or went jogging on the beach back home in Australia. Ashly's suggestion of going ice skating didn't go down too well with him. He hesitated, but then he felt sorry for her, and as he knew that he needed to make friends with Jake sooner or later to get Ashly to fully trust him, he reluctantly agreed.

"Though I can't skate I can sit on the fence and watch you," he tried to sound humorous.

"That's fine with me," Ashly said and jumped out of bed. "Let's get a move on before it gets too late."

"We could meet Jake downtown at Teddy's for lunch — and your mother if she wants to come along," he suggested generously. "I could order a cab for them which would bring them to the restaurant."

Ashly thought that was a good idea, ordering a taxi – at least his big spectacular Bentley wouldn't show up in their street and stir up people's curiosity. She didn't think Iris would like to have lunch in such a posh restaurant as Teddy's. And she was right. When she phoned home to let her mother know about Gordon's plan, Iris declined with thanks. Albeit grudgingly she agreed to have Jake picked up by a cab in order to meet his mother and Gordon for lunch downtown.

"So everything is organised. I ordered a taxi to bring your son to the restaurant in about an hour," Gordon said very pleased with himself on his way to the bathroom. Ashly followed him soon after and they ended up showering together. This time she had great difficulties in fending off Gordon. At the moment her son was more important and she wanted to be in the restaurant before Jake arrived there in the cab.

◆◆◆

During all that time, while his mother was having fun with the poser from Australia, Jake had undoubtedly felt neglected by her. Unlike Gordon, who had vanished into thin air – unfortunately, Jake had thought, only temporarily – Claire and her father had sent a card for Christmas and New Year from Sweden saying: "We love you, we miss you, we will be home soon."

For Jake it had seemed like an eternity until his friend and Ulrik were back in town. Too bad that they had arrived shortly before school started and there had been no chance for him to see Claire any earlier than in class. As it turned out, they both had been bursting with expectation meeting later that week at the Mc Kenneth home where Ashly still supervised their homework and taught them. In fact it was by now not so much teaching any more but more like entertaining, keeping the kids busy with various tasks. Ashly placed importance on teaching languages and cultivating good manners. "Manners matter!" was her latest mantra.

"You'll never guess what I got for Christmas," Jake had greeted Claire and enthusiastically shown her his smartphone when she was at his house last Wednesday afternoon.

"Cool," she responded. "Now we can stay in touch wherever we are."

"Yep."

"I could have sent you pictures from Sweden if I had known that you had a smartphone," Claire said. She was more than happy to be back with Jake after the holiday break.

"Yeah. That would have been cool. I could have shown them to my mum and granny and perhaps they would have wanted to go to Sweden," Jake affirmed.

"Maybe we could go there one day all together."

"That would be wonderful – wouldn't it?" Jake was thrilled to bits by this thought.

"By the way, my dad was very upset about your mum," the girl revealed with a regretful ring in her tone.

"Don't tell me – I suppose because of this poser."

"Yes. I think my dad likes your mum very much and he's very disappointed that she is seeing another man."

"I wish she wouldn't," Jake made an angry gesture. "I don't like Gordon very much. Your dad is much cooler."

"Why don't you like him?"

"I can't really explain it – he seems false somehow. Something is just not right. He shows off so much and it all seems so unbelievable," the boy tried to find words to describe Gordon. "I think he's a real rotter."

"It appears that some women always fall for this type of man," Claire alluded without having Ashly in mind.

"I hope my mum doesn't. But who knows," Jake said, pulling a face. "She talks a lot about Gordon. What a nice guy he is, and how attractive he is, and all that sweet talk."

"It would be a shame if your mum fell for the wrong guy. She is such a nice woman and so intelligent. Still, there's nothing we can do about it," Claire had finished the dialogue with a resigned shrug of her shoulders.

◆◆◆

Jake was busy with his smartphone.

"Granny," he shouted "Look!" As quick as a wink he had taken a picture of Iris, when she was on the phone to Ashly, and showed it to her.

"Your mum just phoned," Iris said, "she wants you to meet her downtown at a restaurant called Teddy's."

"I don't want to go there," Jake replied without hesitation, fervently shaking his head.

"But Jake darling – why not?" Iris wasn't really surprised about her grandson's reaction.

"No, I don't want to go," Jake repeated, looking defiantly at his grandmother.

"But wouldn't it be a good opportunity to find out more about Gordon?" she tried to persuade him.

"Humph," the boy scratched his head. "I could look him up on the Internet."

"That's an idea!" Iris never thought that this new technology could one day become so useful for her. "But you can still do it when you're back from town."

"Granny! I really don't want to face Gordon. It's enough when my mother does," Jake implored, hugging his grandmother.

While holding her grandson in her arms, she tried to encourage him,

"Come on Jake, don't be silly. I don't like this windbag either." And looking in the boy's face she said, "Maybe we're not being fair to him. Just because he is rolling in money doesn't make him a bad guy."

"Maybe, maybe. ... Maybe pigs will fly," Jake replied slightly testy, turning away from his grandmother.

"Oh dear," Iris sighed. She was at a loss. How could she persuade Jake to go to this restaurant? "You would be doing me a favour if you would go," she finally managed to say with her weary eyes resting on her grandson.

"I always have to do what you or mum tells me to do," he became exasperated with his grandmother.

Oh, wow! Iris was stunned to learn that her grandson could be so stubborn. She hadn't seen him in such a mood before.

'Oh dear, I hope he isn't becoming like his father,' she thought, saying aloud, "Jake sweetie, what's wrong with you?"

"I would rather like to stay in and play with my smartphone," the boy grumbled while pretending to be immersed with his gadget.

'Now we have the situation I was afraid of – this damned thing is becoming so addictive,' Iris pondered and felt vindicated in her opinion that all these expensive gimmicks spoil kids imagination.

"I'm merely good for running errands for you and mum," Jake threw at his grandmother in anger. He knew it wasn't fair on her. It was his mother he was annoyed at. Why didn't she go out with Ulrik? Why did she choose this man Gordon instead?

Iris raised her eyebrows given the emotional outburst of her grandson, waiting for more to come.

"I'm the only man in the house," he went on, "and I'm only everybody's darling as long as I do what I'm told to do!" Yes, he was very discontented. "What about me? I have no dad to turn for advice! My mum is having fun with a man who could be my grandfather. And I don't like him!" he continued to air his anger.

Iris had never perceived her grandson so downright rebellious – what was the matter with him? She didn't expect him having growing-up issues yet and thought that he was much too young to be so adamant.

Jake was confused, feeling somehow left alone, if not betrayed by his mother. He was fascinated by Ulrik – a pretty cool customer who, so he thought, could add another dimension to his life. Yet, he feared that if his mother continued to repel Ulrik he would move on with Claire and the young boy would be left with nothing. The thought made him become even more angry with his mother. Couldn't she see that Gordon was an imposter? Shaking his head, he realised that his mother remained a mystery to him.

Preoccupied, he heard his grandmother saying,

"That's not right – and you know it isn't," Iris, though she was somehow upset when faced with the bitter remarks of the young boy, had decided to best ignore his display of temper.

"I don't want to hurt you," Jake said in a sorry voice. "It's my mother I'm angry with."

"You shouldn't be angry with her," Iris replied. Putting her arms around him, she added gently, "Look, I'm not pleased with Gordon myself. But your mother is happy with him. And that's what counts."

After a moment of silence, Jake put what he thought was a serious question to his grandmother, "What about my happiness?"

"Jake dear," Iris begun to speak, trying to gain his attention, "I always have your happiness in mind, because if you're happy I'm happy too".

Jake didn't appear to be convinced. He stared motionless at his granny.

"Happiness attracts happiness," he suddenly muttered, drawing away from Iris.

"We should make a compromise," Iris suggested, "You go downtown to meet your mother and Gordon and find out more about him. And when you're back we can check him out on the internet."

She looked at Jake, waiting for his answer.

"Yeah," Jake said drily and quoted a line from a book which he had recently read, "I want that you do something but you *must* do it voluntarily!"

Iris was puzzled. In a way her grandson was right. How could he do something voluntarily if she *wants* him to do it?

"Yes my dear, I want you to meet your mother downtown," she then said firmly. She thought that Jake seemed to be somehow obstinate today and — case closed — she wasn't going to argue any more with him. "Now go and get ready," she told her grandson with a stern expression that didn't allow for any objection.

◆◆◆

Jake did what his grandmother had told him but of course very reluctantly. The taxi arrived in time, taking him to the centre of town where the restaurant was situated. His mother was already waiting for him outside despite the cold.

"Hi sweetie, I'm so happy that you're here," she welcomed him, hugging and kissing him affectionately. Jake didn't like such a rousing reception and tried to free himself from the clutches of his mother.

"Leave me alone," he said curtly, turning around towards the entrance of this posh restaurant. Before Ashly was able to ask what was bugging him, Jake had already put his hands on the golden shiny door handle and pulled the wooden door open. Seconds later he stood inside the place. The décor was pretentious and the furnishings were exclusive. Jake felt out of place. 'Don't attract attention!' he told himself while he was looking around feeling forlorn. Luckily Gordon had already spotted him and Ashly coming through the door and stood up from the table at the window to call them over.

"Here comes my clever little friend," he said, pretending to like Jake. And while he was welcoming him, he was well aware not to get too close to the boy, knowing that Jake didn't like physical contact.

"Hi," Jake replied, looking down, taking his seat, and thinking: 'I won't embark on your foul play!'

The waiter brought the menu and was waiting at arm's length from the table for the party to order. As Gordon was a regular guest at Teddy's, he knew the menu by heart. And while Jake was still busy studying it, Gordon already ordered for all three. That was so typical of this man. It wouldn't have been him, always seizing the reins.

"Just bring us a platter of your starters," he imperiously ordered the waiter, handing the menus back.

And of course that put Jake off on the spot – how did this haughty prig dare to order for him, not knowing what his favourite food was? Jake sensed that it must be really important for Gordon to impress.

"Have you ever been in a place like this before?" he asked Jake in a very laid-back posture.

"No, of course not," the boy answered firmly and frowned – what a stupid question! Gordon should know quite well that he wouldn't be able to afford eating in such an extravagant place.

As if Gordon had read the boy's mind, he remarked with a broad grin,

"You could afford all this if you made a lot of

money."

"Yeah," Jake answered brusquely. "I'm not into money."

"That's all right. Sooner or later you will be," Gordon returned, smiling affectedly.

Meanwhile the food arrived and it turned out to be an excellent choice. Accompanied by a brilliant white wine (naturally not for Jake) the mixed fish and meats were fantastic in their presentation, served on beautiful dishes. In addition to this sumptuous platter, a good selection of mixed cheeses and bread was also provided.

Jake was particularly struck by the seafood. He mumbled something, which nobody understood, and started pouncing on the food on his plate. Ashly was embarrassed because she thought it wasn't good manners eating before anybody else at the table. This wasn't how she had educated her son. But Gordon laughed.

"Let him go," he said complacently and clicked glasses. "Cheers Ashly."

While everybody was enjoying the food, Jake was audibly munching away on his, and he thought that his grandmother had been right. It was quite interesting to see how his mum and Gordon interacted.

This man wasn't far away from getting all over his mother, even in broad day-light and never mind the bystanders, Jake discerned.

"How was your Christmas?" Gordon tried to start a conversation with the boy.

"That's already long ago," Jake replied short-tempered. He was definitely not in the mood to talk to Gordon and certainly not about Christmas which had been, in Jake's eyes, messed up because of that poser.

"Tell Gordon about your present," Ashly tried to bring some life into the conversation. And seeing the curious expression of her son, she added, "Your smartphone."

"Oh yes my smartphone. I left it at home," Jake languidly said. Being bored, he put his elbows on the table and braced his head in his hands. Again, much to his mother's chagrin; she thought she had taught him it was bad manners to put one's elbows on the dining table.

"I have one as well – here have a look," Gordon reached in his pocket, getting his smartphone out and handing it to Jake with a swanky smile.

"Oh this is the very expensive one," Jake remarked, looking briefly at the thing. "The one I have fulfils its purpose just as well."

"Look here," Gordon was flicking with his fingers on

his gadget, "here we are – pictures from Australia." He turned the phone horizontally around, showing the photos from the Australian landscape to Jake and then to Ashly.

"These pictures could have been taken anywhere in the world," the boy didn't mince words.

"Jake!" Ashly hissed annoyed.

"Well, there isn't a single one showing Gordon," he defended himself, suspiciously eyeing the Australian.

Gordon, however, pretended to ignore Jake's remark. Putting on a brave face, he turned towards Ashly who was deeply impressed with the beautiful landscape.

"Wonderful," Ashly appreciated. "I would like to go there one day."

"Well, why not," Gordon said vaguely.

"I would rather like to go to Sweden," Jake's demur was a dead giveaway.

"Sweden is too cold. Australia is nicer. While you celebrate Christmas and it's cold over here, it's summer in Australia and we go swimming over there," Gordon explained with such conceit that left Jake to feel like a stupid infant.

"Yes, I know," Jake replied reluctantly, being not very eager to talk to Gordon, given his snobbish talk, and adding with a defiant look at the Australian,

"Still, I like Sweden better!"

Ashly wasn't sure what her son was up to. Did he really want to go to Sweden or did he just say so out of spite? She remembered that she liked the country and its people very much when she went there a long time ago. And of course there was Ulrik who had been such a reliable friend all the time.

"Ashly," Gordon interrupted her thoughts. "I have to go to the bathroom", and while he was getting something out of his pocket, he continued, "here's my wallet. Can you please pay the waiter when he comes around." Then he placed his wallet on the table and walked in the direction of the guests' restrooms.

As if it was a cue from fate – Gordon leaving his wallet was just what Jake had been waiting for. Before his mother could say anything he grabbed the heavy wallet.

"Jake, what's wrong with you today?" Ashly asked indignantly. And when Jake didn't respond she admonished him, "Leave it!"

"Why mum? Gordon is such a peculiar person. I want to find out more about him," the boy said, scrutinizing the wallet which on first sight contained a large amount of bank notes.

"It's not very polite of you!"

"He won't know," Jake remarked tersely and when looking further for hints about Gordon, he found a business card from Tim L. Wagner, Art Dealer, High Street, Bangor.

"Mum, look at that," Jake had pulled out the card, showing it to Ashly. "Do you know him?"

Ashly, glancing at the name on the card, was much too nervous Gordon would return and find her spying on him.

"No," she said and was genuinely wondering why she had never heard of this art dealer. "He must be new in town," she said to Jake who was now even more suspicious about Gordon.

As quick as Gordon had left the table he was back. Finding his wallet on the spot, where he had left it, he assumed the bill hadn't been paid.

"We can pay up front", he suggested somewhat bossy, took his wallet and, as if he was in a hurry, he suddenly rushed towards the entrance.

After having paid the bill they realised that Jake had forgotten his skates. The boy secretly laughed up his sleeve but kept a straight face. He had of course no intention of going ice skating with Gordon and thought having no skates was a good exit-option.

"What do we do now?" Ashly asked, feigning despair. She knew quite well that they could rent skates at the Ice-Bowl. In the meantime she must have realised that her son really didn't want to spend any more time with Gordon.

"Very simple," Gordon answered in a tone that allowed no dissent. Since he liked to be the boss, who arranges everything for everybody in order to take control, he continued with a stern expression in his face,

"I call a taxi to pick up the skates at your house and have them brought to the Ice-Bowl."

"Good idea", Ashly gave in reluctantly, "let's check first if Iris is at home."

However, her hopes to spare her son from Gordon were blighted. Of course Iris was home, answering the phone with a weary voice, as the call had woken her from her nap.

"Have a nice afternoon and don't be too late home," Iris said, adding offhand, "Jake has to go to school tomorrow."

◆◆◆

Jake rolled his eyes – the prospect of having to spend even more time with this person didn't amuse him at all. He had hoped to get away with it when his mother noticed that the skates had been left at home. But Gordon had thwarted his plans, for what appeared to be the one and only reason:

spending more time with Ashly. Yet, Jake didn't really want to share his mum. Not with such a man who so seemingly enjoyed attracting attention everywhere he turned up.

The fact alone how he drove the Bentley along at the Ice Bowl looking for a parking spot – Jake thought he could feel the looks of the people who had never seen before such a state coach, as he called Gordon's car. And then – Jake did not believe it! – Gordon wasn't just paying to get into the place, no – he was discussing with the woman at the cash desk about the cheapest ticket! Gordon of all people – as if he had to count the pennies.

The next thing, which annoyed Jake, was that Gordon had not the faintest idea how to skate, but he purported to do so.

"Lace up your shoes right", he reminded Jake with this imperious attitude which he had already put on airs in the restaurant.

"Be careful on the ice and don't bump into other people", was another one of Gordon's alleged words of advice, only aiming to show Ashly how considerate he was, which maddened Jake. He mastered the skating technique very well and didn't need any such instructions, let alone such overbearing orders from a man he didn't like.

'That sleaze bag! It's so obvious that he wants to

impress my mother with his false anxious behaviour,' it occurred to Jake. Again, he could see right through Gordon and he was definitely not going to embark on the Australian's silly games.

The whole ice rink was enchantingly decorated with a winter landscape – little white fir trees with fairy lights, reindeers and sledges with very colourful presents. It was packed with people, showing their amazing levels of fitness and agility, gliding smoothly, sometimes very artistically, over the ice. It was easy for Jake to blend with the crowd. He wasn't so much concerned to bump into people, but much more of meeting those mates on the ice who already gave him a hard time at school. What would they say when they saw his mother with Gordon who was so much older and so overbearing? Then again, he thought, those mates were just as mindless as Gordon – very easily impressed by status symbols and all agog to acquire the top of the range gadgets, clothes, and privileges.

Unfortunately it was unavoidable that Jake did indeed bump into one of his schoolmates. Today of all days, it was one who wasn't well-disposed towards him. The big bloke headed straight for Jake with a broad grin on his face.

"I see you brought your grandfather with you today," he said with a tinge of ridicule, swinging round and forming a very provocative figure of eight around Jake.

'Oh no. Not that as well!' Jake thought, gliding unwaveringly over the ice, hoping not to become a mockery to his classmates thanks to that man Gordon.

"Back off!" Jake replied to him with a half-smile, artistically turning away, leaving the bully standing on the ice by himself.

'Where is my mother?' Jake was now desperately searching for her. Normally the two would have spent a totally cool day out together. But he couldn't find her. After he had done a few rotations he spotted her – what a disappointment for him! She was sitting on the bench with Gordon, intimately hugging. That just did it! Jake wasn't at all pleased with what he saw. He really felt like he was being let down and fumed with rage internally. Nonetheless he attempted to remain calm when approaching them on his skates.

"Your mother is a fine woman," Gordon said flippantly, adding fuel to the boy's fire.

Jake had had enough. He experienced the urge to go home – immediately. He gruffly took off his skates, and, whilst Ashly attempted to catch up with him, he headed to the exit, neither turning around nor saying a word. This man just seemed to rub him up the wrong way.

'Hopefully my mother will spare me this bighead in the future,' he thought, waiting for her outside the Ice-bowl.

Chapter Eleven

Iris did indeed go to see Claudia in her gallery downtown one day in late winter. Good old Iris, who didn't like the frantic activity of the city, went rather reluctantly. 'Knowing the facts will help you plan for the future,' she thought and reminded herself that it was only for the benefit of her beloved daughter that she took the trouble to visit Claudia despite all the hassle. Prepared with best intentions to get on to the track of Mr. Mystery, as Iris called Gordon now, she took the bus to the city one afternoon.

She had told Ashly that she was meeting a friend in town. And although Ashly was wondering – her mother didn't like the city – she didn't raise any questions but offered to pick her up on the way home.

"No, thank you darling," Iris declined her daughter's

offer to give her a lift. "I haven't seen Dorothy for such a long time and I don't know how much time we will spend together." Iris lied without even turning red. Dorothy was her best friend and she saw her regularly, at least once a week, at the bridge evening. She thought she should have invented another friend, but fortunately Ashly didn't notice her mother's mistake.

It was quite a nice day when Iris set out. As everything looked so much brighter and nicer in sunshine, she enjoyed the bus ride, and upon arrival in the city centre she had no problem finding the gallery.
The place wasn't very big and devoid of people when Iris entered. It was all exciting stuff she saw in there, a variety of sculptures and what appeared to be modern art paintings.
"Hello Mrs. Mc Kenneth," Claudia came towards Iris, reaching out to embrace her. "It's quite a surprise to see you in my gallery."
"Well, yes," Iris was concentrating on how to explain to Claudia why she was paying her a visit.
"You know, when we met before Christmas you said we could have a talk about this Australian man, Gordon."
"Oh yes," the young woman seemed to remember. "You didn't like him."

"Well, I still don't like him. He appears to be a rich businessman and I would really like to know where his wealth is coming from," Iris said straightaway. Now that her concerns were in the open, she was relieved.

"Yes, I can understand that," Claudia acknowledged with a friendly smile. "I sometimes wonder myself. Allegedly he is an estate agent, but I don't understand how that can bring so much money," she said, and glancing with her blue eyes at Iris, she spoke on, "As far as I know he is heavily into the arts as well, especially selling artwork to Russia."

"Would that explain his wealth?" Iris asked doubtfully.

"In some circumstances, yes," Claudia replied.

"In some circumstances?" Iris repeated, "And in other circumstances?"

"Well, it all depends on the value of the painting or the object," the gallery owner explained. "If one sells an original Picasso for example, that would be worth millions."

"Sure it would," Iris nodded. "Though, one would have to get his hands on such a masterpiece first." She seemed to think about something and then voiced her misgivings, "I can't imagine that there are so many originals around to make so much money."

"Oh yes, Mrs. Mc Kenneth, you wouldn't believe how big – moneywise – the art market is. Last year it broke all existing records. I think globally it raked in over fifty billion dollars," Claudia told Iris. "And record sales were made with Modern Art, that is to say post-war art."

"Yes I know," Iris said, "from time to time I read about it in the newspaper. Still, it's unbelievable that there is so much money to be made with things like that", and she pointed to a painting which she thought Jake or Claire could have made.

"Well," the young woman responded with amusement in her voice, "there are people who will pay a lot of money for this, as you can see by the price tag."

"So would Gordon get his considerable wealth by not only selling property but paintings?" Iris wondered.

"Definitely," Claudia nodded.

"But where does he get the paintings from?"

"It depends – whoever is selling them. This could be anywhere in the world," the gallery owner insinuated, shrugging her shoulders. And then she bent over towards Iris and lowering her voice she said, "Rumour has it that Gordon was linked to several art heists. Allegedly he is the man with all the contacts in the arts world, especially Russia. The

Russian new elite are extremely keen to obtain artwork from the Western world."

Iris was dumbfounded. If what Claudia had just said was true, then her daughter might be at risk. She looked at Claudia who continued unwaveringly,

"It's said that it is business on mutual terms. Gordon is brokering supply and demand for fine art and hopes to extend his property business to Russia."

"So you mean to say he is selling stolen goods to Russia?" Iris speculated.

"Well, he may not sell it himself but he definitely acts as intermediary," Claudia put her right.

"Maybe that's the reason why he likes to travel and set up small companies?"

"Could well be," Claudia nodded.

Iris had heard enough. It was hard for her to digest all the facts she had just learned.

"Well Claudia, thank you very much for your time. I would appreciate it if you didn't tell Ashly about my visit to your gallery."

"I hope Ashly isn't getting into trouble. I'm glad if I was able to help you," Claudia said and accompanied Iris to the door. Taking her by the arm, she continued in a lowered voice,

"Please don't tell anyone that I shared this information with you. Everything I said must stay in this room!" looking at Iris very distressed, she explained, "It may only come back and haunt me if you were to disclose this to the wrong people."

Iris obviously didn't feel comfortable at all by what she had just heard and stared rather helplessly at the young woman.

"For all our sakes, be very careful what you repeat to anyone!" Claudia resumed with a pressing tone in her voice, while holding the door open for Iris and bidding her goodbye.

The distraught expression on Claudia's face stayed with Iris as she left the gallery. Feeling fairly crestfallen she went to the bus stop, immersed in her thoughts the whole way home. At least, her initial instinct hadn't let her down. Her suspicion that there was something cagey about Gordon had turned out to be justified. Nonetheless, she thought, so far she had no hard facts. Claudia's story might just be a rumour and she understood that she had to be careful not to wrongly accuse the man.

◆◆◆

Iris was home earlier than she had expected, and remembering Claudia's appeal, she thought it might indeed be wise to keep the outcome of her visit to the gallery to herself. But Jake wanted to know where she had been and pestered his grandmother with questions.

"Oh dear," she said, "I totally forgot to ask Claudia about that art dealer – what was his name?"

"Tim L. Wagner," Jake answered. "Forget about him – he doesn't exist."

"What do you mean – he doesn't exist?" Iris asked astonished.

"I couldn't find anybody with this name at that address on the internet."

"That doesn't mean he doesn't exist," Iris objected. "What about Gordon – did you check him out on the internet?" she questioned Jake. Their conversation was interrupted, as Ashly entered the room.

"Have you ever considered that Gordon might be leading you on?" Iris asked her daughter.

"Why would he?" Ashly replied frowning. She was astounded that her mother came up with such a question out of the blue.

"Has it never crossed your mind that there is something dodgy about him?" Iris picked up the thread again.

"What do you mean – there is something dodgy about him?"

"Well, I find it strange that a guy like Gordon is taking you out and you don't even know where his money comes from," Iris raised her concerns with a stern look at her daughter.

But Ashly had too much on her mind, and today wasn't a good opportunity for Iris to talk with her daughter about Gordon.

"Mum, how many times do I have to tell you that I'm not bothered by what he does for a living. Maybe he inherited his wealth," she languidly remarked. Not being inclined to reveal her innermost thoughts, she briskly left the room. But what did she really know about Gordon's activities?

After Iris had made sure that Ashly wouldn't hear them, she and her grandson continued their exchange of information.

"Imagine this," Iris whispered, being well aware of Claudia's alerting words, "Gordon is at the heart of art heists."

"Granny, I told you he's kind of a strange person."

"What did you find on the Internet about him?" Iris looked for the remote control to turn the TV on.

"Quite a lot. Although there are a lot of men with the same name. That makes it difficult to search for the right one," Jake explained low-voiced.

"Go ahead! Don't keep me on tenterhooks."

"Well, he seems to be well established in the art world," Jake started, but he was distracted by the loud sound from the TV. "Can I turn that down a bit?"

"Yes, yes. Go ahead," Iris nodded. She was desperate to hear her grandson's findings.

Jake had found Gordon's name popping up in many society columns.

"I discovered lots of pictures of him – they all seemed to be taken recently – and many articles on Gordon attending arts exhibitions or auctions." He paused, much to the regret of Iris.

"Jake – go on!"

"The pictures all showed him surrounded by some blonde beauty queen types," he eventually said. "That raised my suspicion."

"Yes, I can well imagine – how he is standing there like a playboy. A glass of champagne in one hand and embracing those blondes with the other," Iris agreed.

"What does he want from my mum? She doesn't look anything like these striking beauty queens?" Jake was curious.

"Well, we'll find out, don't you worry. Leave it to me," Iris said, having in mind to discuss things with her friend Dorothy. Then she gave her grandson a tender hug and lowering her voice, she added, "Sorry darling dear, I've had enough for today and I need to relax now."

Of course Jake would have loved to talk his

conclusions through with his grandmother. Especially since having seen Gordon surrounded by these sleazily dressed blondes, with their pink pluming robes looking like nightwear, he couldn't understand why this Australian man was so interested in his mother. But as Iris looked very tired the boy gave in to her request with a deep sigh.

◆◆◆

Iris was tantalized by a lot of questions and tormented with doubt. She was very eager to get to the bottom of the Mystery Man and had arranged to meet up with her good old friend Dorothy ahead of their bridge evening on Thursday.

Dorothy was a little woman, the same age as Iris. They had met many years ago in hospital where both women had undergone an abdominal operation. Fortunately for Iris it had been after she had given birth to her daughter Ashly. Dorothy had not been so lucky and she and her husband stayed childless. Naturally Dorothy, being crazy about children, had adored Ashly all her life and shared Iris' worries. No wonder that she felt the same way as Iris when she heard the story of Mr. Mystery from her friend.

Iris wasn't so blind and obtuse that she wasn't

seeing through the deceptive web that Gordon was trying to weave. And although Claudia had warned her not to disclose anything of their conversation, Iris simply needed to confide in with her best friend. She had already poured her heart out to Dorothy and briefly informed her about the outcome of her visit to Claudia.

Dorothy was already waiting for Iris to turn up in the pub, desperate to learn more about this odd lover of Ashly.
"I don't understand – what is he using Ashly for?" Dorothy said after she heard the full story from Iris again and shook her head. "It all looks as if he is targeting her specifically. But what for?"
"Don't ask me to explain," Iris replied, "I don't know myself. All I know is that there is something strange going on and I'm worried to death about my daughter." Iris, being overly concerned, was imagining the worst case scenario.
"I'm sure there is a reasonable explanation for it," Dorothy tried to comfort her friend.
"Well, what's reasonable about selling stolen goods?" Iris was a bit snappy at her friend.
"I'm only trying to be helpful," Dorothy replied apologetically. She and Iris had already been through so much together that they knew each

other extremely well. As such, Dorothy knew if Iris was in a bad mood there was something really serious troubling her.

Both women were sitting at the little table in the corner of the pub with their drinks in front of them. The lamps on the walls shed just enough light to feel comfortable. After minutes of silence Dorothy picked up the thread,

"Did you speak with Ashly about your concerns?"

"She is too stubborn," Iris shook her head. "I can't talk to her about this man."

"What about fake art work?" the friend inquired. "Have you considered your Mystery Man is selling counterfeits?"

"Dorothy!" Iris exclaimed with a look of shock. She imagined again how her daughter could get caught up in illegal and underhand dealings.

"I only said aloud what I'm thinking."

"I must admit I haven't really thought about it," Iris said rather preoccupied. "But of course I wouldn't put anything past him."

"Still – the question is: what has Ashly got to do with it all?" Dorothy wondered.

"I wish I knew."

"Who could help? What if Ulrik talks to Ashly?" Dorothy suggested and took a sip of her Guinness.

"I don't think so."

"Why not, he's a nice guy."

"Unfortunately Ashly isn't so keen on Ulrik. She seems to be addicted to Mr. Mystery," Iris threw her hands up in despair.

"I mean what else can you do? You can find out anything about the man's past to reveal him to be a scoundrel, or…" Dorothy stopped suddenly.

"Or what?" Iris was eager to know.

"Or talk to Ashly", her friend said slowly and then continued as if she was reflecting on something, "Or even better – confront Gordon with what you know."

"Never mind what kind of shady deals Mr. Mystery is involved in. By all means, I want to save Ashly from doing something stupid."

"Gordon seems to be very clever," Dorothy sank back on the bench. "You better watch out. You don't want your daughter ending up in jail because of her involvement with a criminal!"

"Dorothy!" Iris exclaimed again, shaking her head disbelievingly. She was horrified – her daughter in jail? Never! "Don't paint such a gloomy picture!"

Since Iris' first encounter with Gordon, anxiety and vexation had always been in the background like a shadow. She couldn't resist the feeling that Mr. Mystery was using her daughter for something. But what for and how could she prove what she believed? The whole affair was pretty twisted and had already confused her, and now her friend was totally unnerving her. Gordon was clever – there was no doubt about that. How could she ensure that her daughter wasn't caught in a net that would ultimately entangle the whole family? Panic struggling with dispassion caught up in her mind. 'There is no reason to paint such a sombre picture!' Iris thought to herself, hoping that her nightmare wouldn't come true. Before she was able to converse any more with Dorothy, the door of the pub swung open and, as a crowd of people flocked in, all bedlam broke loose.

Dorothy twirled her watch on her wrist and realised that it was time for their game of bridge.
"Let's go upstairs", she stood up from the bench and pulled her friend gently by her arm.
"Yes, let's enjoy our bridge evening," Iris said with a deep sigh, following her friend to the upstairs premises, hoping to forget for a while the worries which were haunting her.
If Iris had known then that her daughter and her scheming lover where going to spend a weekend in New York, she would have been even more troubled.

Chapter Twelve

The trip to New York with Gordon meant a lot to Ashly, and she kept it a secret that he had invited her for a weekend to the Big Apple. She knew her mother wouldn't have appreciated it. According to Iris, Ashly should have a relationship with a decent man who was caring and sharing. Life was too short for anything less. Despite all of her mother's good intentions Ashly was infatuated with Gordon. She simply loved spending time with this go-getter and was blinded by his good looks.

"Whether you like it or not – I don't care," she often shouted at her mother, hurting her by acting like a defiant child when she once more expressed her reservations about Gordon, leaving Iris in total despair.

Ashly was naturally very excited not only about travelling with Gordon for the first time, but even more so of spending a weekend full of fun with him in New York. Under no circumstances did she want her mother getting between her and Gordon, and particularly did she not want her to become involved in her love-life. For Ashly the trip to the famous city was a gift from heaven and, since she regarded it as a one-off opportunity, she was convinced this would tighten the rather loose relationship with Gordon. Her only problem was how to break the news to her mother who would need to look after Jake. As anticipated, Iris was of course taken by complete surprise when Ashly told her at the last minute about the New York trip.

"Can you explain to me why you didn't tell me earlier?" Iris asked with a piercing look at her daughter.

What was Ashly supposed to say?

"Why should I?" she sullenly answered.

Iris exchanged a quick look with her daughter.

"You know my dear, I don't have to look after your son while you run off with a good-for-nothing," she said coolly, knowing that she may have used the wrong term for the Australian.

"Who says that Gordon is a good-for-nothing?" Ashly countered.

"Is he not? Then explain to me how he makes his money?" Iris insisted, glaring at her daughter with hard eyes.

Ashly chewed her lips. Gordon, the *"good-for-nothing",* was good for at least something. He definitely knew how to satisfy a woman. Even so, what difference would it make to explain this to her mother? Ashly didn't know about Gordon's finances, but she knew for sure that she was definitely not going to abandon her terribly handsome lover. She was instead going to fly with him to New York – no matter what.

"You are making a mistake, wasting the best years of your life. Think about it," Iris tried to engage her daughter's attention.

"So what – it's my life!" Ashly exclaimed annoyed, folding her arms tight across her chest.

Iris tsked, "Tsk!" She wondered why her daughter was acting so cold. Did she not understand that, as her mother, Iris was concerned about her wellbeing? What was wrong with Ashly? All sense of reason seemed to have deserted her.

"Ashly, come on – Jake needs a father and you deserve a good man. Don't waste your time like you did with Rick. You'll find someone who is right for you," Iris said.

"Aha! How can you be so sure?" Ashly snapped at her mother. At the same time she wished she hadn't been so hard on her. Somehow her mother was right. She loved her son Jake more than anything in the world, and not only did she herself deserve a good man, but Jake deserved a good father. Was Gordon a man who was good with children? She didn't care what he did for a living as long as he was a good father. Yet, so far that hadn't been the case. Gordon's lifestyle, which she admittedly enjoyed, was incompatible with a family life. No matter how hard Gordon tried to show off.

Ashly curbed her anger and after a moment of hesitation she said ruefully,
"Mum, please, let's not argue about Gordon. I'm totally infatuated with him. I'm sorry if my relationship with Gordon upsets you."
"It's all right," Iris replied. Sympathy softened her tone when she spoke on, "You should know me – it's against my very nature not to voice my apprehensions."
"Yes mum, I know," Ashly agreed, "But sometimes you are pushing me too hard into a traditional relationship which I don't want." Turning her look towards her mother, she continued, "Look mum, I'm really sorry I didn't intend to have a heated argument with you over a man."
For a moment awkward silence prevailed in the room. Ashly took a long deep breath. It occurred to

her that she would be totally lost without her mother, especially since she was looking after Jake.

Iris, noticing her daughter's quandary, deemed it best not to mention her dodgy lover any more. Trying to get over and done with the awkward atmosphere, she said with a tinge of bitterness in her tone,

"You know darling, one should never start an argument if one doesn't know how to finish it."

Ashly looked at her, slightly confused.

"What do you mean?"

"Well, I appreciate your remarkably candid attitude. It doesn't get us anywhere to argue over Gordon – so let's stop it." Kissing her daughter on the cheek, she resumed, "It's entirely up to you what you do. But you should know: I'm your mother and I love you, no matter what. We shouldn't let any man come between us!"

Ashly ruminated on her mother's words for a while. Claudia had not so long ago said that Gordon put their friendship at stake. And now her mother cautioned her as well. But Ashly didn't want to know. She simply wanted to have a good time with this extraordinary lover, never mind what everybody said. And she didn't want to dwell on what secrets Gordon might harbour.

"I wish you a good time in New York, darling," Iris'

gentle voice called Ashly back into reality.

"Yes thank you, mum – what would I do without you?" Ashly said. Slightly dazed by the argument with her mother, her gaze was drifting off into the distance. She was miles away, full of excitement, looking forward to what she believed would be a romantic holiday with Gordon and could hardly wait to get to the airport the next morning.

◆◆◆

Ashly had travelled many times through Europe and other places, when she was an art student, and so she was very familiar with the busy goings-on at airports. She loved the whole atmosphere before the departure, the little bars and cafes, and the variety of shops displaying jewellery, perfume, books, sweets as well as a lot of other things.

Flying with Gordon was different. When the pair arrived at the local airport he took over the reins as usual which made Ashly, who was so experienced in travelling, feel like a little girl.

"We have to go over there to check in first," he commanded her, and not waiting for her he went straight to the airline's check-in desk where he handed both their tickets over. "No, we have no luggage," he answered when asked by the stewardess, and turning towards Ashly he glared at her with hard eyes, inquiring harshly, "Or do you have any luggage to hand over?" The way he behaved towards her was so unusually unfriendly that Ashly was confused.

"No, only hand luggage," she answered with a smile despite her irritation and showed her little black lightweight trolley, while the stewardess issued the tickets, handing them back to Gordon.

When they arrived at the passport control desk Gordon pushed her.

"Show them your passport, Ashly," he instructed her, while he got his out of his jacket and handed it over to the official.

Ashly had tried her best to stay calm while "good-for-nothing" Gordon took care of everything. Gradually she became annoyed, as Gordon drove her mad with his supercilious behaviour. She didn't like his fuss but didn't want to say anything about it either. Fortunately he didn't get in her way when she was looking in the shops after they had passed through security.

"Nice jewellery," he said when they were standing in one of the many jewellery shops. "Do you like it?" She had been looking at a sapphire ring enclosed with diamonds. These blue stones — she liked them just as much as she liked Gordon's blue eyes.

"Yes, it is very pretty," she answered fascinated.

While she enjoyed looking at the sparkling jewellery in the display, Gordon pushed her again, "Let's go to the gate," he urged her.

Ashly, almost losing her patience, forced herself to sound calm. "There is still plenty of time. Why the hurry all of a sudden?" she asked.

"Then do what you want and stay – but I have the tickets!" He walked abruptly away, heading towards the gates, and left Ashly in a state of total confusion behind. Before she hit the panic button she decided to follow him. She was frustrated and angry that Gordon had left her with no choice. Sitting down in the departure lounge at the gate, she waited for things to come. She didn't like Gordon's controlling behaviour and how he gave himself airs – this was a side of him she hadn't come across before. It somehow reminded her of Rick and his chauvinistic attitude towards women. Perhaps she ought to be more careful? Ulrik jumped suddenly into her mind and how much more easy-going he was. Compared to what she had just experienced with Gordon her Swedish friend was definitely a bastion of calmness. 'Maybe I do him an injustice,' she reflected. She and Ulrik had met briefly after the Christmas break. Ulrik had given her a coffee-table book on contemporary

Swedish art as a present, which he had brought all the way from Sweden. She had hardly appreciated his effort – being so besotted with Gordon. Suddenly she felt a wave of melancholy coming over her thinking of Ulrik. He was definitely not a bad guy. Not like Gordon. Not like Rick.

"Is something wrong?" Gordon asked, interrupting her in her heavy-hearted mood.

Ashly shook her head, "No, everything is fine." She struggled with her emotions and didn't want to talk with Gordon.

One hour later the boarding sign came up and she was glad to finally sit in the aeroplane to New York.

◆◆◆

Gordon had booked first class on a non-stop flight, leaving at 11 a.m. and arriving after an eight hour flight at 2 p.m. local time in New York at JFK Airport. Time enough, so he had said, to explore the big city which Ashly was so looking forward to.

The flight itself was not too bad and it was definitely worth being in first class. They were served very obligingly, with as many alcoholic beverages and snacks as they wanted as well as two big meals in between.

While Gordon used the long flight to do what he

called "*working*" on his smartphone, Ashly browsed through the magazines which had been provided at the entrance of the aircraft.

"Did you know this?" Ashly asked Gordon, showing him an article she had just read – "*Mighty theft nets 163 million dollars in art. Works by Cezanne, Degas, Monet and Van Gogh among the paintings stolen.*"

Gordon looked at the pictures shown with the article.

"Yes," he said, pretending to sound nonchalant, "It was one of the biggest thefts ever in Europe."

"*Paul Cézanne's 'Boy in the Red Waistcoat', was one of the most valuable pieces amongst the four stolen paintings*," Ashly read out from the article. "I ask myself, who buys these stolen works?" she was thinking aloud. "One of the men spoke German with a Slavic accent…" she continued reading. "I wonder if those works are sold in Russia?" she elbowed Gordon who appeared to be engrossed in his smartphone.

"What?" he raised his head.

"These stolen paintings – are they being sold to Russians?" Ashly wanted to know.

"Maybe," he said, striving to sound as if he wasn't bothered and shrugged.

'What a strange coincidence that so many famous paintings, each worth millions of dollars, have been stolen in Switzerland', Ashly thought and tried to continue reading. The article had captured her mind.

"Gordon," she spoke to him, leaning over aside, "do you not find it strange that so many famous paintings are stolen in Switzerland?" Ashly touched upon the article in the magazine.

"I'm more curious about how so many famous paintings are in the hands of the Swiss in the first place," he replied drily.

"Well the Swiss are renowned for being extraordinarily rich and to like fine art," Ashly replied, although she wasn't sure whether they really were well known for liking fine art. 'Everybody rich collects art objects,' she thought. So many times she had wondered what prices paintings, such as van Gogh, Picasso or Edvard Munch reached in auctions. One of the "cheapest" paintings Ashly remembered being sold was a painting by Van Gogh which went for almost ninety-three million dollars. A figure she could hardly imagine. All she knew was that she would never ever earn so much money in her lifetime.

"Most of these paintings are sold in private sales via an art handler," Gordon explained while stretching his legs. "Some of them are successful Swiss businessmen."

"Yes, I know," Ashly replied. She remembered that there had been some "big" cases hitting the headlines of the newspapers on high-value theft relating to several Swiss and Russian people.

"Art theft is a very lucrative business," Gordon interrupted Ashly in her thoughts. "All you need are some highly skilled burglars; a concealer, ideally one with worldwide storage facilities; and a couple of extraordinarily rich people who would go to any lengths to obtain a painting by a famous artist."

Ashly was surprised – Gordon seemed to know a lot about art theft. She looked out of the little window, musing about the man beside her.

The aeroplane was high above a dense blanket of white clouds. It looked like cotton wool, and the sky was, in contrast, intense blue. Somewhere in the distance Ashly could see blazing rays of sunshine. 'Boundless freedom above the clouds,' she mediated, leaning her head against the window. And then she fell asleep, only to wake up shortly before approaching JFK Airport.

It was a stunning view when the plane broke through the clouds, unveiling the unmistakeable majestic skyline of the Big Apple. Ashly looked through the porthole, trying to capture some familiar landmarks like the Statue of Liberty. Unfortunately, all she could see was a sea of skyscrapers. They landed on time, but had to wait ages until they could leave the aircraft and finally the huge and very busy airport. Gordon, organised as ever, had already hired a private limousine with chauffeur which took them comfortably to their hotel in midtown Manhattan.

◆◆◆

Ashly enjoyed every minute of the drive in the limo – it was after all her first time in this famous city. And when they checked in at the Hilton she was simply overwhelmed. It was an exquisite place with spacious rooms, styled with maple wood furniture and big marble bathrooms. The large bed was neatly made and big enough for four people to sleep in.

"What a superb playground," Gordon flippantly exclaimed, bending over Ashly and kissing her neck as he helped her take off her coat.

"Actually I'm a bit tired," she said, stretching on the bed.

"Don't move," Gordon told her, "I'll get us some champagne."

A short time later the waiter brought a bottle of Gordon's favourite beverage, nicely wrapped with a white cloth in a cooler. He looked at the label and handing a filled glass to Ashly, he said,

"Not the best of champagne but good enough to relax you. Welcome to New York."

After he had put the '*do not disturb sign*' on the door, he wasted no time in kissing Ashly passionately, who was lying on the bed.

Pressing his body firmly against hers, her nipples reacted immediately and became aroused.

"Still tired?" he wanted to know, skilfully running his fingers over her soft thighs.

"Oh Gordon, go on," Ashly groaned, feeling an intense excitement coming on. Her panting breath drove him faster and faster, accelerating the intimacy until they reached the height of their pleasure.

Straight after, he didn't wait for Ashly to relax, but rolled over to immediately fall asleep. Ashly was a little bit surprised – usually he was more persistent. Then again, it had been a long day and she was tired as well.

◆◆◆

It was dark when they both woke up.

"What time is it?" Gordon asked drowsily.

"It must be midnight," Ashly replied. But when she turned the light on she realised it was only early evening. "Sorry," she said, "it's only seven o'clock. But it feels later because of the five hour time difference."

He turned over to her, licking her ear gently.

"So what do you suggest we do with our evening?" she asked him, anticipating going out to explore the world's busiest city's nightlife.

"I have to tell you something," he said with his deep blue eyes looking straight into her face. Ashly looked at him aquiver.

"We're going to see a friend of mine," Gordon said whilst stroking her soft white breast. She was still waiting what else he would say. She was torn between her lust, having hot passionate sex with him, or going out to see the famous city by night and having lots of fun together.

"What do you mean – we're going to see a friend of yours?" she asked, her brown eyes wide open when she fully comprehended what he had just announced.

"I've arranged to meet up with my old friend Fyodor Shevchenko in his house. He is VERY rich."

Gordon took Ashly totally by surprise. That was definitely not what she had expected – on the contrary!

"Why didn't you tell me earlier?" she demanded, throwing a cold look at him.

"There was no chance – you were asleep on the plane and then I forgot about it," he replied sweetly.

Ashly could sense it was a feeble excuse and she didn't like his plan.

"I have nothing appropriate to wear," she said to him, as she didn't know what else to say. Feeling thirsty, she jumped out of bed to find something to drink.

"Don't worry about that," Gordon called to her, trying to mollify her, "these people are very sociable."

But Ashly wasn't prepared for a private visit to a "*VERY rich*" Russian's house. Never mind how rich this friend of Gordon was. She was deeply disappointed. She had been looking forward to an undisturbed weekend, without any obligation, only with Gordon, full of fun and excitement. And she certainly didn't expect to be spending her valuable time with some Russian riches. But as it was, she had no choice but to grin and bear it.

◆◆◆

Fyodor and his wife Lyudmila Shevchenko lived on Long Island in one of the grandest houses Ashly had ever seen. The whole house was well-lit outside, and the front featured several white columns, holding the canopy of the enormous entrance area with a massive wooden door leading into the house.

The maid opened the door as soon as the pair arrived.
"Welcome Misses McKenneth, welcome Mister Thompson," she greeted them, much to Ashly's surprise in perfect English. Guiding them into the hall, she added, "Mister and Misses Shevchenko are expecting you."

Ashly was immensely impressed – the entrance hall was very lavishly furnished, and it seemed to her it was as big as the whole ground floor of Iris' house.
A woman, Lyudmila as Ashly later learned, beautifully dressed in a green draped silk-like dress, came down the stairs towards them. For a moment Ashly thought she had seen such a green dress in one of the magazines on the flight, being advertised as "very exclusive" and costing more than she would earn in a month.

"Welcome to our home," the woman said in a deep resonating voice, embracing Ashly and then Gordon each with the obligatory kisses. She was wearing incredibly high-heels which Ashly would never have been able to walk in. Ashly, still stunned, only felt up to whisper, "Hello, nice to meet you", when the woman linked arms with Gordon and her. Lyudmila continued to speak, "My husband will be with us shortly." And with these words she showed the pair into an opulent yet tasteful open plan living and dining area.

When entering the room, Ashly was even more amazed by the unimaginable luxury. This room provided ultimate extravagance and comfort; it was decorated with very colourful, unique furniture, eye catching crystal chandeliers, and museum quality antiques all over the place.

"Take a seat," the lady of the house said, pointing to one of the sumptuous sofas near the fireplace.

Ashly couldn't help but admire Lyudmila's appearance. Her blond curly hair looked like a flowing mane and her dark brown eyes, in contrast to her blonde hair, reminded her immediately of the Van Morrison song "Brown Eyed Girl".

It didn't take long until Fyodor Shevchenko took the stage.

"Gordon my friend," with a roaring loud voice he was in the room, heading towards Gordon. "How nice to welcome you at last to my New York house," the Russian received his friend with cheers, a big embrace, and kisses.

"And you must be Ashly," Mr. Shevchenko said, shaking her hand while softly smiling at her. "I have heard a lot about you – you are a very experienced art historian." He was a big man with dark brown hair and eyes, a strong face, smooth-shaven, and a real charmer!

"I see you have nothing to drink – Lyudmila, please offer our precious guests a drink," Fyodor called to his wife with a wink. "They will run dry just like a stranded fish."

"We were waiting for you, darling" Mrs. Shevchenko replied, shaking her leonine mane and rushing towards her husband to tenderly hug him.

A rapid exchange in Russian followed. As Ashly was fluent in that language she understood pretty well what Fyodor said to his wife, "Be especially nice to them! I'm hoping to do business with this Australian jerk. He is getting me one of Paul Cézanne's paintings, worth about 200 million dollars."

Ashly was puzzled – what was this all about? She had no idea that Gordon was so heavily involved in the art world. And where would he get the painting from? So far there had been no opportunity for her to ask Gordon about the purpose of their visit to his "*VERY rich*" Russian friends.

She felt as if the whole situation was a scene from a play and she was part of it. But which part in this drama was she playing? And, did she feel comfortable in her role? While Ashly was still pondering what was going on, the maid had brought a bottle of champagne in a cooler and set it down on the glass table.

"Thank you Emily, I will do the rest for now," Fyodor indicated to the maid with a dapper wave of the hand. Then he filled four crystal glasses, ceremoniously handing one of them each to Ashly, Gordon, and his wife. With a small toast to good friendship they clinked glasses and sipped at the excellent champagne.

"Our friend here," Shevchenko said, pointing at Gordon, "doesn't speak any other language but English." And with a smirk he added, "So we will be polite and talk in English." His voice was raucous and like all Russians he spoke with that very distinctive accent.

"I do appreciate your effort," Gordon replied, now regretting that he hadn't told Ashly she would be his private interpreter this evening. When they waltzed off to the dining table, with their heavy champagne glasses, Gordon whispered in her ear,

"Tell me everything they say in Russian."

'Too late now,' Ashly refrained to answer.

It suddenly occurred to her why Gordon had brought her to meet the Russians – he didn't speak any other language but English and needed a translator.

'So this is the reason behind your generosity,' she was rather disappointed and wondered whether Gordon had any more unwelcome surprises up his sleeve.

◆◆◆

In the middle of the glass dining table stood a massive crystal bowl – and as Ashly was soon to find out – it was filled with caviar. Little plates with mother-of-pearl spoons were laid out for four people as well as several glasses, of course all crystal catching the light and sparkling like little stars in the night sky.
"Caspian Russian beluga caviar," Fyodor explained, putting a spoonful on his plate. "This one is lightly salted – it is the finest and the most expensive caviar."
The shiny black of the caviar was a delight to the eye and, with their glimmering pearl-white, a very pleasing contrast to the mother-of-pearl spoons.
"Take blini, please" Lyudmila said while passing a plate with small buckwheat pancakes to Ashly. Her striking white gold, diamond and tsavorite bracelet matched Lyudmila's beautiful necklace and delighted Ashly all evening long. She couldn't remember having seen such a gorgeous deep green stone anywhere else.

The caviar tasted like nothing she had ever experienced before. It was absolutely delicious – like out of this world. Ashly lifted a small spoonful, the aroma gently filling her nose – it didn't smell of fish at all. She believed she could savour every single tiny egg, tasting a subtle, buttery flavour, and its juicy pellet, exploding in her mouth, gave her an unforgettable sensation.

"Would you like me to serve the Chardonnay, Sir?" the maid asked after everybody had sat down, relishing the caviar.

"Yes, pour our guests a glass of Pouilly-Fussé," Shevchenko said, waving his hands.

The Russian couple were indeed very generous and very cordial hosts, as it turned out during the course of the evening. It was difficult to tell how old they were. They could be in their late thirties as much as in their late fifties. Ashly thought that both were quite charismatic, talking a lot about their holidays in Monaco.

"Have you ever been to Monaco?" Lyudmila wanted to know from Ashly.

"No," she answered, "I only know it from the Grand Prix motor race and what one reads in the papers about the Prince's family."

"You have to go there," Lyudmila said, and with

great excitement on her face she went on, "The place is sublime with its extravagant lifestyle, non-stop parties, fabulous yachts and super rich people."
"Yes," her husband agreed, "we go there regularly. Then we sail down the Mediterranean to one of the Greek islands which belongs to a friend of ours."

Since Shevchenko had dismissed the maid for the evening, he himself made sure that wine, champagne, and vodka flowed during the entire evening. Ashly noticed the impressive Rolex on his chunky wrist every time he filled her glass.
"I've heard you are an expert on art," he addressed Ashly with a touch of appreciation and affection in his deep voice.
She blushed, "No, not really. I'm an art historian, lecturing at the university."
"Come on, I'd like to show you my pictures," and with a keen expression Fyodor took Ashly by her arm. She was reluctant to follow, as she had already noticed the valuable collection of contemporary art.
"I've seen your pictures," she tried to fend him off. Throughout the house Ashly had spotted numerous paintings and she had no doubt that they all were genuine and some of them, like the Turner, she calculated were worth a fortune.
"Yes, but have you seen my Vasily Gribennikov?"

Fyodor asked with a touch of enthusiasm, feeling proud to have obtained what he thought was a highly valuable painting for his collection.

"A Vasily Gribennikov?" Ashly replied, glancing at him doubtfully with her eyes wide open. Then again, she wasn't really surprised to find a rather "young" Russian artist in Shevchenko's mansion. Gribennikov was born in 1951 and had ascended in a meteoric rise into the world of art and artist. His works had soon become famous and were acquired by private collectors and art brokers.

"Yes," her Russian host confirmed nodding. Feeling honoured he went on, "a genuine Gribennikov, hanging in our bedroom." And turning to his wife he said, "Lyudmila sweetheart, you wouldn't mind if I show our guest my treasures?"

"No, no, go ahead," his wife encouraged him while she and Gordon engaged in small-talk, exchanging views about the different places they had visited.

◆◆◆

Ashly hesitated to follow the Russian into his bedroom. She thought it would be a little bit inappropriate. On the other hand – when might she come across a painting by this artist so close again? Surely, being in a house full of famous paintings, she was excited about seeing the artwork and followed Fyodor to the upper floor, admiring the paintings along the enormous staircase.

'Oh my goodness,' she thought as she entered her hosts chamber. 'Gordon would certainly enjoy having a bedroom like this to play in.' She couldn't help herself envisioning him surrounded by such luxury.
"What do you think?" Fyodor inquired, pointing proudly to the picture, hanging on the wall opposite the huge vintage bed. He could hardly contain his burning desire to hear Ashly's professional opinion.
"It is 'A Night at the Theatre'," she approved, adding after a moment, "Superb. It's one of his oil-paintings that I adore." Ashly couldn't believe that she stood right in front of a genuine Gribennikov, and at the same time she was wondering why her host had hidden such a beautiful piece of art away in his private bedroom. Why didn't he display the picture where everybody could see it? She was beginning to suspect that all wasn't right with the oil painting.
As if Shevchenko had read her thoughts, he explained,
"My wife likes the painting so much that she insisted we put it up where she can see it best."
But his reason was so obscure that Ashly was sure

there must be something suspicious about the oil painting – 'stolen or faked,' she surmised.

"Tell me your opinion," he urged Ashly who was momentarily disconcerted.

"Well, allegedly Gribennikov once said that his paintings must not only please him, but the public as well," she said slowly as if she was pondering every word she was going to say, "And I think he has succeeded in doing so, as you can see with this painting. It captures very well the beauty and the spirit of city life as it was in past times."

"What do you think the painting is worth?"

"I have no idea. Honestly, I have no idea whatsoever," Ashly struggled for an answer. She knew that some years ago one could buy a Gribennikov between for 200 and 1400 dollars. As time had gone by the prices had inevitably increased. There was every chance the painting could now be worth 2000 dollars or even more – if it was real!

"I don't believe you," her host insisted. "You must know something."

"Well, the prices have gone up recently. Now they fetch about 2000 dollars."

Shevchenko's face dropped. He seemed to think about something, scratching his head he asked,

"What do you suggest I do with this worthless piece

of art?" He was visibly very disappointed that the painting wasn't worth more.

"How much did you pay for it?" Ashly inquired.

"A small fortune," he exclaimed in anger with a penetrating look at Ashly.

Obviously someone must have outwitted him. Ashly chewed over who might have sold him the overpriced piece of art and tried to remain calm.

"Perhaps I've lost track of the prices recently," she retracted, "it could be worth ten times that. If I were you I would wait a few years and then have it examined professionally."

Suddenly, she felt rather forlorn and experienced the desire to go home. Caviar, champagne, and all that extravagance wasn't her world! She was most uncomfortable and sought an easy way out of the tense situation.

"Excuse me," she said, unsure how to phrase her need to go to the bathroom, and then she remembered the American way of saying it, "Where can I powder my nose?"

"Of course my dear, come along here," Shevchenko said in a friendly tone, showing her to the bathroom next to the staircase.

At last her mind could take a breather, Ashly believed. But when she had thought that nothing in this house could surprise her any more, she hadn't seen the bathroom. As soon as she stepped into this huge luxurious space, she instantly stopped in her tracks. Such opulence – she had never imagined, let alone seen anything like that before.

Later she learned that a sheer wealth had been spent to decorate this room. The tiles in this deluxe space were all made of Carrara marble. The edge of the bathtub, which was inset in slate like stones, was embellished with glittering stone.

'Diamonds or Swarovski crystals,?' she mused, spotting more glitzy crystals adorning the sink, bidet and toilet. On the taps for cold and hot water were in each case a blue sapphire and a red ruby accordingly. And Ashly was once more stunned that the faucets and other fittings seemed to be made of solid gold.

This was surely the most memorable visit to a 'Ladies Rest Room' she had ever experienced. And to imagine the Russians used this every day! Using the bathroom was – as Ashly later told her mother – a truly unforgettable experience.

◆◆◆

When walking down the staircases, Ashly realised that not only had she had mentally enough of caviar and champagne but also physically. The stairs seemed to move and she felt like she was on a ship on the high seas amidst a heavy storm. She experienced great difficulties speaking, as her tongue felt quite heavy and was somehow hard to control.

"I'd like to go back to the hotel," she said to Gordon when she returned to that prodigious living room.

"No, no, no," the hosts insisted. "You stay here for the night. Everything is prepared for you."

The last thing Ashly wanted at that moment was an argument about where she would spend the night.

"Please Gordon, take me to the hotel," she begged, and surprisingly Gordon obliged her immediately.

He stood up from his chair and said very politely to the Russian couple,

"It was very kind of you to host us all evening. We enjoyed your generous hospitality to the fullest." And putting his arm around Ashly's shoulder, he continued, "I would like to spend the night with Ashly in our hotel."

"Of course!" It was Lyudmila who seemed to understand very well her guest's desire. Looking at her husband, she added, "We enjoyed your company as well and we do respect your wish for privacy, do we not Fyodor?"

And whilst walking her guests to the front door, she cordially said, "You are always welcome. Come and see us again soon."

"Yes," Fyodor agreed, "why not meet up in Monaco in the summer?"

The farewell was just as exuberant as the welcome – with a lot of embracing and kissing.

"Enjoy your stay in New York and have a safe journey home," the Russian couple wished their guests well, waving until the limo disappeared into the black night.

"Yes indeed – a nice and very rich couple," Ashly sighed, sitting relieved in the car with Gordon, as the chauffeur drove them safely through the illuminated city to the hotel.

Chapter Thirteen

Ashly, waking up the next morning in the gigantic bed, didn't believe at first that the evening with this Russian couple had really taken place. What on earth had happened last night? While she was engrossed in thought about her Russian hosts, she suddenly realised that it was already midday and, apart from the drives to and from the hotel, she hadn't yet seen anything of this great city. Gordon lay on the other side of the bed, gently snoring. She was reluctant to wake him and quietly slipped out of bed. After an extensive shower she decided to have breakfast and get ready for visiting the Big Apple. As Gordon was still asleep, she left a note "Back in two hours".

The little spat she'd had with her mother about the New York trip was dwelling on her mind all of a sudden. 'I have to phone home,' Ashly thought whilst waiting for the lift to take her to the hotel restaurant high above.

As soon as she entered the sheltered roof garden, she was captured by the panoramic view which was staggering from up there! She took a few moments to absorb the fantastic impression and then took a seat by the window. Thinking of the vast quantities of caviar last night she spontaneously fancied something down to earth and ordered a traditional American breakfast which was luckily served all day long. While she was waiting for her meal to be served she took her mobile out of her handbag and dialled Iris' number at home.

"Hi mum, it's me. Sorry for not phoning earlier," Ashly attuned to a higher pitch, trying to sound happy when she perceived the familiar voice of her mother. She could hear how Iris breathed a sigh of relief.

"Ashly! We were worried. Just as well that you finally show a sign of life," Iris expressed her anguish. "Wait, I'll pass you on to Jake – Are you having a good time?"

"Well not too bad – I'll tell you all about it when I'm back home on Monday," Ashly said excitedly. After seconds Jake was on the phone.

"Hi mum. Are you ok?"

"Yes love – I'm fine. And you?"

"Everything is ok over here. I was at the zoo with Claire and Ulrik today," Jake told his mother joyously. "It was cool to see all the animals and to be with Ulrik."

Ashly didn't really want to know about Ulrik and therefore replied slightly peevishly,

"I'm glad you are enjoying yourself. Is there anything you want me to bring home from New York for you?"

"No nothing. Just you come home safe. I love you and I miss you very much," the boy said, sounding a little bit wistful.

"I love you too. See you soon," Ashly finished the call because the waitress approached her table with the breakfast: A big slice of bacon – not skinny rashers like at home – a big heap of hash browns, two fried eggs, and a stack of pancakes with syrup, plus a glass of juice in addition to the coffee.

'Oh my god!' Ashly thought – she was hungry, but never expected such a massive plate of food. All of a sudden she wished she was home, having breakfast with Ulrik in the little café near the university, where they had spent some afternoons together, chatting in a companionable ambience about everything that had crossed their minds. She was wallowing in memories when suddenly she heard Gordon's voice behind her.

"Here you are!"

"Gordon," Ashly was surprised, as she assumed him still asleep.

"Yes. Thanks for the note. I thought I would find you here." And while he sat down he asked eyeing at her plate, "What are you having?"

"American breakfast," she replied with a smile.

"I think that's a bit too much for me after last night's dinner," Gordon considered, stroking his chin. "In Australia the majority of urban people would have cereal for breakfast and toast with preserves such as marmalade or Vegemite."

"Yes," Ashly responded, "we would have cereal too and kids love Marmite. I suppose this is the same as your Vegemite".

"I suppose so – wait, I'll get myself a bowl of cereal."

Ashly looked after him. 'A very attractive man,' she thought while Gordon drifted to the breakfast bar. She noticed that he strode with a great deal of pride, like someone easily recognised when walking past, and obviously fancying himself as a womanizer. With his awfully well shaped body he didn't look at all almost twenty years older than she. For a moment she wasn't sure what exactly it was that made him so appealing to her. Was there more than just the sex? She still hadn't had a chance to shed light on their relationship. Their get-togethers were always sexually so exciting that Ashly simply didn't want to spoil the fun. Then again, she started to feel that there must be more to life than just sex and money.

"So what do you want to do?" Gordon asked her, sitting down with his bowl of cereal in his hand.
"Well," Ashly said, "being in New York for the first time, I want to see as much as possible of the city."
"Aye, aye," Gordon replied, trying to sound cheerful, "Your wish is my command."

◆◆◆

"Let's go and start the day," Ashly was very keen to finally get what she came for in the first place – to explore what this interesting city had to offer. There was no time to waste and she rushed to the lift.
Of course Gordon couldn't keep his hands off her. He pressed his body against hers, pushing her to the corner.
"What about a quickie? Have you ever had sex in a lift?" he whispered ravenously in her ear.
Ashly could feel his erection through his trousers.
"No, are you mad!" she tried to fend him off. "Can you not see the camera there?"

"I'm only joking," Gordon said unfazed and, putting a straight face on, he waved to the camera.

The lift stopped and a crowd of Japanese flocked in, all smiling kindly at Ashly and Gordon and gushing about the hotel. As far as Ashly could understand, they were debating on where to go sightseeing today and praising the unique landmarks they had seen so far.

'I want to go sightseeing today as well, no matter what,' she thought while being shoved to the back of the lift by the chirping people.

Gordon gave the Japanese crowd a look that said 'why did you have to interfere with my pleasure?!' Trying to get to the door, he said aloud, "Sorry, this is our floor," and pushed through the bunch.

"I have a surprise for you," he disclosed on the way to their room.

'Oh no, not again!' it flashed through Ashly's mind but she kept quiet, striving to look unconcerned.

"Do you not want to know what it is?" Gordon asked while groping her.

"What is it?" Ashly didn't sound very curious and fended him off. Half the day almost gone and only one more day to come, she was determined to get as much as possible out of her visit to the Big Apple and not even Gordon was going to stop her – she thought.

"Ah, so you are interested?" he was teasing her.

She looked at him. "Come on, Gordon, don't keep me in suspense."

"My friend Fyodor is treating you to a helicopter tour," he said, broadly grinning.

"A helicopter tour?!" Ashly was speechless – that was a surprise! She had not expected such a generous gesture.

"Yes, so that you can see this fabulous city from above," Gordon confirmed.

Of course Ashly couldn't resist such a compelling offer, and regarded it as a peace offering for not having been able to explore New York last night.

"And do you want to hear the other good news?"

"Other good news?" Ashly exclaimed.

"We have enough time for some sex before the helicopter picks us up from the roof of the hotel." A big smile sprung up on Gordon's face, leaving Ashly once more astounded and succumbing to temptation. Not being able to withstand Gordon's irresistible foreplay, she ended up in bed with him, making love fast and furious. Afterwards, lying totally satisfied in his arms and feeling his taut body, she couldn't believe how lucky she was.

◆◆◆

The tour with the helicopter was indeed incredible, soaring high over the traffic below and the crowds of people who looked like little ants. Hovering above and between the skyscrapers, certainly compensated Ashly for what she had missed out on. It was simply amazing – to see all the iconic landmarks such as the Empire State and Chrysler buildings and of course the Statue of Liberty from a totally different perspective. The one hour special tour definitely pushed her adrenalin to the limits, especially as they flew at a low altitude, enabling her to see more of Manhattan and New York's hinterland than she had expected. She was simply blown away and didn't want this adventure to end.

By the time they landed it was getting dark. Gordon suggested walking over Brooklyn Bridge. In the meantime the whole area was illuminated and the view of lower Manhattan and of the Brooklyn Skyline was spectacular. Ashly thoroughly enjoyed pondering over the old suspension bridge hand in hand with a man who offered her such an exciting life. The light, the fresh smell of the river, the atmosphere of the city – she soaked it all in. She was happy, very happy. And there was still more excitement to come, as they went to Times Square with its busy nightlife, theatres, street performances, illuminations and later had dinner in one of the stylish restaurants in the area.

◆◆◆

The next morning Ashly continued her sightseeing tour with Gordon always by her side. They started the day with an excursion to New York's famous shopping row, the Fifth Avenue. The very moment Ashly looked up at the magnificent buildings a wave of uneasiness swept over her and the disturbing feeling that she had been here before dogged her. In all likelihood – that was impossible! How could she have been here before? Strangely, unlike other cities she had visited, the buildings and streets felt immediately familiar and she had no explanation as to why. It took her a moment until, like a faint wisp of fog, she remembered the recurring, odious nightmare some years ago. A tense, jittery feeling seized her. She shuddered at the thought of falling down from one of these skyscrapers. Forcing her mind elsewhere, she linked arms with Gordon and, while resting her head on his shoulders, her tensions quickly passed away when strolling in a relaxed atmosphere and enjoying the window-shopping. It was somehow magnificent to peek into such prestigious designer shops like Cartier, Armani or Lacoste, with Gordon paying so generously for all the bits and pieces she bought. Among other things she purchased a beautiful silk scarf from Fabergé for Iris and a state-of-the-art skate board for Jake which was later delivered directly to the hotel so that she didn't have to bother carrying it.

As she had seen many of the iconic landmarks from the air, she now wanted to have a closer look at some of them on the ground. One of the landmarks on her "must-see-list" was the Grand Central Terminal with its famous opalescent clock in the centre of the main hall, its spectacular structure, the ornate chandeliers, and soaring green ceiling.
It reminded her a little bit of the central train station in Antwerp (Belgium) which was of course a miniature version of this impressive New York building. The Rockefeller Center, with its magnificent artistry, shops, eating places, and ice-skating, was another extraordinary place for her to visit. From one of the outdoor decks on the "Top of the Rock" Ashly had a unique view of the Empire State building and the city's beauty.

"Breathtaking. Simply breathtaking," she said. She felt as if she was standing on top of the world, and at the same moment she was battling with the fear of toppling over when standing near the edge and looking down. The overwhelming feeling that she had been here before lasted a split second. Gordon, having noticed her sudden tension, drew quietly near her and focused her with a perplexed expression.

"What's the matter with you?" he inquired.

"Nothing – I just remembered a bad dream I had many years ago," Ashly tried to sound calm and stared blankly at him, assuring herself that nothing really harmful could happen to her.

"Tell me about it," he demanded.

The sharp tone in his voice instantly discouraged her from confiding in him. Maybe her dream had been a premonition – she tried to convince herself; if so, then it had come true. She was standing on top of a skyscraper, wasn't she? And Gordon was there to prevent her from harm, wasn't he?

Following an impulse, she chose to obliterate the obnoxious feeling, which had captured her for a long minute. Pushing aside the disturbing depths of her bygone nightmare, she took a deep breath and turned towards Gordon. With her face brightening, she said,

"Let's get a move on – this city has more to offer."

She was in an adventurous mood, and taking Gordon by the arm they headed back inside the building.

Not only had the Rockefeller Center a lot to admire, but the whole trip to New York certainly served its purpose of impressing Ashly. She felt the pulse of the "city which never sleeps" and so did she. Her ambition was to see it all – especially such famous art centres and museums like the Guggenheim Museum. Unfortunately there was no time left, but Gordon promised to bring her back for a visit to the galleries.

◆◆◆

On Monday morning Ashly's fantastic short break to the Big Apple was over. Having only had a morsel for breakfast and still half asleep she and Gordon boarded the aeroplane which would bring them back home.

"So what do you think of Fyodor and his wife Lyudmila?" Gordon started a conversation when they eventually were comfortably seated in the aeroplane.

"A very interesting couple," Ashly replied rather aloof, as she tried to catch up with some sleep.

"Have you ever seen such opulence before?" Gordon tried again to involve her in a chat.

"No, never," Ashly answered truthfully. Then she remembered the dialogue she had overheard between the Russian couple. "By the way – where will you get the Paul Cézanne from?"

Gordon looked totally perplexed. What did she know about his business and the painting?

"I don't know what you mean," he said, pretending to be engrossed in reading.

"Well, I heard Fyodor saying to his wife that you would get him a Paul Cézanne, worth 200 million dollars."

"Oh, did he indeed – interesting," Gordon gave a testy reply. Then, after a pause, he decided to explain, choosing his words carefully, "Yes, the Russian asked me some time ago if I could get my hands on a Cézanne. I don't know why – he seems to be obsessed with the idea of having a Cézanne embellishing his wall."

"But paintings by artists of such calibre don't grow on trees," Ashly argued.

"Yes, I know – unfortunately not."

"Where do you think you'll find one?" Ashly insisted.

"I have my sources," Gordon replied and grabbing her hand, he added, "Don't you bother your pretty little head about it. When the time comes, I will need your expertise." His intense blue eyes were penetrating Ashly, while he was gently kissing her hand.

Ashly knew at that moment that she wouldn't get anywhere with him. She had no idea what Gordon was up to. It all sounded strange to her, causing an uncomfortable feeling. All she knew was that she didn't want to get trapped into something awkward. Her mind started revolving around the question if Gordon was the sort of man who would ever put a ring on her finger. Thinking of the nice jewellery she had seen, she remembered that bad feeling he had left her with when she had been looking at that beautiful diamond and sapphire ring. She wanted to know where she stood, though didn't feel like bringing up the subject at the moment. She was in two minds about her relationship with Gordon. He had undoubtedly shown his interest in her, hadn't he? Had he not willingly taken part in all the activities in New York? It must have cost him a fortune to pay for all the admissions. So what?! Ashly couldn't care less – she'd had experienced great fun and enjoyed herself to the full. Now sadly, the drab monotony of everyday life was to catch up with her as they touched ground back at home.

◆◆◆

Gordon ordered a taxi to take Ashly home. For Ashly it was like an ice cold shower. She hadn't expected such an abrupt parting. Gordon briefly kissed her good-bye while helping her into the car. Then he left to catch another taxi for himself. She was still confused when the cab dropped her off at home. Despite being in the middle of the night, the light was on inside the house which meant that Iris wasn't asleep. She came to open the door and affectionately welcomed her daughter.

"Did you have a good time?" Iris asked, cautious not to wake Jake.

"It was wonderful," Ashly gushed, standing in the hallway taking off her coat. She had quickly decided that it was best not to tell her mum about her disappointments, knowing that Iris would have been infuriated.

"Honey, you must be tired – would you like a cup of tea anyway?"

"I would love a cup, mum."

A short time later Iris came back with the tea.

"So tell me, how was New York," she was keen to hear all about it while sipping her tea.

Lots of impressions rolled through Ashly's head. She didn't know how to best describe her extraordinary experiences.

"I brought you a little present," Ashly said and passed the beautifully gift-wrapped parcel to her mother who was for a while busy opening it.

"This is beautiful," she said when she saw the subdued blue and red coloured scarf. "And it feels so nice – it is silk, isn't it?" Iris was holding the scarf to her face. "Thank you so much – I love it!"

"I got it from a shop on New York's Fifth Avenue," Ashly explained and was pleased that her mother liked the present.

"It's very pretty. I see the label *Fabergé* – it was probably very expensive."

"Yes," Ashly confirmed, "it did cost a lot but Gordon paid for it all." And when she saw her mother raising her eyebrow, she quickly added, "As well as for everything else."

"Like what?"

"Just imagine I had a sightseeing tour in a helicopter flying over and around New York. It was simply breathtaking."

"That must have been quite an experience," Iris remarked.

"Yes, indeed mum. A friend of Gordon had organised the fantastic tour."

"I'm glad that you had a good time," Iris said, yawning. She was tired and wanted to go to bed. Ashly, on the other hand, was completely awake and lively, telling her mother about the trip with Gordon.

"Yes, it was a most amazing opportunity to go on

the helicopter tour and to see all the remarkable landmarks of New York from above…. Standing on the Top of the Rock was like standing on top of the world," she gushed, reliving her memories.

"Top of the Rock?" Iris asked with a perplexed expression.

"Yes, the Rockefeller building," Ashly explained. She hesitated for a moment. Should she tell her mother about her recurring nightmare and the funny feeling she'd had, although she had been in New York for the first time? She knew Iris would want to know more about it and if Gordon played a part in this dream. As she thought it was too late and much too complicated to quarrel with her mother on the details, she dropped the whole subject.

Ashly was glad to be back at her mother's home. It was cosy, warm and inviting. Ensconcing herself on the old, very comfortable couch, she looked around – the room was furnished according to its purpose – a living room. People lived in this room. It wasn't a huge hall filled with museum like art objects, pink sumptuous sofas, and crystal chandeliers.

"Mum, you won't believe the extravagance I've seen."

Iris looked at her, once more raising her eyebrow, curious to hear what her daughter was going to tell her.

"Yes, the first night we went to see Gordon's Russian friend and his wife. Mum – such opulence!" Ashly described her visit to the Russian couple's house.

"The house itself was unimaginable – and you should have seen the hall! It was as big as the whole of your ground floor. And as for the bathroom! You won't believe it – it was all so flamboyant, fitted out with gold plumbing fixtures, decorated with diamonds and other precious stones."

"Never!" Iris had serious doubts, "Who would be so decadent, bathing in such lavishness?" she asked, at once noticing it was in the truest sense of her words – some people actually *bathed* in luxury. She couldn't, by any stretch of the imagination, envision a bathroom decorated with gold and diamonds as described by her daughter.

"Yes, yes, mum. I didn't want to use the toilet," Ashly confided, "The bathroom was an unforgettable experience." After a moment of silence she continued enthusiastically, "And all the paintings – some of them are worth a fortune. Unimaginable!" Ashly shook her head, still not being able to understand how people could be so filthy rich. In the end it slipped out that Gordon was going to get a painting for his Russian friend, worth more money than one could ever imagine.

'Gordon again!' Iris thought, rolling her eyes and momentarily wondering where he would get the artwork from. Aloud she said, "Well dear, I don't know about you, but I'm tired and now I'm going to bed. Tomorrow is another day when you can tell me all about your trip."

Chapter Fourteen

Weeks passed and Iris realised that she still hadn't the slightest idea what to make of her daughter's relationship with Gordon. While she saw her daughter getting deeper and deeper into Gordon's world, Ashly seemed to be very happy and having the time of her life.

"What is Mr. Mystery up to?" Iris kept asking herself. Neither she nor Jake noticed anything extraordinary. No art robberies, no counterfeits hitting the headlines, no news on paintings being sold for big money.

Life in Iris' old yellow house went on as usual. The days passed quick and uneventful. Summer was approaching with all its vibrant colours and Iris appreciated being in her garden. As usual, Claire and Jake spent Wednesdays together. Ashly saw Gordon regularly and spent as much time as possible with him, whereas Iris enjoyed her game of bridge on Thursday evenings.

Ulrik, in addition to when he brought and collected Claire on Wednesdays, showed up occasionally to see how the Mc Kenneth family were doing, always trying to avoid Ashly. In fact he was deeply disappointed. Ashly kept popping up in his thoughts. He had missed her enormously while he was in Sweden and had considered asking her out in the near future once he was back at work. But whenever he approached Ashly for a date, she always seemed to have an excuse. He was soon downhearted at her constant refusal. If it hadn't been for his daughter, Claire, and Jake who got on so well together, he would have left the country rather sooner than later. His mistress also put him off from week to week – he felt pathetic without her. As a result he buried himself in his work and became more and more depressed and miserable.

One day his colleague Natasha confronted him in the canteen of the university. Ulrik had queued up with his meal tray at the till when Natasha said from behind,
"You're not looking your usual self, what's going on – need a shoulder to cry on? Or is it something I shouldn't ask?"

Oh boy – she touched upon the right subject!

"Long story", Ulrik answered, looking over his shoulder.

"How long?"

"You don't want to know."

"Try me."

Their little talk was interrupted. As it was Ulrik's turn to pay, he wasn't able to respond to Natasha. After awkwardly getting his wallet out of his pocket and paying for his food, he waited patiently with the tray in his hand for Natasha. The hall was packed. The students were pushing and shoving and Ulrik, balancing his tray, tried to find seats for them. Eventually there were some empty places near the exit which they were pleased to take.

"So, tell me – what's going on?" Natasha prompted him to speak, glancing at him with her big brown eyes.

"What can I say – it's Ashly. She's troubling me."

"In what way?"

"She avoids me, doesn't want to talk to me – or her mother," Ulrik explained while he was eating his lunch.

"That doesn't sound good. Did you ever tell her how you feel about her?" she asked, coming right to the point.

"No, not really…," he trailed off, turning to the food

on his plate.

"Did you take her out, to a nice romantic restaurant for example?" Natasha was keen to know.

Ulrik wasn't sure if she was just prying or genuinely interested in helping.

"How can I? She keeps putting me off from week to week," he snorted, staring right at Natasha's face. He was slightly indignant to say the least.

"You have to give her time," she advised him, licking her spoon and relishing her dessert.

"How much more? This has been going on for some time now," Ulrik replied fretfully.

"But something must have happened to make her avoid you," Natasha said with utter conviction, returning his gaze. "You and Ashly have always been such good friends."

"Yes," Ulrik, bending over the table, said grim-faced, "she is seeing someone else and apparently they had a good time in New York."

"Oh dear, you should have told me to begin with." And because Ulrik wasn't responding, she went on, "Do you know anything about him? What does he look like? How old is he? What does he do for a living?"

"My goodness, what a lot of questions!" he said with a dour expression.

"Well?"

Ulrik hesitated, then he vented slightly outraged, "This bloke is much older than Ashly. I suppose she likes him because she grew up without a father and now found her 'daddy'," he sneered.

"Being older doesn't make him a bad person," Natasha demurred. "Surely there must be more to it than that if she's attracted to him. What does this guy have that you don't?"

"For a start a lot of money," he remarked bitterly.

"How nice for Ashly." And when Natasha saw Ulrik's glowering look, she quickly added, "I mean a lot of women would like a sugar daddy."

"I'm not sure if he is a sugar daddy or a wolf in sheep's clothing."

"Why do you think that?"

"That's just an idea," he waved his hand.

"Does Ashly know what she is doing?" Natasha asked.

"I doubt it." Ulrik looked at his watch. "Lunch break is finished," he observed and got up from the chair, followed by Natasha.

While they were drifting towards the exit, Ulrik addressed her,

"Listen, if you hear anything about a job going somewhere far away let me know."

"For you?" Natasha asked with her brown eyes wide open in disbelief.

"Yes."

"Oh Ulrik, you're not throwing everything here away just because a woman spurns you?!" Natasha was speechless. She and Ulrik had been working together for so long now. She hated saying farewell to people she had grown fond of!

"Yes Natasha, I would really like to leave the country. I've thought about it a lot and I think now the time has come for a change."

◆◆◆

It was one of those days when Ulrik picked up Claire at the McKenneth's house. On his way he had bought a bunch of flowers for Iris as a thank-you gift since she too was looking after his daughter. He quite liked the bubbly little lady, because she reminded him a lot of his mother.

Ashly was just about to leave the house, when Ulrik knocked on the door. She wasn't very pleased to see him and was certainly not expecting him with a bunch of flowers. Lately she felt stalked by him, which of course wasn't true – on the contrary, Ulrik tried to avoid her.

"Don't worry," Ulrik hastened to say, "The flowers are for your mother."

"Who is at the door?" Iris shouted from the living room.

"Ulrik," Ashly answered curtly and left the house in a hurry.

"Ulrik, come on in," Iris called him in a friendly voice, her face brightening when she took the flowers. Unlike her daughter, Iris was always happy to see this nice cultured man from Sweden – now even more so, as she had been waiting for an opportunity to talk with him confidentially. After weeks of careful consideration she had decided to confide in him and to let him in on her worries about the Australian. As soon as she was alone with him she began to speak in a shaky voice, as she was still shocked and not sure how to describe what she had learned in the meantime about Mr. Mystery. She knew that Ulrik regarded him as a rival and would most certainly not like to talk about Gordon. Did she really want to bother him? Her eyes searched for something to rest on.

"Ulrik," she eventually said, trying to control her voice, "can you spare me a couple of minutes of your valuable time?"

Ulrik looked at her, and with the sparkle in his eyes he looked so funny that Iris lost her inhibitions. She spouted out, "I fear for my daughter."

"Why, what's wrong with Ashly?"

"Well, it's not so much Ashly, but I have to talk to you about Gordon."

"No!" Ulrik said dismissively and turned away, "No way!"

"Ulrik, please, I have to talk to you," Iris begged him. She knew he would not like it. "It's important."

Turning towards Iris, he frowned at her,

"Why would I want to talk about Gordon of all people?" Ulrik was certainly not impressed by the thought of talking about Ashly's 'sugar daddy'.

"Because I think he's somehow involving Ashly in some kind of underhand business deals," Iris replied. She was visibly distressed.

"Well, I could have told you that he is cold and calculating, only doing what suits him best, but – ," he stopped abruptly when he noticed her apparent sadness and anxiety.

"I'm so worried that Ashly is getting into trouble," Iris beseeched Ulrik who stood at the door obviously not wanting to be impolite.

"What sort of trouble?" he inquired.

"Well, I can't affirm it, it's all just rumours. I really shouldn't be telling you this, but as far as I know Gordon could have been involved in several art heists," Iris explained, suddenly experiencing an annoying dryness in her throat, "And it seems that he's selling off the stolen goods in Russia." She coughed several times. Ulrik wanted to help, but she refused his helping hand and sat down on her chair.

"Wow, that's quite a story," he regarded with mild derision in his tone. And with a look of disbelief he added barbed, "You have to tell Ashly, not me. I have enough on my plate without getting dragged into any kind of awkward business!"

Iris was visibly baffled. Groping for words, she eventually said,

"I would if Ashly wasn't so stubborn. She doesn't listen when I try to talk to her. I don't know what hold that man Gordon has over my daughter. She's completely different. And Jake is suffering the most."

Ulrik froze in place. After a moment of silence Iris begged him,

"Could you not talk to her and bring her to her senses?"

Ulrik laughed. "Me? Even if she listens to what I have to say, she will never let go of Gordon. What would you do then?"

"I don't know. I'm still trying to find out what he wants of Ashly."

"That's obvious, isn't it?" he said and, noticing Iris raising her eyebrows, he explained, "Ashly speaks several languages fluently. He probably needs her language skills for his purposes."

Iris nodded, realising that she wouldn't get any further with Ulrik.

"That could be it," she simply said, not really convinced. On the contrary, she was deeply disappointed and felt she had reached a dead end – what else could she do to persuade Ulrik to talk to Ashly?

"Well," Ulrik said, while he went slowly to the front door, "think about it."

◆◆◆

In the end it was Claire who pointed Jake in the right direction. It was a sunny day and the two were sitting on the porch of the treehouse when Jake poured out his woes to Claire.

"My mother," he said genuinely upset, "she is so oblivious to the fact that this Australian is using her."

Claire didn't respond immediately. She instinctively grasped that her friend needed to express his worries about his mother and Gordon. Sitting close by him she was waiting patiently for what he was going to say.

Jake was only able to bare fragments of his thoughts.

"Things aren't so good at the moment," he continued, his face down and his legs dangling in the air. "My granny is worried about my mum as well. My mum is accusing us of begrudging her any happiness."

Then out of the blue he said,

"I remember a dream I had last night," and he looked at Claire. "A wolf attacked me."

"That's horrible," Claire exclaimed with an apprehensive expression. "What happened?"

"I vaguely remember. It was dark and I was lost in a forest. And then all of a sudden a shaggy animal turned up and gazed at me," Jake paused for a moment, faltering he went on, "I tried to run away but I was unable to do so. I couldn't gain any ground."

His face turned into a scowl as he tried to visualise fragments of his dream. Hardly being able to conceal his discomfort, he continued, "And then that big grey wolf came running towards me."

"That sounds like a horrible nightmare," Claire compassionately exclaimed.

"Yes, it was. Fortunately I woke up before the animal got to me." Jake, looking at his friend, was dazed. "I don't know if that means anything. What do you think?" he asked her.

"Apparently it's quite obvious, isn't it?" Claire

replied slowly, gathering her thoughts and looking very seriously, while Jake waited eagerly for her opinion.

"The wolf seems to be your mother's lover, this man Gordon," she said.

"Um, is it so easy?"

"Yes, don't you see it yourself?"

"And the dark forest?"

"That's your unconscious. The dark depths of a part of your mind which you can't grasp ... hidden meanings and emotions – a dark threatening place ... unseen dangers," Claire disjointedly explained.

"You may be right," Jake admitted with a pensive face. "Subconsciously I sense that there is danger connected with Gordon."

After contemplating for a while he remarked,

"Then again, I can't see any danger coming from Gordon. Yes, there is definitely something strange about him – but real danger?" he wasn't so sure. Well, his grandmother was always thinking of the worst scenario. Jake, on the other hand, was rather doubtful. Gordon was kind of a self-opinionated overachiever, a pushy show-off. Was there something Jake wasn't aware of yet? Was Gordon possibly even more dangerous than he thought?

"You told me that this man isn't trustworthy. That he's boasting and using your mother for something which at present you aren't privy to," Claire argued.

"Yes, that's right. This Australian is purporting to be loaded, and it's hard to believe his money comes from just the estate agency business," Jake readily confirmed. He thought hard for a moment. Glancing doubtfully at his friend, he expressed his reservations, "Not that I know of any danger my mother might be exposed to."

"Danger means that something harmful or unpleasant could occur to your mum," the girl pointed out.

"She was already harmed enough by that despicable liar Rick," Jake said with a fierce anger in his eyes, scornfully spitting. And because Claire was frowning, he made a snarky remark,

"The guy unfortunately is my father."

"Well, well," she said with a touch of dislike in her voice.

"The whole situation scares me. You would think my mum realises that she's wasting her time with those types of creeps," the boy resumed. He was pretty disappointed in his mother.

"Surely, she's too intelligent not to notice that she's being used," Claire suggested, trying to resolve her friend's misgivings.

"I doubt it," Jake said and voiced another of his thoughts, "Your dad mentioned to my granny that it could be my mother's language skills which are useful to Gordon."

"Yes," Claire agreed. In almost the same moment she had an inkling rushing into her mind and said, "I have an idea – what if this Gordon sells fake art?" she paused, obviously thinking about something, and then continued, "And your mother is renowned for being an art expert, speaking several languages – what if he uses her to certify that the counterfeits are real?"

"What did you just say?" Jake looked at his friend electrified by the thought!

"I mean if he is selling allegedly genuine paintings to Russia or wherever, when he knows they are fakes, he needs someone to certify the authenticity of a faked painting," Claire explained her thought.

"Good grief!" Jake nodded and tapped his forehead. "Why didn't I come up with this genius thought?"

Claire laughed. Before she was able to say any more, Jake had already climbed down from the treehouse, and was picked up by his mum soon after.

◆◆◆

Ashly stood at the door in front of Ulrik's house to collect Jake.

"*Hej*," he said to her in Swedish as usual, "Why

don't you come in?"

She hesitated a moment, then she thought 'why not' and stepped in. The little entrance was rather dark, as the weak light, falling through the stained glass window of the door, didn't shed much sunlight.

"*Hej*," she replied, "I don't have much time."

Ulrik was used to her saying that. But this time he didn't get discouraged so easily and insisted that she should listen to what he had to say.

"Come into the living room – I would like to talk to you," he invited her.

"No thanks, I'm fine where I am," Ashly said, wondering what Ulrik would have to say this time and hoped it wasn't yet again about their relationship. "What do you want?" she asked him abruptly, unhinging him slightly.

Ulrik hemmed and hawed for a moment, and then stuttered hoarsely,

"Your mother begged me to talk with you."

"My mother?" Ashly rolled her eyes, "What on earth has she got to do with you?"

"She is worried you might get into trouble," Ulrik explained calmly

"Why would I?"

"Well, she isn't sure about Gordon." Now it was out in the open.

"Not Gordon again!" And seconds later Ashly said firmly, "I'm kind of tired – always Gordon. Can you not understand that I am merely enjoying myself? There is nothing amiss with Gordon!"

"Nobody is challenging you over Gordon," Ulrik tried to appease her. "If you enjoy yourself with him – that's fine with me."

"So what do you or should I say my mother want of me?"

"She thinks you are in danger," Ulrik informed her.

"Me? In danger? Why would my mother think so?"

"That's because she's still wondering what Gordon wants of you."

"Does she not understand – we just want to have fun together."

"Is there nothing else?"

"Like what?" Ashly asked harshly.

"I mean workwise," Ulrik didn't know what else to say. He felt quite uncomfortable and hesitated to continue.

"Workwise?" Now it was for Ashly to wonder. "Do you mean the texts I translate for him occasionally?"

"I don't know. It's your mother who is worried."

"Well, Gordon has introduced me to some influential people from the art world," Ashly pondered aloud. "To my knowledge they all speak highly of me and trust me in my work."

"If this is so then there's no reason to worry," Ulrik admitted with a wan smile. "Anyway, it's not my intension to stand between you and Gordon." And then Ulrik let the cat out of the bag, "I will soon be leaving the country."

He had enunciated each word slowly and was now fixing Ashly with a triumphant gaze. Of course he was exaggerating. He hadn't even heard of another job yet, and who knew when an appropriate job would come up. Nonetheless, his announcement had the right effect – it totally surprised Ashly and in a strange way saddened her.

"You will what?" she exclaimed, staring at him with a perplexed expression. She definitely hadn't expected this.

"Yes, as soon as a job comes up somewhere far away from here, I'll be gone."

Ashly was much too shocked to reply. She called for Jake and quickly turned towards the entrance door.

"Watch out that Gordon doesn't misuse you," Ulrik said tenderly and added while closing the door behind her, "just be careful."

❖❖❖

Ashly felt she was in a trance heading to her car. Jake, walking beside her, must have sensed that his mother was immersed in her thoughts. He didn't dare to approach her, although he desperately wanted to get Claire's detection about Gordon off his chest.

Ashly took a deep breath when they both sat in the car. Putting her safety belt on, she muttered,

"Oh well – all talk and no action." She simply couldn't imagine Ulrik really leaving.

"Mummy what are these things you have to do for Gordon?" Jake asked innocently, not being aware of what Ulrik had just told Ashly.

Ashly's mind was occupied with driving. "Jake, please. You won't understand," she said, concentrating on the traffic.

"You always say that if you want me to be quiet," the boy said slightly frustrated.

"What is it you want to know?" Ashly caved in.

"What sort of work do you do for Gordon?" Jake persisted.

"Nothing much – just little pieces of translations," Ashly clarified while waiting at the traffic lights. She looked at her son, gently stroking his hair. With her mind far away, she tried to understand what Ulrik had just intimated.

"Have you ever thought that Gordon is selling

counterfeits?" the young boy ventured his suspicions, instantly alarming his mother.

"Darling dear, why should he?" Ashly replied astonished, putting the car into gear and driving on.

The vibe of discomfort and sadness engulfing her, caused by Ulrik's announcement, was swiftly blown away – Gordon! she suddenly realised. Indeed it had never occurred to her that Gordon might be using her in the selling of fake art. Their recent visit to the Shevchenko's emerged from her memories. What about the Cézanne which Gordon had promised to obtain for Fyodor?

"Well," Jake started to speak, carefully considering each word he was going to say, "How can he afford such a luxurious lifestyle by being only an estate agent – that doesn't earn him all the money, or does it?"

"He sells big mansions – that renders him a good return," Ashly explained.

Jake wasn't pleased with his mother's answer. He had tried every option in order to understand Mr. Thompson. He could smell a rat. What does this Gordon really want of his mother? What did he intend by taking her out to such posh places and introducing her to all these strange people? The boy wasn't at all happy with his mother's choice of lover. By any means – was his mother serious about being with such a man? 'Too many questions and no answers,' he thought. Not giving in so easily, he curiously asked, "What sort of texts are you translating for Gordon? Have any of the texts to do with his estate agency business?"

"No, not any," Ashly answered truthfully and was for the first time astounded as to why Gordon had never given her any work linked to his estate agency trading. "The translations are all art related," she added pensively.

"Like what?" Jake probed his mother. His suspicion increased from minute to minute.

"Well, little pieces like appraisal reports of a painting, or an expert opinion."

And then it crossed her mind that Gordon had asked her recently to render an expert opinion on several paintings from a variety of rather unknown artists. As she trusted Gordon, she simply did what he had asked her to do – sign each translated certificate with her name. She had thought nothing of it, particularly, since the paintings had all successfully passed a number of different tests.

'Maybe I should just be a little bit more cautious in the future,' a new thought crept into her mind as she parked the car in the old garage.

◆◆◆

"Granny, what's wrong with you?" Jake asked when they arrived home. He looked warm-heartedly at her and felt a little bit uneasy, because she didn't look well.

Iris was sitting in her recliner, her hand with the newspaper hanging over the arm of the chair, and the little reading lamp shining some light on her grey hair.

"I just had a nap," she said. One could tell by her voice that she must have been fast asleep. "I must have fallen asleep thinking of your mother," she yawned. Unaware that Ulrik had spoken to Ashly in the meantime, she went on, "You know, I'm still bothered that Ulrik doesn't speak with your mother." Yawning again, she quipped, "I feel so tired. Must be late spring fever."

Ashly had followed Jake into the living room, whilst the boy left to play upstairs in his room.

"I feel a bit tired as well," she concurred with her mother. "I suppose I'll have an early night." She felt like crying. During the last hour her world had been dramatically shaken up. First, the news from Ulrik that he might leave the country; and then, her son asking troubling questions about Gordon. It was simply too much for her and she wasn't prepared for times like this!

"Turn the light on," she said to Iris while drawing

the curtains, "it's dark in here."

She felt cold and Iris must have noticed it.

"Look at you – you are shaking," she observed. "A good cup of tea will make you feel better, darling," she continued while climbing out from her comfortable chair and walking away to the kitchen.

Ashly sank on to the sofa, staring into the distance. It seemed like hours before Iris came back with the two cups of tea. She looked at her daughter.

"What's wrong with you, honey?" she asked apprehensively.

"Everything and nothing," Ashly replied in a quiet voice, holding the warm teacup in both hands.

"Something is troubling you," Iris knew her daughter. She wasn't her usual self.

Ashly glanced at her mother. She wanted to tell her that everything was ok. But how could she when she knew full well herself that nothing was the same any more. She was still shocked about Ulrik's plan to go away. How could she explain this to her mother? It would only upset her. And then Gordon – the thought that he was being less than honest with her was creeping in and niggled her.

"Maybe I'm coming down with flu," Ashly said, hoping that her mother would swallow her clumsy excuse.

Iris took a deep breath. Since her daughter's return

from New York she hadn't been the same. Whatever she did – she couldn't get through to Ashly to find out what was troubling her. Iris felt totally helpless. The whole situation reminded her somehow of Rick, with all the arguments they had been having recently about Gordon. She was bothered by the way her daughter looked when she talked about this man. Ashly always argued and shouted at her mother, "Don't tell me anything bad about Gordon!"

"Honey, what is it?" Iris tried again. "You're not the same since your trip to New York."

Was her mother right? Was it possible that she had changed? And if so – how much? Ashly was unable to comment. What could she possible say that wouldn't infuriate her mother? She stared at her for a long moment, all sorts of thoughts chasing each other, yet none found its way to her mouth. With a lump in her throat she finally blubbered out, "I can't tell you – not yet."

What was going on with her daughter? Iris was wondering. She went over to the sofa, gently hugging Ashly who was shivering.

"Honey, everything will be fine," she comforted her.

Like the bursting of a dam Ashly started to cry. Tears were streaming down her cheeks as she held on to her mother's arms. "Mum it's so terrible," she cried. What could probably be so terrible to make her daughter cry? Iris, having been worried for ages, was immediately thinking of a worst case – this bloody man Gordon again! – but tried to stay poised and waited patiently for Ashly to tell her. "Everything will be fine, honey," she soothed her again while Ashly wept inconsolably.

All of a sudden Jake stood in the doorway.
"Is everything all right with my mum?" he asked squinting and seemingly aghast. He had been in his room upstairs when he heard his mother sobbing and came running down the stairs. Childhood memories, long thought buried, surfaced all of a sudden. The last time Jake witnessed his mother crying had been eight years ago in Rick's house.
"Yes, yes, love," Iris assured her apprehensive grandson who snuggled up beside his mum on the settee.
Still, Jake couldn't so easily be deceived. He sensed immediately that there must be something serious which fazed his mother. And he bet it was Gordon.
"Mummy I love you," the boy whispered while bending over to put his arms around his mum, holding her fondly. He was puzzled – what was going on? There was something he wanted to say.

But he was somehow rocked back on his heels. Watching his mother crying, he just couldn't find any words to ease her. Instead he tenderly stroked his mother's face.

"Jake sweetheart," Ashly hugged him and wrapped him in her arms. Tears were still spilling over her face. What was she going to tell him? What would he be capable of understanding? That Ulrik and Claire were going to leave? Ashly knew that would break her son's heart. She wasn't sure herself what caused her to crack down, crying and sniffling like a little girl. She glimpsed a quick flash of fear in Jakes eyes, reminding her to pull herself together. After a short pause she pushed herself up from the sofa and, standing in front of the fireplace, she dried her tears.

"Everything is fine," she said, forcing herself to sound composed, "It's nothing important. I'm just not feeling too well. It has been a tough day with a lot of problems..." – she hesitated and then quickly added, "at work."

A fleeting look of misgiving crossed Jake's face. Ashly strove to reassure him that there was really nothing to worry about. She tried to produce a laugh which only made her mother and son frown.

"Honestly. I'm all right," she then said grandly,

"A good night's sleep and I'll be fit again tomorrow."

"Well darling – we'll figure it all out tomorrow," Iris stood next to her daughter now. What was the point in going on? She looked warmly at Ashly when she continued, "Honey, you best go to bed and sleep it all off whatever it is that's bothering you."

"Yes. I'm so tired. I just want to sleep," Ashly said and hugged her mother. Her voice dwindled away when, on the way to the door, she gently kissed Jake and said her goodnights to him.

Iris watched her daughter leaving the room, shaking her head with consternation. She was worried!

◆◆◆

"What's wrong with mum?" Jake asked distressed. He felt somewhat sorry, having probed his mother so tenaciously about Gordon earlier on.

"I bet Gordon has a finger in the pie," the boy voiced his thoughts.

"I don't know what has upset your mum so gravely" Iris despairingly answered. "It could be Gordon – anything is possible. Don't you worry darling. We'll find out sooner or later."

She picked up the remote control to turn the TV on. Usually at this time of the day she watched the newscast. Although today she thought she couldn't cope with any more bad news. She had enough problems herself at the moment.

Jake was desperate to tell his granny what Claire had shared with him about Gordon.

"Guess what," Jake couldn't wait any longer to disclose his secret. And before Iris had a chance to turn on the TV, he excitedly said to her, "I was talking with Claire about it all. Listen granny what I have to tell you," and pulling Iris' arm, the boy explained to her with his voice cracking, "If Gordon is selling allegedly genuine paintings he needs someone to certify that the false objects, he is selling, are genuine. And that's why he needs my mum – he is using my mum for her expertise. BINGO!" Jake had a big smile on his face when he dropped his bombshell.

"Hang on, hang on," Iris demanded, "say that again please, but slowly." Her mind was still occupied with her daughter so disconsolately crying and she wasn't prepared for what her grandson had just revealed so quickly.

"I mean he needs my mum to certify that his fake paintings are genuine," Jake repeated, winningly looking at his grandmother.

It took Iris a moment to comprehend

"I see!" she mulled over her grandson's assertion. "Yes, that could be it," she acknowledged. "Either that or he is forging her signature." Iris couldn't imagine her daughter voluntarily signing for a fake painting.

"Forge her signature?" Jake frowned.

"Yes – why not? He only needs one of your mother's signatures to then continue faking all further signings."

"Humph, I never thought about that," Jake admitted somehow puzzled and let out a soft moan.

"I don't think that your mother is so spellbound by Gordon not to know what she is doing. Don't you think so?" She noticed that the boy was engrossed in thought. Gently tapping his nose, she blew softly at his forehead. "Go away you muddling thoughts or I'll get our ghost to haunt you," she teased him and tried to cheer him up.

"Granny….," his eyes searched her face. "What are we going to do about it?"

"About what?"

"Gordon, using my mum for his shady dealings."

"Well, at the moment we have no proof. We must be very vigilant," Iris said with a weary sigh.

"Yes. We have to do whatever it takes to find out what Gordon is up to," Jake agreed.

Iris didn't respond right away. She was much too afraid of the consequences and imagined worst case scenario.

"Mr. Mystery thinks he is very clever," she

murmured. "I have always a bad feeling about this man."

"So do I," her grandson agreed.

◆◆◆

The phone rang. "Who is this so late?" Iris wondered while rushing to answer the phone. It was Dorothy.

"Did you see the news?" she asked.

"It's Dorothy," Iris flicked her head, indicating to Jake that it was bedtime for him, and then she turned back to the phone.

"Unfortunately not... I was going to but I became tied up with matters concerning Ashly. She has been feeling a bit down tonight and I tried to soothe her," Iris explained to her friend. "Why – what's the news?"

"What's the matter with Ashly? How is she?" Dorothy asked alarmed instead of revealing what she had seen on the TV.

"Nothing very important," Iris said, not sounding very convincing.

"Has Gordon caused her trouble?" Dorothy stuck to her guns.

"I hope not," Iris replied, "Ashly was in a terrible state. I haven't seen her crying like this since she's been living with me."

"Oh dear – what can I say. I somehow wonder if this Gordon is the right man for Ashly anyway. Knowing your girl, it must be something really serious if she's so distressed," Dorothy expressed her sentiments, adding compassionately, "I can well imagine how you feel, my dear."

"Yes, the whole situation between Ashly and her lover is putting quite a strain on me too... All these gloomy thoughts which are torturing me. I have a feeling something is brewing. That said, let's change the subject – What about the news?" Iris wanted to know.

"Oh yes, the news – there was an art heist in Switzerland. The second within a couple of years. I thought you might want to know," Dorothy hastened to say. "A number of Cézanne paintings have been stolen from a private collection."

"Oh well, that's all we needed tonight," Iris said in an exhausted tone. And as if she could see her friend's question mark in her face, she added, "I can't take any more tonight, Dorothy. God needs to rub me out and draw me over again."

"Oh dear," was all Dorothy was able to comment. "Is it that bad?"

"Yes and no. Everything is falling into place and I'm falling apart," Iris replied with a touch of self-mockery in her voice.

"Aren't we all?" Dorothy readily agreed and quickly added, "Falling apart."

"I assume that's the way it is when one gets older," Iris calmly replied.

"Sure it is. Nevertheless, keep on running, dear," Dorothy encouraged her friend. "So tell me, what's eating you?"

"Alas! Dorothy," Iris initially didn't know where to begin and then she sputtered, "First of all, my daughter – seeing her in such a frustrated and despairing state. I can only assume it has to do with Gordon. And then my grandson tells me such a preposterous story that Gordon may be using Ashly to sell fake paintings. And now you phone to tell me about an art heist." Iris stopped with a weary sigh.

"That's indeed a lot to take in all at once," Dorothy assented and added after a short pause, "Even so it looks as if it's all connected."

"Yes. But how?"

The two women were convinced that there was more to this story. Though for now, neither of them was sure how to put the pieces together.

"Well, it appears we can't solve the mystery tonight. Don't let these worries get on top of you. Everything will be fine," Dorothy tried to pacify her friend.

"Yes," Iris sighed again, "I'd like to think that. The

whole situation is much too much for me! I hope I can see a clearer path tomorrow after a good night's sleep."

"Have a good night, my dear," Dorothy said, "Maybe things will start to make sense in the clear light of day!"

Chapter Fifteen

As usual, Ashly left the next morning early for work. Fortunately Jake would be picked up by a child-minder which Gordon had insisted on and so generously organised for the mornings. Paying for a minder meant actually nothing to Gordon. He just wanted to have more time with Ashly when she stayed at his place overnight. And pretending to take some responsibility off her shoulders, he had at one stage even suggested arranging for a nanny for Jake. She had thankfully declined, believing that a nanny would really be over the top. Her son didn't need a nanny. Iris was looking after him, and apart from that Jake had a mother, namely Ashly.

The day was rainy and overcast and was just in keeping with Ashly's mood. Driving her car through the heavy rain, she was very upset and depressed. Her life was turning into a nightmare and she needed time to rethink the current events and to gather her thoughts. Never in a million years had she thought that Ulrik would ever leave. And if it was true that he was leaving, then not only her life but more so Jake's life would be changed in a most dramatic way. She was sure neither Jake nor Iris would like it. Iris had become so acquainted with the alluring, well-mannered Swede – it would probably break her heart if she had to say farewell to him for good.

'Well you can't blame him,' her sub-consciousness was telling her.

Eventually she found a parking space at the university and hurried up the stairs to her office. Would she be able to concentrate on her work, being so consumed with racking thoughts about her relationships – the passion, sex and extravagance on the one hand, and the patient, cordial, and sophisticated friend on the other hand.

'I have to put this rather intricate affair out of my mind for now,' she reminded herself while hastily bundling a few papers together. All in vain – she experienced the strong desire to leave the workplace, go home, and go to sleep.

"Pull yourself together," she heard herself saying.

She looked out of the window – people were rushing, with their open umbrellas fighting with the heavy wind and rain. Normally she would have gone for a walk to clear her head. But this weather didn't permit it. The very moment she turned her computer on, and heard the welcoming sound signalling that all was set on the pc, she felt sick. The machine was ready to work but Ashly was not.

"I can't cope with this," she said to herself and then she realised that she hadn't had anything to eat this morning. 'No wonder I feel so weak.' She looked at her watch – there was enough time to run over to the canteen and get a sandwich.

The wind was blowing heavily in her face as she made her way across the campus. A group of students were gathering at the entrance to the canteen. 'Why do people always have to stand at the doors and block the entry?!' she was in an angry mood and pushed her way through.

"Hello Ashly," she unexpectedly heard the friendly voice of Natasha, one of Ulrik's colleagues, beside her. "The weather is awful today, isn't it?"

"Terrible," Ashly agreed, "Very depressing."

The weather was usually a topic she didn't care to talk about. There is nothing one can do about it – one has to take it as it comes, she would normally reply. However, today she was happy for the distraction and to have – what she expected was to be – a harmless conversation. But Natasha wouldn't be the person she was if she hadn't jumped at the chance to talk with Ashly about Ulrik. She was much too worried that her longstanding, best colleague was going to leave for good. For that reason Natasha got right to the point. Facing Ashly she said, "You don't look too well. Just like Ulrik. What's wrong with you two?"

What was Ashly going to say – that she was totally lulled by an enticing lover who provided her with a kind of thrilling jet set lifestyle and she was, despite all this, secretly yearning for Ulrik? That was preposterous!

"Natasha, please, I'm not in the mood to talk about Ulrik," Ashly brought herself to say, closing her lips into a thin line across her mouth.

The other woman wasn't so easily deterred, "But you know that he is thinking of leaving the country."

"Yes I heard it last night."

"So what do you have to say about it?" Natasha placed her finger right in the open wound, scowling at Ashly.

Ashly took a deep breath – what could she possibly say to defend herself? Did she have to defend herself anyway? Why? She had done nothing wrong – or had she?

"If Ulrik wants to leave then he must do so," Ashly

answered brusquely.

"You are not serious!" Natasha was appalled. "Ashly – I know you better. You are not so cold hearted." She looked angrily at Ashly who only shrugged as if to say, 'That's no concern of mine'.

A long silence, then Natasha picked up her thread again,

"Ashly, think about it! What about Claire and Jake? The kids are the losers – not you and Ulrik."

"Yes I know," Ashly replied with a flat voice and then offered, "Look Natasha, if you want to talk about it let's meet somewhere else. Not here in this busy canteen." She felt that it might be a good idea to talk it all through with somebody who also seemed to have a vital interest in Ulrik staying in the country.

Apparently Natasha didn't want to let Ashly go so easily. Then again, she couldn't refuse her offer, meeting somewhere else.

"What about the Café Brazil?" Natasha suggested, showing her willingness to comply.

"Yes. That's a good idea. Would early next week be okay with you?" Ashly hoped that matters would be more settled by then.

"Let me think," Natasha opened her diary and shaking her head – next week seemed so far away – she suggested, "Why not meet today for lunch?"

Unlike Ashly she didn't want to wait until Ulrik had actually left. On the contrary, she was determined to prevent him from going away.

Half-heartedly Ashly agreed. With a forced smile she said,

"OK, see you half past twelve at the Café Brazil." Then she took her sandwich and rushed back through the rain to her office.

◆◆◆

Fortunately by midday the rain had dispersed and Ashly made her way to the little café to meet Natasha. She was already waiting there and beckoned Ashly who was searching around when she entered. Ashly observed that Natasha looked pretty sexy when she sat down. Her loose, low neckline jumper covered discretely her voluptuously curved feminine body and her high heeled sandals perfectly matched the Audrey Chino style trousers.

Time was short and the reason, why Natasha wanted so desperately to talk with Ashly, was very complicated. Under no circumstances did she want Ulrik to leave and it all depended on what Ashly had to say. Natasha, though she tried to stay calm, spoke rapidly, as if she would come quicker to a conclusion before things would get even worse. Ashly, feeling very agitated too, faced her with a great deal of trepidation, but retained her poise.

"Ashly, do you really want Ulrik to give up everything here and burn all his bridges?" Natasha asked. "It will come to me as a relationship break-up." The bitterness in her voice was unmistakable.

"Give up everything? Break up like in a relation-ship?" Ashly hadn't seen the current difficulty from that point of view. Visions of her own breakup from Rick emerged. The abuse and arguments she and Rick had been having. It had been the most upsetting time in her life. One fine day she had left Rick and everything else behind... *Break up* sounded so harsh, so like *no return* – like *terminally ill*... But the situation with Ulrik was different, wasn't it? He wasn't breaking up with her as Natasha insinuated. She was exaggerating, wasn't she?

"But surely he isn't going to burn his bridges!" Ashly objected.

While Ashly was still coming to terms with what she had just heard, Natasha was bending over the table, looking in Ashly's face, nodding.

"Yes, he is!" she confirmed sternly. She was greatly perturbed to become estranged from Ulrik and continued, "Ulrik leaving might lead to a parting of our ways as well."

"Of course he's not!" Ashly replied, feeling unwell and tired. And then, defiantly looking at Natasha, she added, "It's not my fault that Ulrik wants to leave."

"He is throwing in the towel," Natasha adhered to her grounds, "Giving up everything here and never coming back!"

Her words hit Ashly hard.

"Okay, then what have I got to do with it?" She remembered a proverb from one of her German friends, 'do not prevent travellers from their journey'. Aloud she said, "Don't let the door hit him on his way out." As soon as the words slipped her lips she regretted it, knowing it was unfair on Natasha.

"Ashly, you simply don't want to understand me!"

The worst was that Ashly did understand, in fact she understood quite well. However, she was torn between Gordon, offering her a glamorous lifestyle, and Ulrik, whom she – for some obscure reason – always had turned down.

"What makes you think that?" she asked, striving to sound totally unconcerned.

"You are so cold, so aloof," Natasha was searching for words to describe her impression of Ashly, "… it's as if the whole situation isn't touching you."

"How about you? What's your interest in Ulrik?" Not being nettled by Natasha's flaming words, it was Ashly's turn to raise questions now.

"Well, that's very easy," Natasha replied heartfelt, "if Ulrik leaves I'll miss him deeply. He isn't only one of my best colleagues, but the finest by far."

"I see," Ashly acknowledged, pretending she hadn't known.

"Yes," Natasha swooned over Ulrik, "he is a good sport, conversant with any subject – he knows very well what's going on in the world and what's going on inside people." And if that wasn't enough, she added, "Whenever I need a friend, and I mean *a real friend*, he is there for me, listening to my worries. And apart from all that he's one of the best lecturers we have!"

Ashly could see that Natasha was fighting with her emotions, choking back her tears. She hadn't been prepared for such an emotional conversation and tried to think of something appropriate to say. During the moments of silence Ashly fiddled with her napkin. Natasha was right. Ulrik was a real friend. Compared to Gordon he was more conventional. There was nothing insincere about his friendship. He was genuinely a good man, no bragger or swagger, easy going and pleasant to be with. And yet – Ashly was lost. She could say that, yes, she would do everything to make him stay, but that would be a big lie.

"Don't you think you are playing with his feelings?" Natasha said, trying to catch Ashly's eye. And because Ashly wasn't reacting, she added, "Ashly, you know Ulrik loves you," it was a desperate attempt to call on Ashly to do something.

"What do you want me to do?" Ashly looked at Natasha. Her question was rather rhetorical, as she knew quite well there was nothing she could possibly do to make Ulrik change his mind.

"Maybe you could talk to him? Ashly, please..."

"I'm confused," Ashly admitted at last. "I know that Ulrik is very fond of me. Even so, I never thought he wanted more than the friendship we have. I don't think I've done anything to lead him on."

Right now Ashly couldn't take any more. After a moment of consideration she said, "It would be so much easier if Ulrik wasn't so attracted to me."

"You're not telling me that you never noticed Ulrik's affection for you?" Natasha said emphatically, her eyes carrying a mixture of blank astonishment and anger. It sounded almost like an accusation when she continued, "As far as I know he loved you pretty much from the very moment he laid eyes on you,"

"Well, I did notice he was attracted to me," Ashly acknowledged, trying to shirk from Natasha's look.

"It was a long time ago. But when I started to go out with Gordon I thought Ulrik's feelings would cool down."

"You broke his heart," Natasha's words hit Ashly like thunder. "Ulrik is purely too decent to tell you."

"Why are you not dating him?" Ashly surprised Natasha with her question.

"Why should I? He doesn't love me." Natasha's blood was up – how on earth could Ashly say such a thing!

"Are you sure about that?"

"Yes! He loves you," she was profoundly convinced and left no doubt that Ashly was Ulrik's true love.

Ashly took a deep breath. That didn't make things any easier.

"Natasha, you're right. Ulrik has been such a good friend to me and I don't know why I don't feel the same way as he does." Somehow Ashly hoped that the other woman would understand that there was a reason for her ambiguous feelings.

"Do you love this man Gordon?" Natasha asked with a penetrating look at Ashly.

Ashly wished she could find a way to avoid answering. 'Do I love Gordon?' It was the one question Ashly kept asking herself repeatedly. Could she see herself married to him? No! She really couldn't imagine it.

The sound of shrill voices, as a group of young students entered the café, distracted her. Ashly was in a rather forlorn mood. And on top of that in the background the radio played Chris De Burgh's song *Tender Hands,* instantly reminding her that there had been times when she was tempted to lean on Ulrik, wanting him to hug and kiss her. Clearly a sign that she didn't love Gordon, or was it? 'That's all I needed', she thought while listening to the song, suddenly experiencing a touch of melancholy and feeling even more at a loss as how to answer Natasha's question.

"Well, let me put it this way," Ashly picked up the thread, "Yes, I'm enjoying myself with Gordon...," she stopped and after a moment of consideration she continued, "But *love* – that word is not part of our affair." She wanted to wrap up the awkward conversation.

Natasha shook her head. "Is that all there is?" she asked with her dark brown eyes wide open. Ashly's answer was beyond belief and left her feeling sad. She knew in that moment that she was definitely going to lose a friendship she had come to cherish. Ashly really didn't care about Ulrik – on the contrary, she was consumed by living the high life and enjoying herself with a man she didn't even love!

"Look Natasha, I appreciate your concerns for Ulrik. But I don't need any more problems at the moment," Ashly said in a low voice. She was in a terrible state and all she wanted was to go home and to sleep it off. 'Maybe it is all a bad dream,' she wished.

"I just wanted to help," Natasha said with overblown sincerity. Realising that she was getting nowhere with this conversation, and after throwing some money resentfully on the table for Ashly to pay the bill, she left the café, wishing that she could have changed the outcome!

◆◆◆

Most days Ashly liked her job. But today wasn't one of them. Especially after the conversation with Natasha she felt very unsettled. How could she play with Ulrik's feelings?

All of a sudden she thought of her relationship with Rick – the way he had treated her and showed her that he definitely didn't love her, and yet she had been dangling in indecision whether or not to stay on with him.

With a deep sigh she asked herself why she had tolerated such a nightmare. Remembering the heartbreak she had endured with that man, she recalled the sense of hope that she had clung to in the bad times. Hope – that small word with such a deep meaning. The hope that her life would improve and the love she sought from Rick would one day magically appear. Unfortunately, the truth was that it never did and in the face of all hope she had to admit some relationships fail.

The thought she might have done the same to Ulrik, what Rick had done to her, gnawed on her mind. Had she hurt his feelings by putting him off? Ulrik's behaviour suggested that he had been hoping she would reciprocate his interest in her. But Ashly had never picked up on his feelings and never actively promised him anything.

When she had first come across Ulrik she precluded another relationship. After all the hardship she had experienced with Rick she was too afraid to commit to a serious romance. Ok, having been single when she had met him didn't mean that she wanted to stay that way all her life. But obviously she must have failed to convince Ulrik that all she wanted at the time was a little bit of fun and sex, and that he wasn't the right person.

So they stayed friends, with Ashly being oblivious to his advances until the day when Ulrik's announcement somehow plunged a dagger into her heart. She still doubted that Ulrik was serious – burning all his bridges seemed so far-fetched. Never for one moment had she thought that he could throw her into such emotional disarray. Lost in thought she was questioning why he was so attracted to her. What made her so appealing to him? She regarded herself as nothing special, a sensible, adaptive, and down-to-earth person. Did Ulrik really love her, or wasn't it because he was a single parent and she was good at looking after his daughter Claire? Whichever way she looked at it, she couldn't come up with an adequate conclusion.

She was also annoyed how Natasha had talked to her. The way that woman wanted to discuss Ashly's private life wasn't what Ashly had expected. What if Natasha was to blame for prompting Ulrik to "burn all his bridges" as she had phrased it? Exactly! Natasha saw Ulrik more often through work and spent more time with him than anybody else. And did she not look so sexy? With her fiery brown eyes – could she not sweet-talk Ulrik? All these torturing thoughts were running through Ashly's mind at once.

"I need time for myself to clear my head," she spoke to herself.

◆◆◆

Instead of driving home, Ashly had a sudden urge to go for a walk by the sea and so she headed off to the country park at the waterfront. The storm and rain of last night had littered the beach with piles of seaweed. There was no way she could walk through that mess to get down to the water, hence she rambled on the little paved meandering walkway, immersed in thoughts.

What was she supposed to believe? While she was fascinated by Gordon's lavishness, Ulrik had always been a reliable and dependable friend. She couldn't say the same about sexy Gordon. There had been many times when she tried to ring him or had sent him little texts which he didn't answer and as a result left her frustrated. When she later mentioned it to him he explained convincingly that his phone was turned off because he had been with an important client.

'Gordon is full of negative surprises,' Ashly thought, remembering how bad he was at time keeping. He had let her down on several occasions when they had arranged to meet as he was invariably late. His feeble excuse was always that he had been held up in a traffic jam or by a client. And then there were the days when Gordon simply disappeared for long periods of time, insisting that business had taken him out of town at short notice.

She took a deep breath and absorbed the fresh air from the sea. She wished herself far away – on a desert island in the middle of an ocean where she would feel safe and nobody could touch her... sunny, blue sky, palm trees, white beaches as far as the eye could see, and clear emerald green water... She saw it all in her mind's eye. But would she be happy on her own? She was passionate about Gordon; enraptured by his personality and lulled into his sweet-talk which didn't allow any questioning of his integrity. Despite his age he had a strong body and he was so damned good looking. A brilliant lover and one could truly say a real colourful character. Just thinking of his brawny-armed embraces when they made love launched Ashly into a delicious shiver of lust. There was no doubt – Ashly was fascinated by Gordon. A fascination, which she understood, she couldn't easily withdraw from. And why should she? She admitted almost in disbelief that she was addicted to him. In all honesty he hadn't done her any harm up to this point, and she realised she had enjoyed some of the best times in her life with him. But was it really such a good time or was Gordon too good to be true? A warning from her friend Claudia suddenly came to mind, 'All handsome men are cheaters.' Then again, why should all handsome men be cheaters, and why was she particularly attracted to him? Ashly had no answer and wished from the bottom of her heart that her friend's words were not always true!

The sun was setting and more and more people had decided to take advantage of a walk by the sea, either walking their dogs or just strolling along. They all greeted her in a friendly manner and paused to have a few words with her about the weather. Despite her cordial nature Ashly was not in the mood for any small talk today. The gigantic clock on the old church was striking, without Ashly paying attention how many times it had struck. Somehow it reminded her of a big antique grandfather clock with its oscillating pendulum. And that was exactly how she felt – like playing with a pendulum. Just like the ticking of the clock, *Gordon, Ulrik, Gordon, Ulrik* the pendulum swung consistently strong both ways.

◆◆◆

In some way Ashly sensed that her life was going in a direction which she hadn't wanted. No matter what she thought, she was getting nowhere.
'Let's call it a day,' she said to herself and decided to drive home.

Nobody said anything at home about the previous evening. Ashly put a brave face on, hoping to make Iris and Jake believe she'd just had another tough day at work. Jake knew his mother occasionally worked longer hours when students turned up after a lecture or class to discuss issues of their academic research. He was therefore not surprised to see her coming home late.

"How was your day at school, sweetheart?" Ashly enquired. She was anxious that Claire may have mentioned something about her father's intentions to leave the country.

"I was debating with Claire today how private ownership came into existence," the boy told his mother.

"Oh good grief, that's a very controversial subject," Ashly said and was relieved – at least it appeared that the girl hadn't said anything about her and her dad going away. Maybe Ulrik would change his mind, Ashly hoped.

"Can I assume you had a good day at school with your friend?" she then went on. "How is Claire?"

"She's all right," Jake answered rather uninterested. "Have you ever heard of the fisherman who was the first person to become a millionaire?" he suddenly came up with a question which totally confused his mother.

"No," Ashly answered puzzled.

And then Jake told his little story,

"You know, in the old days there was once a fisherman who caught more fish than he and his tribe were able to consume. Therefore he sold the surplus and with the money he made, he bought more boats, made more nets, employed more people, and became richer and richer." The boy looked at his mother, expectantly waiting for her to answer.

Since Ashly wasn't prepared for a discussion with her son, she only remarked,

"That's a very simplistic example. How does one make money if money wasn't even invented yet?"

"Well," Jake continued undaunted by his mother's remarks, "they had other means of barter. They used precious stones, wine, and spices. And those who kept the means of production to themselves were the ones who gradually gained power over others."

"Yes, and nowadays it's not so much *means of production* but money which makes the world go round," now Iris joined the discussion. "Everything has to be flashy, big and bigger," she complained. With a significant look at her daughter she continued, "And women fall for those signs of wealth."

"Height and might already played a major role in

early history in order to suppress and impress people," Jake backed his grandmother. "And then there were those people who didn't get enough and always had a strong desire to impress others with their glamour and make them awe."

"I don't know what you two are up to," Ashly said, shaking her head. The whole situation was getting tense.

"All the monumental architecture for example, and the entire majestic demeanour – this was purely to cement the power of the rich over the poor in place. And it mimicked nature – the survival of the fittest," Jake aired his anger about mediaeval society. "Yeah, but look what had happened – all these mega beasts, like the mighty dinosaurs, they all died but tiny insects survived!"

"Which teaches us that nature doesn't need '*Pomp and Circumstance*'," Iris resumed the debate. "Only humans are so greedy that they make war, rape and steal..." she abruptly trailed off. The heist in Switzerland had jumped her mind.

◆◆◆

"By the way, have you heard about the art heist – what do you think about it?" Iris was keen to hear her daughter's opinion.

The heated dispute had cooled off in the interim.

"Which art heist?" Ashly replied genuinely surprised.

"Did you not hear it on the news?"

"No, I really don't know what you're talking about, mum."

"There were several paintings stolen... in Geneva, I think. INTERPOL is involved as it is the second big art heist or so within a couple of years," Iris explained.

Ashly didn't understand straightaway.

"You mean in Switzerland?"

"Yes Geneva – that's in Switzerland, isn't it?"

"What sort of paintings?" Ashly wanted to know.

"As far as I remember those of a famous painter – I can't recall his name. He was French or so," Iris put her hand on her forehead, trying to remember the name. "Something like Chaser, Che...Che..." The name was on the tip of her tongue but just couldn't come to mind.

"Do you mean Cézanne?"

"Yes, now I remember, it was Paul Cézanne," Iris confirmed, pleased that her memory hadn't failed at last.

"He was a French artist and Post-Impressionist painter who lived in the nineteenth century," Ashly explained to her mother. "He is said to have paved the way for what is now modern art."

"I have never heard of him."

"Well, I saw some of his paintings in Paris at the Musée d'Orsay," Ashly went on, adding with a pensive look, "His paintings are valued very, very highly." After a short pause she asked her mother excitedly, "Where exactly were the paintings stolen from?"

"From a private collection – I don't think it was a public place like a museum or gallery."

Was there more to this story? Ashly knitted her brow. It gave her food for thought. She was putting the pieces together – Gordon's connections to all these wealthy people. What had he recently explained to her about art heists? 'All you need are some experienced burglars; a concealer, ideally one with worldwide storage facilities; and a couple of extraordinarily rich people who would go to any length to obtain a painting from a famous artist.' Gordon, who was allegedly the owner of an estate agency operating world-wide with links to removal companies, had plenty of such storage facilities. And had his super rich Russian friend in New York not asked him to get a Cézanne? Instinctively it was clear to her that Gordon was behind the heist. Who else? The facts were on the table. She thought it all added up! For a moment Ashly was slightly fazed by her guesswork. The fact that she had never mistrusted him made her angry. Gordon – what sort of a person was he?! There was no doubt, he was good at coining phrases and he was a terrific lover. Little by little she became aware that she could indeed have been taken in by a con-artist. Gordon – he gradually turned into a man who purported to be rich. What was he really? This time the pendulum swung in favour of Ulrik.

"Ashly dear, what's wrong with you? Why are you so agitated about that heist?" she heard her mother asking.

"Nothing mum," she replied with a sweet smile. "I just need a little bit of time to digest everything that has happened to me recently."

Iris was patiently waiting what else her daughter would say.

"This story about the theft of such a highly prized collection of paintings is very disturbing. I'm concerned, as an art historian, where these paintings are now and," Ashly went on and looked straight at her mother, "who is prepared to buy them? This sort of theft inevitably results in a sale on the black market."

"Yes, darling, I understand full well your concerns," Iris agreed, "after all, art is your profession and career."

Meeting her daughter's eyes, Iris knew instinctively that there must be more to this story and sincerely hoped Ashly wasn't entangled in Gordon's web of lies.

Chapter Sixteen

Ashly was determined to shed some light on the complexities surrounding Gordon's financial dealings. She was angry and rehearsed in her mind what she was going to say to him the next time she saw him. No longer did she want to be kept in the dark. So far, she had simply enjoyed a taste of the high-life and the sex with him, but this would have to come to an end. She wanted to establish clarity – was he truly involved in the heist in Geneva, or not? She may have allowed things to go too far already by not paying attention to what her mother, her son, and some of her friends had always told her about Gordon. Whenever Iris had warned her – "You should never have become involved with this man", she had given these words of warnings many times – Ashly had refused to listen. She didn't want anybody spoiling the time of her life with this colourful figure, this hot Australian lover. He had introduced her to such interesting people and sweetened her life by taking her out every so often, either to exclusive restaurants or nightclubs. They had flown to New York to spend the weekend there in hyper-stylish venues with superb restaurants, and he had promised they would return to visit art galleries and such places. Not to mention of course their meetings at irregular intervals in his penthouse suite where she thoroughly enjoyed the lovemaking with him.

But then, bit by bit her liaison had become overshadowed by suspicion. Everybody around her believed Gordon wasn't the perfect guy he appeared to be. Ashly herself started to ask what else he wasn't telling her. In the past, things weren't going to work out as smooth as she had thought. Gordon was very adept at avoiding questions he didn't want to answer. Whenever she had thought she could talk seriously with him he had manipulated her, changed the subject, and quite cleverly ignored the questions. She knew he was sweet talking her and nothing was going according to *her* plan. This time she was determined to resist his allure and get answers for her questions

"Gordon, we have to talk," she addressed him one day, determined not to become distracted this time.

"About what?" he asked her, gently kissing her neck and sending pleasant shivers down her spine.

"What about this latest art heist?" she insisted, having difficulties fending him off. She loved the smell of him, "Stop it – I'm not stupid!"

"Of course you're not," Gordon replied with a confident smile, running his fingers across her shoulders down to her breasts. "I know how to make a woman happy," he continued and pulled Ashly over to his bed, passionately kissing her nipples.

Just when she thought she could resist Gordon, his hand reached down between her legs and began slowly massaging its destination. It was again too good to be true. Gordon was such a brilliant lover with such irresistible techniques Ashly would never forget. How could she possibly end this relationship? Her willpower deserted her and she knew her resistance was at low ebb. In no way could she foresee putting an end to this pleasurable affair.

After the amazing sex Ashly rested totally satisfied in Gordon's big bed, and glimpsing the ceiling, she was reminded why she came here in the first place.

"Have a glass of champagne," Gordon interrupted her thoughts.

She took the glass he handed her and, looking into

his wonderful blue eyes, she forgot for a moment that there was something about Gordon that said *'don't trust me'*. He bent down to kiss her. His scent was so seductive that Ashly had trouble composing herself. In spite of her feelings of pleasure, she endeavoured to find out what Gordon knew about the art heist in Switzerland. Was he deliberately distracting her from obtaining any information?

"Gordon, please…," Ashly tried again while he showered her with kisses. In the end she shoved him away, much to his surprise.

"What? What's wrong with you?" his voice sounded angry and as he took up an intimidating position, the whole situation became unexpectedly rather scary for Ashly.

With the white linen blanket covering her naked body, she sat up in the bed and forced him to make eye contact with her. Her voice was steady when she spoke with a confidence that surprised even her.

"What is wrong with you?" she countered his question.

"Nothing," Gordon answered, turning his head away from her so that she couldn't see in his face what was really going on.

"Fair enough," Ashly uttered, "then why can't you tell me what you know about that recent art heist in

Switzerland?" She was convinced he knew more than he was letting on.

"Because...!" he snapped at Ashly and turned his back to her.

The atmosphere was very tense. Gordon, who had withdrawn in the meantime from Ashly, remained resolutely silent. Curbing her urge to find out the truth, she realised that this was neither the time nor the place to have a serious conversation with him.

"Let's go for a meal at Teddy's," she suggested, hoping that the informal atmosphere of the restaurant would allow them to ease the tension between them and offer a better environment in which to discuss this obviously difficult subject.

Gordon reacted with a sulky look but immediately agreed.

◆◆◆

While Ashly sought to get some sense out of Gordon and his connections within the art world, he was once more working the room. With his macho attitude he was received with cheers from the bar staff at Teddy's and instantly became entangled in the latest buzz. Ashly realised straightaway it might not have been such a good idea to have suggested this lively place, especially since Gordon was so well known by everybody.

"I guess it's very busy here today," Gordon addressed the staff. "We would like to eat a little something."

A little while later, they were seated at a small table near the bar where as usual Gordon ordered a platter and some white wine.

"Cheers my dear," Gordon raised his glass to Ashly, "you worry too much."

Ashly didn't hesitate. With a serious look she came right to the point,

"Gordon, I have the impression you are involved in some nefarious dealings and I would like to know the truth."

"The truth about what?"

"This recent art heist," Ashly explained in a low voice, as she didn't want others to hear what she had to say, and bending over to Gordon she continued, "where a couple of Cézanne paintings were stolen. It was the second big heist within a couple of years."

"What have I got to do with it?" Gordon asked, feigning innocence.

"Well did you not promise your Russian friend Fyodor that you would get him a Cézanne?"

"Yes I did – so what?"

Before Ashly could say anything a dolled up blonde approached the table.

"Gordon, darling," she exclaimed, coming up to Gordon. Bending down to embrace him exuberantly and sounding shrill, she continued, "Where have you been all this time? We missed you so much."

Ashly had never seen this woman before. Who was she? An old flame of Gordon's she should be worried about? With her full breasts, her rather tawdry pink dress, the exceptionally high heels, the heavy make-up, and especially her over-mascaraed black eyelashes she appeared to Ashly as if she may be an escort of some kind.

'Yes, where have you been, dear Gordon?' Ashly thought to herself, 'in Switzerland stealing paintings by Paul Cézanne.'

"Gloria, you're looking great," Gordon at last elevated himself from his seat to hug the woman. "Have you met Ashly – she is advising me on modern art and other things," he said, twinkling mischievously.

"Ah, I see – other things. So you don't need us any longer?" Gloria flung a flippant remark. Looking at Ashly with a cool gleam in her eyes, she greeted her kindly in a smoky voice,

"Hello darling, nice to meet you," for a moment Gloria paused. Fluttering her heavy eyelashes, she added, "Keep an eye on our friend here and take good care of him,"

Then she turned towards Gordon,

"Well sweetie, I won't keep you two lovebirds any longer. Enjoy your evening. See you soon, darling." And with two kisses on Gordon's cheeks she left the table, striding towards the exit.

"Who was that?" Ashly was of course keen to find out.

"Gloria – one could say an old friend of mine," and looking into Ashly's face he added, "whenever I feel lonely she or one of her friends would come round to my place."

'Yeah,' Ashly thought – she sometimes had a wanton imagination, 'whenever you feel horny you would just summon one of those prostitutes.' But aloud she said sarcastically, "Oh poor Gordon, I didn't know you would even feel lonely."

"Yes sometimes I do," he confirmed in such an amiable way that he almost convinced Ashly. Gordon being so soft – she doubted indeed. That was a side of him which she hadn't noticed before.

"You know, men just do stupid things sometimes," Gordon went on, leaning over to take Ashly's hand. He was making her nervous. There was something in his tone that troubled Ashly.

'What on earth does he mean now?' she couldn't make up her mind what Gordon was referring to – stealing paintings or being with whores. It wasn't

the first time she had difficulties understanding him.
"Stupid things like what?" Ashly asked with a harsh sound in her voice.

'Why don't you come to the point?' she thought while a peculiar feeling took hold of her that things could get very ugly.

Gordon was clever enough to know what Ashly was aiming at. He was hesitating whether or not to let her in on his secrets. She probably wanted to know where he sojourned when he was occasionally out of town. However, the question was: could she cope with the truth?

Ashly was waiting for an answer while Gordon stared blankly at the bar, deliberating his next step. What did she want him to say? In fact, he thought, he didn't have to answer to her at all. Would she believe his story anyway?

"Tell me," she demanded, trying to catch his eye.

"Do you really want to know my opinion on the latest art heist in Geneva?" he asked her cagily, avoiding her gaze.

"Yes," Ashly nodded, tensely waiting for his story.

Gordon took a moment's thought and paused for effect. Then he began to speak slowly in a distinct voice, without looking up,

"I'm afraid it's out of my hands. I don't know much about that particular heist."

Lifting his head he glanced at Ashly, would she believe him? Ashly watched. She was waiting for him to say more.

"Somebody beat me to it and took the paintings before I even had a chance to get close to them," he disclosed, hoping Ashly wouldn't question him further.

"Aha!" Ashly replied, looking accusingly at Gordon, "So you admit that you are involved in stealing?" She fumed and brandished her finger in the air. "Not just petty thievery, but theft on a grand scale as far as I can see. Those paintings are worth several million dollars."

"Don't get so upset," Gordon countered, his smile vanishing. "Where do you think the money comes from to afford my lifestyle? Eating out in expensive restaurants and visiting exclusive nightclubs?"

He bent over and his intense blue eyes penetrated Ashly's eyes.

"You are about to break the rules, my dear!" he accused her hissing.

'Rules – which rules?' it crossed Ashly's mind. With a steady voice she replied,

"Gordon, you're not serious. You steal valuable paintings and now you're accusing me of breaking rules..." Ashly was completely lost what else to say. The occurrence many years ago, when she had been accused of handling a fake Paul Horton, which basically wasn't true, and the associated trouble it had caused, popped suddenly into her head. All she knew at the moment was that she didn't want to get involved in any underhand dealings – never mind *the rules*!

"So what?" Gordon was enraged, his blue eyes glittered dangerously. "I thought you liked being taken out to all these glamorous places and enjoying everything without question."

Ashly was quiet. Her brain was working full speed. She summarised – so far she had spent a wonderful if not bizarre time with Gordon. All she had to do occasionally was to translate a small art related text into Russian or vice versa into English. As business was not really her thing, she had simply done whatever Gordon had advised her to do. Sometimes he had asked her to render an expert opinion on a painting, mostly modern art. Very rarely had he wanted her expertise on older oil paintings. There was no doubt about it – she utterly enjoyed the glitzy time with Gordon. However, things had started to change and she didn't like it. How much longer was she going to play his game? Or maybe she was overreacting? Again, she was plagued by questions – that dreadful inner strife which she didn't want to endure any longer.

"I can't do with you being a liar," she decided to say after a while.

Gordon was angry. He should have never got himself into this conversation. Just by saying that he couldn't get close to the paintings, Ashly had jumped to the conclusion that he had stolen them!

"Who says that I'm involved in theft?" he demanded to know, not bothering to hide his anger.

"Are you not?"

"No!" he said emphatically with a quick glance at Ashly.

He was in a quandary. Should he let Ashly know that he urgently needed a painting by Cézanne for his rich Russian friend in New York who would pay him several million dollars? Yes, the heist in Switzerland would have been a good opportunity for him to obtain an original at a good price. Otherwise he had to forge one. In any case, he needed Ashly with her expertise. For him everything he had done so far with Ashly was an investment. He had gradually introduced her into the Russian art scene as a good, reliable art historian. And with Ashly's signature under the documents they wouldn't question or doubt the authenticity of any of the paintings he sold them. Gordon smiled to himself. So far Ashly had kept to the rules. He had more than one card up his sleeve, and if things didn't go according to *his* plan he had something more sinister in mind.

"Ashly trust me," he tried to appease her with a sweet smile, "I want you to believe me. I wasn't involved in the theft."

Was he bluffing? Ashly started to have misgivings and she was determined not to fall for his well-rehearsed excuses any more.

Bad news for Gordon – "I think we need a break," she said while considering if this was really the right thing to do.

"There can't be any necessity for that!" Gordon exclaimed with a threatening ring in his tone. Yes, he was fuming!

The situation was tense. Ashly, now feeling pressurized, was even more determined to distance herself from him.

"Frankly there is," she countered with a stiff smile, "I need some time to sort myself out."

"I have a better idea – we go home and have sex," Gordon suggested in a desperate attempt to appeal to her and tempt her with what he knew was something she could rarely decline.

"No Gordon," Ashly replied firmly. "I really need a break." She instinctively feared that things could get worse for her and pulled, what she called, the emergency handle.

He stared brazenly at her.

"You're not serious."

"Yes, I am. I have decided to put a temporary halt to our relationship," she said firmly and left the table.

◆◆◆

Ashly felt relieved having finally managed to tell Gordon she needed a respite from their relationship. Whereas she regarded it merely as a little holiday from her bizarre relationship with him, he was of course furious that Ashly had proved so strong-willed. She had pricked his pride and he felt his ego had been offended. Under no circumstances did he want to put up with this situation. He was angry that Ashly had so cold bloodedly rebuffed him, and was out for revenge. However, after some serious consideration he concluded that he still needed her for his own purposes. He had some influential clients who were desperate to buy art work from him, and each of them were prepared to pay him a fortune. It had been a major setback that he really hadn't had a look-in as far as the spoils of the latest heist in Switzerland were concerned. Someone else had been quicker than him. And now Ashly was causing additional trouble. So far, she had always played by the rules and had willingly signed the verifications of authenticity of paintings. If this was going to change now, he had to find a new way of authenticating the art works. For a moment he curbed his urge for revenge and considered if he could sweet-talk Ashly into continuing their relationship. She hadn't said it was definitely over – she only wanted a break. 'So be it', he calmed himself down. Otherwise, if Ashly refused to cooperate, he would simply forge her signature. He was working with some of the best forgers in the world. Forging a signature wasn't a big deal for these people.

Ashly wasn't knowingly aware of any of Gordon's ongoing forgeries. She simply sensed something wasn't to her liking. Then the whole situation with Ulrik, potentially leaving the country – it was all getting too much for her. She recognised how badly she had neglected her family because of her amorous escapades with Gordon. What had he really ever done apart from treating her to a lavish lifestyle from time to time and indulging her sexual desires?

'Diamonds are a girl's best friend' she smiled bitterly when she recalled the situation in the jewellery shop at the airport on their way to New York. 'First I was fired up for the beautiful sapphire ring and then Gordon dropped me like a hot potato,' it flashed through her thoughts. She was somehow disappointed and very angry. Fortunately she was neither the sort of woman who could easily be thrilled by generous presents, nor did she expect any sort of "big" presents from Gordon. Still – something was missing. Perhaps her mother was right – she should look out for a relationship with a decent man; one who was caring and sharing. Anything less wasn't good enough. For all that – could she really see herself married? No, not just yet! A good friendship, like the one with Ulrik, was sufficient. She didn't want to be pushed into anything serious or even marriage.

Suddenly she caught herself thinking of Ulrik. She became deeply concerned about what it would be like when he wasn't around any more. The thought made her agitated and fearful – what if Ulrik *was serious* and he was indeed going to leave the country? So far she hadn't taken him seriously. Perhaps she should rethink and imagine what her life would be like without him.

◆◆◆

Jake and Iris were naturally very happy when they found out about Ashly's decision to have a break from Gordon. Iris went straight to tell her friend

Dorothy.

"Imagine this – the Mystery Man is gone!" she exaggerated with a sweet smile in her face.

"Is he?" Dorothy was of course pleased about the good news.

"Yes!" Iris confirmed. She was proud of her daughter, "Ashly gave him the push."

"I don't think he was such a good choice for Ashly anyway," Dorothy remarked calmly.

"He definitely wasn't. Since she had been with him, she had changed so much. Just think what my girl may have got involved in…" Iris trailed off with a deep sigh.

"Ashly isn't stupid," Dorothy ascertained, "She wouldn't let herself get into trouble. Would she?"

"No, of course not!" Iris said firmly, and then asked her friend, "Did it ever occur to you how much this man's wheelings and dealings could have drawn Ashly into real trouble?"

"Oh dear! Well, we don't know anything about his ongoing business transactions. But it all seems dodgy and I dread to think what Ashly might have gotten into," Dorothy shook her head. She was convinced Gordon's dubious dealings could have proved dangerous for Ashly. "Have you any idea how Gordon took it? He may be out for revenge. Men like him do not take a snub easy."

Iris exhaled and staring at her friend, her voice shook with panic as she exclaimed,

"Dorothy! Don't say that – Revenge! I've just had enough of this Mr. Mystery and I simply can't take any more."

It had been a difficult time for Iris and she was hoping that her life would return to normal now that the case of Mr. Mystery was, in her opinion, resolved and closed. She certainly didn't want to reopen it.

Dorothy swallowed. According to her, Iris worried too much.

"I don't think your concerns are quite appropriate," she told her friend. "Don't take it so seriously. Things have changed now, and hopefully Ashly won't fall for such a man again."

"I'd like to think so too," Iris spoke in a halting voice. "I hope she'll find a nice man." And of course she had Ulrik in mind.

"Yes," Dorothy agreed immediately, "somebody who wants to be part of her life and makes us all feel better." She recollected how difficult the time had been for Iris and herself since this Australian stranger had entered into Ashly's life. Iris was a woman with a strong heart. Even so, Dorothy had noticed that her old friend had lost weight and her rosy cheeks had become pale. The strain had left its mark on Iris.

"To be honest, I've been feeling far from well recently," Iris confided in her friend, "Hopefully my nightmares are now over and I can sleep properly again."

"Yes, there are far better reasons than to rack your brain over that man Gordon. But remember – sleeping and eating are a must! Especially at our age," Dorothy admonished her.

"Oh, that reminds me of a dream I had," Iris interrupted her friend and waved her to be quiet. "There was a figure, all in white. I think it was an angel, calling me to come in...," Iris, with her eyes closed, tried to remember, "There was somebody beside me... I don't know who that was and what the angel wanted of me... It was all white. Like a ball of cotton wool, like clouds. The angel had opened his hands and was welcoming me..." Iris tried to put into words how she felt, "It was horrible... as if the angel had come to take me..." She kept it to herself that she had clearly seen Dorothy standing at her side in the dream. Now she feared that something dreadful may happen to her dear old friend. And that was what worried her most.

Dorothy listened, holding her breath. She, like Iris, believed that when an angel turns up in one's dream the message that is relayed must be heeded.

"Iris, don't you start all that. Our bridge round is getting smaller because so many people are dying," she said alarmed.

"Well, we reach the age when these things happen. The many old friends leaving us just shows that we too are getting older," Iris remarked with a touch of irony.

Dorothy couldn't make sense of what her friend was saying,

"Bear with me on this."

"Well, it's true! We become fewer and fewer," Iris explained with an ambiguous smile.

◆◆◆

Jake had been dying to tell Claire about his mother breaking off her relationship with Gordon. Like his grandmother he was convinced that his mother had finished the relationship with her lover for good – a relationship which he had always regarded as temporary anyway. Now, that Gordon was gone, he wished that his mother would start to date Ulrik and that they all would live like in his granny's fairy tales, 'happily-ever-after'. Especially since Claire had over time become inseparable from him, he hoped that their friendship would never end and perhaps one day they would all be one family.

"Guess what," he addressed his soulmate with a big smile, "my mum split up with Gordon."

"What a wise decision," the girl acknowledged and showing her delight, she added, "I knew she was a reasonable woman."

"I suppose this braggart is going crazy, now that my mum has jilted him."

"Oh dear," Claire said, trembling at the thought, "I hope he is not stalking your mum."

"Ha!" Jake exclaimed quite amused, "That would be the day."

Claire looked at him baffled,

"What do you mean? Can you enlighten me?"

"Think about it! That would be a good reason to report him to the police," Jake explained, triumphantly grinning from ear to ear.

"You may be right – I never saw it that way," Claire agreed, squatting down to her friend in the treehouse.

"I could never have seen Gordon as my father," Jake snapped. "Imagine...," he stopped abruptly.

"Imagine what?" Claire wanted to know.

"Well, how this poser would have been as my father," Jake aired his thoughts. "I had enough of him when we were at the Ice-Bowl." He shuddered as if to shake Gordon off.

"Do you ever see your real dad?" Claire asked

carefully.

"No, never," Jake answered, shaking his head and adding, "I really wonder how it would be to have a dad."

"Isn't it funny," Claire said with a smile, "You're missing a dad and I'm missing a mum."

"Yes," Jake readily agreed, "we could all be one family." And after a moment of silence, he added quietly, "In fact you and your dad – you are my family."

"Ah, that is so sweet of you," the girl hugged her friend. "By the way, my dad would definitely like us all to go to Sweden for the summer holidays. Did you know that according to legend the night before Midsummer's Day is a magical time for love?" Claire looked expectantly at Jake.

"What do you think?! Of course I know about your Swedish traditions. When the sun never sets and you dance around a suspiciously phallic pole," Jake countered with a big smile over his face.

"I know for sure that my dad would very much love to take your mum for a dance around the Maypole," the girl carried on, and looking at Jake chuckling, she added, "and I would like to do the same with you."

Jake didn't take the bait but smiled as he answered, "Oh yeah, have some more riotous entertainment in the evening, eh!"

"Yes, why not? That would be fine with me," Claire wasn't deterred.

"Yeah, good idea. But unfortunately not possible," Jake replied not very happy, "my mum has already booked us into a seaside resort for the summer, where I can have fun on the Big Dipper!!"

"You don't seem to like it?" Claire observed with a curious expression on her face.

"No. Not since my horrifying experience with this *Flying Carpet* some time ago," Jake confessed grimacing.

The two friends sat silently side by side when Jake broke the silence.

"You know, being a dad doesn't mean being related by blood. It's how you love someone."

Claire was honestly surprised and didn't know what to say. Even more so, as she didn't dare to tell Jake that in the coming holidays she would stay longer in Sweden than ever before, because her dad was in no rush to come back home. And then there was still her father's intention of taking a job in China, as soon as a suitable position became available. He wanted to get as far away from Ashly as possible.

Claire chewed her lips; she was somehow lost for words. After a moment of deliberation she changed the subject in order to avoid responding to Jake.

"Isn't it odd that we regard good looking people as

more trustworthy?"

"I know," the boy answered drily, "it's called the *halo – effect*. But if it is true, then Gordon must be a very trustworthy person. And isn't it strange that nobody, apart from my mother, had fallen for him?"

"Yes, that's right – when I saw him, he was indeed fabulous looking. I mean for a man of his age. Not bad," Claire admitted with a touch of admiration in her voice.

"Now, don't you start as well and fall for such a man," Jake told her teasingly.

"No, no, don't worry," Claire laughed. "External beauty doesn't matter to me."

◆◆◆

Ashly was in her room upstairs when she heard the front door slamming.

"Jake," she shouted down, "Did you have a good time at school?"

"Not too bad. I spent the afternoon with Claire," the boy mumbled languidly to his mother.

"How is your friend Claire?" Ashly asked. "Is she all right?"

'What a stupid question!' Jake thought and refused to answer.

"Can I assume that Claire is still your friend, or?"

Ashly provoked him playfully to bring him out of his shell.

"Yeah, we are friends," Jake finally replied. "Yeah, boys and girls are just friends."

'That's true,' Ashly was thinking of her late relationship with Gordon, wishing they had been as innocent friends just like Jake and Claire.

On her way downstairs Ashly heard voices. It was her mother chatting to Ulrik. What was she telling him? Soon after Ashly had told Iris that she had decided to have a break from Gordon, she had enquired if Ulrik knew about it and what he thought of it all.

"It's none of Ulrik's business what is going on between me and Gordon," she had told her mother angrily and thought she had made it quite clear that she didn't want any gossip spreading.

Who knows what Iris had told her friend Dorothy? Ashly could well imagine how the two would enjoy conversing over Gordon, the baddy. He was bread and butter for their gossip. For the two old friends, who had nothing much exciting going on, the latest news must have been like a thrilling mystery story.

'Let them have their fun,' she thought, at the same time asking whether she might have made a fool of herself being too indecisive and not having been able to make a clean cut with Gordon. Instead she had dithered for ages just like when she was with Rick. She felt suddenly rather ashamed.

"Hej Ulrik," Ashly greeted him in Swedish as she entered the living room. 'He's a good looking guy,' she realised. However, for now she'd had enough of men.

"Are you going to Sweden in the summer holidays?" she asked courteously

"Yes, yes. Definitely! As every year," he answered with a sheepish smile and quickly added, "But this time we are staying longer."

"Oh, are you," was all Ashly was able to utter.

"You know that you're always welcome to join us," the Swede invited her in a polite manner that was so typical for him. "We could dance around the Maypole," he added with a smile, knowing that it would remain wishful thinking. On balance, he was still very fond of Ashly, and it seemed that he couldn't escape from the only woman he had ever desired as much since his wife had died many years ago. Ashly was the only person, apart from his daughter, who had a firm place in his heart, and he continued to hope that she would return his feelings.

"Yes Ulrik, I know," Ashly replied, "Maybe next time."

He had heard this phrase from her so many times

and he was yet again deeply disappointed. He recalled what Natasha had advised him, "Give Ashly more time." His colleague had made a desperate attempt to stop him from going away and leaving everything behind. At the moment there was no suitable job anyway. China might be coming up in the near future. Should he not rather reconsider his plan? Had he considered all his options? Yes, he had and he didn't want to make a fool of himself any longer. Let Ashly be happy with Gordon. It was Natasha who had pointed out to him that Ashly may not even be happy with the man. The only thing her comments had done was to fire up Ulrik's hopes once again, which sadly was all in vain. In the end he gave up, realising that trying to get close to Ashly was like a minefield. Whenever he stepped forward and spoke to her he got hurt.

"Well, whenever you change your mind and decide to take down your walls, give me a ring," he finally said with a dash of bitterness and hurriedly left without a further glance.

Chapter Seventeen

Weeks turned into months and life at the McKenneth's had become quite tranquil. Since it was out in the open that Ulrik was looking for a job far away, he didn't drop by so often to say hello to Iris. She had difficulty getting over it. She really adored that fair and square Swedish guy and would definitely have loved to see him as her son-in-law.

"Have you considered that you aren't getting younger and a nice man on your side would do you good?" she asked Ashly repeatedly.

"Mum, why do you keep asking me that?"

"I just want you to do the right thing."

"Well, everything will fall into place when the time is right," Ashly expressed her view in a rather dour tone. She was tired of her mother's continuous admonitions.

In the meantime Claire and Jake were both going to grammar school which meant they didn't need to be looked after by Ashly or her mother any longer. The childminder, which Gordon had once organised for Jake, had also become obsolete. Ashly had decided that her son was now old enough to find his own way about and quite capable of taking the bus. She still saw Ulrik from to time, but it had obviously become significant less often.

Gordon had approached Ashly a few times. He didn't stalk her and she had of course not broken up with him, as everybody around her alleged. Nonetheless, they had agreed to stay loosely in touch through this time. It had become sort of an on-off relationship which they maintained. More *off* than *on*, because Ashly was determined not to let him get too close to her. But just when she thought everything was going fine and according to plan Gordon phoned her one morning in her office at work.

"Ashly dear," he oozed charm, "I need you. I have a problem with a painting and urgently need your expertise." He must have noticed that Ashly was totally taken aback because he hastened to add,

"I'll take you somewhere fancy – to New York for example, if you help me out on this. Promise!"

Ashly hesitated – his sweet talk was so different today. Did he really need her professional advice or was there more to it?

"What is it that you want me to do?" she asked curtly.

"I need you to certify the authenticity of a painting by Jasper Johns."

"Jasper Johns?" Ashly repeated, raising her eyebrows. "Do you mean the one who painted *The Flag?*"

"Yes exactly. That's the one."

"How did you come across a painting of his?" Ashly was very curious. She personally didn't like Johns' work which was best described as *pop-art*. "I suppose it is a painting, or?"

"Yes," Gordon reassured her, "A late work of his, rather unknown."

Ashly became suspicious. She wasn't very familiar with Johns, but she knew for sure that his — what she regarded as "weird" — paintings were much favoured by private collectors and were extremely difficult to acquire because of their rarity.

Gordon, waiting eagerly for an answer, pressed her, "So what do you say — can you come over to my place to sign the painting off?"

"If you expect a serious answer you have to give me a little time to think about it," Ashly replied briskly. She was annoyed.

"Ok, ok," Gordon, hoping to keep the peace, tried to appease her. He really needed her, "Whatever you

say dear. When does it suit you? And remember I'll treat you to another weekend trip to the Big Apple."
"I'll see what I can do," Ashly replied and hung up. How did he always manage to do it – twist her around his little finger?

◆◆◆

Somehow Gordon's request preyed on her mind. Ashly wasn't the sort of person who put things into cold storage. She was mulling over whether or not to spend the weekend with him. After all, a little bit of sex now and then wouldn't do any harm, she thought. So far Gordon had surprisingly played by her rules and abstained from sexually turning her on or teasing her. Well, he had tried to. Ashly had always hung up on him when he had become too persistent.

"Let him wait – that will spur his appetite for you," one of her friends had recently suggested when they were chatting about how to proceed with this handsome lover.

"Don't fall into his trap. He is using you!" her friend Claudia had strongly warned her over and over again. Ashly didn't want to listen and instead accused her friend of being envious and as a result evoked a violent altercation. A long period of frosty silence had ensued until Ashly had realised it was too ridiculous to argue over a man – especially this one – and possibly even lose her good friend because they disagreed about Gordon's motives. Remembering the proverb that it takes two to make a friendship and keep it alive, just as it does a quarrel, she and Claudia had fortunately reconciled.

"Go for him," a different friend had encouraged her, "Get as much pleasure as possible out of this gorgeous Australian. He might be using you – so what stops you from using him?"

Yes, if Gordon was playing games she could too, Ashly thought for a moment. Then again, she wasn't so sure and tended to agree with Claudia whose urgent words of warning stayed with her. What if he was using her? It might be an expensive gamble to get close with him again. There were still too many questions to be answered. How deep was his involvement in the second art heist in Switzerland, for example? But maybe she was on the wrong tack and should perhaps reconsider that he might be innocent?

'Whatever,' she thought with mixed feelings, 'I could do with a little bit of entertainment.' Seconds later she decided to send him a text. '*How about Saturday?*'

Surprise, surprise – Gordon, who had never been quick to answer Ashly's calls or texts, must have waited for her message because he swiftly replied, '*Ok. Around noon at my place.*'

All Ashly had to do now was to explain to her mother that she was going to meet Gordon on Saturday. 'A difficult task to undertake,' Ashly thought on her way home.

Explaining to Iris did indeed not go down too well. She was naturally taken by complete surprise, because she thought Gordon was dead and buried.

"How come that he has kindled an interest in you again?" Iris sighed, "Ashly honey, I hope you are doing the right thing."

"Yes mum, I hope so as well," Ashly replied with a smile, leaving her mother in the dark as to why she was seeing Gordon.

◆◆◆

When Ashly arrived at Gordon's place he didn't lose any time and instantly lured her over to his bed. His vivid blue eyes glinted with lust as he locked his hands behind her neck, kissing her gently. A delicious shiver seized her when he embraced her, making it impossible for her to move. And she wasn't sure if she wanted to disentangle from his strong arms anyway when he pulled her down on the bed, ripping off her clothes.

"You are making it very difficult for me to say *no*,"

she admitted when he was all over her, passionately kissing her.

"I missed you," he whispered, softly stroking her body. "Do you like me kissing you? Say that you missed me too." He didn't wait for an answer but went straight down, burying his head between Ashly's warm thighs.

"Ah, that's so good, so good," he went on fervently kissing Ashly. Her moans teased him into fiery desire. Noticing her arousal, he positioned himself on top of her and, sliding into her, he gently rocked her. It was difficult for Ashly not to scream too loud when she got carried away in pleasure.

"That was something else – sensational," Ashly said appreciatively. She greatly enjoyed feeling his wonderful body pressed tightly to hers as he was lying on top of her.

"I'll go and get us some champagne," he announced with a releasing movement and jumped out of bed. 'Well,' he thought on the way to the kitchen with a wicked grin, 'my job is done. Now it's her turn to do hers.'

With her head in the clouds, Ashly, enjoying Gordon's comfortable bed, looked out of the window. The sky was clear and blue. Luxuriating under the white linen sheets, she mused: had she allowed Gordon to go too far? No question – as always she had thoroughly enjoyed his love making. In some way, however, today was different. She was afraid to be left once more with no answers but only questions. And she didn't like the thought of it! She became aware that she would have to face reality, whether she liked it or not. Forget about craving spice in her life – it became more like salt in a wound. She, Ashly McKenneth, had to stand up and make a clean sweep of this false-hearted relationship. Was it a relationship at all? Was there anything she would have done differently so far? She felt suddenly as if she had to choose between Gordon and Ulrik. Then again, she didn't want to jump to conclusions. Gordon was a good lover, very seductive, and she hadn't been able to resist. But *exactly that* would have to change, she promised herself.

Gordon came back with the champagne.

"Everything all right?" he asked, his blue eyes piercing her.

"Yes, yes," Ashly assured, feeling like a child who has been caught with its hand in the cookie jar. She took the champagne glass which Gordon reached to her with a secretive smile on his face.

"Why do I always get the impression that you are hiding something?" she asked him, sipping the champagne.

"Maybe I am," he replied with a cryptic smile.

This time Ashly wasn't taken in by his seductiveness. "What about the Jasper Johns?" she asked, forcing herself to sound casual, while she left Gordon's luxurious bed, heading to the bathroom.

"I'll show you later," Gordon shouted after her when she disappeared into the shower.

◆◆◆

Relishing the feeling of the warm water running down her back, she gave it some thought. She was sure that Gordon wouldn't like her idea to finally split up.

'Let's see what that Jasper Johns is all about,' she decided. Wrapped up in Gordon's fluffy white bathrobe, she left the bathroom and walked slowly towards him, summoning a weak smile.

"So where is this artwork?" she asked while getting dressed.

Gordon came back with the painting. Stencilled words and numbers were covered under layers of explosive blue, red, and orange paint. It was immediately clear to her that it was a Jasper Johns. But was it real? If it was real, she was sure that it should be in a museum, like the Museum of Modern Art in New York. It simply didn't belong in Gordon's hands.

"Where are the papers from the tests?" she demanded, determined that without all the tests, she wouldn't sign the authentication.

"I have all the papers apart from one," Gordon answered, passing her the documents.

He was waiting patiently, while she took her time to go through the forms. Something wasn't right here. Yet she couldn't figure out what it was – the papers seemed genuine.

"I have grave doubts about the authenticity of the painting," she finally expressed her opinion, thus driving Gordon mad.

"But it is genuine – how can you doubt it?" Gordon became het up, his voice turning shrill.

"Well," Ashly remarked calmly, "there's still one more test pending."

"So what? That isn't of any importance, or is it?" he asked, his blue eyes glittering dangerously.

Ashly cleared her throat. She wasn't sure what to say. Her suspicion that Gordon was involved in some kind of skulduggery gained ground. Her face troubled, she sensed foul play.

"Ashly, dear come on – I need you to sign this painting off as genuine," Gordon changed tack, trying to beseech her. "It's for a rich client – for Fyodor and his wife Lyudmila Shevchenko. You know – the couple you met in New York."

Oh, yes Ashly remembered very well that filthy rich couple. How could she ever forget? Well, she thought, the Russian was once shocked to find out that he had been short-changed with a painting by Vasiliy Gribennikov. Finding out that this Jasper Johns was a fake would surely not go down well with him either. But she, Ashly McKenneth, wouldn't want to be held responsible for any wrong doing!

"He'll pay me one million dollars in brokerage fees. Such a deal doesn't often come my way," Gordon tried to persuade Ashly.

"I can't sign fake artwork!" she said, shaking her head and heading towards the door.

"Just a moment!" Gordon grabbed her by the arm. "Don't jeopardise my business!" he exclaimed with an intimidating tone in his voice.

"Your business – What about my reputation?" Ashly was infuriated. She wasn't going to risk her career for this man. At that very moment the scales fell from her eyes. How could she have been so dazzled? How could she have trusted Gordon's false words?

Gordon, taking up a threatening position, shouted at her,

"If you try to expose me you're wasting your time!" It was a feeble and desperate attempt, but it wasn't going to hold Ashly back. His anger was boiling.

"No Gordon, don't you worry – I won't expose you and your dirty deeds," Ashly replied with overblown sincerity, almost feeling sorry for him. "I simply have had enough of your wheelings and dealings."

"Oh, have you? All of a sudden, eh?" he turned nasty. "You'll be sorry!" Gordon threatened her, gripping her shoulder and shaking her.

"You are hurting me," Ashly objected, trying to get him to release his grip. "It's not just me – it's my son as well. He needs a father he can look up to. I doubt you are the right man."

"You and your damned brat," Gordon shoved her furiously towards the door. "Get out!" His rage palpable, he pushed her hard through the door and slammed it full tilt behind her.

Ashly was appalled. What had just happened? She hadn't expected Gordon to display such violence. While she was running down the stairs she felt empty and depressed. Worse – she somehow felt stupid that she had trusted this man and clutched at his demeanour as such an expert lover. There was nothing sexy about Gordon any more. He had just shown his true face and she had finally realised what he really was – cold blooded and ruthless. A bragger of the highest order, obsessed with money and sex. Fortunately the cold air, as Ashly headed to the taxi, made her feel better. 'At last I have become aware of his character before reaching the point of no return,' she thought and took a deep breath. There was one thing for sure – she'd had enough of spicy allures!

When she arrived home she didn't want to tell her mother about the scene with Gordon and tried to hide how utterly disappointed she was. But the very minute she quietly hugged her, Iris promptly noticed that her daughter was deeply upset and insisted Ashly told her the truth.

"See I told you, he wasn't the right man for you!" Iris remarked after finding out what had happened.

"Yes, you were right, mum," Ashly said regretfully, "Everything you said would happen did happen."

"Well," Iris replied, "whatever happened – life goes on. What about a cup of tea, honey?"

Chapter Eighteen

As time went by, Claire became more and more aware that she needed to tell Jake about her father's plans to move as far away as possible. She knew this would bring about a terrible change in their friendship and break Jake's heart. Then again, nothing was decided yet. And since she didn't want to be the bearer of bad news, she had kept putting off the serious talk.

It seemed strange to her – her father's plan to take up a job in faraway China, didn't take her too much by surprise. Since she was so interested in Chinese philosophy, she wasn't only ready to explore new places but actually liked the idea of living in China, the home of such famous philosophers as the ancient Confucius and Laozi.

One sunny day Claire carefully approached Jake and tried to bring the tricky problem home to him. Like so many times in the past, she started a conversation about a book she had recently come across.

"I had a heated discussion with my dad last week about a novel by a German author which I found very weird," she said.

"Let me guess – you don't mean Herman Hesse?" Jake asked with a tinge of disbelief. "I know this author. My granny has several of his books on her shelf."

"Yes, that's the one," she confirmed.

"Oh yeah, he is weird. I opened one of his books and tried to read it, but didn't understand what it was all about and quickly put the book away," Jake confessed, nodding bemused.

"My dad told me that his books are quite heavy stuff and difficult to understand. One might have to read it again to fully comprehend the message," Claire suggested.

"Maybe," Jake didn't really seem to be listening to what his friend was saying.

"As far as I understood from my dad, it's quite interesting how at one stage the author compares life as going through rooms," Claire chirped undeterred. "Once a room is explored you move on to the next one. That's how I feel at the moment. I've explored all the rooms here and now it's time for me to move on, exploring a new room."

"Yes, everyone has to go step by step his own way," Jake said rather morosely.

Never in his wildest dreams did he think that Claire would really move on and leave him behind. He drifted off into thoughts, until something deep down inside alerted him that Claire's going away might be a possibility. He became uncomfortable and even more caught up in thoughts. It wasn't so long ago that he had overheard a conversation between his mother and grandmother about Claire's father. Jake hoped, now that Gordon was gone, his mother would fall for Ulrik. But she wasn't the least bit interested in this nice Swede and Jake feared for the worst. So many times he had been imagining how it would be to spend his summer break with his friend. Perhaps they could all go together on a holiday to Sweden? He would have loved to! But when he had heard that his mother had rejected Claire's father, the young boy saw his dream burst like a bubble.

He experienced his anger rising at the thought his mother was somehow opposing him. Why couldn't she make an effort and show at least a little bit of fondness for Ulrik? Life would be so easy, he believed.

◆◆◆

Everything was so simple – at least for Jake and Claire that was. According to them, their parents were a perfect match. *They were made for each other!*

"As above so below," Jake philosophised while squatting on the treehouse porch, immersed in thought.

"What do you mean?" Claire asked him, furrowing her brow. "Do you mean that hard to watch thriller?"

"No, no – not that cheap horror rubbish. I mean the analogy – My mother is an art historian and your father is an archaeologist," Jake began to explain. "She is interested in everything artful *above* the ground and he is interested in everything *below* the ground."

"Ah, you mean what Isaac Newton once said: That which is below is like that which is above and that which is above is like that which is below," Claire answered back.

"Yes! Exactly! It's an ancient wisdom and means that everything on earth has its parallel in heaven. The galaxies up there," Jake pointed to the sky, "and the microbes below," he continued, pointing to the ground.

"Could one also say as large so small?" she wondered.

"Yes. Or as without so within," the boy confirmed and added, "everything is possible, as long as it's an analogy."

"I see," the girl said slowly. "So you mean my father and your mother are an analogy?"

"Well, not as persons," Jake responded, giggling. He was somehow at a loss with his own line of reasoning and tried to put his thoughts into words. Then, as if he had just come to a conclusion, he murmured, "There is nothing on earth that isn't in heaven."

"It would require magic," the girl took up the thread, "if *my* father and *your* mother were to get together. I know my dad was pretty disappointed ever since their first date and has suffered all the time because of your mum, and, you know, because of that man Gordon." She didn't dare telling Jake that her father's disappointment resulted in his wilful intent to move as far away from Ashly as possible.

"Yes I know," the boy asserted. "Unfortunately my mother seems to have a problem with your dad." The regret in his voice was unmistakable. A little while later he became enthusiastic. "Imagine this: If I want something to happen I must firmly believe that it will happen."

"You may be right. Magic and imagination …," she

hesitated for a moment before speaking on, "Do you think we should believe that a miracle will occur and that our parents get together?" She herself didn't really believe that her father would miraculously change his mind. Then again, one never knew.

"Wouldn't it be great? You and I would become siblings," Jake said, joyously looking at his friend.

"Yes!" she confirmed, somehow thrilled by Jake's thought. "It would be perfect for all of us," she paused distracted and then picked up the conversation again, "From another point of view, *desire and will* are in stark contrast to Buddhism. You know Buddhism," she thought aloud, "where the big thing is happiness. One of its key essentials is to let go of everything which makes you suffer. That includes actions as well as thoughts and feelings." Would Jake understand this hint that sooner or later he may have to let go of her?

As Jake didn't respond she continued,

"It's like crossing a river on a raft. Once you have reached the other side you don't need the raft any longer. So you let go of it. Otherwise it becomes a burden if you had to drag It behind on your way ahead."

"Yeah, unless you want to go back," Jake argued tartly. He was a bit grouchy today without knowing why.

What was wrong with him? Claire was astonished and so she replied,

"But you cannot go back! It will never be the same because everything is continuously changing in a split second."

Jake looked at her, raising his eyebrows up.

"Just look at a river," she explained, "its water is running ceaselessly and although it looks the same it's not." Then, she turned to Jake and asked him, "Anyway, why would you want to go back when you had decided you wanted to move forward?"

"I don't know. Maybe, because I left something behind or because I'm looking for somebody! Anyway, everybody is an individual and as such responsible for his own destiny." For a moment Jake came back as usual with rational arguments. "It's like a vicious circle: Your thoughts impact your feelings, your feelings impact your behaviour, and your behaviour impacts your actions."

"According to Buddha the purpose of life is to be happy. If you are happy from inside that will have an impact on the outside," the girl replied.

"Yes you see," Jake argued. He jumped up and stamped on the treehouse floor. Now being grumpy, he exclaimed, "I'm not happy at all!"

Claire looked at her friend and was speechless for a moment. This spontaneous outburst was quite contrary to his usual behaviour.

"Yes," he shouted while turning towards her, "I'm worried – worried, because my mum doesn't love your dad and worried that you will leave me."

This would have been a good opportunity to tell Jake the truth about her father's intentions. Claire was hesitant. As much as she looked forward to China, she felt sad just thinking that she might not be able to see her friend any more. As a matter of fact, her father had so far only *considered* working in China, but not yet decided. Everything might still be possible, she thought. So why should she trouble her friend?

"Well," she tried to calm him down, and with a charming smile she continued, "don't you worry – a bad penny always comes back."

Jake had cooled down in the meantime and he corrected her,

"It's a saying and you should say: *A bad penny always turns up*."

"Anyway, I like '*comes back*' better," the young girl said and looked at him.

For a moment their eyes met, but Jake broke off and swung down from the treehouse.

"Hey, my bad penny," he called up at her, "what about going shopping and spend some pennies tomorrow?"

"Why do you want to go shopping?" Claire asked. She was astounded, knowing that Jake didn't really like shopping.

"My granny's birthday is coming up and I need a present."

"Oh yes," Claire slapped her palm on her forehead, "I totally forgot about Iris' birthday."

◆◆◆

The next day, when Jake and Claire came up with the idea to go shopping downtown, Ashly was bemused where her son's sudden interest in shopping came from. She didn't make much of it when talking about it with her mother.

"It's all part of growing up," Iris reassured her. "Don't you remember how you liked to go downtown after school?"

Yes, Ashly did. She remembered vividly how she and her schoolmates had got into trouble because one of the girls turned out to be a kleptomaniac. Wherever they went the teenager would steal items so cleverly that nobody even noticed it. When the truth about the girl's behaviour had come to light, all the other girls turned away from her. 'What a poor girl,' Ashly thought, pondering for a second if Claire would have such a tendency. No, no – she rejected her thought out of hand – Claire was far too bright to get into such trouble.

Of course, it never dawned on the two teens to go on a shop lifting spree, but they were about to look for a present for Iris' upcoming birthday. Before they got anywhere near a shop, they almost bumped into Gordon. Claire spotted him first. Poking Jake, she called out, "Look, there is Gordon."
The downtown shopping area was a small strip of shops, not at all very special. One wouldn't expect to find Gordon here.
"Where?"
"Over there, at the shop."
"That's the address of Tim L. Wagner, the art dealer, who doesn't exist," Jake was baffled. "What is Gordon doing there?"
"Let's go and find out," Claire encouraged her friend, grabbing him by the arm and pulling him over the street.
In the meantime Gordon had left the shop, unaware that he was being shadowed by the two teens. He wouldn't have known Claire anyway, and Jake doubted if Gordon would have recognized him. The boy watched as the Australian walked to the parking lot, opened his car door, and drove off in his posh Bentley.
Nothing on the outside of the shop indicated what

kind of shop it was. The kids peered curiously through the dirty window, without being able to see much. It appeared as if the shop was being refurbished.

"Strange, very strange," Jake observed. He was hesitant to enter the place.

"Come on," Claire was all agog with curiosity, and becoming increasingly adamant, she pulled Jake by his arm into the shop.

"What are we doing here?" Jake, following her reluctantly, whispered anxiously. The shop was almost empty. Only a few slim rectangular packages, all different sizes, covered in brown wrapping paper were leaning against the naked walls. 'Paintings,' it leapt in his mind. Turning towards Claire and pointing at the packages, he asked astound,

"What are these?"

"Paintings?" Claire suggested, creasing her face into a frown.

"That's what I thought," Jake agreed in a whisper. "We should leave." He felt most uncomfortable in this odd place.

"No!" Claire insisted, "Relax. We're not leaving until we find out what this is all about."

"There look, there's a painting," Jake pointed at one of the square objects, standing on top of a pile of packages, opened. "I wonder if this is a genuine piece of art," he aired his suspicion.

"Can I help you?" a loud male voice from behind suddenly surprised the two teens.

Jake was startled and spun round,

"Um, yeah," he hemmed and hawed and, searching for words, he asked, "Is this painting genuine?"

"I'd think so," the slender, weaselly looking man answered, glaring with hard eyes at Jake and Claire who stood in front of the picture in question.

"What is in these packages?" Claire, sweetly smiling, was curious to know and pointed at the pile of objects.

"Art exhibits," the man, looking tough, said slickly, "They're being prepared for dispatch."

"Quite a lot," Jake remarked drily. He had counted at least seventeen bulky parcels.

Claire turned to the packages and peered at the address labels, checking where they were being sent.

"I see these exhibits are going to Russia," she said with a glimpse at Jake. The two teens looked at each other, laughing nervously.

"Can I ask why you are so interested in my business?" the shop owner quizzed them brusquely.

"I don't think these pieces of art are all genuine," Claire said pertly, eyeing the man with suspicion.

The bloke coughed – Claire knew she had hit a raw

nerve!

"What makes you think that?" he finally managed to say, sounding annoyed.

"Well," she resumed in a superior tone, turning to the bloke, "one wouldn't leave them standing here unattended if they were valuable." Examining a couple of them more closely, she spoke on, "And apart from that – where are the certifications of authenticity?"

"What would you know about such things?" he reproached her, cleaning his glasses. "And apart from that", he then repeated to Claire, "I already told you these exhibits are being picked up for dispatch."

At the same moment Jake stepped in, "My mother taught us all about the ins and outs of art." He looked triumphantly at the man, "She is an art historian, lecturing at the university."

"Ah, so you think you know all about selling and dispatching paintings, eh?"

"No, but I can sense skulduggery," Jake said undeterred, looking straight in the man's face.

"Skulduggery, eh? How can you be so sure I'm involved?" the weaselly looking shop owner drew near to Jake with a deep, piercing gaze.

Now Jake felt constrained. "I just assumed, because I saw Mr. Thompson coming out of your shop." He thought it might be best to tell the truth.

"Ah, interesting. How do you know Gordon?"

"My mother knew him," Jake explained tersely.

"Your mother? She isn't by any chance Ashly McKenneth?" raising his eyebrows, the man asked.

"Yes, she is," Jake replied, nodding affirmatively.

"I know your mother. She has a good reputation as an art historian," the bloke acknowledged. "In fact I've heard a lot about her."

Jake winced and then darted a questioning look at his opponent.

"What do you mean?"

"Wait, I'll show you something," the man rushed to what appeared to be a little office at the rear of the shop, obviously looking for something. "Here, I've got it," he shouted, waving a handful of papers.

"Look here," he showed one of the documents to Jake, pointing to the signature, "isn't this your mother's signature? She signed this painting off as being genuine."

"Claire, look at this," Jake was thunderstruck. There was no doubt – it was his mother's signature attesting the authenticity of a Jasper Johns painting. But the date – "See the date," Claire pointed out, "This was only recently. Your mother wasn't with Gordon then, was she?" she asked doubtfully.

"No, she wasn't!" Jake was one hundred percent

sure. "That must be the piece she refused to sign because she thought it was *NOT* genuine." He couldn't get his head around how his mother's signature could appear on that document. "Basically", he then said, turning towards Claire, "we must have been taken in by a forgery."

"See, I always felt that there was something not quite right about this Australian," Claire whispered and dragged Jake to the door.

◆◆◆

"Why shouldn't we report him to the police?" Claire asked when they were sitting in the living room, back at Iris' house.

"My mother might be compromised. It's her signature on the document," Jake replied, obviously he was very worried.

"But surely we should tip off the police," Claire resumed cool-headed.

"And my mother?" he objected. He was a bit on edge and worried as to exactly what might come next. "She would get into deep trouble and not only lose her reputation but her job as well."

"Sooner or later the truth will come out," Claire insisted unruffled.

"Yes, unfortunately for my mother. If this forgery is

uncovered – who knows what trouble she will get into," the boy voiced his concerns with a very agitated expression on his face.

"I wonder how these forgers are operating," Claire thought aloud.

"I have no idea," Jake responded, shrugging his shoulders.

Unexpectedly, Iris came in from the garden.

"How nice to see you, Claire," she greeted the girl with a friendly smile. "How was your downtown shopping?"

"Granny, we have a problem," Jake took the floor before Claire was able to answer.

"What is it?" Iris asked.

And then the two teenagers informed Iris what they had discovered, alternately nodding as one or the other told the sordid story. Iris listened in silence. She hadn't expected Gordon to turn up again and was of course not pleased to hear about his shady deeds. But had she not known all along? She took a deep breath.

"So what do you think we should do?" Jake broke the silence.

"Well, at least your mother has realised the perilous gamble with Mr. Mystery and stopped it before it was too late," Iris said, looking at her grandson. Jake and Claire nodded, waiting with bated breath to hear what else Iris had to say.

"It appears that this man must have forged both – the painting and your mother's signature under the assessment. What a shark!" Iris was aghast at the thought.

"Ah, YESS! That would explain it all!" Jake exclaimed assenting. And of course, since, in his mind, his mother was totally innocent, he sighed with relief.

"At least we have *that* question answered," Claire agreed, "It's pretty obvious, isn't it – Gordon was using Ashly. It's hard to believe that she meant nothing to him."

"Gosh, just imagine if my daughter would have gone any further with this smooth operator…" Iris abruptly trailed off.

"And just imagine – we wouldn't have known about it if Claire hadn't spotted Gordon downtown today!" Jake said.

"I hope that villain gets his just rewards!" Iris said. She despised the man. In her heart she was wounded at what he had done to her daughter.

"I guess we should tip off the police, even if we have no evidence," Claire proposed, gazing at Iris and Jake.

"We could do it anonymously," Jake seconded.

Iris didn't feel very comfortable at all with this proposal.

"It might be difficult to prove that Ashly wasn't involved. She had once been falsely accused of wrong doing," she gave cause for severe concern. Under no circumstances did she want the incrimination from the past to be repeated. Horrible visions, how her daughter might be heading to prison, danced in her head. She kept asking herself, 'What is right – what is wrong?' This situation was infuriating! Then she recalled what Dorothy always said, 'As long as you know what you're doing, you do the right thing.' Yes, but what was she doing?! 'The spirits that I called...' Iris remembered a line from a book, thinking that she would rather have a ghost in her house than being plagued by her daughter's ex-lover. Would that conman Gordon never stop haunting them? What would the implication of reporting him to the police be? Would things get better or worse?

Jake and Claire could hardly wait to hear what Iris would say.

"Granny, what do you suggest?" Jake raised the all-important question, looking expectantly at her.

With a very deep sigh Iris came finally up with a decision and said,

"Ok, I'll not allow my daughter to be ruined, but we have to put a stop to that scoundrel's activities," and with a serious look at her grandson she instructed him, "Jake, go ahead and report the whole case to the police. If possible do it anonymously."

◆◆◆

"What do you think we should do?" Jake consulted with Claire after they were alone.
"Let's check if we can file a crime report online," she suggested.
"Good idea."
"As always," Claire grinned.
"It's dead easy," Jake said when he had found the Crimestoppers' website. "We just have to fill in the questions." Looking at Claire he went on, "You know all the why's and wherefores ..."
"They want to know as much detailed information as possible," Claire pointed to one of the blank fields.
"And supporting evidence," Jake mumbled, "we have none. Why didn't we take any pictures?!"
"I find it difficult to explain which crime has been committed," Claire observed. "Especially since nobody got really hurt."
"Yeah, only a bunch of rich people got stung," Jake huffed.
"Let's see what we can write ... It's about a suspicious or unusual activity. Wouldn't you say so?" Claire pointed out, looking over Jake's

shoulder.

"Location, time and description of those involved," Jake read out to her. While Claire told him what to write he was filling in the spaces: Bangor High Street, eleven o'clock, Gordon Thompson, Australian national, and Tim L. Wagner, art dealer.

"Contact details," he turned towards Claire as he had reached the last question, "What do we write here?"

"Hm," Claire was thinking. "But we do want Gordon's days to victimise innocent women to be over," she said, "and that means we should be able to stay in touch with the police."

"So you reckon we should leave our contact details?" Jake was terribly conflicted as he didn't want his mum drawn into something which might turn out to be hard to deal with.

"Yes, of course. Maybe we should even go to the police station and report our observation and suspicion in person," Claire suggested.

"Whoa!!! Not so quick!" Jake objected. "What about my mum?"

"What about her? Talking to the police in person may help to provide the full picture and spare your mum from trouble," Claire argued. "Above all, our main concern is to bring Gordon to justice and help to protect other women from becoming his victims."

Despite the nagging thoughts, which consequences the whole incident might bring about for his mum, Jake was somewhat persuaded and half-heartedly agreed to go with Claire to the police station the next day.

Upon their arrival, he explained what his concern was all about.

"I'm in a quandary," he started in a low voice, "I would like to report a crime, but without getting my mum into trouble."

The police officer, smiling amused, seemed to understand and after assuring that all the information was treated confidentially, he called an officer dealing with fraud.

It took Jake and Claire the whole afternoon to answer all the questions, especially since it was difficult to explain plausible that Ashly hadn't been involved in the swindle – how was it possible that a renowned art historian and intelligent woman had fallen into a trap? The officer roamed over the two teenagers with a baffled look and jotted down something.

"That's an impossible story," his tone didn't sound encouraging.

Jake wished the whole thing would never have started, but refused to give up so easily. "Look," he stated, "my friend and I gave you all the information you requested. My mum was an apparent victim of that man Gordon Thompson. All I want is to bring him to justice and keep her out of trouble."

"I will see what I can do," the officer responded, his eyes fixed on Jake. And while guiding the two teens to the door, he assured, "I'll do my best not to get your mother into trouble."

Jake took a deep breath, standing outside the police building.

"Phew!" he expressed his apprehensions, "I hope this doesn't erupt into more hassle."

Chapter Nineteen

The whole incidence of Gordon's forgeries had taken a great toll on Ashly.
In the end, the police had decided to build a case and during the lengthy police investigation into the matter she had become very perturbed, leaving her to feel as if her whole life was off balance. Since the police hadn't been able to trace Gordon or any of his forged art works, they had finally concluded the case. Luckily for Ashly, Gordon had disappeared, hopefully never ever to surface again. And Ashly, being in the end acquitted of any suspicion, had decided she needed some laughter back in her life.

It was a nice sunny afternoon. Ashly had been invited to an early evening hangout with friends and they all met in a pub downtown. As the place was full with people, it was very noisy. Everybody seemed to have gone for a drink after work on that day. The eccentric group – Ashly and five mates who called themselves "artists" – found a little table where they altogether squeezed in. They were excitedly chattering, and Ashly could hardly make out what her jolly crowd was talking about, when all of a sudden an uneasy feeling took hold of her. It became so persistent that Ashly, who had just ordered another glass of wine, decided to abandon the evening.

"Dear friends, I would like to go home," she tried to escape the place.

"You can't leave us now," her friends cheered. "The evening has just started and we want to have fun!"

"No, please let me go. I have a terrible feeling something might have happened at home," she insisted.

"Ashly, dear, it will still be there when you get home," one of her friends tried to make a joke.

That didn't go down too well and spurred her on even more.

"And I thought you were my friends!" Ashly fired at the group.

"But we are – aren't we?" another friend said gaily, looking around seeking approval.

"If you were my friends, you would jump up and accompany me home. Because if my feeling is right and something has happened at home, I may need

the backing of a friend," Ashly told them off.
The cheerful crowd was staring at her. Then one broke the awkwardness and offered to take her home.
"No, but thanks anyway, I have my car. See you around next time," she asserted herself and hastily left the table.
"Yes, see you soon, Ashly. Take care," her friends called after her as she left the cosy pub in a panic.

◆◆◆

'Calm down, everything will be fine' Ashly tried to persuade herself, hastening to her car. She was so anxious that she could hardly get the key in the door. As never before, she drove home in a hurry, feeling so nervous as if she had an anthill inside her. The traffic was terrible. Nearly every traffic light was red, forcing her to wait, and thus escalating her nervous tension each time. Fortunately she had not drunk the second glass of wine. The way she was driving may have attracted the police. After what seemed hours to her she was finally near home. Taking a deep breath, she drove around the corner into the street leading to Iris' house, and then she saw it – the police car.
"No," she told herself, "that's not at our house!" But

it was. And as soon as she realised, her immediate concerns were for her mother and her son.

"Oh my God, something dreadful must have happened," she screamed when she stopped the car in the street, jumped out and started running towards the house. Her first impulse was that the house had been burgled. But there was no damage on the front door or in the hallway. She followed the voices into the living room. Iris wasn't there – her chair was visibly deserted. Where was she?

"Mum," Ashly called. And then turning to the two policemen, who had been waiting patiently, she shouted, "Where is my mother?"

"I'm sorry to inform you," one of the men addressed her, "there has been an accident."

Ashly was much too apprehensive to understand straightaway.

"What accident?" she demanded, her voice shaking with emotion.

"A car drove into Mrs. Mc Kenneth while she stood at the bus stop earlier this evening," the other policeman explained, keeping his voice low.

"Why was that? What was my mother doing at the bus stop?" Ashly was asking, anxiety tormenting her. Then she remembered that it was Iris' bridge evening and she must have been on her way to the venue.

"It was a hit and run incident," one of the policemen stated, "All we know is that it was a dark car with a little blue and white badge on the boot."

"Yes, according to one eyewitness, the black Audi sped off after hitting the woman. Whoever it was, had left her lying unconscious on the pavement. It was thanks to the eyewitness that an ambulance was called immediately," his colleague added.

"How is my mother? Where is she?"

"She is in a critical state in the City hospital. That's all I'm allowed to say," the first policeman answered short and crisp.

Ashly felt powerless. Right now she didn't know what to think or what to say. 'Dorothy,' it flashed suddenly through her mind, saying aloud,

"I must ring my mother's friend. She is probably wondering why my mother didn't turn up at the bridge round."

"I informed Dorothy," she heard Jake saying, "I was about to phone you, when she turned up here."

It was only now that Ashly became aware of her son and Dorothy being in the room.

"Ashly, I'm so sorry," Dorothy came with her arms open to embrace her. Big tears running silently down her cheeks.

"I'm driving to the hospital," Ashly said hurriedly, hoping it all was some horrible nightmare and her mother would be fine and everything would be back to normal tomorrow.

"I'll come with you," Jake and Dorothy called out simultaneously, hastily following Ashly.

◆◆◆

Ashly was speeding through the night to the hospital. She refused to think the worst. Her mother had always been inclined to 'worst case scenarios' – she had not. She shuddered at the thought of her mother lying severely injured in hospital. She didn't like hospitals anyway; that very distinctive odour of antiseptics, the long corridors with their bays, harbouring multifarious sick people, and doctors and nurses around them like busy bees in a beehive.
– 'Who does?' she thought

Dorothy was sitting silently in the passenger seat. 'Poor woman,' Ashly felt sorry for her. It must be hard to imagine her closest friend in such a critical state.

She tried to put on a brave face when they arrived at the hospital.

'After all, things may not be so bad', she thought on their way through the building. It took the little group some nerve racking time to find Iris eventually in the intensive care unit.

Ashly was the first to burst into the room, after the nurse had prepared her for the state her mother was in. It was indeed a terrible picture – Iris lying motionless in the white bed, unconscious and surrounded by numerous machines, all beeping and pumping, keeping her body functioning. It looked so alarming – her mother being connected to a whole series of tubes, wires, and cables. Obviously she was unable to breathe on her own.

Ashly was astonishingly composed, throwing a desperate look at Iris. She had never seen anybody in such a terrible state, let alone her mother.

"Mum," she said, stroking her mother's hand, "mum it's me, Ashly, your daughter. I love you." Tears were streaming down her face. She didn't know what else to say or do, being cautious not to touch Iris' hand with the needle connected to the drip feed.

Meanwhile Jake and Dorothy had entered the room. "Don't be afraid to see Mrs. Mc Kenneth with all the tubes and wires. These are life-saving measures," one of the nurses had explained to them. Still – it was too much for Dorothy. She broke down in tears. "Iris!" she cried, her voice shaking with pain. "Who did this to you?"

Somebody from the nursing staff tried to comfort Dorothy who broke down and sobbed uncontrollably.

"Perhaps it's better if you leave the room," the nurse suggested in a low voice and guided Dorothy gently out of the room.

Jake was also in a state of agitation and close to breaking out in tears. Was his beloved granny going to die? 'No', he pondered, praying that this would never happen. 'Whoever did this – I want this person brought to justice!' He wasn't in a rational state of mind, his body and brain screaming for vengeance. 'Cool it,' he then told himself. This situation, he knew, was tough. Desperation and appetite for vengeance would only make it worse.

"Granny, you're not ending up in the graveyard," he whispered, bending down to stroke her forehead. His voice was full of grief when he continued, "Where was your guardian angel? You always told me that everybody has a guardian angel looking after them – where was yours when you needed it?" Staring at his grandmother, with all the tubes and wires appearing so frightening, he wished himself somewhere else – somewhere in the countryside, at the lake where he went fishing with Ulrik and Claire. They hadn't been out there together at that peaceful place for a long time. ... Never in his life had Jake felt so lost and alone.

"Granny, please get better. I love you," he said,

struggling with his emotions.

It seemed so unreal. An awkward silence prevailed in the room, only to be broken by the constant noises from the various types of technical equipment. Iris lay in the bed, not responsive, her eyes closed, breathing through one of the machines supplying oxygen to her body.

"Jake, darling, come on – let's go. There's nothing we can do at present," Ashly seemed to be the only person at the moment who was strong enough and reasonable in view of this extraordinary difficult situation.

She tried to brace herself when the doctor spoke to her, after what seemed hours of waiting outside her mother's room. The whole situation was very tense and made her feel as if her heart was torn in pieces. 'Hope – never give up hope,' she tried to pacify herself.

"Do you know what is wrong with your mother?" the seemingly young doctor asked her.

Ashly shook her head, "No."

"She was knocked down by a car. Her head must have hit the ground very hard and when she fell, she must have hit her back on the curb," the doctor explained, "As a result she has multiple serious injuries, broken ribs, and collapsed lungs. But most worrying is the fracture of her skull, which means that she has a serious concussion, and she may be left with hearing and vision loss problems."

'If it's only that,' Ashly thought for a second, 'we will learn to live and cope with what lies ahead.' Although the doctor had spoken slowly and very clearly, Ashly was much too agitated to understand the full extent of what he had so kindly explained. She looked at him helplessly.

"We don't know for sure yet. Because of the injuries to her spinal cord your mother may be permanently paralyzed," the young doctor continued to give an account of Iris' injuries. "We may have to transfer her to our major trauma unit, as all these life-threatening wounds and multiple fractures could result in serious disability or even death."

"Doctor, you scare the life out of me," Ashly was totally crestfallen and confused.

"I am obliged to tell you," he replied drily.

"You mentioned death – what are my mother's chances of getting well?" she wanted to know.

"That is hard to say. At the moment she is stabilized and we are administering Morphine to her. It all depends how she does overnight," the medic said. And when he noticed Ashly's anxiousness, he quickly added, "Look, there is nothing you can do for your mother tonight. You should get some rest for yourself."

"Yes, thank you doctor," Ashly finished the conversation, torn between dread and optimism.
Seeing Iris in such a terrible state was a grievous blow for the three and they left the hospital in very low spirits.

◆◆◆

The night was mild and clear when they were heading home. All that mattered now was that Iris would recover from her injuries. Needless to say neither Ashly nor her son or Dorothy found any sleep. The worry that the hospital might phone at any time kept them awake, and visions of Iris, how she was lying so brutally injured in her bed, were haunting their thoughts.
The following weeks were marked by fear and hope. The house simply didn't feel the same with Iris missing. Everybody wished a miracle would happen and Iris would at least wake up from her coma. But there was no improvement. On the contrary – Iris' condition worsened. And one day the doctor suggested to Ashly,
"You might consider switching off the machines."
It took her some time to digest what she had just heard and get the picture. Should she be made responsible for the life or death of her mother? No! No way! She wasn't going to kill her mother! She

was still optimistic that things could take a turn for the better.

"Mum," Jake said, "if granny doesn't wake up from the coma, she may as well pass away peacefully. All these machines – what good do they do? And even if she does wake up – her life wouldn't be the same. She would be totally dependent on other people for help.

"I don't know. I simply don't know. I have a bad feeling about switching off the life-saving machines," Ashly muttered. She was unable to think reasonably.

Only a few days later the unavoidable couldn't be put off any longer, and the inevitable caught up with Iris' family.

Ashly wasn't in the room when the phone rang. Jake heard it and fear gripped his stomach immediately. 'No, don't tell me that...' he thought when he lifted the phone.

"Mr. McKenneth?" he heard a woman's voice at the other end, "This is Dawn from the hospital speaking. There is no easy way to tell you that your grandmother passed peacefully away in the early hours of the morning. I am so sorry for your loss."

"She passed away?" he repeated faintly, feeling as if he had been hit with a brick, and after thanking the nurse he quickly hung up. He shook his head in disbelief. "No, no way was she gone!" he exclaimed, tears running down his face. He sank down on the chair – his granny's chair – and buried his head in his hands. It took him a moment to work out what he had just been told on the phone. He stared motionless into space until he heard his mother coming down the stairs.

Ashly, seeing her son bereft in the chair with his head down, wept silently. She knew it must have been the phone call they all had been dreading for weeks. Unable to say anything she sank down on the settee. She should be crying out aloud that her mother was gone – shouldn't she? She should show how heartbroken she was that her mother wasn't there any more. But she couldn't. Succumbed to grief, she dipped into the past, vividly recalling her mother being her best friend. She had never been stuck for somebody to watch Jake. Iris had always been there to fill the gap. And her mother would stand by her in the most difficult times. Ashly cast a glance around the room and took a deep breath – all the happy years they spent together in this snug house.

"Was that the phone call from the hospital?" she asked shakily. "Granny – is she..." Ashly was unable to finish the sentence.

"Yes, mum," Jake answered, fighting with his tears,

"sadly it's true – granny passed away."

Ashly, like her son, was devastated. Tears were spilling down her cheeks.

"What now?" she asked, trying to stifle her grief, not really expecting any response from Jake.

"It was the best for granny," Jake nodded slowly, looking down.

"Yes," Ashly agreed hesitantly. Despite that sense of loss and all her grief she felt somehow relieved at the thought that her mother must have sensed her distressful doubts about switching off the machines and had granted her a last favour by saving her from having to make such a decision – a decision which would have been the hardest ever in Ashly's life.

◆◆◆

In the subsequent days Ashly was busy arranging her mother's funeral. Iris' tragic death, following the accident, hit Ashly so hard – she hadn't even had a chance to talk with her about her last wishes.

"Decisions, decisions," Ashly wailed despairingly, lifting her hands up to her head. The very idea of arranging her mother's funeral was both stressful and draining for her. There were so many questions to ask about the funeral: what type of coffin would Iris have wanted and would she have preferred to be cremated or rather buried? Every day her mother wasn't there Ashly realised how much she missed her. Not just that, but she noticed how much she needed her mother's invaluable advice and support. She started crying, as she just realised that she had never told her mother how much she admired her for her tender, love and care, and her astuteness.

It was difficult for everybody to believe that Iris was gone for good.

Who was that damned driver who had taken his granny away from him? Jake mourned for his beloved granny, unable to describe the feelings that went through him since he had seen her last: lying in the hospital bed – white like the blankets, but as if she was peacefully asleep.

Poor Dorothy – she felt the same as Ashly and Jake, grieving her loss and being completely bewildered. The unforeseen death of her best friend, with whom she had walked such a long way, was heavily eating on her, and the hit and run accident preyed heavily on her mind.

"Snatched from this life," she repeated to herself several times, crying and wiping her tears with a handkerchief. "I never thought that your mother would be right, even beyond her death," she snivelled, "our bridge friends are getting fewer and fewer."

"Dorothy perhaps you can help me with this – did my mother ever mention to you anything about her funeral?" Ashly, who was at a total loss with the funeral arrangements, hoped to get some support from Dorothy in this difficult situation.

"Well, not directly," Dorothy wiped her nose and replied haltingly, "You know how one talks when someone passes away – Iris mentioned that she would want a quiet funeral ... her ashes buried in the back garden."

"So she wanted to be cremated?"

"Oh, yes," Dorothy confirmed. "We had lots of discussions about that. I personally wouldn't want to be burned. But Iris always said that it would be better to be cremated and get quickly over with rather than being buried and slowly eaten by all sorts of insects."

Ashly shuddered at the thought of a body being burned. Though, lying in a black box, covered with tonnes of soil, wasn't a pleasant option either. On the whole, it was a question of where does the *physical body* go after death? 'The body', she thought, trying to compose her mind, 'is just a husk which keeps a human being together. There's more than just bones and skin – there's also mind and soul. What happens to the soul of a dead person?'

"I agree. Cremation would be the easiest way to bury my mum," Ashly said, turning her head to the more practical tasks ahead.

"As far as I know Iris wouldn't have wanted a pompous funeral. A simple memorial would definitely take her wishes into account," Dorothy affirmed.

"My mother would have liked us all to be happy and celebrate the life she had lived, wouldn't she?"

"Definitely," Dorothy started crying again by the thought that her best friend was gone forever. "Ashly, darling, you should use a funeral director," she recommended, snivelling and blowing her nose again. One could see how difficult it was for her to come to terms with Iris' death.

"Yes, I guess I'll have to do so," Ashly replied in a halting voice and set about doing just that.

◆◆◆

Despite Ashly's efforts to keep it a quiet funeral, so many people, who knew and loved Iris, turned up at the memorial service to show their respect. In order to fulfil her mother's last wish and to celebrate the life Iris lived, Ashly had asked for a civil funeral. The Celebrant gave a wonderful tribute to Iris and her life... *There is a lot I could say about Iris... It is difficult to describe her in a few words... She was an incredible character with lots of talents who fascinated people with her spirit... Her sense of justness was enormous and so was her wisdom...*

Everybody struggled to cope with the death of Iris. For the Mc Kenneth's it was a painful and distressing time. Jake was riven by grief. He really wanted to cry but found it hard to do so. It was Claire who tried to soothe his pain, and for Jake it was one way to share his feelings, blissfully unaware that there was worse to come his way.

Iris' death had left the girl shattered too. She had known her more than seven years and Iris had become like a second grandmother to her.

"Do you remember the discussion we once had in the treehouse, when we spoke about Buddhism?" she asked her friend gently.

Jake was however in no mood to discuss philosophical questions at the moment.

"Let go," she told him in a low voice, "To love a person means to let go..." Her well-intentioned words were ambiguous. Claire might not have been aware that she had unintentionally just made a reference to the fact she would have to let go of her friend shortly.

Jake brushed his hair from his forehead and roughly

wiped away his tears.

"What would you know," he snapped at her. "How could my granny do this to me – leaving me alone? I wish she was back." His grief was devastating.

It was a difficult situation for Claire. She couldn't think what to say. How could she describe the feelings she had for Iris *and* for Jake? Then she looked past him and said, gazing into the distance,

"Granny is dead and cannot come back. Not in the way we want her to."

Jake stood there; with his arms tightly crossed he experienced a flush of inexplicable discomfort. It was wrong, all wrong. He wanted to cry. Tears were filling his eyes. He dropped his arms and let Claire wrap her arms around him.

"She left us a treasure – all these invaluable memories of her," the girl tried to pacify him, despite having difficulties with her own emotions. She vaguely remembered the loss of her mother and the pain and emptiness her death had left at the time. Deep down Claire was sure her mum was looking out for her, and that thought had always comforted her and given her peace when she needed it the most.

"Do you remember the day when we went downtown to the movies to see *The Nightmare before Christmas*?" she gave her best to take Jake's mind off things.

"Oh yes, we had so much fun speaking in that funny language which even we didn't understand," he replied chirpily. Then he exclaimed with a black look, "That was also the day we spotted Gordon with my mother!"

"Sure it was," Claire nodded. "Anyway, Iris you and I were a good team to find out about this man's misdeeds – weren't we?" she said cheerfully and nudged him gently.

"I wish he could have died instead of my granny," the bitterness in his tone was undeniable. "And then that damned driver who took away my granny," Jake exclaimed, adding angrily, "I want revenge!"

"That wouldn't bring granny back," Claire said, "let justice run its course." She breathed in, a deep, shaking breath. Then she looked down, noticing her shoes – dirty from the graveyard where they had just buried Iris' ashes. She wanted to scream, wanted to get rid of that dreadful feeling, that haunting memory when the urn had been let down in the hole and Dorothy crying, "That's all that's left of my friend."

'Don't even think about it,' jumped through her mind. She pushed her feelings aside and said with a weak smile,

"Granny isn't dead as long as she lives on in our hearts. Remember the fairy tales she used to tell us?"

"Oh yes," Jake answered, picturing how he and Claire had snuggled up on the cosy, old settee and his grandmother, with her glasses on, had read out the tales from her *big book*. After a while he continued with a soft smile around his lips, "And the stories always ended with the line 'and they lived happily ever after'."

"Yes I remember," Claire said bemused. "I'm sure Iris would want us to do the same." She didn't dare to divulge to Jake that her father was considering working in China, which implied leaving Jake and everything else behind. 'Not yet,' she thought, chewing her lips.

Lifting his head, Jake looked at his friend, raising his eyebrows. Obviously he hadn't understood what she was trying to tell him.

"Well," Claire began to speak, "just like in her fairy tales, granny would have wanted us to live happily." She deliberately didn't mention the all-important word 'together'. How would a happily living together be possible if they lived apart in the future?

"Never mind," she continued softly, as she didn't receive a response from her friend. And then, out of the blue, she added faintly,

"You know, a bad penny always comes back."

Yet Jake was too devastated, mourning his grandmother's passing to comprehend the full dimension of what Claire had just said.

Chapter Twenty

In the painful aftermath of Iris' passing, Ulrik continued to be a steadfast friend to Ashly, not having the courage to tell her anything about his plans of taking up a career in China. Apart from one, the rare offers hadn't been very appealing, and so far he had hesitated to accept any of them. Then the unforeseen death of Iris – he hadn't wanted to burden Ashly with his intentions. She obviously needed support at this hard time, following the loss of her mother. His condolences at the funeral had been truthfully sincere, and he had received the impression that Ashly appreciated him being there for her. He still very much hoped that Ashly would love him for other reasons too; regrettably he never got anything in return.

"Has any other man ever done that for Ashly?" one of his mates had asked him not so long ago. "You're casting pearls before swine."

For goodness sake! What was he supposed to do? "Don't read anything in to it," Ashly had many times warned him when he had tried to win her affection. Yes, he would have loved to court her and didn't want to go on just being friends with her. But his friend's bold remarks had opened his eyes. Why wait any longer for a woman who may never return his feelings? Obviously his love was unrequited! Of course, he was disappointed. Indeed very disappointed! Ashly unfailingly avoided any intimate situations with him. 'It may go on forever,' he speculated. In addition, his secret lover had broken up with him after all these years of hourly enjoyment in the hotel bed. Her husband must have got wind of his wife's playing away and had threatened to divorce her. There was nothing left to hold Ulrik here.

After turning his thoughts over and over again, he finally came up with the conclusion that he might just as well start a new life somewhere else. Lost in contemplation, he realised that he couldn't turn the clock back. When it came to decision-making Ulrik often regarded himself as inflexible as a tank. Once he set his mind on a certain direction, he could — just like a tank — not easily turn around and change direction. At present, his mind was set on getting away as far as possible from Ashly – so why not apply for the latest position in China which had been in the offing for some time now?!

With a great deal of trepidation he submitted his application, not knowing if he would be successful and set the ball rolling. A few weeks later he received the good news and was offered a contract. For a moment he vacillated to sign the papers, but the offer was too good to reject, and so he finally decided to go ahead with it.

When he told his daughter about his irrevocable decision, she was excited by the thought of living in China. She, like the rest of the Mc Kenneth family, was mourning Iris' death. By grabbing the chance of living far away, she sought to flee the excruciating pain of granny's passing. To her, China was basically something exceedingly unusual.

"Who goes to China?" she asked enthusiastically, looking forward to a new challenge. Ulrik, however, was astonished that his daughter seemed to take the migration to a faraway country so easily.

"What about Jake?" he asked rather vaguely, because he didn't want to discourage her from their move to the Far East.

"Yes," Claire agreed hesitantly. Excitement fighting

with doubts caught up in her mind when she continued, "That might be a problem. But what choice do I have?" She glanced at her father, not really expecting him to answer.

Ulrik was glad that his daughter was so reasonable. Claire had given him no trouble – not like Ashly, when he revealed his plans to her.

He turned up at Iris' old house one day, very much to the surprise of Ashly. Since he had never been a man of many words, he laid it on the line that he was leaving the country to work in China. Although Ashly had been aware of his insinuations in the past, the news hit her like a bombshell.

"I just came to say goodbye to you," Ulrik said, polite as always, when Ashly opened the door.

"Goodbye?" she wondered, "Why is this?"

"Claire and I are leaving for China. I was offered a good job there which I can't refuse." Standing on the doorstep, he staked everything on one card, confronting Ashly with his intent.

Ashly stared at Ulrik, her eyes wide open. She had never heard him so measured.

"You're not," it was more a desperate question than a serious statement.

"Yes – we are leaving shortly," Ulrik confirmed steady as a rock. Having made up his mind to take the job in China, his plans were irrevocably fixed.

Ashly swallowed. She stared at him in disbelief. Never had she assumed that Ulrik would really leave. Then again, she should have known better.

"What about Claire and Jake?" she asked abashed, knowing full well it would break her son's heart when his soulmate left.

"Well, Claire is looking forward to China. If you don't mind I would very much like you to tell Jake," Ulrik said and drew near Ashly to hug her.

She flinched appalled.

"Why me? You and Claire are the ones leaving and breaking everybody's heart!" Ashly was angry. Poking her finger on Ulrik's chest, she continued reproachfully, "You should have the decency to tell Jake."

"Ashly, you know this isn't true," Ulrik defended himself. "YOU leave me with no other option but to go as far away as possible! It's YOUR responsibility to explain to your son."

His words hit her hard. This was all going horribly awry. She looked at him, unable to say anything. Her heart raced at high speed and her throat felt like she would choke, which made it impossible to get a word out. What could she possibly say to persuade him?

"Aleae iactati sunt," Ulrik said wryly. Normally he

wouldn't show off with his Latin. Yet, in this case it was true – the dice were cast. "I'll keep my email address. In case YOU change your mind and want to contact me," he told Ashly. Then he turned around and walked without wasting any more words to his vintage Volvo, turned the engine on, and unhesitatingly drove off.

◆◆◆

What had just happened? Ashly was much too ruffled to think straight. Ulrik and Claire were leaving. And so very far away – China. It seemed like they were going to the end of the world. And she hadn't kissed him goodbye. She was in complete turmoil. All sorts of thoughts bustled in her head, preventing her from thinking clearly. What was she going to say to Jake? Surely Claire had informed him already, had she not?

Yes, Claire had, since she knew her father's decision was final. Gingerly, shilly-shallying, fully aware that there was no easy way to tell Jake about her moving to China. "Jake, we have to talk – you know the bad penny which is coming back ...," she had approached him twice lately, never to be taken seriously by Jake.

Why should he listen to her? Claire wasn't a "bad penny" and Jake didn't like her saying so! He turned away from her, grim faced, not heeding any of her warnings and instead simply ignoring everything she said.

Then came the day she couldn't avoid the truth any longer and told him,

"I'm going to leave you." And as Jake didn't respond, she continued, trying to cheer him up, "China will be great. We can write emails."

But again, he didn't react.

Silently he took the pendant she gave him – one half of a broken heart, as a sign of their true love – and vaguely perceived Claire's last words,

"I'm sure we will meet again."

Unmoved, he looked at the pendant in his hand. His thoughts were dark – his granny had just left him. If Claire was going to leave him as well, he would be absolutely shattered. Instantly he realised that she meant so much to him. He didn't want to lose her and the very moment Claire had told him that she was leaving for China, he felt like he was swallowed by a sinkhole. Unable to say anything, he had only stared blankly at her. And then they had parted tight-lipped, leaving him to firmly believe everything would be as always and he would see her after the weekend at school. Alas, by the time he realised that the chair next to him in the classroom would stay empty, Claire had already left for good.

◆◆◆

Ashly realised what was at stake. With a tinge of guilt she carefully tried to speak with her son when he was home from school. It came to him as a terrible shock, and he went berserk the very moment he fully grasped that Ulrik and more so Claire had left for good. His dream of having a nice holiday together in Sweden had brutally come to an end.

"That's all your fault!" he accused his mother instantly. He was furious at her and shouted repeatedly, "I hate you. I hate you!"

After a heated spat with his mother, he slammed the door in anger and, while bursting into a flood of tears, he ran upstairs to his room. Throwing himself down on the bed, he hid his head under the pillow and remained there, fighting with the pillow and his tears for quite a while. He was depressed and angry. Most of all, he was angry with himself when he realised that he had been too stubborn to take a note when Claire had tried to tell him she was leaving for China. Just like his mother, who had never listened to what her mother said about Gordon, Jake hadn't listen to what his friend had to say to him. The stubbornness seemed to run through the family. Even so, this late insight didn't bring Claire back. She was gone! The thought swept a wave of sadness over him. Then again – would she not be bored to death living in China? Would she not rather stay here where they had been so happy together? Jake knew it was impossible, but nonetheless he hoped that a miracle would happen, making Claire to change her plans at the last moment. But the girl had been far from doing so. She and her father had left at the weekend, her eyes fixed on China and the prospect of new exciting challenges over there.

Unlike Claire, who was looking forward to her new life, Jake was shaken to the core by the news of her departure. The following months were like a never-ending nightmare for him. Ashly could see the pain in her son's eyes. Instinctively it became clear to her that wallowing in memories and getting caught up in each other's blame wasn't appropriate right now. Without Ulrik at her side or her mother to resort to, her life was truly off balance. And so was her son's. She had always tried to keep him free of emotional complications. In the end it appeared the complications had become overpowering. She realised that she had to reclaim her life, which meant changes had to be made for herself and for Jake.

"I wish this whole mess had never happened," she said and slouched her shoulders, feeling full of despair, now even more so as she could no longer consult with her mother. Incredible frustration welled up inside her.

However, the love for her son made Ashly push aside for the moment all the misery of the past months. There was nothing she could have done to prevent her mother's death following the hit-and-run accident. And then the episode with Gordon – the hot lover from Australia! She had enjoyed a crazy time with him, but totally misjudged him. He had spiced up her life a little bit too much. Should she condemn him for what he had done?

Shrouded in thoughts, she remembered all of a sudden the words of Edith Piaf, the "Little Sparrow", whose grave she had seen in Paris, "*Je ne regrette rien – I regret nothing*".

"That's right," she exclaimed after a while of contemplation. With her posture upright and a smile on her face, she clapped her hands and declared,

"Every cloud has a silver lining!"

Ashly certainly didn't want to make a career out of

being unhappy. All that mattered now was: what was she going to do? Putting the past away, she focused on her next task — to get back on her feet and not let anybody or anything get in her way.

◆◆◆

While Ulrik and Claire had been busy with their departure to China, Jake was totally heartbroken. Since the death of Iris, the house had felt empty and cold. The boy missed his granny sorely and now his soulmate Claire as well. Especially at school it became soon apparent for him how much he truly missed his friend. The place next to him stayed empty. He had nobody to talk with. There was no *'see you tomorrow'* any more. Claire had always been someone really special to him and thoughts of her kept tossing around in his head. Now that she had gone, he missed her from the bottom of his heart.

"Claire, I miss you. I wish you were here. Why did you clear off?" he kept asking in despair.

He was totally miserable without her and felt like an empty shell. Life wasn't the same any more. Whatever he was eating tasted like straw. Not that he actually knew how straw tasted, but his food was dull – just like his daily life.

On top of his gloomy days he had sleepless nights. Restlessly he lay awake in his bed, going back through the happy times with Claire, becoming more and more aware of how much she really meant to him. His emotions kept him twisting and turning in his bed – something he had never experienced before. Now and then a woman turned up in his dreams, sometimes haunting him. All he remembered, when he woke up the next morning, was that it hadn't been Claire.

At the tender age of fifteen Jake was becoming keen on girls and dating, although he knew it was impossible to find a friend like Claire again. There were some nice girls in his school who had cast a desirous eye on the handsome young Jake. But none of them unleashed the interest, let alone the passion in him!

"He is so wickedly sweet," the girls were sweet on Jake and eager to date him. With his black hair he looked like his father, but his facial features were much softer than Rick's. And he also seemed to have the same charisma as his father, since so many girls were crazy about him when they heard that Claire had left. Jake never had a serious crush on any of the girls and never got himself involved in any serious relationship. Nothing compared to Claire, her wits and charm, her red hair and freckles.

After a while he started to feel isolated and lonely at school and everywhere else.

He rapidly lost interest in his environment and, by neglecting his schoolwork, his performance in school worsened sharply. Only Claire mattered to him, feeling his heart beat faster every time he thought of her. After school he often prowled around the places where he had been with her, only to become more and more frustrated and angry with himself. Sometimes he played truant, rushing to Claire's old house with the sign that the house was for sale clearly visible, until one day the sign was gone and the house had obviously been sold. Standing in front of the house, Jake wallowed in memories how they had been sitting in the treehouse, debating over anything and everything. Ah, what a wonderful time they had spent together! Why had he not paid more attention when Claire told him that she would leave him one day? Could he have stopped her from going to China? He remembered Claire's words – if you really love someone you have to let go. If China meant so much to her, he didn't want to be the person who kept her from such a great adventure.

Driven by love-sickness, he every so often went to the nearby lake, where he and Claire had been having so much fun together when fishing with

Ulrik. Sitting on one of the rocks and staring at the calm water of the lake, he tried to soothe his irrecoverable loss by hoping to see Claire right now. 'Believe in miracles, because they do happen,' he tried to persuade himself that Claire would turn up any minute. But no – she had disappeared, leaving him with a broken heart in the truest sense. Not only with the pendant, she had given him on the very day she had said goodbye to him, but also with a dark hole in his heart which was clouding his mind. Yes, he had great difficulties coming to terms with his emotions. All his life he had been taught languages, philosophy, maths, and all about art, yet nobody had ever explained to him what to do with his emotions if he should be lovelorn. Following a first impulse, he never wanted to see Claire again.

'She is gone – far away, unreachable,' he convinced himself. She didn't care about him – or did she? He was fighting with his agonizing grief. In reality he would have loved to phone her, just to listen to her voice. He wished he could tell her how he felt, how much he missed her. He wished he could hold her close, realising at the same instant that he had never felt this way about a girl before and that he had never given Claire a real kiss.

In all his despair he recollected Claire's words: "A bad penny always comes back."…. He blamed himself for having corrected her with a tinge of drollery, "A bad penny always turns up…" Having regarded Claire always as his treasure, she was by no means a bad penny to him! Never in his wildest dreams did he think that she seriously meant to go away. "Damn it," he hissed, "I should have figured it out before it was too late! Bad penny or not – come back or turn up. It doesn't matter. All I want is Claire."

Jake felt like a fool when walking back home from the lake, frustrated and angry with himself. Imploringly hoping for the best, he remembered bits and pieces from his childhood. Had his mother not done the same – always hoping for the best? "Never give up hope" she had said so many times to him. Until now, Jake had never really been aware what his mother's words of advice actually meant. Holding the one half of the broken heart pendant, which he carried in his pocket, tightly in his hand, he tried to remember Claire's last words before she left for good. What was it she had said? They will meet again? With a big sigh he thought, 'Who knows if the two hearts will ever be reunited?'

Life wasn't fair at the moment and nobody realised it more than Jake.

Chapter Twenty-one

Months turned rapidly into years. Since Iris' death Ashly, Jake, and Dorothy had lived through incredible changes in their lives. The sense of loss had left a big gap in all their hearts. The three had to find their way through bereavement, sharing their feelings and assisting each other in those hard times. Dorothy had always been a close friend of the family and that bond had become even stronger since Iris had passed away.

While they were mourning Iris's death, experiencing excruciating pain with a feeling of condemnation for the person who caused all the misery, the police investigation into the fatal hit-and-run accident had unfolded. The video camera at the crossing had put the driver of the black Audi clearly at the crime scene. A young man, aged twenty-eight, had hit Iris and fled the scene at high speed. He had been charged with manslaughter and dangerous driving and after a long court procedure sentenced to six years in jail.

The case was closed, but Jake's wounds were still open. In addition to his grandmother's death, he had been left with a mood of total frustration after Claire had gone without a second glance backwards. Feeling that she had somehow left him in the cold, he had great difficulties getting back his get-up-and-go. His life had literally split into thousands of pieces and things could possibly not get any worse.

As their everyday life had been so harsh on them, Ashly knew full well that she had to get a grip on this difficult and distressing situation very soon. Subsequently she moved without dithering from the very moment she had decided to get back on her feet. First she took Jake out of school before he was thrown out because of his bad behaviour and poor performance, and then she took a sabbatical year, swapping her lecturing job for wanderlust. She thought it would do her and Jake good to travel around the world and surely Iris would have fully agreed with her decision.

"Enough is enough," Ashly told Jake one day in spring. It was the second time in his life that the young lad experienced his mother being so strong-minded. The last time was when they had left Rick's house, which was over fourteen years ago and Jake would never forget it

"The past years haven't gone too well. We need to do something else to get back on our feet," Ashly announced. And with a resolute look at her son she went on, "Gordon had once meant the world to me, but bitterly disappointed me. Now I have decided that we will travel the world."

It took Jake a little while to fully comprehend what his mother had just suggested. Travelling the world – had he understood right? He knew when his mother had this look on her face she was determined not to mess about but to promptly put words into action. There had been times when he felt that his mother had let him down. This was however different! He had no doubt about it any longer – his mother was great. Full of enthusiasm he immediately agreed to her proposition and replied,

"Mum, I love you to bits." Thinking her move was really, really terrific, he drew near her and, whilst cheerfully hugging her, he added, "This is the best idea you've ever had!"

"Well! Sitting here and doing nothing is getting us nowhere," Ashly admitted with a big smile.

For such a long time she had been longing to travel the world and, as if it occurred to her overnight, she realised that fulfilling her long-cherished wish was the best she could do for Jake and herself. Her dream would come true at last! She could hardly believe it. 'If I didn't know better, I would think my mother had a finger in the pie,' she thought.

"YES!" Jake sputtered aloud; his voice went head over heels with enthusiasm. "Travelling is a very good motivator for something much bigger and better than singing the blues at home." Smiling quietly at the thought that now, after all those years of endurance, his wish of not having to go to school was about to materialise. 'Funny how everything falls into place!' he concluded. The thought of backpacking with his mother gave him wings. It had been a long time since the happy days, where they both had fun together. As well as having a good time with his mum, he expected his travels to be a splendid opportunity to put Claire out of his mind.

◆◆◆

During the following months mother and son launched into action. Not only did they have to organize everything for their journeys but also for Iris's old house and garden as well. Being in two minds, they didn't know what to do with the property. Since they had become so accustomed to it, selling it was not an option.

"What do we do with granny's wonderful garden?" Jake was worried. The only thing that had kept him going after Iris' death was that small paradise, her jungle. In so far, the garden was indeed a problem. As it was spring, everything had started to sprout and flourish. Who would look after the whole property while they were away travelling? They were however fortunate, very fortunate indeed, because they found a young couple of passionate gardeners who agreed to rent the place as it was for one year.

"I hope you don't mind the ghost living in the old house," Ashly said with a wink when handing over the keys. Seeing the young woman's perplexed face, she quickly added, "I'm only kidding. My mother always thought that there was a good presence in the house. We never experienced anything uncomfortable or malevolent."

Iris, though she hadn't been very rich, had left the house and a substantial amount of money from her life insurance to Ashly and Jake. Heartbroken, yet looking forward to their adventurous travels, the two made a list of their goals, highlighting the places they most wanted to see. Then they cashed the money from their inheritance, booked the flight tickets accordingly, and after some weeks of preparation they eventually said good-bye to Dorothy who, with her deep rooted kindness, had remained a staunch friend.

"Ashly, dear, I hope you and Jake enjoy your trip around the world – perhaps you can let me know from time to time that you're all right," Dorothy asked, her mind was full with worries about the well-being of the two globetrotters.

"Yes, we'll call you and let you know how we are," Ashly readily assuaged her concerns and affectionately embraced the petite woman. She didn't mind to call Dorothy frequently from abroad. On the contrary – she had long sensed that her mother's old friend maintained contact with Ulrik and Claire and she was curious to occasionally hear how the two were getting on in the Far East.

It was only one more night until they would leave much of their old life behind. Tomorrow they would leap into the unknown, embarking on an ambitious travel adventure. With their bags packed for a long haul trip around the world, they were nervously waiting for the day to break. In the early morning Ashly and her son headed to the airport, catching their flight to their first destination – South America.

◆◆◆

As soon as Jake had seen his mother's agenda — what she wanted to see and what she wanted to do — he felt like the character Phileas Fogg, the protagonist in the 1873 Jules Verne novel *Around the World in Eighty Days*. His mother was going to push him from country to country, from place to place. Only in their case they flew the other way round, starting by travelling to the West. Jake had a little spat with Ashly before their departure as to why they weren't flying to New York first. He would have loved to see the famous city, but Ashly steadfastly refused to do so. And, although they had all the time in the world — Jake thought what they didn't see today they would see tomorrow — his mother seemed to be in a rush, never staying too long in one place and dragging her son to museums and art galleries wherever she found one on their trip through the South American continent.

When visiting numerous sites and museums they saw some really bizarre objects, which neither of them had seen before, like prehistoric stones with carvings; ancient bowls, featuring hundreds of triangular carvings; enlarged skulls, and many more mysterious objects

In hindsight, Jake appreciated his mother's efforts to have taught him different languages. During their explorations he could put it all into practice, being able to communicate with the indigenous people. It had always been easy for him to talk with people from different walks of life and that gift of the gab came in handy now. As he so quickly bonded with people, he learned a lot about the local history, culture and daily life. Something was especially striking – there were lots of similar stories, legends, symbols and designs of monuments, all thousands of years old and more or less always connected to gods or the homes of gods. Pyramid shaped temples were for example as common in Mexico as they were in Asia. And there were also similarities of circular shaped structures appearing all over the world. This was by far the most interesting part of their adventures, as it was thought-provoking – was there some hidden meaning, some messages which Jake didn't understand? He would have enjoyed sharing his impressions with Claire.

"Claire, where are you?" he whispered more than once and wished he hadn't so stubbornly deleted all her contact details in his smartphone. Having been so traumatised shortly after she had left him, he initially never wanted to see her again. But the truth was that he deeply missed her and sometimes he would have loved to get in touch just to let her know how he felt. His stupid action was eating away at him and now he regretted his decision, realising that Claire was indeed unreachable.

However, there was no time to wallow the doldrums. Ashly dragged him to the next ruins, some remains of megalithic structures of ancient cities. Blocks of stone so sophisticated that they must have required engineering knowledge. Jake heard from the local people that no one until now knew what these ancient, almost industrial, constructions were meant for. To him these stones looked as if they were made by giants, and he remembered the times when his granny had told him stories about giants who built bridges over the water to welcome their sweethearts. His mind drifted off. He imagined what it would be like if he was one of those giants. He would put on his boots and walk in seconds from one place to another, looking for his sweetheart. Regrettably, reality wasn't so fortunate for him, because his mother made him visit yet another museum. Not to mention the many temples, scattered all around the world, which Ashly intended to see.

◆◆◆

After having travelled the length and breadth of South America they headed to the United States and Canada. Travelling a lot on the Greyhound buses en route from New Orleans to Seattle, they experienced some incredible landscapes. Mountains high and rivers wide was a mild description of the vast areas. In California, the Golden State, Ashly had the spontaneous idea to go on a tour, which included mountain-climbing and paragliding. Jake would have rather spent his time on the beach with a surf-board. But Ashly lured him away by promising to do white-water rafting and fishing for trout in Canada. And so they journeyed on, after – what Jake called – having taken a breather for a couple of days, heading north where another walk on the wild side awaited them. Whilst hiking up the mountains and taking a rough ride in a kayak down the rivers, they had an awesome time and enjoyed the Canadian nature in all its magnificence. A few weeks later they took an overnight flight from Vancouver to New Zealand, the next place on their schedule.

◆◆◆

When they reached New Zealand in the morning the first thing Jake spotted was a poster announcing an All Black rugby match. He was over the moon by the thought to watch the match and felt his heart beat faster as he said to his mother,

"I want to see this match. When will I ever get

another chance watching the All Blacks live?"

Ashly was giddy with excitement. This was her first time to visit the other side of the world and it never dawned on her to watch Rugby.

Glancing at Jake as if to say, 'Do we have to do this?!' she shook her head.

"Yes mum – this is a one off chance!"

While Jake was totally passionate about seeing the game live, his mother was by no means thrilled. However, as his facial expression seemed to entreat her not to decline his wish, Ashly had no choice but to give in.

With a gentle smile she said,

"Why do I always get the impression that you can twist me around your little finger?"

"Because you are the best mum in the world," Jake replied, his face instantly brightening, he gave his mother a big bear hug.

And so it happened – tada! – that Jake and his mother watched the All Blacks perform the Hakka war dance live before the Rugby match on Sunday. Of course Ashly had seen that peculiar act before on television. She knew that the dance was a traditional ancestral performance, done by the players before a match, with fierce looking faces, vigorous movements, involving stamping of the feet, and accompanied by rhythmical shouting.

Originally that dance was done by the Māori people of New Zealand before battles to frighten off the opposition. And yes, it was a totally different experience to see the men, dressed in black with painted faces, perform the Hakka live. The atmosphere was electric.

'I'll never understand this sport,' Ashly thought, 'too many rules and much too technical.' If it hadn't been for Jake she would never have attended a game where thirty big men are running and fighting for a ball which looked like a large egg. But she thought she owed it to her son who was so eagerly watching the famous All Blacks playing rugby, and, after all, it was kind of compensation for dragging the boy persistently to places she favoured. Funny, it was Ulrik who had once tried to explain to her the origins of that sport. Her good old friend Ulrik – how was he? Ashly was wondering. It wasn't the first time that she thought nostalgically of him.

Following the Rugby match, the two undertook a few excursions to incredible islands, allowing themselves the luxury of staying in exquisite resorts. It was a wonderful spell for both of them.

"Now this is how I imagine paradise," Jake said, sitting relaxed in his swimming trunks on the little porch of their overwater bungalow, from where he

had a striking view over one of the lagoons. He started to dream…. finding himself in the middle of a crowd of people, all having books and reading…
"Claire – is that you?"
A splash of water woke him up.
"The water is fantastic – very warm. You should come in and have a swim." It was his mother laughing loudly and waking him so abruptly just when he was about to reach out for Claire.
"You wait," he guffawed and with a huge jump he landed next to his mum in the aquamarine ocean, splashing her with water.

◆◆◆

Life had been so easy going for Jake until now when he started to feel as if his mother was stretching him to the limit. Although he had always been eager to quench his thirst for knowledge, he sometimes just wanted to relax on one of the beautiful beaches of the paradisal islands which they visited in between the sightseeing tours. He simply wanted to dive into the calm blue water and dream about how nice it would be to spend all that time with Claire. But his mother, with her revived appetite for travel and adventure, dragged him to their next destination Hong Kong. Jake was moaning – what would they do there besides buying cheap counterfeits?

"Why don't we go to Australia?" seeing his mother's facial expression, he knew straightaway that he had asked the wrong question. Ashly winced when she heard the word "Australia" associating it instantly with the duplicitous Gordon. How could she have fallen for such a man? It still nettled her. Too many bad memories surfaced and she refused to go anywhere near that country.

"No way will I set foot on that corner of the world," she said, and with determination in her voice, adding, "We are going to Hong Kong. I need to buy an outdoor outfit for harsh winters."

Jake was curious – why would his mum want to purchase any clothing for winter? In Hong Kong! What had his mother in mind now?

He had absolutely no idea that Ashly had seen an advert in a magazine during one of the many flights, "*Dog sledding tours for divas in Norway*". That had given wings to her long cherished wish to see the Northern lights.

'Why not go to Hammerfest?' she had spontaneously envisaged a trip over Christmas and instantly contacted her friend Claudia at home, asking if she would join her on an adventurous trip for women only at the Nordkap. Ashly loved the thought of travelling with her friend as they had done in the old days. But Claudia had been reluctant to go along. She was still agonising over the heated argument the two women once had, when Gordon had entered the scene. They had almost fallen out over his purposes, and stubbornly refused to speak with each other until they discovered that no man was worth putting a solid friendship at stake.

"Can we talk about it, when you're home?" Claudia had asked instead of agreeing, unfortunately putting Ashly's hopes to the test.

Ashly, not wanting to push her friend, had tactfully said her goodbyes and focused on their visit to Hong Kong.

◆◆◆

After a long flight from Auckland they landed in the morning in Hong Kong. Jake woke up just in time to have a breathtaking view of the island's skyline, with a multitude of skyscrapers housing the headquarters of multinational banks and companies.

"There you have your fisherman, having hoarded the means of production", Ashly laughed at her son, alluding to the fierce discussions they'd had in Iris's living room.

"Well, you wouldn't think that only a handful of families concentrate the world's total wealth in their hands," Jake remarked drily whilst looking out of the aircraft window and pondering what his granny would have said.

When stepping outside the airport he was hit by a frenzy of activity. Having just been to places which were as calm as paradise, he didn't like spending much time in such a busy centre of commerce.

"Let's go and see the Tian Tan Buddha statue and then quickly leave this hectic place," he said, sliding in one of the waiting cabs which would take the pair downtown. Fortunately for Jake, it was merely a stopover, where they would spend a couple of days only.

As Ashly had announced earlier, she demanded that they went shopping as soon as they arrived at the hotel. No! Jake wanted to yell. He didn't like being forced into buying things which he didn't want or like.

"Leave me out. Don't terrorise me with your consumption," he was quite angry with his mother. How did she dare to make such a suggestion – him and shopping? No way!!!

But Ashly soon lured him to the main shopping area and, with the sheer variety of clothes and accessories on display, their bargain hunting turned out to be truly a tempting scene to behold.

"I have to get an outfit for polar winter," she explained to Jake, hoping to strike a good bargain in this shopper's paradise.

"Polar outfit – what for?" Jake asked, creasing his face into a frown. The weather was sunny and hot and definitely no change was forecast. Why would his mother need clothes for polar temperatures?

"I want to travel to the Northern hemisphere later," Ashly said, with a sweet smile on her lips adding, "above the Arctic Circle."

"Sweden?" Jake asked, getting all excited because he was thinking of Claire.

"No, Hammerfest."

"Hammerfest – you mean Norway?" Jake stammered as his face fell.

"Yes, Norwegian Lappland," Ashly confirmed, thinking to herself if Claudia wouldn't come along with her, it might even be Sweden.

Jake was too perplexed to object – his mother didn't seem to include him on this trip to the "North Pole" as he called it. What was she up to?

He had really no choice but to follow her reluctantly through the malls and cubbyhole stalls, flagship stores, and factory outlets. At last they found a shop with outdoor clothing, where Ashly purchased all the warm clothes she would need for her *dog sledding tour for divas* in Norway.

Since she didn't want to carry the bulky stuff to

their next destination, Cambodia, she organised for the whole lot to be shipped directly to Dorothy whom she phoned from time to time as promised.

Chapter Twenty-two

Travelling through South East Asia was really something out of the ordinary. Ashly and Jake went to see many interesting places, obtaining a whole variety of different impressions in each country. Having heard so much about Angkor Wat – the heart and soul of Cambodia – they could hardly wait to see this archaeological wonder with its more than forty-five temples.

One of the must-see on Ashly's list was to witness the sunrise at Angkor Wat. However, it took some gentle persuasion to convince Jake for an early morning jaunt to the temple, fitted out with only a torch.

A tuk-tuk, an auto rickshaw on three wheels – a vehicle so typical of Asia – took them in the dark of the night through the jungle. The road to the temple was well travelled by people from all over the world, all hoping to capture the magnificent sunrise over the world's largest and still operating religious monument. Jake wasn't sure what to expect. He was loudly complaining that he had to leave his comfortable bed at four o'clock, only to be encircled by complete darkness and peculiar sounds echoing around him.

"The early bird catches the worm," Ashly said to him when they were waiting in the dark, hopping from foot to foot and urging the sun to rise.

"In the truest sense of the proverb," Jake replied drily, hearing the strange chirping noises around him. He felt as if little eyes were peering out of the bushes and trees and thought the sound was coming from birds. Later he learned that cheeky monkeys were camouflaged against the foliage and they mimicked bird-like noises.

The wait paid off! When the sun began to rise, Jake realised that he wasn't the only one trudging along in the dark to watch how the majestic temples were illuminated on the horizon. The sky suddenly filled with shades of blue, purple and crimson, and the silhouette of the grandiose Angkor Wat was reflected in the surrounding moat which was filled with lotus flowers. Hundreds of people had been waiting for that absolutely enthralling moment, and, as the crowd went into raptures over the unique view, there was a lot of "aaahs" and "ooohs".

"Well, after all, getting up so early didn't seem to be such a hardship. It was actually well worthwhile," Jake admitted. While joining in with the crowd's ecstasies he too was thrilled by the mesmerising spectacle he had just witnessed.

The colourful sunrise wasn't the only show Ashly and Jake enjoyed. The architecture of the whole temple complex, the vitality, the diversity of the people, and the Buddhist monks with their orange robes, gave an incredible atmosphere to the place. After the crowd of tourists had dispersed the two went on to explore the areas around the temple complex a bit further, climbing on top of the constructions, searching for mystical inscriptions.

"Unbelievable – the religious art displayed here," Ashly mumbled in admiration, walking around the ancient site.

By late afternoon they were both tired and sweaty. Calling it a mind-blowing day, they hailed one of the many taxis standing around to take them back to the hotel where they repaired to the pool, sipping well-deserved iced coffee with sweet milk.

◆◆◆

Cambodia turned out to be a terrific adventure – Just as Ulrik had described it to Ashly. All of a sudden, a ringing tone in her ear became unavoidably noticeable. Iris had always said, a ringing tone in the ear means that somebody is thinking of you.

'Ulrik,' was Ashly's first impulse. Putting the magazine, she was languidly reading aside, she found herself thinking of him. 'Why did I never travel with Ulrik?' The thought unexpectedly jumped into her mind, becoming almost overpowering. She tried to picture the time with him way back. He had always been a dependable and reliable friend and it had been great fun to be with him. Strange, Ulrik had always been so nice and it was only now that she started to realise it. Curbing her sudden urge to contact him, she jumped into the refreshing water of the pool, forgetting the past. Everything was going fine – so why should she spoil her holidays?

After almost four weeks of touring the country, their stay came to an end. Ashly and Jake would never forget this charming place with its beautiful coastline, the infectious optimism and smiles of the people, and the abundance of natural attractions. And last but not least its sublime temples of Angkor which – as Ulrik had once explained to Ashly – are only matched by a couple of spots on Earth, like Machu Picchu in Peru, or Petra in Jordan. It wasn't easy to leave this impressive country, heading on to India which turned out to be another breathtaking stop with ancient sites no less outstanding than the ones in Cambodia.

◆◆◆

The two tourists had already experienced Hong Kong as a somehow commercially busy place, aligned to the twenty-first century. Now India was busy as well, but not in the way they would have imagined it. The first thing, which struck the two when leaving the airport in Chennai, was the distinctive smell of spices embellishing the air, the withering heat, and the striking colours of people's sarees and turbans. It was definitely an enigmatic place where the calmness of ancient tradition met the hustle and bustle of a modern society, by far exceeding their expectations.

Many years ago Ulrik had recommended to Ashly to visit the Southern part of India, as it was more original than the North and its people were very relaxed.

'It might be an initial culture shock anyway,' Ashly remembered how Ulrik had advised her. 'India is very diverse, friendly, and very poor, yet one of the most amazing places on Earth I have ever been to.'

'How right he was!' Ashly thought, now being in India herself. She had chosen to travel to South India, not only since Ulrik had favoured it, but because of its distinctive architecture with its famous ancient Dravidian temples which were renowned for being as high as modern skyscrapers.

"You wouldn't think that people, thousands of years ago, were able to build such beautifully crafted buildings," Ashly whispered awestruck, standing in front of the sculpted, pastel-coloured deities and other figurines which decorated one of the oldest of all pyramid shaped temples in India.

"This is surely the most impressive complex I have ever seen. These colours – they are fantastic!" Jake agreed. He, like his mother, was totally in awe of the outstanding, colourful sight of the place and its detailed carvings.

"How amazing – what passion for detail the ancient people must have had in building their temples to commemorate their gods," Ashly said, smiling approval whilst looking up at the building in admiration.

"I really ask myself," Jake picked up the thread, "if the ancient people were able to build such impressive complexes, let's say they would have needed tools to do so – where did all that knowledge go to?" Seeing his mother's surprised face, he added, "I mean it took thousands of years until people were able to build modern skyscrapers. What had happened in the meantime?"

"Good question. I've never thought about it," Ashly admitted. She was deep in thought, gradually understanding why Ulrik was so passionate about archaeology – that robust appetite for discovery and that crucial moment of excitement when unearthing some of the greatest artefacts and celebrated treasures. Did she not feel the same when holding an ancient relict in her hands?

When touring across the South of India, mostly visiting temples, standing in front of them, and marvelling at the very colourful and very skilful sacred sites, Ashly could barely hide her enthusiasm.

"Those temples all emerged thousands of years ago!" she contemplated aloud.

She was totally impressed by the scale of the well preserved ancient sites. One temple was more stunning than the other, with their typical Dravidian architecture so characteristic for that part of the country, and Ashly was simply overwhelmed by their sheer magnificence. Nudging Jake, she pointed at the fabulously detailed carvings,

"Look at that, all those sculptures of deities, kings, warriors and dancers, all painted in such bright colours. This ambience... all this reflects the Hindu way of life..." she trailed off absorbed in thought.

◆◆◆

While continuing their journey through South India, they noticed how vibrant this part of the country was, always seeing throngs of native Indians waving with a friendly smile, and jostling crowds either on bikes or on foot, crouching to pick crops or working in their open shops, people with animals or people standing at one of the many market stalls peddling their goods. And then of course the sacred cows – they were all over the place, wandering about freely. Whatever it was – the view was always extraordinary, full of life and colour. Ulrik had once highlighted this part of India and Ashly certainly didn't regret having travelled to it.

"Well, I don't know how you feel about it," she said to Jake, "India is truly an exciting place, filled with undiscovered stories, astonishing people, and iconic objects. It's nothing like anywhere else and well worth visiting."

"Yes, it's got that sense of mystery which makes it a brilliant experience," Jake replied languidly, as he wasn't interested to join his mother's taxing conversation. His mind was occupied with the inspirational experience he had just made with India.

'It's a pity that I can't share my impressions with Claire,' he regretfully thought while sitting in the sun, waiting for the train to take them back to Chennai. He felt so relaxed that he didn't want to move on. But his mother insisted, since they were already half way there, to take off to their next exotic destination, Sri Lanka.

◆◆◆

It was as if Ashly was trying to make up for all the bad times she had experienced back home, she was determined to see as many places as possible, always imagining it would be the ultimate experience.

"The best way to travel this beautiful tropical island is by bus," she announced, and pulling Jake by the arm she added with a smile, "Come on. Don't fake weariness."

Jake was indeed very tired and still wrapped in thought about that unforgettable place India where he would have loved to travel with Claire. He was sure she would have been enthralled the same way he was. With a sigh he looked at the one half of the broken heart pendant which he was still carrying with him. Would his broken heart ever be mended? As if his mother had read his mind, she said,

"Why don't you contact Claire? You could send her a message."

But Jake declined.

"Maybe later," he assured his mother.

"You don't need to prove how strong you are," Ashly encouraged him. "Do what your heart tells you."

"Yes, mum I know. But at the moment I'm not in that frame of mind to contact Claire," he mumbled, quickly suggesting with a look at his mother, "Let's see what Sri Lanka has to offer."

Having been so intrigued by Cambodia and India, Jake didn't imagine his mother's sightseeing plans could get even better. Yet, as it turned out, their trip to Sri Lanka was indeed another stunning experience; this rather small strip of land provided a lot of attractions. With the pace of life feeling surprisingly much less frantic on this little paradise, Jake hoped his mother would calm down. She was always full of excitement as to what they were going to do next.

Luckily, Jake was able to prevent Ashly from travelling crisscross by public transport around the island. He had already enjoyed – what he ironically called – "*a joyride*" with a tuk-tuk in the busy capital, Colombo. And imagining that such a lame conveyance or a bus would take them around the Hill Country with its tea plantations convinced him not to do so.

"Did anybody ever tell you that buses are very slow, because they constantly pick up and drop off people, and are always so packed that one feels like sardines in a tin?" he pointed out to his mother and in the end successfully persuaded her to refrain from her plan.

"We could hire a local driver and thus save time by not having to wait for buses," she suggested.

"Yes," Jake agreed, "We wouldn't have to worry and could see more places."

"Then let's not waste any more time," Ashly cheered and launched into action.

◆◆◆

During their two weeks stay they undertook a lot of activities, such as visiting cultural sites in remote locations to closely look at stupas, the bell-shaped Buddhist commemorative monuments, or riding on elephants in jungle-like areas with monkeys jumping in and out of trees. They experienced where the tea came from in the Hill Country, and, at the end, they found time to either surf or simply relax on one of the beautiful beaches where sometimes they saw elephants walking along at a leisurely pace.

"There is one thing for sure – you haven't been an elephant in your former life," Jake teased his mother, lying on the beautiful white beach, watching the animals.

"What makes you think that?" she wanted to know with a baffled look.

"Well, you're much too frenetic. Look how sedately the elephants walk," he replied with a smile, wiggling his toes.

"But I have a good memory. Just like an elephant I don't forget," Ashly countered. Her mind was suddenly spinning around the words Ulrik had left her with. *"Whenever you decide to take down your walls, give me a ring."* ...

"Fancy a swim, mum?" she heard Jake's voice and at the same time she felt some water being splashed on her naked skin. Jumping up startled, Ashly rushed down into the calm sea. Laughing and gasping she ran after her son, trying to splash him with lukewarm water. But Jake was too good a swimmer, and diving down he escaped his mother's feigned cries for revenge. They both had a lot of fun in the water, quickly dispersing Ashly's rueful thoughts of Ulrik.

Then came the day when they had to say goodbye to this beautiful island. Both, Ashly and Jake, were reluctant to leave and thought Sri Lanka was simply a dream with its golden, calm beaches, the lush green palm trees and plantations, the remote temples, and of course the extremely friendly people.

"I would very much like to come back here and get married," Jake said on their way to the airport, receiving a funny look from his mother.

"I didn't know that you were such a romantic," Ashly remarked amused.

Jake didn't answer. He ensconced himself in his seat on the aeroplane bound for South Africa and tried not to think about Claire. Unfortunately he couldn't stop it.

◆◆◆

Since Ashly had promised Jake that they would have a time full of adventures when travelling to the four corners of the world, they were now heading to the southern tip of the African continent. It was to be the last leg of their journey around the world, and Johannesburg turned out to be a total disenchantment for Jake after that beautiful break in Sri Lanka. As soon as he stepped out of the aeroplane he felt uncomfortable.

'This place doesn't feel nice,' he thought and was confirmed when going through the passport control. The officers did their job with a stern look – just like at home. No such friendly smiles as in Sri Lanka.

"Why did we have to come here?" he asked his mother, moaning and groaning.

"Because Johannesburg has an incredibly rich history and cultural heritage, and I want to visit some of these places," Ashly replied with determination. "Just like you wanted to see the All Blacks live in New Zealand, I now want to see the Cradle of Humankind and the Origins Centre."

Noticing Jake's perplexed look, she added,

"The Cradle is a site with human skeletons, millions of years old, and the other is a museum, showcasing the origins of humanity in Africa."

With a smile she opened the door of the old cab which drove them from the airport to their hotel downtown. It was raining. Grey clouds smothered the sky and made everything appearing dull. Through the rain-drenched window Jake could see the skyline of Johannesburg in the distance. As they came closer, it turned out that the city itself seemed quite European and busy.

'No wonder it's called the "New York" of Africa,' he thought.

He felt uneasy again. Despite the interesting scenery

he didn't like the place. Maybe he was prejudiced knowing the country's history of Apartheid which he thought was still visible.

"It's just like home – with the rain," Ashly tried to break the silence.

"The only difference is that it's warmer. I have noticed that a lot of plants here also grow in granny's garden," Jack replied, thinking of home. Not being in the mood for a conversation, he added mumbling, "This horrible weather makes it easier for us to go home."

Looking through the steamed up cab window, he once more thought of Claire. He would have loved nothing better than to hire a little van and drive away with her. The twilight took him into the land of dreams. He was imagining how he would explore the world with his soulmate and take her to the end of the rainbow which was just appearing in the sky. His gentle reveries were interrupted by his mother's announcement of her sight-seeing agenda... Argh! Claire – it was too nice a dream. Now he would have to trudge around all the places, the museums, and art galleries with his mother instead.

The miserable weather must have stoked Jake's mood. For no apparent reason he felt miserable too. After a long drive they arrived at the hotel in the evening, nightfall mantling the whole area. Having been advised by friends at home not to use public transport as a tourist and not to walk around after dark, they had no choice but to spend the evening in the hotel, thus adding to Jake's discomfort.

Fortunately the next day the weather changed and so did Jake's mood. It was a bright, sunny day when he and his mother set out to explore Johannesburg, visiting famous art based locations.

On Saturday morning they went to a huge market which was offering artisan food, clothing, and crafts. No, it was no mistake Jake found out – the market was indeed called *Neighbourgood Market* because it was presenting an abundance of different goods. It was certainly a wonderful place to stroll around with all the friendly people behind the many stalls, the unique smells, and really good authentic food.

At one stage Jake thought he spotted Claire standing in front of a stall which was selling artisan craftwork. He could only see her back – it was a woman with a red curly ponytail hairdo. For a moment he caught his breath.

'That's her. That's Claire!' He was so delighted that he stumbled as he walked towards the woman, striving to touch her. Just as well, she turned around before Jake could grab her from behind. The situation which followed is best described as if Jake had seen a mirage. His face fell when he realised it wasn't Claire. He mumbled "sorry" and, leaving the woman baffled, he quickly walked away.

"I must contact Claire," he said to his mother who had noticed that he was visibly flustered. It took him a couple of minutes to calm down before he continued, "But not now – I'll do it when we get home."

Ashly, glancing with amusement at her son, had witnessed the whole incident and wasn't sure what to say. Claire was too sensitive a subject to touch upon and she thought it would be better to remain silent.

As if Jake had read his mother's mind, he said unexpectedly,

"I would rather be in Sweden now."

Oh, oh – Ashly was very surprised and wondered where her son's sudden affection for Sweden derived from?

"Well, we will see…," she stopped abruptly, attempting to pacify Jake who seemed to be inattentive.

"Who knows," she then added, "we're heading in that direction."

Jake turned his head and looked at his mother. He wasn't sure what to make of her words.

"What do you mean – *heading in that direction*?" he asked.
"Well, you wait and see," Ashly said amusedly. She had of course her little secrets which she wasn't willing to reveal, not even to her son, not just yet.

◆◆◆

During their two weeks stay in Johannesburg, the home of Nelson Mandela, it was almost a crime not to visit the Apartheid Museum and later the Origin Museum. As both centres ranked high on Ashly's must-see agenda, she and Jake went off to visit the thought-provoking places.
Standing at the entrance of the Apartheid Museum, they were randomly given a white or non-white admission ticket.
"What is this for?" Ashly asked astonished, only to find out seconds later she was to enter the centre through a separate entrance for black people.
Jake on the other hand was entering through the white people's entrance.
"That gives you a real sense how Apartheid was," he said, shaking his head in disbelief.
"Yes, one wouldn't think that it's just a couple of decades ago that this inhumane regime was ended," Ashly expressed her opinion, looking at the pictures

which were in great detail telling the story of South Africa's immediate past.

Having glimpsed something of South Africa's nearest past, they went a couple of days later to the Origins Museum, spending the whole morning delving into the remote past of mankind.

"The origins of man... Emerging from Africa... Now being able to build atomic weapons, flying to the moon, and even to Mars," Jake was pondering out aloud whilst standing in front of a millions of years old skeleton on display. "It's hard to imagine that allegedly we are all descending from apes."

"Yes," Ashly agreed, "how did that hairless, upright walking, intelligent Homo sapiens come into existence? One wouldn't think that we, the Homo sapiens, all originated from one place in Africa and, when having become fully intellectual, spread out into the world."

"We should have come here first," Jake observed. Being deeply lost in thought, he continued, "We should have started our journey around the world from here and then followed the trails of humans."

"You're probably right," Ashly replied, "but we didn't know before that this place here is so educational."

After a good night's sleep they went on to visit the Cradle of Humankind. Another place on Ashly's must-see list which truly made them wow. Even Jake was totally taken in by this intriguing World Heritage site, loaded with dozens of different types of hominid fossils.

"One wouldn't believe that these bones are millions of years old and belonged to our ancestors," Ashly said, rapt in contemplation.

"And the missing link between ape and Homo sapiens is still not found," Jake contributed. Pointing to the bones, he added, "I would never be able to identify a bone as a valuable find. How does one know if it's human and not animal?"

"You learn to get an eye for such things, which are sometimes very painstaking, when you study archaeology," Ashly explained, "It's a pity that Ulrik isn't with us. He could give you details."

Jake thought he could hear some remorse when his mother mentioned Ulrik.

"Well, you had your chance," he pertly remarked with a cheeky glance at his mother.

"Let's move on to the caves," Ashly urged while heading on.

Jake's initially tight mood totally dissipated when taking a captivating tour around the fossil areas with a deep descent into the underground, shedding more light on the earliest ancestors of humans. And Ashly felt her heartbeat quickening at the sight of the artistic remains. She was totally taken in by the petroglyphs – images carved into the rock by the first humans.

"These sketches are ten to twelve thousand years old," she regarded with admiration. "It's truly unbelievable how sophisticated our ancestors were."

"And all that can be traced back to a single woman in Africa," Jake read out a text from the explanatory notes.

Having spent a day out on the different sites, it took Ashly and Jake some time to fully comprehend what they had learned at the Cradle of Humankind. Both were very thoughtful during the drive back to Johannesburg, sitting silently in the car and admiring the scenic beauty of South Africa in the setting sun. They had been to so many impressive places in South Africa, not forgetting the sensational Kruger National Park with its "Big 5" – elephants, lions, leopards, rhinos, and buffaloes. Having stayed only two nights there, in a round thatched-roof hut, watching wild animals roaming around, both Ashly and Jake would have loved to spend more time in that vast game reserve. In the end, Jake's initial reservations about South Africa turned out to be unfounded, and it wasn't easy for the two globetrotters to accept that they possibly never see any of the breathtaking views and the nice people, they had met, again. Tomorrow would be their last day in South Africa. The day after, they would board the plane, taking them home and their travels would come to an end. Having enjoyed a taste of the big wide world, they were now looking forward to get home.

Chapter Twenty-three

It had been a great experience, perhaps the greatest ever for both Ashly and Jake, travelling throughout the world. South America had been full of surprises. Each country had its own unique charm and attractions. And so had Asia. They definitely would have loved to see them all – the Milkyway over Lake Titicaca in Peru, the Galapagos Islands in Ecuador, the Great Wall of China, the Himalayas, the Sahara Desert and many more such breathtaking places. They had experienced things they would never have imagined. They had immersed themselves into the unknown, visited places that left them speechless, took adventure tours, and relaxing holidays. Sometimes it had been a wild ride, which taught them to see the world with different eyes, and sometimes they felt like they had been in paradise and didn't want to leave the place. Unfortunately all good things come to an end and so had their journeying, notwithstanding leaving them with a quest for more daring adventures.

The encounter of awe and wonder had undoubtedly broadened their minds and made them kind of modest. In the end the globetrotting did what neither Iris nor Ulrik had been able to accomplish. It made Ashly think a lot about Ulrik. She had felt miserable without him and she gradually realised how much she would have loved being on a holiday with him... Maybe in Sweden, dancing around the Maypole. Maybe ... Ashly had never expected to really miss the fair and square Swede and she was certainly not prepared for any bad news.

When the two globetrotters arrived back home in the afternoon on a wet and windy day in late autumn, they went straight to see Dorothy who had become almost like a mother to Ashly.

"Welcome home. I'm so glad that you're back home safe and sound," she received them warm heartedly in her peaceful bungalow, and just like Iris, offered them a good cup of tea.

Whilst sitting around the fireplace Ashly and Jake related how they had explored some of the most memorable parts of the world, capturing moments of action and leisure. By the time the two world travellers had finished enrapturing Dorothy, it was fully dark, the flames were dancing in the fireplace, and all their faces shone with happiness.

"Oh dear, time to go to bed," Dorothy reminded her guests how late it was, adding with a yawn, "I have prepared bedrooms for you."

"Yeah," Jake agreed, "Let's call it a day – Good night everybody." He was really exhausted and, looking forward to a good night's sleep, he swiftly left the room.

"Ashly, do you have a moment?" Dorothy asked before Ashly was able to follow her son. Noticing her look of astonishment, Dorothy quickly added, "I don't want to worry you, but there has been an accident in China and we've heard that there are many people dead."

'No!' it came to Ashly as a shock, 'not Ulrik!' She closed her eyes, feeling her heart racing. She hesitated, and then asked Dorothy,

"Have you heard from Ulrik or Claire – are they all right?"

With her face troubled Dorothy replied,

"No, that's what's worrying me – I've not heard from them for a while."

"How do you know about the accident?" Ashly inquired. Her voice was shaking. Memories of her mother's sudden death surfaced, throwing her into a state of panic.

"It was on the news this morning."

Ashly stared at Dorothy, waiting for her to say more.

"There was a fire at a warehouse containing chemicals, which sparked a series of blasts," she explained, "Hundreds of people are reported injured or dead."

"How terrible," Ashly commented, shuddering at the thought that Ulrik might be amongst the dead or injured.

"The explosion was apparently so strong that thousands of people fled their shaking sky-scraper apartments, fearing that an earthquake had hit them," Dorothy went on to explain.

"China is a big country," Ashly said, her voice almost failing her. She was tired, but the thought of the disastrous explosion kept her awake. Hoping that the catastrophe had not occurred anywhere near Ulrik, she added, "It all depends in which region of China it had happened."

"As far as I understood, it was at a port near Beijing," Dorothy replied with a quivering voice, seconds later adding, "It's near where Ulrik lives."

The statement wrecked at a blow all Ashly's hope!

"Should we phone Ulrik?" Ashly asked, trying to conceal her feeling of unease. Putting a brave face on, she continued, "Have you got his number? I only have his email address."

"Yes," Dorothy replied levelly, "fortunately Ulrik gave me a phone number shortly after arriving in China."

"So you stayed in touch with him all the time?" Ashly pretended to sound surprised. She had long since figured out that Dorothy served like a kind of messenger between all of them.

"Of course I did," Dorothy confirmed with an assuring nod.

Despite being tired and feeling depressed, Ashly was eager to get on the phone. It suddenly struck her that she shouldn't think any longer of how things might be, but to face them as they were. There had been a disaster in China, with many people dead, and she feared Ulrik or Claire might have been caught up in it.

"Let's face it and phone Ulrik," she said, striving to stay poise although she was fraught with worries and uncertainty.

"No, not now," Dorothy repelled, "China is eight hours ahead of us. You may wake Ulrik if you ring him now. Do it tomorrow."

Ashly's face fell. Having been so worried about Ulrik, she had been ready to phone him on the spot. Then again, waiting until tomorrow? 'Tomorrow... tomorrow never comes,' she thought.

"Would you not like to know if Ulrik and Claire are well?" Ashly voiced her concerns.

"Yes dear, very much so..." Dorothy stammered. She obviously didn't feel comfortable at the thought something might have happened to Ulrik or Claire. Being in two minds, she explained, "I'm only a bit worried that Ulrik might be peacefully sleeping in his bed and we would disturb him..."

"I'll send him an email," Ashly finally said with a reassuring look at her mother's old friend.

"That's even better," Dorothy confidently agreed at once. She felt indeed very relieved – had she not managed in the end to get Ashly to contact the nice Swedish fellow?

◆◆◆

Remembering Ulrik's words – *"Whenever you decide to take down your walls, give me a ring"* – Ashly's mind was wandering. Was it the right thing to do – contacting Ulrik after all that time? It might turn out to be a mistake... Ashly was hesitating.

'Oh well,' she thought when sitting down and pondering what to write, 'I'm not ringing him because I took down my walls – I'll send him an email because we are all worried over here and we need to know if he and Claire are safe.'

She was simply dying to know how Ulrik was and

the explosion in China seemed to be a good-enough reason to find out. Her heart was racing and her hands were quivering when, after some careful consideration, she actually typed a trivial text:

Hey Ulrik, if you are still my friend please contact me. We heard about the disaster in the news and we are worried if you and Claire are safe...

Playing with her hair, she hesitated to press the "send" button. For a moment she wished she could hear Ulrik's husky voice. Was there a way to meet again? Ashly contemplated. The thought of seeing Ulrik again lingered temptingly in her mind all of a sudden.

'Sometimes you have to just follow your gut,' she remembered her late mother encouraging her. And as if by magic she quickly sent the message off to Ulrik.

"Now I have to wait and see," she said to herself, scrambling into the bed which Dorothy had so kindly prepared. She closed her eyes and thinking of Ulrik, the man she had once rejected, she hoped that her optimism wouldn't let her down.

'Everything will be fine...' was her last thought before drifting off into sleep.

Ashly wasn't sure how long she had slept when she woke up to what appeared to be the middle of the

night. Haunted by a terrible dream she was covered in sweat. It took her a moment to regain her thoughts. Bits and pieces from the nightmare emerged – a giant pendulum with a sinister smile, swinging UL-RICK, grinned at her while she had been fighting with flames... It left her with a bad feeling and she couldn't remember whether the flames had to do with the explosion in China, or whether her imagination was playing tricks and the flames were a sign of her passion for Ulrik. It dwelled heavy on her mind!
'I have to phone him….,' Ashly told herself before she went back to sleep.

◆◆◆

Waking up in Dorothy's comfortable bed, with the sun flooding the room and the aroma of tea tickling her nose, made her aware how wonderful a cup of tea would taste. She hesitated to leave the warm bed. Wrapped in the duvet, she was contemplating how good it was to be home. Yesterday, she and Jake had arrived back from their journeys around the world. A whole lot of things had been very impressive – far too many to absorb in a short time – and Ashly still hadn't quenched her thirst for more adventure. The trip to Norwegian Lapland – dog sledges for divas – was still in the offing.

'This must be great fun,' Ashly smiled for a moment and reminded herself to contact her friend Claudia who had reluctantly agreed to think about it when Ashly had phoned her from abroad. Ever since they had almost fallen out with each other, because of the Australian, the two friends had considered a mutual holiday. But unfortunately, the passion for travelling together, as in the old days, had faded. Would Claudia now come along on such a trip?

Ashly's thoughts went to Ulrik.

"Ulrik!" she exclaimed, jumping out of bed and reaching for her smartphone. With a buzz of excitement she turned it on, searching for news from Ulrik. Sadly there was none. Not a good start to the day.

A knock on the door brought her back to reality.

"Ashly dear, would you like a cup of tea?" Dorothy asked. Her voice was so soft and warm, making Ashly feel easy.

"Yes, thanks. I'm coming down."

"Any news from Ulrik?" Dorothy inquired while handing a cup of tea to Ashly.

"No nothing," Ashly replied, shaking her head. "I don't know if it was such a good idea at all for me to contact Ulrik," she continued with a hint of sadness.

"Was it Mark Twain, or who was it, who once said: *'You will be more disappointed by the things you didn't do than by the ones you did do'*," Dorothy tried to cheer her up.

"Mark Twain said it," the two women heard Jake's voice. "And if you ask me – they are true words!" Jake spoke on while taking a seat at the table in Dorothy's kitchen.

"Jake, good morning dear, what would you like for breakfast?" Dorothy asked with a friendly smile.

"A cup of tea and some porridge will do me fine," he said, and with a look at the faces of the two women he continued, "What's up with you two?"

"What's up with us?" Ashly said, expressing surprise. How did her son know about her worries?

"Well your faces aren't brimming with glee," he drily answered, "So there must be something upsetting you."

The two women faced each other, and then Dorothy said with a deep sigh,

"Oh dear, Jake you are as observant as always."

"Yes. Nothing gets past me!" Jake replied with a big smile flickering over his face. And as the two females remained quiet, he asked seemingly curious, "Well?"

The radio was discreetly playing in the background. Before any of the women could answer, the Chinese tragedy hit the news broadcast again, reporting that the firefighters were still trying to extinguish the flames.

For a moment absolute silence lingered in Dorothy's kitchen.

"What was that about?" Jake said to no one in particular with a perplexed expression.

"Yes, you heard right – there has been an accident in Beijing," Ashly begun to speak.

"Has anybody contacted Claire and Ulrik?" Jake wanted to know, feeling alarmed and hoping that there was nothing to fear.

Ashly nodded, "Yes I sent an email to Ulrik."

"Did you not speak personally with him?" For a second or so Jake felt shattered. But then, deciding it was time to find out what was going on in China, he left the breakfast table and went to get Dorothy's phone.

"Odee, I am sure you have their phone number," he said, with a look of anticipation at Dorothy. She was used to being called "Odee" by Jake. The boy had once created that name, because she started almost every sentence with "oh dear".

"Oh dear, yes Jake, I have," Dorothy hastened to say, getting the number out of the drawer and passing it to him.

Jake took a very deep breath. Lifting the phone, he

was for a split second tempted not to dial the endless long phone number.

"Don't be a coward," he mumbled while his heart was racing at the thought of soon hearing Claire's voice.

He took another deep breath and finally made an effort to punch in the numbers Dorothy had given him.

After what appeared ages to Jake a woman's voice came on, saying something in what he assumed was Chinese. And as it sounded as if it was an answering machine, Jake quickly put the phone down.

"What happened?" Ashly wanted to know with a curious look at Jake.

"I don't know – a Chinese answering machine," he explained.

"Oh dear – that was Claire," Dorothy clarified with amusement in her voice. Looking at Jake, she said, "Hand me the phone. I'll speak with her."

And so it happened that a little while later Dorothy was the one to establish that Claire and her father were safe and sound.

"Wait a second," she said into the phone, "I'll hand you over to someone who is dying to know how you are..." With a big smile in her face she pressed the phone to Jake's ear. There was no way he could refuse any longer to speak with his old friend Claire.

"Claire," he said gingerly, "how are you?"
"I'm fine and you?"
The ice was broken. Finally, after all!

Chapter Twenty-four

"Thank you for your hospitality, Dorothy, but we want to get back to our house," Ashly gently said when Dorothy offered them to stay another night. Since her husband had divorced her and had run off with another woman, half his age, Dorothy had lived on her own in the comfortable bungalow, and was always pleased to have people stay with her. Ashly was grateful for Dorothy's offer. It was understandable that her mother's old friend would have liked them to stay longer. But she didn't want to overstretch the hospitality more than was necessary, and, as their own home was waiting for them, Ashly and Jake took their luggage and left.

It was a cloudy day, the blustery storm from last night had not eased, when the two instantly wished they were somewhere else where it was warm and sunny. But once they were back in their own house, and finding it as well as the garden very well looked after, they quickly cheered up. The young couple, who had been living in the house, had already moved out at the weekend and had left a note saying they had greatly enjoyed looking after the property and had much fun with the ghost, which had neither shown up nor caused any trouble at all.

It took Ashly and Jake a couple of weeks to adapt to being back home and getting used to their daily routine. First and foremost, people and friends, all wanted to know about the exciting places the two globetrotters had been to. They devoured the stories Ashly and Jake told them, conjuring up their best and most hilarious memories. Jake was especially delighted in giving accounts of "horror-stories", such as: *"Do you remember the green Mamba creeping towards you"*... or *"Do you remember the fried scorpions, we were offered to eat."*

After a few weeks, life gradually returned to normal. Ashly, who was back to her old job, bumped into Natasha one day. She felt a slight blush coming on. Under no circumstances did she want to get dragged into a conversation about Ulrik. He had in the meantime responded to her email, only asking if she still had her walls up. Of course that hadn't gone down too well with Ashly who had hoped he would have been more gracious. The two women grinned at each other. Natasha responded with overblown affection, asking Ashly how her extended holiday had been.

"Good, good. Thank you," she replied with a steady voice, hoping that Natasha wouldn't come to speak of Ulrik. At the same moment she remembered when she and Ulrik had first met in the little café nearby. That was a long time ago. Things had changed, she told herself. Then again, she couldn't help it – all of a sudden the memories surfaced and dwelt heavily on her mind.

Natasha hesitated to continue chatting with Ashly. The two women had really nothing in common apart from Ulrik being a friend to both of them. She took a quick look around. There was nothing catching her imagination to conduct further conversation with Ashly who appeared so distant.

"Ok, then have a nice day," she said with a supercilious shrug and teetered away on her high heels.

◆◆◆

While Ashly was back in her old job at the university, Jack was hanging around not really knowing what to do next. Having seen so much misery and hardship in his young life, he considered studying social policy at university. According to him poverty and suffering went side by side with unimaginable extravagance and excess. And his travels around the world contributed to his thinking – surely there was enough of everything on this globe and it only had to be redistributed more equitably in order to make the Earth a fairer place. He soon came to realise that power and greed were so prevalent that it would probably remain a dream to change the world for the better. Bearing that in mind, he enrolled for a degree in Social Science.

There was still plenty of time left for Jake to decide what to do in the interim, because university wouldn't start until autumn next year. Unless he wanted to go on living at his mother's expense, he had to find himself work to bridge the gap. He was lucky – thanks to his language skills and his travel experience he was quickly offered a job, working as a journalist for a local newspaper, which he was more than happy to accept.

Even though his mind was all over the place with his new demanding job, he was sure about one thing – he missed Claire. Having grown into a handsome young lad, he was a very charismatic person with a special appeal to girls, which sometimes even Jake himself didn't understand. Despite the girls being awed by his charm, his heart belonged to Claire and Claire only. She had left him once with a broken heart – and that was in the truest sense of the word. Looking at the split heart pendant, which he had carried all around the world, he remembered to contact his treasured friend.

◆◆◆

According to Claire life in China was not as expected, and the fact that she wasn't very happy, raised Jake's hopes that she would be back with him soon.
"School over here is totally different," she told Jake, "very rigid, hard training and no choice."
He had no idea what she was talking about and didn't know how to reply. To him, China was a faraway country which he didn't care a fig about at the moment. All he wanted to know was if his friend still remembered him and the great times they had together. He couldn't forget the many happy moments that had lined their childhood path. How did she feel about it?
"You wouldn't believe it – but I have to get up early every morning for outside exercise with hundreds of

other students at the school commons," Claire went on complaining. "The school system kills student's imagination. Individualism as such doesn't exist here."

Jake had listened patiently. He was more interested in finding out what Claire was doing when she didn't go to school. Was she seeing someone?

"What keeps you over there?" he raised the question. Of course he was particularly keen to hear if there was a chance to see his old friend again and if so when that would be.

However, Claire left him guessing, as she was cagey about her future plans.

"My father's contract will be coming to an end and I certainly do not want to stay on here any longer," she said, leading Jake to assume that his childhood sweetheart was emotionally not tied to China.

"When will that be?" he wanted to know. Agog with the expectation of seeing Claire again, his heart was racing.

"I don't know. If his contract isn't extended he may be finished next summer, or the year after," Claire chirped.

BANG! Jake's floating hopes of seeing Claire soon were dashed. For a second he was tempted to hang up on her. 'Be careful – don't get hurt again!' his inner voice whispered.

Fortunately Claire must have sensed his discomfort, as she quickly went on with a clear voice, "Whatever happens we will be in Sweden as usual in the summer."

"Ah," Jake faltered, and then forcing himself to sound casual, he said, "My mother is going to Lapland."

"Lapland?" Claire asked astonished, "Where to and when?"

"She hasn't made up her mind if she wants to go to Norway or Sweden," Jake explained levelly. "She has to convince her friend Claudia first to come along on a dog sledding tour for divas," he sneered at the thought of the two women sitting in the big sled trying to control a bunch of dogs.

"That sounds interesting," Claire commented. "Perhaps we could arrange something so that my father and your mother could meet each other?"

"Yeah, good idea. The only hitch is that this short trip is for women only," Jake enlightened his friend.

"Hm," Claire seemed to contemplate. "I think my dad would very much like to see your mum. We have to find a way for them to meet."

Why was it always his mother and Claire's father? Why wasn't it possible that simply he and Claire could arrange to see each other? Reluctantly Jake agreed, "Yes, let's think about how we can make that happen."

Disappointed, he finished the call. Though promising to get in touch shortly, he was way too upset that his heart might get broken again. "Damn it!" he shouted, throwing his half of the broken heart pendant into the corner.

◆◆◆

Ashly, bursting with vigour, was still passionate about an action-packed break and had eventually succeeded in talking Claudia into a joint holiday in Lapland. As it had turned out the dog sledding for divas was solely offered in Norway, hence solving the problem for Ashly not having to choose whether or not to go to Sweden.

"This is fantastic! This is great! This is so wonderful," Claudia was bitten with enthusiasm when they arrived at their final destination. The wilderness, the snow, the calmness, and of course the Huskies – it all contributed to an adventurous escape from the daily routine of the two women. It was clearly an absolute recuperation for their body and mind, and it was no surprise that the two friends were more than enthusiastic about their five days of nature travel.

Going on a holiday with Claudia was just like twenty

odd years ago when they were students, travelling through Europe on a rail-pass.

"Do you remember that sleazy joint in Paris where you were covered with bug bites?" Claudia wallowed in memories one evening when they were relaxing in the sauna at their hotel.

Oh yes, Ashly remembered!

"Yes," she said with a vague smile, "those were the days. We were young and naive."

"We still are young," Claudia objected passionately, "Young at heart, and hopefully a lot wiser."

"If you mean we don't get carried away so easily by shady characters, you are definitely right," Ashly agreed.

"Only by sensational lovers," Claudia babbled away, abruptly pausing for a moment when she saw Ashly's face dropping. "Oops, sorry, dear – I didn't mean anybody in particular."

"Don't you ever remind me of that Aussie," Ashly hissed with an angry look, brushing the sweat out of her face.

"No I won't," Claudia promised and forcing herself to sound casual, she asked, "What about Ulrik?"

"Ulrik, he is ...,"Ashly started and exhaled to blow the wet hair from her forehead.

"What?" Claudia was curious to know.

"He isn't really a womanizer."

"Is he not — I thought he was very handsome," Claudia said and turned towards Ashly, "I wouldn't push him out of my bed."

Ashly was slightly fazed by her friend's frank confession. She never really thought about what other women liked about Ulrik. She had him made up in her mind as a regular sort of guy, a friend and nothing more. It suddenly occurred to her that he seemed to have that certain 'je ne sais quoi' charisma on other woman. Now she was surprised to learn that Ulrik might well be a passionate lover and started to see him in a different light.

"Would you not," she teased her friend.

"No," Claudia confirmed, licking the beads of sweat off her lips, "I think he is an attractive guy."

The sauna was steaming. Ashly, sitting on the wooden bench and sweating, was for a moment wrapped in thought. What did she like about Ulrik? She had always been oblivious to his advances, never given him a second thought. What was she afraid of? ...*Tick-tock, Ul-Rick...* Her subconscious distantly piped up.

"Maybe I should give him a chance," she admitted with a suppressed chuckle.

"Give him a chance?" Claudia said aloud. Fervently shaking her head, she went on, "Come on Ashly — give the two of you a chance!"

A quick exchange of looks.

"It's not easy," Ashly exhaled. She had had enough of steam and sweat.

"Why don't you tell him what you feel? The sooner you speak with him, the sooner you two can be happy together," Claudia vented.

"I will think about it," Ashly replied non-committally. Jumping down from the bench, she added, "I need a drink now. Are you coming with me?"

◆◆◆

The short winter-break had been a real delight for the two friends. Unfortunately, back home it didn't take long before the daily life turned into dull routine again.

Claudia had ardently recommended Ashly to approach Ulrik – why not have a holiday in Sweden? Why not spend time with him? Yes – why not? Ashly thought twice about it and then contacted Ulrik one day out of the blue. She must have been out of her mind, because she actually had the courage to phone him. And before she could reverse her intention, Ulrik answered.

"Don't hang up on me," she said, her voice faltering, "I'm sure you are mad. But I want to talk to you."

It has been so long since she had heard Ulrik's husky

voice.

"Ah," he said, "so did you decide to take your walls down?" Leaving Ashly totally perplexed, he gently continued, "Sorry, I didn't mean to be so gruff. What's up?"

"I have just returned from Lapland," Ashly started and, realising it was a crucial moment, she was carefully searching for words before continuing, "I still have my winter outfit. You know, I bought it in Hong Kong. I got it for a reasonable price over there ... and I thought I might like a holiday in Sweden." It was as if she stood beside herself – why on earth did she not simply say that she wanted to see him? Why did she not say that she longed for him? Why did she have to beat about the bush?

Ulrik on the other end of the phone had listened patiently. Why was that woman bothering him with talking about her clothes?

"If this is the true reason why you are phoning me, you are wasting your money," he said and added sharply, "and my time!"

By no means had Ashly intended to have an argument with Ulrik. It was only that she was too afraid to admit that she was in love with him. Everything seemed to be going wrong – again! These tricky heartstrings! Ashly struggled for words.

"Well, what about a holiday together in Sweden?"

"With or without walls?" Ulrik inquired with a tinge of mockery.

"Without walls," Ashly replied and fazed Ulrik who hadn't expected Ashly to ever say so.

Seconds of silence. One could have heard a pin drop.

"Are you sure?" Ulrik asked sheepishly.

"Yes!"

Seconds of silence again.

Ulrik was contemplating; his brain was working full speed. Was she serious, he was trying to figure out, or was this just another one of her spiels, intending to make him listen to her excuses and empty promises? So many times he had invited Ashly to join him for a summer holiday in Sweden, and she had never ever offered a gleam of hope that she would like to come along, let alone come along with him! Was she serious this time? Did she really want to have a holiday with him?

"I'll be back in Sweden in the summer," Ulrik eventually said, hesitating, and then, trying not to flounder, he continued, "If you wish to come then..."

"Yes I wish," Ashly replied cheerfully, adding in a soft tone, "very much indeed."

It all turned out so well. At last Ashly had spoken

with Ulrik, honestly admitting that she wanted a holiday with him. What a relief! A wave of emotions suddenly came over her. It took her some time to mull over everything before phoning Claudia to tell her.

"Good, good. Great news! So when are you going?" she asked and was very happy that her friend sounded like her old self again.

With a deep breath Ashly said, "In June. I want to be there for Midsummer and surprise Ulrik."

"Surprise him? I thought he knew that you were coming."

"No, he doesn't know exactly when I will arrive," Ashly enlightened her friend.

Chapter Twenty-five

The months until June seemed to Ashly as if they would never come. She could hardly wait to see Ulrik again. And, because she wasn't very patient, the time until then was a real test of her endurance. Even more so, since she wanted to keep it as a surprise for Ulrik, having already booked a flight so that she would be with him at Midsummer – the night when, according to legend, the future husband would appear in a woman's dream after she had picked seven different species of flowers and laid them under her pillow.

Keeping it as a surprise, meant that she couldn't make Jake privy to her plans. The young lad was once more wondering about his mother's behaviour. Whenever he tried to speak with her about Ulrik, or a summer holiday in Sweden, she was always very short with him, not revealing her intent. So good was Ashly's camouflage that in the end it left Jake to assume his mother had finally decided to stop contacting Ulrik.

'Women are strange creatures,' he thought depressed. 'One never knows when a NO is a NO until it is final. And then there is no way back and nothing can change their minds.' While Jake was lost in thought he hoped beyond all else that in the case of Claire, he would be proved wrong.

Thinking of Claire, he pondered if he should contact her. It had been some time since he last heard from her. In the meantime his sentiments had settled and he had rescued the pendant which he had thrown away in frustration. Looking at his watch, he realised it must be early in the morning in China. He hesitated for a moment. Then again, as he knew that Claire was an early riser, he gave her a ring to surprise her.

"Here is your other half," he said when he heard her voice, looking at the pendant.

"You don't say. I would never have guessed!" Claire reacted cheerfully.

"I have to tell you something. It's about my mother," Jake disclosed, the frustration in his voice was unmistakable.

"Ashly – is she all right?" Claire asked apprehensively, thinking something dreadful might have happened to Jake's mother.

"No, she's not," Jake rashly replied, and by stretching the truth he made Claire believe it was something gravely serious. "Her mind is completely gone," he added with a note of sarcasm in his voice.

What on earth was going on? Claire wondered, eventually managing to express her concerns.

"What is the matter with your mother?"

"Oh well, she has finally broken up with your dad," Jake let the cat out of the bag.

A loud gasp on the other end of the phone.

"Why do you always have to exaggerate?" Claire accused her friend. She was annoyed.

"What do you mean – me exaggerating?"

"I thought something dreadful must have happened to your mother."

"Well, for me this is dreadful enough. If she has broken up with your dad, all my plans to visit Sweden in the summer are dashed," Jake said angrily.

"If you wish so desperately to have a holiday in Sweden – why don't you go on your own?" Claire asked indignantly.

"Because apart from you and your dad, I don't know anybody there," he answered stroppily.

"Well," she resumed resolutely, "you'll have to wait and see."

For a brief moment there was silence. Jake was kind

of upset. The conversation didn't go as he had wished.

"Ok, I'll wait and see," he faltered. "I hope I don't have to wait too long until I see you," he then continued with a sigh.

"Who knows," Claire finished their chat in a mysterious voice, leaving Jake to believe she might have something special in mind.

◆◆◆

It was one summer evening when Ashly decided to reveal the secret. She had left her son dangling long enough on tenterhooks. Jake was home from his work and while relaxing on the back porch with some refreshments, his mother waved with something looking like flight tickets.

"Surprise," she laughed, drawing near Jake, "guess what I have here."

"Flight tickets?" the young lad asked doubtfully, adding with a frown, "You are kidding."

"No, I'm not," Ashly asserted, her brown eyes glittering with fun. "We are going to Sweden."

"No way – I don't believe you!" Jake jumped up from his chair, totally mad with joy.

"Yes, yes," Ashly exclaimed, overwhelmed by her son's outburst of happiness, "We are going next week to be there for Midsummer."

"I have to contact Claire and tell her."

"No, wait – I want to surprise Ulrik," Ashly explained to him, "Don't say a word. Not yet."

It was difficult for Jake not to share his mother's plans. He would of course have loved to tell his childhood sweetheart about the trip to Sweden, as he was so much looking forward to seeing her again. Wallowing in memories, he remembered how much they shared during their childhood years, having gone through thick and thin together. He was unable to tell how he would feel being with Claire right now. Would there be any difference? His mind went astray – had she not once said she would like to take him for a dance around the Maypole, that suspiciously phallic shaft? 'The night before Midsummer Day – that magical time for love,' he was absorbed in thoughts and memories. Bitten with enthusiasm, he slipped into reverie, seeing himself dancing closely entangled with Claire. He hadn't felt so cheerful in a long time at the prospect of seeing her. Carried away with his own emotions he suddenly experienced doubts. How would Claire feel about him? Did she want to see him in the first place? She didn't seem keen on replying to his texts and messages which he had recently left on her phone.

"There is always a happy ending!" he said confidently to himself, pushing his uncertain thoughts aside. But little did he know that his feelings for Claire would have to face once more an acid test.

◆◆◆

A few days before leaving, Ashly rang Ulrik just to let him know when they would arrive in Malmö. She took him by surprise again and he was totally over the moon when he was told about their visit. The time until their departure dragged. They were so enthusiastic and could hardly wait to finally be in Sweden. Jake was dying to see his friend Claire; and Ashly and Ulrik were excited about meeting again for the first time in five years. They felt like teenagers looking forward to their first date – flushing and having butterflies in their tummies.

As soon as they had boarded the aircraft, Ashly's heart began to pound. She was extremely nervous, not knowing what to expect. When she suddenly realised that she knew very little about Ulrik, she became even more edgy. 'He could be married with a bunch of children in the meantime and I wouldn't know,' she mused, acknowledging that her thoughts were ridiculous.

Fortunately her worries were all in vain, as she was

soon to find out.

The flight was on schedule. When they landed, they headed straight to the exit with their hand luggage.

A quick look around and there he was – Ulrik, standing amidst a crowd of people waiting at the arrival area, casually dressed, light trousers, t-shirt, sandals, which made him immediately appear youthful.

"Hej Ulrik," Ashly called out in Swedish as soon as she spotted him. Fervently waving at him, she rushed with excitement towards him.

Ulrik was totally ecstatic to meet Ashly. She hadn't changed – only become more beautiful in all those years, he hadn't seen her.

"Hej Ashly," he responded with a big smile. Gently hugging her, he was searching for words, "At last! You made it – you are in Sweden. Finally, I can welcome you here."

Then turning towards Jake, he added cheerfully,

"It's great to see you too."

"Is Claire not here?" Jake wanted to know, glancing suspiciously at Ulrik.

"No," the Swede faltered and looking down to avoid Jake's look, he continued, "She had to go away for a few days."

BOING – Jake felt as though he had been hit by a brick. He bit the bullet – what else could he do?

Determined not to let the bad news spoil his first visit to Sweden, he decided to have a good time and put on a brave face. Of course he was deeply disappointed — what was so important that Claire wasn't in Sweden? Was she possibly avoiding him? He couldn't help himself, but he was seething with rage.

Ashly, by contrast, was on cloud nine with Ulrik. She was startled by his warm reception. Holding on to his arm, they strode along to the exit.

"So what do you say — can we try again?" he asked her, his eyes sparkling with joy.

"Yes," she said, feeling brilliant.

Still smiling at each other, they had to disentangle to climb into Ulrik's car, parked in the car park. Within an hour they arrived at his parent's house, where Ashly was struck by the thought that her mother would have liked Ulrik's old parents who so affectionately welcomed her and Jake.

◆◆◆

Midsummer Eve was coming up the next day and Ashly asked Ulrik,

"Do you remember what you once told me about Sweden?"

"Not exactly," he answered slightly embarrassed. "I

said a lot of things to you."

"True. But you never asked me to dance around the Maypole with you," Ashly replied, nestling up to him.

"Did I not? I'm sure I did," he said with an astonishing look.

"No, you didn't," Ashly insisted, and gently smiling she added, "you might have thought about it."

"Hm," the Swede mumbled. After seconds of consideration he continued with a bright face looking at Ashly, "I would always have loved to dance with you anywhere – even around a Maypole."

"Then why don't you ask me again?" Ashly said keenly, continuing with an amorous glance, "Since I took my walls down there is no reason for you to be afraid."

Taking her gently into his arms, his brown eyes fixed on hers, Ulrik hastened to ask,

"Would you like to dance with me around the Maypole"?

"YESS!" Ashly exclaimed overjoyed with happiness.

It was fantastic! Ashly never thought that Ulrik could be so exciting. He was a great dancer. Leaning on him, she inhaled his musky fragrance. It was a very pleasant scent. Sort of beguiling, reminding her somehow of Rick, or was it Gordon, whom she had forgotten in the meantime. Rick or Ulrik – anyway, the similarity in the two names didn't matter any longer. If her subconscious was playing tricks on her, that was going to stop now! She was at last sure – with Ulrik it was different. It wasn't a craving for sex and fun. It was something else. Something Ashly had always wanted, but never dared to ask for: real love.

Gently embracing Ashly, Ulrik danced with her in his arms around the Maypole for a while, until bedlam started and the crowd of Swedes vivaciously hopped in a circle. She deeply enjoyed the little dance. It was like being in another world – so romantic and harmonious. Was Ulrik, all things considered, the right man? YES! Ashly wanted to yell. Ulrik – his beautiful hands, his sound body, his brown hair and the sparkle in his eyes – everything just cried 'Come and take me!'

What followed was a night filled with love and romance – so wonderful, Ashly had never experienced before. Ulrik was full of amorous attention. His foreplay drove her mad. With a caress, far more gentle than a feather, he touched her neck before carefully fondling her breasts, as if they were something to easily break. She felt his soft hands reaching down between her legs. Then he gently kissed her, stopping only for a moment to look up at her as if to ask 'do you enjoy it?' Yes, yes, yes! Ashly, smiling down on him, wanted to shout. She gasped in anticipation to finally love him like no man before. Her fingers twined in his hair, she was longing for him – for god's sake take me! And so he did.

Ashly had her eyes closed. With Ulrik lying on top of her, she was wonderfully in love with him. It was such a peaceful moment she didn't want it to end. She felt like "Sleeping Beauty" awaking from a deep slumber, when Ulrik gently kissed her on the cheek. He looked at her with a captivating smile, softly whispering in her ear: "I love you."

◆◆◆

Jake, who had quietly watched his mother entangled dancing with Ulrik, remembered how he and Claire had always been convinced that their parents were a perfect match. He had hoped all these years that his mum would reciprocate Ulrik's feelings and that the two would get together one day. And didn't it come true finally?

'Everything is falling into place,' he silently observed and recalled his granny's remarks: 'One has to strive long enough for it to happen.'

How right she had been. He wished his granny could

see the two adults so deeply in love. And where was his match? Nostalgically he looked at his half of the split heart pendant. Childhood memories surfaced when he and Claire were listening to his grandmother's stories which always ended in the lines "and they lived happily ever after." So many times he had nudged Claire, as if to say "that could be us." 'She probably doesn't forgive me for the many bruises I gave her when I nudged her,' Jake thought, not knowing whether to laugh or to cry.

There was nothing to lift his heart up, when all of a sudden he heard a female's voice behind him.
"Hi Sweetie," a blonde girl brushed past him with a charming smile. "Would you like to dance?"
Jake, with his raven black hair and charming good looks, had immediately attracted attention. All the Swedish girls seemed to have a crush on him – especially since he chatted so comfortably in Swedish, telling them anecdotes about his travels around the world. He visibly enjoyed being in the limelight. Even more so, as he was convinced Claire had let him down. She obviously didn't care one bit about his feelings – so why should he be considerate? But it wasn't that easy – Claire's magic worked even over the miles.

Closing his eyes, Jake blissfully imagined the girl, he was dancing with, was Claire. He was almost tempted to give in to the girl's flirtation, when it became clear to him that his heart belonged to Claire. What had he let himself in for? He tried to find excuses. But Willa, his dancing partner, laughed and assured him that she wouldn't have dragged him to her bed anyway.

"I know that you're in love with my friend Claire. Unfortunately she couldn't be here to-night," she said, all of a sudden appearing reserved and leaving Jake to speculate what was going on.

"Where is she?" he asked.

"Sorry, I had to promise her not to tell you anything!"

"Come on! That's not fair on me!"

"Well, all I can say is that you just have to wait and see," Willa said with a deep look in his face. She knew it would have been only right to tell him the truth, but she was betwixt and between honesty and the promise to her friend. Being terribly conflicted, she continued with her eyelids drooped, "Look, I'm really sorry. But don't you worry – Claire is fine. Come on and enjoy yourself."

Jake didn't know what to reply – the whole world had turned against him and apart from getting drunk, he didn't know what else to do.

Like a shadow, anger and acrimony followed him in the background all through the night, until he tottered to bed. The next morning he woke up with a headache, reflecting on his visit to Sweden. Considering his situation dispassionately, he was in a mess. Excessively passionate he had boarded the plane to Sweden a few days ago, aglow with enthusiasm to meet his sweetheart. Up one minute – down the next. He was of course totally frustrated when he learned that Claire wasn't there and nobody would tell him exactly where she was. His mother, on the other hand, seemed to have had a great time – again. And he? He felt left out – again.

"Jake darling," he heard his mother calling him, "hurry up, we have to catch our flight."
He was reluctant to respond but got hurriedly dressed. Feeling like a fool, he wanted to obliterate everything reminding him of Claire and Sweden from his memory! All the way home, he was in the doldrums. No Claire – no fun! He didn't speak a word with his mother, but stared blankly out of the window as the aeroplane was landing.

◆◆◆

At home he went straight to bed, only to dream of Claire – how they danced around the Maypole. He thought he could actually feel her. Then the dream went on – they were separated. He had to cross a river, but he had let go from his raft and couldn't get over to the other side where Claire was waiting for him. 'Let go!' she called out to him.

When he woke up, he felt immediately disenchantment creeping through him. Yes maybe he should let go of Claire. What had prevented her from being in Sweden? She had quashed his hopes so many times. He couldn't bear it any longer. He was once more deeply disappointed and swore to himself that this was the last time!

He felt bad, very bad. His mouth was dry and it took him a while to gather his senses. There was no time left to go into the deeper meaning of his bizarre dream. Looking at his watch, he realised he was late for work at the local newspaper. Hastily he jumped out of bed and dashed to the bathroom, trying to concentrate on the job he had to do today. His task was to write an article on the cultural activities taking place all over the town at the moment. Fortunately, he had already prepared most of his piece before leaving for Sweden. All he had to do now was to finish off some more research in the library where he was heading in a hurry.

The town was packed with little stalls and platforms. As he was in a rush, he was annoyed that he had to make his way through the throng of the crowd. And then, pushing forward, he suddenly spotted her among an assembly of people – a young woman with beautiful long red hair. Jake stopped immediately. With his eyes wide open in excitement he thought that might be her, Claire. But no, not again – so many times he had been mistaken; always thinking all women with red hair would be Claire. While he hesitated the young woman turned around. Jake was electrified. He was unable to think clearly and then it hit him – it was her!

"Claire? What are you doing here? What a wonderful and complete surprise!" he stammered, still unable to believe it was Claire in person.

"I missed you," she said, drawing near Jake with her green eyes glistening with joy.

"Why didn't you phone or text me?" Jake wanted to know eagerly.

"That would have spoiled the surprise – I came over here for the literary festival with some friends," she explained, aglow with enthusiasm. "And I didn't expect to bump into you here. I was going to knock on your door later today."

"Oh my god – I have waited for you for so long," Jake spoke passionately, finally managing to gently embrace the young woman.

"Yes I know. You'll never have to wait again..." Claire promised. And after a long pause she continued with a sweet smile, "See, I was right – a bad penny always comes back!"

This time Jake didn't disagree. He took the girl of his dreams in his arms and as he was kissing Claire, he had this thought he had never before given her a real kiss.

Life was wonderful!!!

Acknowledgements

I was very lucky to have met the right people at the right time. Without their patience and encouragement this book would never have been written. To all of them I owe my special thanks.

Carmel Perry, who set the ball rolling by suggesting to me, after my recovery from ovarian cancer, to write a book in English and gave a brief outline of her ideas.

I am deeply grateful to my trusted test readers, editors and proof-readers for their vital support, without which it would have been much harder to accomplish the book.

Linda McKennett, my earliest reader who was courageous enough to work through the jungle of words of my first draft and leave much appreciated feedback.

Rosemary Mclenaghan, everybody should have a neighbour and such a fantastic editor like her. She thoroughly edited the manuscript.

Jean Wood, her detailed work and feedback encouraged me to make much needed corrections.

Ethel and Gordon Robinson, with their proof-reading they put the final touch to the manuscript.

Siggrid Lorenz, who was always there for me to discuss the manuscript at various stages.

Gabriele Helbig, for her valuable feedback.

To my friends:

Beverly Osborn, my Facebook-friend, whose painting and stories of her old house inspired me to write about it in my book.

Natasha Francis, for contributing with information on China and archaeology.

Trefor Phillips, for the information on gifted children, teachers, and schools.

Last but not least my very special thanks belong to all the people from the **Macmillan Support and Information Centre** in Belfast, who helped me to get back on my own feet. Especially:

Terry Deehan, who helped me with her patient counselling to clear my mind and to focus on important things in life.

Elaine O'Roarty-Downey, who, with her excellent massage and enthusiasm, encouraged me to look forward and finish my novel,

and **Nicola Taylor**, who was always there for me at the reception desk, enthusiastically reminding me to bring my book to life.

It was a great experience for me to work with all these supportive people!

ABOUT THE AUTHOR

Carmen S. Bauer was born in 1956, in Wiesbaden (Germany), where she grew up with a younger brother.

She studied Political Science at the University of Hamburg and at the London School of Economics and Political Science. After graduating with a PhD, she worked in an array of jobs, her last job being in Brussels, where she came across different nations and cultures.

She abandoned her career in Brussels to live in Northern Ireland with her partner and never regretted having moved to this lovely place on earth.

Whereas her jobs always required writing a lot for other people, she started publishing her own works after settling in her new home. Her earliest book "Yorkshire Terrier – Zwerge mit Löwenherz" was first available in 2011 in Germany.

When she is not writing, or walking her dogs, she is a passionate gardener.

Printed in Great Britain
by Amazon